What the critics are saying...

NOCTURNAL URGES...

"A vampire thriller that keeps readers guessing right up to the final moments of this extremely well-written and – executed novel... Kudos to Elizabeth Donald on her debut novel, 'Nocturnal Urges.' This is a writer to keep an eye on..." ~ *Loveromances*

"From the very first page, this book takes you into heat... I truly loved this story, and I found myself reading page after page towards its completion. I highly recommend this e-book from Cerridwen Press for a little nocturnal fun any time of the day or night." ~ *Romance Divas*

"The unexpected way this story evolves is magnificent..." ~ *Coffee Time Romance*

"Elizabeth Donald's 'Nocturnal Urges' has a little for everyone. An old-fashioned whodunit with the violence we've come to expect in any vampire novel; a love affair against the odds; and a vampire with a tortured past. Her characters run the gamut of emotions. The passions contained in this story are hot and will have you hot-blooded... 'Nocturnal Urges' is definitely a keeper for those of us who crave vampirotica." ~ *Vampire Book Club*

"There is much more to this tale than just vamps and sex. There is an against-all-odds deep and caring relationship found in the pages of this story, as well as a suspense-filled 'whodunit' mystery woven into the already-detailed storyline…'Nocturnal Urges' is a hot, sexy, edge-of-your-seat-type read that will hold you captive from beginning to surprise ending." ~ *Fallen Angel Reviews*

A MORE PERFECT UNION…

"Elizabeth Donald's second installment in the 'Nocturnal Urges' series is a fast-paced murder mystery sure to appeal to both lovers of thrillers and lovers of vampires…Populated with wonderful secondary characters, Ms. Donald has the perfect grasp of what a series really means. Funny, scary, passionate and quirky, "A More Perfect Union" is worth the price of admission into Elizabeth's wonderful world." ~ *Ecataromance.com*

"Elizabeth Donald once again takes readers on a remarkable ride through the shadowy world of vampires, while exploring some of the darker sides of humanity…This is a beautifully-written book with an enormous amount of depth and detail that really bring Ms. Donald's vampires to life." ~ *Just Erotic Romance Reviews*

NOCTURNE

Elizabeth Donald

Cerridwen Press

A Cerridwen Press Publication

www.cerridwenpress.com

NOCTURNE

Elizabeth Donald

Cerridwen Press

A Cerridwen Press Publication

www.cerridwenpress.com

About the Author

80

Elizabeth Donald is a writer fond of things that go chomp in the night. She is the author of the award-winning Nocturnal Urges vampire mystery series and numerous short stories and novellas in the horror, science fiction and erotica genres. By day, she is a newspaper reporter in the St. Louis area, which provides her with an endless source of material. Her web site is www.elizabethdonald.com, and readers can find out more by joining her YahooGroup at groups.yahoo.com/group/elizabethdonald.

Elizabeth welcomes comments from readers. You can find her website and email address on her author bio page at www.cerridwenpress.com.

Author's Note

80

I always wanted to watch someone accept an Oscar by saying, "I have no one to thank. I did it all myself." Maybe Hollywood stars have that much ego, but I know very well that I would never have published NOCTURNAL URGES or A MORE PERFECT UNION without the support of others, so many that I could not name them all in this space.

Special thanks to my family, for their unending optimism and support. To my beloved son, Ian, who puts up with the travel and the eternally-present laptop. To marvelous editor Mary Moran, who makes my best work so much better—without Mary, I'd truly be lost in a sea of commas. To the terrific people at Ellora's Cave and Cerridwen Press, who took a risk on a completely unknown author and have given me such wonderful support. To Beth Kaio and the Writers' Circle, who have given me critiques and support throughout the years. To my fellow Sleepwalkers: Frank Fradella, Kit Tunstall, Jeff Strand and Jay Smith, for their continued advice and fellowship. To my fellow Dragon Ladies: the real Anne Freitas, Kelly Parker and Dana Franks, who shift into high gear at conventions and make some mean margaritas.

Finally, to my wonderful readers. I am blessed with dedicated, creative and slightly insane fans who don't just sit back and listen on the Literary Underworld list. I bounce my ideas off them, and they always have something helpful or witty to say. Roughly half the characters in this series are named after these amazing people, to honor them for their very real contributions. Thank you all, and I hope you'll stay with us for more adventures among the vampires of Memphis.

Here's to nightmares and margaritas at midnight.

Elizabeth Donald

www.elizabethdonald.com

groups.yahoo.com/group/elizabethdonald

Contents

Nocturnal Urges

ဆာ

Chapter One

The silk scarf pressed lightly against her eyelids, forcing them to close. Isabel tried to blink, her lashes twitching against the smooth, taut fabric. When she tried to open her eyes, to sneak a peek down the sides of her nose, she found that he had let the lower part of the scarf fall over her face, obscuring anything from view.

"Trust me." Duane's hands fell away from the scarf.

Isabel reached out, trying to sense where he was. Her hand encountered a broad chest, a muscled arm, and then he guided her hands back to her lap.

The bed shifted, and she sensed him kneeling behind her. "Remind me why we're doing this?" Isabel asked.

"Just as a warm-up," Duane said, his breath gliding over the back of her neck.

"Tease," Isabel said, and caught her breath as Duane's fingers skated lightly over the line of her shoulder, bared in the light sleeveless top she wore.

Duane kissed a gentle line along her shoulder to the place where her neck lay bare. The moist tip of his tongue teased her neck, high up where the pulse beat quickly. Shivers ran through her skin and she exhaled, slightly dizzy. "If you're trying to get me to stay in tonight, you're succeeding," she said.

He whispered in her ear, in between light, quick darts of his tongue. "No," he said. "But I'm not pushing. If you really don't want to, we won't."

Isabel couldn't see, couldn't tell where he would kiss her next. A touch on the shoulder, a lick at the back of her neck, his hand gliding along her thigh. She felt the warmth expanding between her legs, and suddenly going out didn't seem like such a great idea. "What I'd really like to do is get naked with you, right now," she said, smiling.

Duane pressed his teeth lightly against her shoulder. "Baby, I can't wait," he said. "The first time is the best."

Isabel laughed a little. "But will they blindfold me?"

Duane's hand glided up her leg, along her side and brushed lightly over her breast as it wandered up to the blindfold. She gasped just a little when he pulled the scarf free.

"Too kinky?" he asked, his brown eyes amused. He had a classic face, with a square chin and chiseled nose, sandy-brown hair that he let grow a little long, curling a bit around his face.

Isabel smiled. "Oh, no," she said. "Let's keep it in mind."

Duane smiled back, but this time his face was serious. "Are you okay with this?"

"I'm twenty-five years old and I've never been bitten," Isabel said firmly. "Frankly, I'm annoyed I haven't gotten around to it yet."

Duane's eyes cleared. "Great. Then we should get going."

He stood up and walked over to the dresser, where his jacket lay. Isabel sighed just a little—she was turned on, tuned to a high pitch and tense with anticipation. She'd really rather just grab Duane and throw him down on the bed, but he'd planned this to celebrate six months together, and she didn't want to disappoint him.

Isabel stood up and checked her appearance in the full-length mirror beside her bed. Her cheeks were a little flushed, and she had to tuck a black lace slip strap back under her sleeveless navy top. Her black hair was a little out of place, and she smoothed it back from her face.

"Is this all right?" she asked, indicating her casual shirt and short denim skirt.

Duane glanced over at her. "It's perfect," he said. "Besides, you won't be wearing it that long."

Isabel followed him through his apartment and downstairs to the street. The night was clear and cool, a sure sign that Memphis summer had finally waned into the few scant weeks of fall before the winter cold struck. Duane lived right on Main Street, the only downtown street blocked off from auto traffic, except for the trolley that tourists rode from Beale Street to the Pyramid.

They walked under old-fashioned shepherd's-crook streetlights, and in between the buildings, they could see glimpses of the Mississippi River.

"Isn't it a little weird? You know, doing it with *them* in the room?" she asked.

Duane shook his head, but she couldn't see his face. He always walked a step or two ahead of her. It was one of his quirks that drove her crazy. "Not really," he said. "It's not like they're people or anything. Think of them as oversized marital aids."

Isabel couldn't help it, she burst out laughing. "Marital aids with teeth? Is that on the brochure?" she asked as they crossed a street, heading toward the music district.

Duane laughed with her. "It would be if Miss Fiona could get away with it!" he said.

"I know this is silly, but…" Isabel's voice trailed off.

Duane stopped, and turned to face her. "You can't catch it, Isabel. I'd never even consider taking you if it was possible. I've been bitten at least a dozen times, and I'm as human as you are. You've had the vaccination, so you're safe. I promise."

Isabel nodded, feeling silly for even asking it. "You just hear all these horror stories," she said.

Duane shrugged, walking up the street again. She had to hurry to keep up with him. "That's the religious crazies, saying they're demons sent to steal our souls or whatever. They're not evil; they're just animals, doing what they do."

"But not people? It's not like sex with people, like a four-way or anything?" Isabel asked.

Duane snorted. "Hey, if you're into that stuff, you should've mentioned it before, baby," he said, and she could actually hear him waggling his eyebrows, it was there in his tone, although she couldn't see his face.

"In your dreams, darlin'," she replied. "Is it close?"

"Just a few blocks past Beale," Duane said, turning a corner. "They have a hell of a band."

Up ahead, Isabel saw the club, large and recessed from the cheerful, artsy shops of the tourist streets and the pounding jazz of nearby Beale Street. It was on the south side of the street, but Duane led her to the north side to walk up the sidewalk.

"Why are we..." Isabel began, but then she saw them. Four young people in clean, collared shirts and blue jeans stood just beyond the club's property line, wearing placards that read FANGS ARE WORSE THAN GANGS and YES, THEY DO BITE.

One of them saw her looking at the signs and waved his tracts at her. He was a tall one, with a dark beard and intense eyes. "Miss! Don't go in there! It's not worth your soul!" he shouted.

"Just keep walking," Duane muttered.

But Isabel couldn't help it—she risked another glance back. The young man saw her and loped across the street toward her. Her heart started beating faster.

Duane hurried them along, but the young man caught up to them. "You're not going in there, are you?" he asked, almost conversationally.

"Back off, buddy," Duane said, his voice noncommittal.

The man then dismissed Duane, focusing on Isabel. "The leeches steal your soul," he said, his eyes burning into hers. "You will think of nothing else. It's worse than drugs, worse than sex. It's your soul, miss. It's not worth it."

"That's enough," Duane barked, and the man backed off a step. He quickly shoved a tract at Isabel, who took it without thinking. Then he ran back across the street to his friends, who began chanting, "Humans aren't food! Humans aren't food!"

Isabel absently put the tract in her pocket. "Sorry," she said.

"Don't encourage them," Duane said. "If they think they've got a possible convert, they'll be all over you."

They were directly opposite the club now, and the music pounding from inside the building seemed to beat through her very skin as they crossed the street toward the entrance. The club seemed as though it had its own shadows, cloaking it from the clear light of the streetlamps. The design played up the Gothic angle, with ersatz gargoyles along the roof and "stone" outlines painted on the walls. The doorway was arched with torches on either side, and above it was a sign with NOCTURNAL URGES painted in blood-red dripping letters.

"Subtle," Isabel said.

Duane shrugged. "We don't come here for the décor," he said, paying the bouncer. Isabel tried not to be obvious about staring at him, trying to see his teeth. The bouncer was tall and heavyset, but when he handed Duane his change, Isabel saw that his nails were long and pointed.

Duane led her through the arched doorway into a huge, darkened hall filled with smoke that smelled oddly like incense, rather than cigarettes. The light was dark and red, lit from flickering electric "torches" in wagon-wheel chandeliers high above their heads. The walls and floor were painted red, with black curtains on the walls and black swirls painted on the dance floor.

The band up on the stage was playing loud and fast, with pounding drumbeats and an electronic rhythm that seemed without word or plan, just driving on and on. There were at least a hundred people out on the dance floor, gyrating to the music, and many more at tables around the edge of the floor, each with a black lace tablecloth and small candles—red, of course—casting shadows between them. Beyond the ring of dance-floor tables, a few steps up led to another level of tables, all filled with couples.

All through the club, small recessed doorways were closed, nearly hidden in shadows.

Duane led her through to an empty table near the dance floor. Isabel sat down gratefully, preferring to watch the room for a moment or two. She didn't try to talk to Duane—the enormous sound coming from speakers all around them made any discussion impossible.

The music never seemed to end. It pounded on, and Isabel could feel the vibration of it rolling through her skin, through the chair in which she sat, beneath the soles of her feet. Although the people on the dance floor were of every age and background, somehow the music rolled over them and made them into one, as if they each knew how to move without disrupting the rhythms of the others. It was fascinating to watch, in the flickering candlelight and the shadowed glow from electric torches high above them.

Duane was writing something on a piece of paper. Isabel touched his hand, and he looked up at her, leaning over so she could shout into his ear. "What are you doing?" she nearly screamed.

He turned to shout into her ear. "Our order!" he yelled. "You're still up for it, right?"

Isabel nodded quickly, and he returned to the paper, marking X's on the form. But the butterflies in her stomach were fluttering quickly now, and she was less sure than ever that she wanted to try this. It was nothing, everyone had done it—but she was unnerved by the protesters outside, by the dark shadows in this room, by the muted mystery of the closed doors.

But then there was the music. It rolled through her, making her heart beat faster for reasons that had nothing to do with fear. On and on, quickening her pulse, sending shivers down her spine if she concentrated on it.

Isabel glanced up at the stage, and noted with no real surprise that each of the band members had pale skin and long fingernails. A small placard before the drummer read CREATURES OF THE NIGHT. *Of course*, she thought.

She turned back to Duane. "Want to dance?" she shouted, and had to repeat herself twice before Duane understood her.

"No time!" he shouted back. "No waiting list tonight! We're up next!"

Isabel nodded, biting the inside of her lip to keep from being nervous. It didn't work. She fought the urge to grab Duane and take him back home with her, away from this strange place, back to his quiet, modern apartment where a blindfold suddenly didn't seem that kinky.

A hand rested on Isabel's arm and she jumped a little. "Don't worry," said the red-haired woman beside her. "I'm not going to bite you." She was shorter than Isabel, with generous curves readily visible beneath artfully draped, shimmering green robes. Her pale skin was nearly translucent, and a flood of dark red hair curled around her shoulders.

"Hey, Fiona!" Duane shouted.

The red-haired woman smiled, and Isabel saw the pointed teeth. She tried not to stare. "Mr. Russell, welcome back," Fiona called. "And you have brought such a lovely companion with you."

"First-timer, so make it a good one," Duane yelled, smiling.

Fiona rested a hand on Isabel's arm, and Isabel tried not to flinch. Fiona seemed to speak in a normal tone, but Isabel heard every word nonetheless. "Don't worry, my dear," she said. "At Nocturnal Urges, we are here for your pleasure."

She released Isabel's arm and handed her a form. "Please ask if there's anything you don't understand," she said, and tapped the form.

Isabel nodded, and looked at the form. CONSENT AND RELEASE, it read at the top. The letterhead read NOCTURNAL URGES VAMPIRE SERVICE, FIONA KNIGHT, PROPRIETOR.

She scanned through it—a lot of legalese, indicating she was there of her own free will, that she had not been bitten in the past two weeks or given blood in the past six weeks, that she was over twenty-one, that she had had her immunization at the age of two along with everyone else in America.

She filled out her information, and when it asked which gender she preferred, she checked MALE.

"What does this mean?" she asked Duane, tapping the pen against the line that read LEVEL OF SERVICE.

"They want to know how far you want to go," he shouted.

Isabel frowned. "What do I put?"

"Level one," he yelled. "Bite only."

Isabel blinked, and circled LEVEL ONE on the form. "What else can they do?"

Duane grinned. "I haven't tried anything else," he yelled. "I heard you can get fucked if you really want."

Isabel grinned and glanced around, as though anyone could possibly hear them over the pounding music, still vibrating through the air. "Is it legal?"

Duane shrugged. "Everything's legal in here!" he yelled.

She signed ISABEL NELSON at the bottom of the form, and watched him sign DUANE RUSSELL on his. Almost immediately, Fiona reappeared to take their forms. "Follow me!" she called, and Duane stood up.

Isabel stood to follow them, but her knees were suddenly a little weak. She took Duane's hand gratefully, relishing its solid comfort in the swirling shadows of the club. Fiona led them around the dance floor to a dark, recessed door. Isabel blushed, looking around to see if anyone was watching them. She felt as though the entire club would know what she and Duane were here to do. But no one was looking at them.

Fiona unlocked the door and led them into the room. It was lit only by a candelabra on a small table against the wall. Shadows danced around the room, which was painted to look as though it had been hewn out of stone. A huge four-poster bed hung with black drapes was against the far wall, and a soft bench without a back or arms sat in the middle of the room.

The music was a little quieter here, but Isabel could still hear it pounding beyond the door.

"Your attendants will be with you shortly," Fiona said and slipped out, closing the door behind her.

Isabel looked around, hugging her arms nervously. Duane came over to her, running his hands over her bare arms. "You're not afraid, are you?" he asked.

"No," she lied, forcing her arms to relax.

"Good," he said, and stroked her arm gently, up and down, using the soft pads of his fingers instead of the tips, where a jagged nail or hardened callus can roughen the skin.

Damn, he always knows how to get me, Isabel thought, letting the shivers relax her. It had been this way with Duane since the beginning, a naked heat that seemed to grow each time they made love instead of quenching the fire between them.

Duane unbuttoned his shirt, slipping it off his bare, muscled shoulders. She ran her hands over his chest, playing with the light mat of hair down the center. He lowered his head to kiss her, and her mouth welcomed his with heat and passion, melding into one.

Then the voice spoke. "Forgive the intrusion," she said, and her voice was like the cool brush of silk across bare flesh, both enticing and chilling at once. Isabel looked around and saw a young woman standing beside the bed. She was small and slim, nearly frail, with skin like thinned milk and silky golden hair fanned out in cornsilk strands across the wine-dark dress she wore. Almost conservative, it was a simple scooped-neck dress with capped sleeves and a long skirt, but its deep wine color was a startling contrast to her milk-pale skin.

"Just in time," Duane said with slight difficulty. "What's your name?"

"Elyse," she said, stepping forward. "He is Ryan."

Isabel looked around, but didn't see anyone else. For that matter, she hadn't seen Elyse enter the room through the only doorway.

"I am Ryan," said another voice, and suddenly Isabel saw him, standing in the shadows beside the bed. The first thing she noticed was his hair, dark and cropped close, but with a touch of wave to it that almost seemed as though it was meant to grow long and curl about his shoulders like a man in a romance movie. Then she looked at his face, into his dark eyes, and wondered how she could have noticed his hair first. His was a face that belonged in an old photograph, dark and intense, as though he were in sepia tones in an old family album. His eyes were dark in the dancing shadows. But as he moved into the light, she saw they were a deep azure blue like the sky on a clear summer day.

"Me first," Duane said. "So she can see how it goes."

"As you wish," Elyse said, gesturing to the chair. Duane led her over to it and quickly slid off his slacks. He sat in the chair, his legs slightly apart. Isabel stepped close to him, a little shy with other people in the room.

"They're not there, not really," Duane whispered, and Isabel nodded. She drew the sleeveless top over her head and let it drop. She kept her eyes on Duane, pretending that there was no one in the room but him, and vampires didn't exist.

Isabel stepped closer to Duane, unzipping her skirt and letting it drop to the floor with her panties. She started to slide the strap of her black lace slip off her shoulder, but Duane shook his head. "Keep it on, baby," he said pulling her onto his lap.

Isabel straddled him in the chair, feeling the hard branch beneath the thin cotton of his shorts press against her. He rubbed it against her gently and she pressed hard against him, her hands clenching involuntarily against his shoulders.

She wanted to dismiss the vampires and make love to him, but he stilled her rocking hips, holding her steady.

"Elyse," he said, and the pale vampire slid up behind him. Her translucent-pale hands glided down over Duane's arms and across his chest, between his body and Isabel's. It was strange, as though Elyse were intruding on a private moment between them. But as Elyse's hand passed close to Isabel's bare arm, she could feel something pass over her skin, an electricity generated by the vampire as she moved over a living body.

Elyse moved around them, standing behind Isabel for a moment, and Isabel fought the urge to turn and watch the vampire. "Look at me, Duane," Elyse purred, her voice cool as silk sheets on a rain-pounded night. Isabel watched Duane's eyes meet Elyse's, and there was a sudden calm, an almost beatific trance over his face.

Elyse slipped back behind Duane and lowered her mouth to his neck. She breathed lightly, and Isabel felt Duane grow harder and hotter beneath her thighs. Elyse licked along the juncture of his neck and shoulder, delicate as a cat licking cream.

Elyse smiled, revealing the sharp white points of her teeth. Her head darted downward in a swirl of cornsilk hair and she plunged her teeth into Duane's neck. Her lips pressed down and sucked the blood welling from Duane.

Duane cried out, a hoarse moan that came from somewhere deep in his chest. Beneath her thighs, Isabel felt that hard rock swell and explode, rocking beneath her, wetting her skin, his muscles jumping and clenching against her. His hands gripped hard on Isabel's hips, and he cried out again as Elyse sucked one more time, a long draught before licking the wound clean.

The haze cleared from Duane's face, and he leaned forward against Isabel. "Oh God, baby," he murmured. "I can't wait to watch you go."

Elyse had retreated a step, giving Duane a moment to regain his composure. Isabel's heart was beating too fast. Ryan was crossing the room toward her. *What if it hurts?* she thought. The music was suddenly too loud again, pounding through the door into her mind, driving her heart faster and faster.

Ryan's steps slowed as if he had heard her thoughts. He reached out a single finger, touching her lightly on the lips. "I will never harm you," he said softly, and instinctively, Isabel believed him.

Ryan moved forward slowly now, stepping beside Duane, who was loose and satiated beneath her. Duane's hands were stroking along her thighs and up her sides, then back down again, growing warmer beneath her thighs.

"Look at me," Ryan said. If Elyse's voice had been silk, Ryan's was like warm flannel, comforting and soft. Isabel raised her gaze.

Ryan's eyes were no longer blue, but black, as if the small black circle at the center had expanded to fill the deep azure blue of his eyes, and nothing was left but darkness. She had never seen eyes as dark as his, dark enough to see her own reflection in them, even in the dim candlelight. In his eyes, she saw herself, skin flushed with heat. It was as though the room was spinning, and only the chair and Ryan's eyes kept her from falling down. Vertigo swirled through her head, but at her center, she was still and calm.

Elyse had returned to her place behind Duane, gliding her hands up and down his arms and chest. Ryan moved behind Isabel. Although some part of her still recoiled in fear, that calm place in her midsection remained — and her skin shivered with the fire that had been lit within her.

Ryan's hand moved over her shoulder, gliding down the bare skin of her arm. He barely touched her, but the skin beneath his hand trembled and shuddered. It was as though he created an electrical field with his hands, stirring the nerves of her skin to exquisite life, and wherever his hands roved, her body trembled.

He stroked along one arm, then back up the inside, along tender, untouched skin. Then he stroked the other arm, and back up the inside, then both at once. He drew his hands up over her shoulders, to the smooth skin along her shoulder blades, and she couldn't help crying out at the sensations rippling down her back.

Ryan slid one hand around her neck, where the pulse beat a rapid patter beneath the hollow of her throat. Slowly it wandered downward, over the upper swells of her breasts to the tender valley between them. The loose silken lace of her slip fell lower, and the electrical storm created by his hand moved to the right, enveloping her breast and the taut nipple, sending shooting bursts of pleasure throughout her body.

Beneath her, she felt Duane stir to life again, hardening between her legs. She opened her eyes and saw him watching her, fire burning in his eyes. She was helpless beneath the storm of sensations Ryan had created on her skin. She felt the ache between her legs, the familiar heat of unfulfilled want, swollen and hot.

Duane's hands shifted down beneath her slip, raising up a moment, and she felt the cotton shorts slide away, leaving nothing between them. His hard, warm flesh pressed directly against her, and she cried out.

Ryan's other hand had moved beneath her slip, filling her left breast with that electrical fire, that dance of nerves and heat that made her heart pound and her hips rotate desperately against Duane. It was as though she felt some deep-seated itch that she could not scratch; something that only hot desire could fill.

Isabel felt Ryan's tongue, surprisingly warm and delicate, licking a long line along her shoulder, up to the place where her shoulder curved into her neck. Shivers ran down her spine and she cried out wordless sounds of pleasure.

Duane's hands were on her hips, lifting her up, and he thrust into her, hard and strong. She settled down on him, rocking back and forth. She felt the press of two hard, sharp points at her throat, and forgot to be afraid.

Ryan's teeth sank in, and a bright sharp pain darted across her neck, bringing a momentary lull to the pleasure. Then his mouth closed over the wound and the pain instantly vanished. The warm, moist pressure of his mouth tugged sensually at her skin, and she had the feeling of something being drawn out of her, some great velvet thread that began coiled between her legs and drew up through her stomach and chest, around her breasts and up to the place where Ryan sucked at her throat, drawing through her a velvet friction within her skin.

The roil and shudder began in her lower belly, growing and thundering through her until it filled her limbs and skin and seemed to explode from her mouth as she cried out into the air, a shattered explosion that cycled again and again, clenching and releasing as Duane exploded within her, brought by the violent eruptions within her body.

Isabel cried out again as the glorious fever ebbed. She felt Duane collapse against her chest, his head moist with sweat and his mouth open with his own breathless exhalations.

Lightly, Ryan's tongue licked the wound on her neck, catching some small drop that lingered on her skin. That one touch set off a cascade of shudders throughout her body, down beneath her skin to the place where Duane had withdrawn from her, now spent. Duane was in some other place, his eyes closed.

A swirl of warm velvet around her, and Isabel looked up to see Ryan, gently placing a wrap around her bare shoulders. Wordlessly he faded back into the shadows, and though she watched carefully, she could not see him leave. Elyse also faded into shadows, and Isabel knew when they were alone.

Carefully she extracted herself from the bench, but her legs were wobbly and unsteady. She made her way to the bed, pulling the velvet wrap around her. Duane had sunk down onto the floor, resting against the bench in his exhaustion.

Her limbs were heavy, suffused with warmth. She wanted only to curl up and sleep. But more than that, she wished Ryan were holding her, that the room was theirs for the night and she could…

What?

Duane. She wished that *Duane* were holding her, not Ryan. Isabel blinked, and shook her head. *I must be more tired than I thought.*

She lay down on the bed, curling into the velvet wrap. She watched Duane stir a little, sitting up next to the bench.

"Damn, baby," he said softly. "I'm never going to be able to walk out of here."

She smiled a little.

Duane stood up. "You okay?" he asked, pulling on his pants.

"Yeah," Isabel said, still curled up in the velvet wrap.

"Shake a leg then," Duane said. "We don't get to stay long."

Isabel gave up. She stood up, and reached for her clothes. Duane had never figured out that she liked to be held afterward. When it was over, it was over, according to him. To be fair, she'd never made a big deal out of it. She didn't want to be one of those whiny you-don't-bring-me-flowers-anymore women.

Sometimes, though, you just want your guy to pick up on what you want without spelling it out for him.

Isabel zipped up her skirt, wishing there was a bathroom somewhere so she could freshen up a bit. Somewhere, the pounding music came to a sudden stop, replaced with thundering footsteps and raised voices. Until the music stopped, Isabel hadn't been quite aware of its constant pressure, the rhythm behind the walls that seemed to radiate sex.

"That's weird," Duane said. "I wonder—"

He didn't get to finish his statement, because the door flung open and a short, severe woman in jeans and a jacket stood braced in the doorway. Her hand rested at her hip, and Isabel knew without being told that the woman had a gun. Isabel pulled the velvet wrap around her shoulders, acutely aware that she was wearing only the slip and her skirt.

"Everything all right in here? Are you both okay?" the woman asked.

"Yeah," Duane said. "What's going on?"

The woman shook her head in a fast, businesslike manner, and Isabel realized she was a cop. "Please don't leave this room, sir. You or the lady. Someone will be back to talk to you in a minute."

She stepped back, and the door swung closed.

"Shit," Duane said. "A bust."

Isabel gaped at him. "You said it was legal!"

"It is," Duane said. "But plenty of people bring stuff that isn't legal here. The bite's legal, and vampire prostitution is legal, because they can't carry disease or impregnate you. But nothing's gonna stop some idiot from bringing fireweed to the party and ruining it for the rest of us."

Isabel pulled her shirt back on. "You're sure? I really wasn't up for getting arrested tonight."

Duane smiled. "But you liked it? It was good?"

She ducked her head, oddly embarrassed. It had been his idea, so it seemed silly to be shy about it. But her legs were still shaky, her stomach still full of butterflies, her head still a little swimmy from the most incredible orgasm of her life. "It was good, better than good," she said.

Duane went over to her, and she nestled into his arms gratefully. He stroked her hair and kissed the top of her head. "I knew you'd like it," he said.

The door opened again, and the cop came back in. "Sorry about the disturbance, folks," she said. "I'm Detective Anne Freitas, and I hate to do this to you, but I need you to stick around for a few minutes."

"What's going on? We haven't been outside this room for a while," Duane said, and Isabel blushed a little.

Freitas seemed unfazed. She was a little shorter than Isabel, her reddish hair cut sensibly short. "How long?"

Duane glanced at his watch. "An hour, maybe more."

Freitas pulled out a notebook and started writing. "You're Duane Russell and Isabel Nelson, correct?"

"Yeah," Duane said. Isabel stayed quiet.

Freitas wrote something down. "And who was with you?"

Isabel dropped her eyes, and Freitas picked up on it fast, her laser gaze boring into Isabel.

"Two vamps, legally paid for," Duane said.

Freitas kept her eyes on Isabel. "Names?"

Duane shrugged. "I don't remember."

Isabel looked back at Freitas. "Ryan and Elyse," she said softly.

Freitas kept staring at Isabel. "They were here the whole time?" she asked.

Isabel nodded. "They just left a few minutes ago."

Freitas stared at her a moment longer, then looked at her notebook and wrote some more. "And you're sure it's been an hour."

Duane shrugged. "Give or take a little. Ask Fiona, she'll know what time she brought us back here."

"Fiona's busy," Freitas said absently, making another note. "Anything unusual tonight, anything out of the ordinary?"

Isabel couldn't help a small giggle, mostly from nervous tension. Freitas zeroed in on her immediately—Isabel had the feeling this woman noticed everything. "Something funny, Miss Nelson?"

"Nothing was unusual," Duane interjected. "Just the same as every night."

"So what's so funny?" Freitas asked.

Isabel ducked her head. "It's just…you asked if anything was unusual, and this whole place is so unusual it just struck me funny," she said.

Freitas stared at her a moment, then pulled out a Polaroid photograph and shoved it at Isabel. "Know him?" she asked.

Isabel looked at the photo and her giggles died as if doused with cold water. The photo showed a middle-aged man lying in a pool of blood, his corpse-pale face frozen in a rictus-grin.

"Oh my God," Isabel heard herself say, and the photo fell from her nerveless fingers onto the floor.

Duane stooped down to pick it up, looked at it, and jerked as though it had burned his fingers. He shoved it back at Freitas. "Jesus! What the hell is that?"

"Do you know him?" Freitas repeated.

"No, no," Isabel said, feeling strange and lightheaded. She must have stumbled a little, because Duane suddenly had his arm around her shoulders and Freitas was leading her to a chair.

"Are you okay, miss?" Freitas asked.

"Yes," Isabel said, embarrassed. "I just got a little dizzy, that's all."

"It's that damn picture," Duane snapped. "You had to shove that in her face, officer?"

"I'm okay," Isabel protested.

Freitas was staring at Isabel's face. "First-time bite?" Isabel nodded. "It's minor blood loss. You'll feel okay in a few hours. Be sure to drink plenty of fluids and don't have any alcohol."

Duane laid a hand possessively on Isabel's shoulder. "Can we go now, officer?"

Isabel was suddenly, inexplicably annoyed. "She's a detective, Duane."

Duane blinked, and Freitas did a double-take. "That's all right, miss. Happens all the time." Freitas handed Duane a business card. "Please contact me if you think of anything we should know about tonight."

Duane rolled his eyes. "How could we know anything, we've been in here all night!" he snapped. "What happened to that guy anyway?"

Freitas pocketed the photograph. "Murdered in the alley behind the club. Looks like a vamp-kill."

Duane shook his head. "Fucking animals."

Isabel stared up at Duane, stunned. "I thought they were safe," she said quietly.

Freitas was glaring at Duane. "That depends on your definition," she said. "They know a vamp-kill is an automatic death sentence."

"Can we go now?" Duane asked, and his tone was rude enough that Isabel was embarrassed.

Freitas closed her notebook. "Yes. Thank you for your cooperation," she said in a neutral tone.

Isabel stood up, holding on to Duane's arm. As they passed Freitas, the detective slipped her another business card. She pocketed it without Duane noticing.

Walking out into the club, the entire atmosphere was different. The torches were overcast with large fluorescent lights, and the band was sitting on the edge of the stage, talking to two police officers. Small groups of patrons were standing around the dance floor, as police milled about. Something indefinable had left the room, that sense of mystery and magical danger had dissipated along with the shadows.

For some reason, Isabel was sad to see it gone.

Chapter Two

ରୀ

Ryan bent over her, his eyes deepening to that total black color. A gentle smile barely showed the points of his teeth, and Isabel was not afraid.

He lowered his mouth to hers, and she felt the gentle pressure of his lips molding to hers. His whole body hovered over hers, barely brushing against her naked skin. She felt the electric heat of him tingling in the tips of her breasts, the curve of her abdomen and the long muscles in her thighs.

She seemed incapable of moving, pinned and pliable beneath Ryan as his hand wandered over her skin. She felt that electric warmth moving down her neck, between her breasts and lower, until it settled between her legs, and she broke the kiss with a cry of sudden sensation.

"Beloved," Ryan whispered against her throat, the moist heat of his breath caressing her skin. He pressed his lips against her throat, his tongue dancing a line along her neck.

Isabel was still unable to move, her arms languid and heavy beside her. His mouth traveled lower, licking and kissing a slow line over the upper swells of her breasts to the tender skin between them. She felt the expanding warmth between her thighs, and he gently pushed her legs apart, settling between them.

"Yes, beloved," she murmured.

Ryan caught her nipple in his mouth, rubbing it with his tongue until it hardened into a tiny, sensitive bud. Isabel wanted to reach down and pull him into her, to feel that aching emptiness filled with him. She wanted him to slide into her, to grasp his hardness and feel its velvet-smooth strength as it thrust into her.

But her arms would not move, she was still a prisoner of his power over her.

She looked down at him, at her breast caught in his mouth, and opened her mouth to beg him to enter her. But her words dried up as she saw his teeth sinking into the soft skin of her breast, just above the nipple. Blood pooled up from the bite and he drank greedily, his lips closing over it as a slight line of blood trickled down between her breasts. There was no pain.

Isabel tried to speak, to push at his head, but that languid stillness remained like an invisible down pillow pressed against her. Then the pleasure began, vibrating between her legs, and she cried out at the building sensation within her skin even as her mind cried out in horror, aghast at the blood now running across her chest, the blood turning reddish-black in the light, the blood —

Isabel jerked awake with a tiny gasp, her heart pounding in the darkness. She heard Duane's heavy breathing beside her and knew immediately that he had not awakened. She reached beneath her thin nightshirt and felt the skin above her nipple.

It was smooth, unmarked and uninjured. But the nipple below it was hard and hot, sensitive to the touch.

She exhaled, tension leaving her muscles, and she let her hand rest over her breast for a moment. She touched her breast lightly, the real sensations of pleasure rolling over the dream-touches and fading them from memory. Her heart still pounding, she realized she was still highly aroused, charged with a deep sexual energy still unexpended.

She looked over at Duane's sleeping form, turned away from her. *I wonder if he'd mind if I woke him*, she thought, sliding her free hand lightly over his muscular back.

A brief memory of the dream, Ryan's mouth sucking blood from her breast, tried to intervene in her mind and she pushed it away relentlessly. The combination of terror and ecstasy was sharp and bitter in her mind, and the pressure between her legs was still unrelieved.

"Duane," she murmured, and he did not stir.

Slowly, she slid a hand over Duane's hip, down beneath his boxers, and found him flaccid and sleep-warm. She danced her fingers lightly over him, taking him in her hand, gently stroking him. She felt him stir and begin to harden in her hand.

She worked him lightly, slowly, feeling him grow hotter, firmer beneath her fingers. His breathing changed, and she realized he was awake. She stopped for just a moment to draw her nightshirt over her head and pressed her body full against his back.

Isabel licked the curve of Duane's ear, listening to him catch his breath. He was fully hard now, his hand clenching the pillow, and she moved against him tight and strong.

"God, baby," he murmured, and rolled onto his back. Isabel slid over him, pressing herself against him, rubbing herself against him in a smooth rocking motion.

Duane dipped his head between her breasts, molding them with his hands, his mouth opening to taste her. She froze for a moment as his lips closed over her nipple, and the image of Ryan tried to intervene. She bit hard on her lip and the dream receded beneath Duane's kneading fingers and tight, sucking mouth.

She slid her hand down between them and guided him to her. He thrust up hard into her, and she cried out in short, gasping breaths. He rocked beneath her, his hands moving down from her breasts to the curve of her hips, steadying her as he slid in and out, filling her over and over again.

The ache was gone, replaced by a delicious fullness and gasping joy. She rode him harder, heat and sweat covering her body. She took his hands in hers and pressed them up over his head, jerking her hips harder against his rising body.

Her nipples hovered bare inches from his face and he caught one in his mouth, sucking it hard and making her cry out.

The rhythm of his hips sped up beneath her and she knew he was close. His hands broke free of hers and clasped onto her shoulders, pushing her down hard so he could bury himself deep within her. It kept her still, unable to move freely, as though trapped beneath his hands. He jerked and cried out beneath her, and she felt him explode within her, his head thrown back in ecstasy. His hands relented as he came. Isabel continued thrusting, rocking harder, feeling her orgasm swell within her, until she too exploded in wave after wave of bursting sensation.

The tension in her muscles slowly ebbed. He slipped from her, still breathing hard, and she slid to his side, up against his chest.

"Damn," he said softly. "What time is it?"

Isabel didn't want to turn and look at the clock. "I don't know," she said.

Duane sat up, leaving her leaning against an empty pillow, and glanced at the clock. "It's almost two in the morning," he said, getting up to go toward the bathroom.

Isabel lay still for a moment, feeling a little lost as the sweat cooled on her skin. The aching emptiness was gone, but at the same time, there seemed to be some other emptiness Duane hadn't touched, something left unfulfilled.

He came back in, wearing a fresh pair of boxers. He slid back into bed, and kissed her on the cheek. "You sure know how to give a man a good surprise, baby," he said, and turned away on his side.

For a moment, Isabel considered asking him to hold her, or scooting over toward him so he couldn't possibly ignore her. Then she sighed quietly and got out of bed, still naked. She went into the bathroom and turned on the shower, letting the water warm.

She stared at herself in the bathroom mirror. Her black hair was tousled and wild, heat still flushing her face and body. She ran her hands lightly over her skin, feeling the light sweat and the smell of sex still on her body.

There was a light mark on her breast. A faint, reddish mark.

Of course there is, she thought.

The mark was slightly above the nipple. Just a faint reddish tinge.

Wasn't Duane sucking on the nipple itself? she thought, and the memory sent a faint twinge of electricity through her still-warm body. But was it Duane's mouth she was remembering or Ryan's?

That's silly, she thought. *It was a dream.*

* * * * *

"You look better."

Isabel looked up from her desk to see Det. Freitas standing over her. "I beg your pardon?"

Freitas leaned against the cubicle wall. "You look a lot better than the other night. You feeling okay?"

Isabel glanced around to see if anyone was listening. The office was a honeycomb of cubicles, hiding any number of eavesdropping ears, but no one within her line of sight seemed to be paying attention. "I feel fine, thank you," she said. "Is there something I can do for you, Detective?"

Freitas shrugged. "Feel like a cup of coffee?"

Isabel didn't feel like a cup of coffee, but she was desperate to get Freitas away from her co-workers. "I've got a lunch break in ten minutes. I can leave early."

Freitas nodded, and Isabel quickly collected her purse. They walked through the honeycomb in silence, for which

Isabel was profoundly grateful. She waited until they were out on the sidewalk before she spoke. "I'm sorry, Detective, I didn't mean to be rude. It's just…"

"You don't want your friends to know about your weekend plans," Freitas finished.

Isabel shrugged. "It's just they're not really my friends. They're people I work with, that's all, and I don't want any rumors running around about me."

Freitas gestured to a nearby café. "That place has great coffee," she said.

They were seated quickly and Isabel ordered a sandwich, although she wasn't very hungry. Freitas ordered a ham-and-cheese omelet with extra onions while stirring sugar into her coffee.

The waitress left, and Isabel stared at Freitas for a moment before speaking. "I suppose I'll find out eventually, but is there something you want to talk to me about?"

Freitas sipped her coffee. "Maybe I just wanted to see how you were doing. You didn't look so hot at the club."

Isabel cast her eyes down. "I was tired."

"You didn't look that thrilled to be there," Freitas said.

Isabel shook her head. "Is that what this is about? You think someone made me go? I was there of my own free will, and I had a good time."

"Whatever you say," Freitas said.

Isabel couldn't help asking. "So that guy, the one whose picture you showed me…"

"Yeah. Sorry about that," Freitas said.

Isabel waved her hand dismissively. "No, I just wanted to know if you caught the guy who did it."

"What makes you think it was a guy?" Freitas said, glancing at her.

Isabel blinked. "I don't know, I guess it could be a woman," she said. "Did you catch him? Her? It?"

"Nope," Freitas said. "No hims, hers or its. Third body this month at Nocturnal Urges, and I'm starting to get itchy about it."

"Three!" Isabel said, shocked.

"Yup." Freitas swirled her coffee in her mug. "All three, male patrons. At this point, I'm a step away from consulting a psychic. Don't suppose you have ideas?"

Isabel shook her head. "They steal your soul," she murmured.

"What was that?" Freitas asked.

"I'm sure it's nothing," Isabel said.

"No such thing as nothing, what are you thinking?" Freitas asked.

Isabel hesitated then remembered the man in the photograph, and the blood. "It's just…if it wasn't vampires…"

"And that's a big if," Freitas interjected.

"If it wasn't the vampires, it could be someone trying to make it look like the vampires," Isabel said. "There were these protesters…"

"Yeah, the Students Against Vampires," Freitas said. "Call themselves SAV, spelled 'save' without the E. I think they ought to learn how to spell before they try to save *my* soul."

Isabel giggled a little, and Freitas smiled with her. Then for no reason, they were both laughing, and in that laugh, some of the tension eased. The food arrived while they were laughing, and Isabel found herself laughing all over again at the incongruity of their conversation in this light, airy café with French art prints on the walls and white wicker furniture.

"They're mostly harmless," Freitas said when the laughter faded. "Wave their signs, bother the clientele. They don't cross the line, at least not that Fiona's been able to prove."

"There was this one guy," Isabel said. "Dark hair, beard. Real intense. He came over to talk to us on the other side of the street."

"Legal, if annoying," Freitas said.

"Yeah, but he was really intense. Said the vampires would steal my soul," Isabel said, and her voice faltered a little.

"Yeah," Freitas said, looking rather intently at Isabel. "That's a common line. Along with, 'Fucking animals'."

Isabel dropped her eyes. "That was rude of him," she said softly.

"But it's what he thinks, isn't it?" Freitas said. "That's all the vamps are, animals."

"Aren't they?" Isabel asked. "No, I'm really asking. I don't know any vampires, but…"

"You were at the club," Freitas said, spearing a chunk of ham with her fork. "You saw them. Are they animals?"

Isabel suddenly saw Ryan's eyes turn black, felt that jolt between her breasts, the shivers down her spine. "I… I don't know," she said.

"Uh-huh," Freitas said. "Let me tell you what I know, Miss Nelson. Vamps have minds and bodies, just like us. They live and work, have jobs and apartments, just like us. They've got an unusual diet, that's for sure, but so do vegetarians and kosher Jews, so I'm not going to throw stones. They do good things and sometimes they do bad things, just like us, and then it's my job to go do something about it."

Freitas stopped eating for a moment and looked at Isabel. "There's all kinds of animals, human and vamp. You can't tell an animal from a man just by looking, Miss Nelson."

"Isabel," she replied. "You can call me Isabel."

* * * * *

"Watch your step," the uniform warned her, handing over a clipboard as he stood watch in the alley.

"Thanks, Wyben, I've never been to a crime scene before," Freitas snapped, glancing at the notes scrawled on the clipboard.

"Sorry, ma'am," the kid said. "It's just real slippery."

Judging by the blood smeared along Wyben's pants, he'd figured that out the hard way, she thought. The two short steps leading into the abandoned building were slicked with blood, almost invisible against the dark, filthy cement in the shadows cast by the orange streetlight.

"Photogs done?" Freitas asked.

"Yeah," Wyben said, looking a little green. "M.E., too. Soon as you're done, they'll bag him."

Wyben was trying to look tough, but even in the crappy orange light Freitas could see he was pale. She tried to think of something steadying to say, but quickly gave up. Comfort wasn't one of her strengths.

Freitas stepped — carefully — over the blood-soaked steps and into the shadowy space beyond. A few jury-rigged lights had been set up, and three officers held up their flashlights, sending dancing shadows around the abandoned building. A photographer was carefully loading his equipment back into a bag and everyone was walking on eggshells.

Freitas tried to avoid the runnels of blood all over the floor, but finally gave up. *Crappy shoes anyway.* She walked straight through the blood toward the body, laid out under the best of the lights.

"Dead no more than a few hours, the blood's only tacky," said the medical examiner, squatting beside the body. Freitas thought only three types of people could squat gracefully—little children, the mothers of little children and Joann Betschart, a medical examiner who didn't like to kneel in blood and shit. If Freitas tried squatting like that, she'd end up with a big smeary bloodstain on her ass.

"Vamp?" Freitas asked, staring at the guy's torn-up throat. No way he'd been any older than twenty. His blue eyes stared sightless, frozen in nearly comical shock at whatever had been his last sight on earth.

"Unofficially?" Betschart said. "It's someone who really likes to bite. Not a dog or other predator—that's a human bite radius. Not enough tissue left for a match, but I bet if you find the sick son of a bitch, you won't have any trouble figuring out it's him."

Freitas leaned over, shining her flashlight right at the torn flesh of the throat. In the harsh relief of concentrated light, the wound looked like someone had jammed a monster firecracker down the guy's throat and set it off.

"Tell me he's never been to a particular club near Beale," Freitas said.

"Can't help you there," Betschart said. "He's got old bites."

Freitas leaned closer. "How can you tell? His neck's hamburger."

"Wrist," Betschart said, lifting the meaty arm. Freitas shone her flashlight at it, and sure enough, there were the telltale pockmarks of a regular feeder.

"Doesn't mean NU," Freitas said. "He could have a vamp lover."

"That's your department," Betschart said. "I just work here."

"It'll be NU," Freitas sighed. "Wonder what this one did to get munched."

Betschart shrugged and straightened up. "Kept breathing?"

"Ha. That's funny, Joann, you gonna come back for a curtain call?" Freitas took a closer look at the bites on the wrist.

"Testy, Annie, you might want to get more fiber in your diet," Betschart said. "I'll send my boys down for him. Wyben outside has his vitals."

"Yeah, I saw the sheet," Freitas said, running her flashlight around the body in a quick, cursory glance. "No wife and kids this time, praise the Lord and pass the blood."

"It's gonna stink to high heaven in here by Tuesday," Betschart said. "They'd better get a HAZMAT team in."

"Better yet, just tear the whole nasty-ass place down, this building gives me the creeps," Freitas said. "Blood barely changes the decor, and by the way, why is there so much of it? Don't suppose Dead Man Bleeding had any company?"

"Nope," Betschart said. "There's two gallons of blood in the human body. You take one glass of orange juice, drop it, and it'll cover half the kitchen floor. Two gallons'll mess up half your house quite efficiently."

"I can always count on you for gruesome, useless trivia, Joann," Freitas said, following her out.

"See ya next body," Betschart said, turning the opposite way.

Shit, Freitas thought. *Four.*

* * * * *

The water flowed over Isabel's fingers, and she jerked them away quickly. She turned down the hot water a little and added two scoops of bubble bath salts to the water.

Humming to herself, she switched on the radio and let jazz music fill the room. She lit a candle beside the oversized oval tub.

In the mirror, she saw the fading marks on her neck.

It had been two weeks since the night at Nocturnal Urges and the marks were already healed over. Only a faint reddish tinge remained.

Isabel sighed and unwrapped her robe belt. Of course, at that moment the phone rang in the bedroom. She dove for it, keeping an eye on the water level in the tub. "Hello?"

"Hey, baby," Duane said. "What're you doing?"

"Taking a bath," Isabel said, walking back into the bathroom with the cordless phone. "It's a very exciting evening."

"It would be if I was off work," Duane said. "I'd come over to your place, sneak upstairs while you were in the tub…"

"Oh stop, you're just teasing me," Isabel chided.

Duane deepened his voice and added a fake accent somewhere between French and German. "Zen I would slide up behind yu, cover your eyes vith my hands and make luuv to yu in ze vater…"

"You're so mean," Isabel said, testing the water again.

Duane dropped the silly accent. "I'm trying to get back on days, baby," he said.

"S'okay," Isabel said. "Good to have you out of my hair once in a while."

Instantly, the accent was back. "Nevaire, nevaire, my darlink," he said. "Yu are mine, mine, mine!"

Isabel couldn't help giggling. "Can anyone hear you? Because you sound completely ridiculous."

"No, my darlink, ze information seestems department ees completely empty, because only schmucks like me must vork this shift," he said.

"My bath is ready, and I can't take ze accent any longer," Isabel said. "Go earn money, behave yourself."

"Your vish is my command, my darlink," Duane said. "Enjoy ze bath."

"Goodnight, silly," she said.

"Goot night."

Isabel clicked off the phone and set it beside the tub in case he called back for more goofiness. She slipped off her robe and let it drop to the floor, sliding a foot into the bubbles and the warm caress of the water. It was just right, almost too hot but not quite.

I'm so lucky, she thought. *Duane is so…*

No words came to mind. She sank into the tub, the water flowing over her, and she felt the familiar prickles of goose bumps along her legs and arms as the water warmed her.

Duane was smart, funny and sexy as hell, she reflected. He made her laugh and he made her cry out in passion. He was good-looking as well—half the female workers at their company were jealous to see him drop by her cubicle.

Isabel sighed, smoothing her hands down her thighs, gathering suds and drifting them up over her chest.

So what's wrong?

Nothing was wrong, she thought. She couldn't be such a perfectionist as to find something wrong with Duane. She'd gone from relationship to relationship, always finding some fatal flaw as soon as things got serious. But Duane had been around for six months and so far, no flaws had appeared. He'd even introduced her to the bite.

Instantly, the sensory memory took her over, and she felt the sharp press of teeth at her neck, that coil within her loosening and drawing beneath her skin, the growing tension of pleasure through her body, almost as if it were happening again.

You're crazy, girl. No orgasm is better than a real, solid relationship. Duane's a good guy, a keeper. Are you looking to be alone?

Isabel let her eyes drift closed, leaning back against the wall of the tub as a husky female voice came from the radio, mellow and smooth. She drifted her hands over the suds, over her breasts, and thought about what Duane had said. She imagined him sneaking into her bathroom, his hands sliding into the water, and she let her own hands drift over her abdomen and down between her thighs.

"Mmm," she murmured, imagining he was there, touching her, his black eyes intense above hers, black hair cut too short around his face.

Her eyes flew open, reasserting reality and banishing Ryan's face from her mind.

"Dammit!" she said aloud. "Would you leave me alone?"

No one answered.

Isabel sat up, her body now tense and unrelieved in the tub. A thought came to mind, a simple image.

The bed. That black-iron bed with four posts, lit only by the candelabra.

Ryan lying naked in the bed, reclining on his side, with the black satin sheets discreetly swept over his hip. An inviting smile graced his mouth as he beckoned her to join him.

No. It's cheating.

Isabel absently smoothed sudsy water over her shoulders.

It's not cheating. It's just another bite. Only this time I'd be alone.

She splashed fresher water on her breasts, rinsing away the suds.

It's going behind Duane's back. It's wrong.

She opened the drain. It had been a very short bath.

Marital aids with teeth. That's what he called them. It's no different than…than using a vibrator would be. And he wouldn't mind that.

She stood up in the tub, letting the water and suds course down her body. Grabbing a thick towel, she patted herself dry. The bath made her skin smell like flowers, a light musky scent that made her feel attractive and feminine.

He thinks they're animals.

She reached for her jeans, but at the last moment, looked into her closet instead. She pulled out a sleeveless black dress she hadn't worn in a long time. It had a long, swirling skirt, and Duane didn't like it. "I like to see your legs," he'd said. Thinking of Duane, she stopped for a moment, her hand sliding over the fabric of the dress.

He goes by himself.

Duane had said he'd been bitten at least a dozen times. That meant he had to be going by himself.

That settled it. She pulled on the dress and a fresh pair of panties, deciding at the last minute to forgo a bra. After all, it was just a short drive downtown.

* * * * *

Walking in downtown Memphis was an entirely different experience alone.

The streets seemed different, with muted colors and sharpened echoes. The light took on a different quality, bright enough to be daytime, but still with shadows. She noticed the footsteps and voices of other people, whether they were walking along the next block or sitting on a park bench, waiting for the tourist trolley to come by.

Main Street was winning its battle between urban decay and old-fashioned grace. For every shuttered, gated shop with a FOR LEASE sign in its soaped-over window, there were three shops of trinkets or toys to grab the unwary shopper. Recent years had brought new money in the form of shops and restaurants, but history was built into the very streets. The cobblestones and streetlights tried to recapture the days of the Old South, but ominous sounds from the alleys and streets nearby reminded her that it was definitely the modern era.

All along the way, like a murmur beneath raised voices, the river flowed past the city. Isabel caught a glimpse of it from time to time, glancing to her right as she crossed another street. Its faint rushing sound was both huge and still at once, something eternal in the ever-changing city.

Isabel was mindful of the fact that she was alone. She had to park several blocks away from Nocturnal Urges. Smart enough not to bring her purse, she kept her hands in her jacket pockets around a small wad of cash and her keys. She walked quickly and purposefully, passing the small park with a lighted fountain where lovers would cast their coins into the water, making a wish.

She passed the Beale Street jazz district, and turned down the sidewalk toward Nocturnal Urges. Her steps faltered, however, on seeing what had taken over the street.

A crowd of people shouted from the block just west of the club, just as they had before. Sure enough, she recognized the man with the dark beard, screaming and waving a placard that read DON'T CROSS A HUMAN.

But on the other side, another crowd shouted just as loudly, waving its own placards. SAVE THE BITE read one and MORALITY IS SKIN DEEP read another.

Isabel stopped, considering making a break for it. But somehow, the thought of her empty apartment was unbearable, and she started walking again, down the middle of the narrow street.

"Stop!" shouted the man with the beard. Isabel ignored him and kept walking. "Save your soul! Don't give in to the dark ones!"

But it was a man from the other group who approached her this time. He was very tall, blond with a gaunt face. He held out a flyer, and with a sudden jolt of adrenaline, Isabel saw that his nails were long and pointed.

"Save the bite," he chanted, shoving the flyer at her. "Turn back and leave this place."

Dark Beard was coming toward her as well, and Isabel was growing more nervous by the moment. "Come with us and we'll protect you," Dark Beard said, holding out a cross toward the blond one.

The blond one shook his head. "Jonathan, Jonathan," he said. "How many times do I have to tell you? It does nothing to us."

Jonathan held out the cross even more tightly. "Get back, Drew," he snarled.

Drew reached out and wrapped his fingers around the cross. Isabel stared at his long nails, almost claw-like around the small wooden cross.

Jonathan jerked the cross away, and Drew opened his hand. There was no mark.

"Demon," Jonathan breathed, and Drew's light smile faded, hiding the small points on his teeth.

"That's enough, break it up," said a deep voice from behind her, and Isabel turned to see the vampire bouncer, much too close to her. "You boys know the rules. Stay on the sidewalk, don't harass the customers."

"Of course, Brent, my apologies," Drew said, and drifted back toward his crowd on the east side of the street.

Brent? Isabel thought, staring at the muscled bouncer. *The Vampire Brent? You've got to be kidding.*

"You too, Mr. Osborne," Brent said, and Jonathan nodded, fading back toward his sidewalk. "My apologies, miss. May I escort you to Nocturnal Urges?"

"Uh, sure," Isabel said, following Brent the Vampire Bouncer up to the front door. She fumbled in her jacket pockets for cash.

Brent held up a hand, and she stared at his pointed, claw-like nails. "No cover for ladies who have to walk the gauntlet," he said, tilting his head toward the protesters, who were now trying to out-shout each other from opposite sides of the street. "Miss Fiona's orders."

"Oh," Isabel said. "Thanks."

She passed Brent and stepped through the anteroom into Nocturnal Urges. Immediately, she sensed that strange urgency, through the music pounding from the stage. The Creatures of the Night were in full force, and there seemed to be even more bodies writhing on the dance floor than the night she had come with Duane.

For a moment, Isabel felt awkward, as though there was a neon sign over her head shouting LOSER HERE ALONE. She slipped along the side wall, trying to be invisible. She sat at a table as far into the shadows as she could go and slipped off her jacket in the warmth of the club.

Looking down, she saw she still had Drew's flyer in her hand. Grateful for something that would make her look occupied, she read it.

SAVE THE BITE

The need is overwhelming, isn't it? You want it again and again.

There is a reason.

Do NOT be fooled by those who would trivialize the bite of a vampire!

It is a deep and spiritual moment, more than sexual, the bonding of human and vampire souls in mutual passion.

To sell the bite is prostitution, nothing more — and worse for a human, who is paying to be used and cast aside like nothing more than unwanted food.

It is never too late to stop. Contact Vampires Against Mortal Perversion and ask how we can help you stop.

Andrew Sanford, VAMP president

Isabel frowned, a little uncertain. The tone made it sound as though the bite was a drug. *Of course it's not*, she thought. *I don't have to be here. I could walk out anytime.*

Isabel quickly folded the flyer into her jacket pocket as a young woman with musky dark skin came up to her table. "What can I bring you?" the woman asked.

Isabel looked up at her. "Uh…bourbon and diet soda," she stammered.

The young woman looked at her with knowing eyes, and Isabel flushed. "I'll get that right out to you," she said, and laid a slip of paper and a pencil on the table. She walked away and Isabel hesitantly turned over the paper. Sure enough, it was an order form.

She filled out the form, checking all the right boxes and her credit card number. When it came to preference, she hesitated again. She began to check "male", and at the last moment, scratched it out and added, "Ryan".

The word just sat there, staring at her, as though accusing her of some grave misdeed.

It's not too late, she thought. *I could still walk out of here, leave a few dollars for the drink and go.*

The young waitress was on her way back, weaving through the dancers and the crowds and the pulsing, pounding music coming from the Creatures of the Night.

I could go. There's nothing to stop me.

The waitress was there, and she laid the drink down carefully. She reached for the paper, and Isabel made a move to stop her.

The waitress' hand froze in midair. "Are you ready?" she asked.

"Yes," she said, not sure why. She didn't feel ready for anything, except maybe ducking out through a side door.

The waitress scooped up the paper and gave her a smile that was probably meant to be reassuring, but revealed her small, sharp white teeth. She vanished into the crowd, and Isabel's heart resumed its pounding.

Too late, too late, can't stop it now, she thought. The vibrations of the music pounded through the floor beneath her table, thrumming into her chair and vibrating against her lower body.

Of course I can stop it. I'll just tell Fiona when she comes. I'll say I've changed my mind. They can charge me for it if they want, but I'll just leave.

Fiona was coming, her lush, ripe body wrapped in red silk that accentuated her green eyes and red hair. The dress was meant to show off the vampire's ample cleavage, and even Isabel couldn't help but notice the smooth curves bared to the air.

"Follow me, dear," Fiona said.

Isabel opened her mouth to protest, but instead her legs seemed to lift her up of their own volition. Again, she felt as though people were watching her, as if anyone looking at her would know what she was here to do.

Fiona reached the same recessed door as the other night. Isabel started to speak up, but Fiona opened the door and disappeared inside. Isabel followed her with a tiny sense of relief — somehow it seemed different away from the dancing crowds, more private, as though what happened within the chamber would be her secret.

"Ryan will be right with you," Fiona said, and slipped out the door.

Alone, the room seemed even more anachronistic, like something out of a movie or a quick trip back in time. The four-poster bed was turned down invitingly, the candelabra flickering dancing shadows on the walls. Isabel sat on the edge of the bed, her heart still pounding.

I'll tell him, then, she thought. *Tell him I've changed my mind, he can keep the money.*

Unconsciously she clutched the flyer in her pocket.

"Do not be afraid," came that soothing, warm-flannel voice from behind her. Somehow, she recognized its timbre, although she had only heard him speak once. His voice wrapped around her, soft and comforting, yet tangibly enticing.

Isabel wanted to say she was sorry she wasted his time, but for some reason she couldn't speak. She heard him come around the side of the bed, but she was frozen, afraid to look at him.

He hovered just beyond her sight, just beyond arm's reach. It was as if he was waiting for her to approach him.

Fucking animals. That's what Duane thought. What if Ryan became angry? Would he hurt her? Would he be able to stop hurting her?

"I would not hurt you," came Ryan's warm voice, deep and soothing.

"Can…can you read my mind?" Isabel asked hesitantly.

A low chuckle tumbled along her nerves, and she smiled in spite of herself.

"I don't need a sixth sense to see your fear," he said, and came into view. He stood a respectful distance away, not moving toward her. "I remember you."

Isabel flushed, as the memory tried to reassert itself. Ryan's breath on her neck, and Duane's face contorted in pleasure beneath her… Duane…

She started, and the flyer fell out of her pocket. Ryan glanced down at it, and chuckled again.

"You have been reading about us," Ryan said. "Drew is quite persistent."

"Is it true?" Isabel asked, daring to look directly at his fine, chiseled face. She was struck again by that sense of time in his face, as though his eyes belonged to another era, some time long past. "I mean, which of them is right? The humans say you can take over my mind, the…the vampire says the bite is supposed to be an act of, you know, love."

Ryan sat in the chair opposite her, seeming not at all surprised to be having a conversation with his lunch, she thought. "I absolutely cannot take over your mind, miss," he said. "Nor would I."

"Can you bite each other?" Isabel asked.

Ryan shook his head. "No," he said. "That which gives you pleasure is death to us. If any vampire were to drink my blood, it would offer him no sustenance. But for me, it would mean my death."

Isabel digested that for a moment. She wanted to ask, *Why have you been all I can think of for weeks?* but she didn't quite dare.

"What about the other? The bite as intimacy?" she asked.

Ryan shrugged. "Perhaps it is, at its finest," he said. "There are those who can form such a closeness with only one person that when they feed, it is spiritual and emotional as well as sexual and sustenance."

"But not all the time," Isabel pressed.

Ryan laughed, and she saw the fine points of his teeth. But now they did not seem frightening, but only part of his features. "No, of course not," he said. "Otherwise we could not do what we do here."

"I don't understand," Isabel said.

"Consider," Ryan said. "If a human makes love to another human, it may be a deep, abiding spiritual and physical encounter, yes?"

Isabel loved listening to his voice. She nodded yes, just so he would keep talking.

"But it is not always so," Ryan said. "Sometimes— often—a man and a woman may partake of each other's bodies, but not their souls. There is nothing wrong with it, nothing harmful or shameful. It is a physical release, nothing more or less."

"So it is kind of like prostitution," Isabel said.

Ryan's eyes flickered for a moment, and she was suddenly nervous again. "Not so harsh as Drew would have it," he said. "He is a moralist, and as such, believes that all should live according to his beliefs."

Isabel cast her eyes down. "I'm sorry if I offended you," she said quietly.

Ryan didn't answer, and the silence grew taut for a moment. She looked up at him, trying to gauge his expression.

"Thank you," he said quietly.

Isabel blinked. "For what?"

This time it was Ryan who averted his eyes. "It has been a long time since anyone…since a human asked me a question, or wished to speak with me at all, in this room," he said, his voice dropping a little in hesitation. "I cannot recall a time when anyone apologized to me. You gave no offense at all, but I thank you just the same."

She loved his voice, the sudden uncertainty in his tone and even his formal tone seemed perfectly in character.

"But of course you have come for a reason," Ryan said, beginning to stand.

"But…" Isabel stammered, her heart suddenly beating fast again.

Ryan remained still. "It is your choice, miss," he said. "I would not press you at all. No one should come to us unwilling. It is our deepest law."

Marital aids with teeth. Isabel was suddenly ashamed of herself.

"Isabel," she said. "Please call me Isabel."

He nodded, quite somber now. "It is an enchanting name."

"Is it… Do you enjoy it?" Isabel asked. "The bite, I mean."

Ryan inclined his head. "It is food, and more," he said.

"But the… I mean…"

Ryan reached out, and his hand floated in the air near her. She immediately felt electrified, her skin hypersensitive beneath the jacket and thin black dress. "You are not taking advantage of me, Isabel," he said, lightly accenting her name. "I would not be here if it was not my wish."

His hand stayed there, without advancing. Slowly, she reached out and touched it. Instantly, a jolt of sensation leaped from his hand to hers, that powerful electricity she remembered from the last time.

"What is that?" she breathed.

"We do not know," he murmured, pulling her to her feet.

Isabel's heart was pounding. *Am I really doing this?* she thought, slipping her arms out of her jacket and letting it fall to the floor.

Ryan's hand slid up her arm, sending shivers across her skin, arcing across her back and making her nipples harden painfully against the fabric of her dress.

"Are you sure?" he asked, still a step away.

"Yes," she breathed.

But his hand didn't move. She looked up at him, and his eyes were that deep azure blue, enormous, filling her own gaze with an instant connection she felt to the base of her spine.

"Are you sure, Isabel?" he repeated, and in his eyes she saw the absolute truth—he would go no farther than she wanted.

"Yes," she said, and smiled, as much to alleviate his concerns as her own jumping fears. With the decision made, somehow the butterflies quieted in her stomach and her heart slowed its frantic race.

Ryan stepped closer, and his eyes darkened, beyond blue to black, dark and mysterious. It was like ink swirling into two pools of blue water, spreading its tendrils, deepening until they filled her world.

She felt that soft lassitude in her limbs, heavy and languid. He led her gently to the bed, and she sat on the end, pulling her legs up onto the mattress. He slid behind her, and she felt his spare form against her back in a sudden jolt of electric heat along her body.

Ryan's hands moved gently along her arms, making the light hairs along them prickle. He slid his hands to her waist, pressing gently against the curve of her hip. He leaned forward and pressed a light kiss on the curve of her neck, and a sudden bolt of pleasure came from somewhere in the center of her back and straight up to the back of her neck.

Isabel cried out softly, and she felt his soft lips smile against her skin.

His hand moved around to her stomach, still creating that electrical storm through the fabric of her dress. He smoothed his hand upward, so slowly she wanted to cry out again, sliding it up to rest just beneath her right breast. She arched her back, bringing the aching nipple into sharp contact with the sliding fabric.

"Ryan," she breathed.

"Is this what you want?" he asked, and she almost laughed. As if she could possibly have the strength to stop. Duane's face tried to intervene, and she pushed it away without difficulty.

Ryan's hand moved up swiftly to cup her breast, and the electric heat sank into her skin with sudden, jolting fervor. She breathed sounds of pleasure as his fingers gently rubbed over the nipple, which was so hard and sensitive it was nearly painful. Ryan seemed to sense that, and touched her so lightly that he never overstimulated her, never pressed too hard or too roughly, but kept the right amount of pressure to keep her aroused and seemingly incapable of silence. Her voice cried out wordlessly, as though she had no control over it, and when his other hand moved up to capture her other breast, she let out a moan that would have embarrassed her if the pounding fervor of the music in the club beyond had not surely drowned her out.

Ryan's mouth was moving again, pressing against the back of her neck, the exposed skin at the top of her back, licking little patterns along her shoulder line.

His hands slipped off her breasts, moving down again to her hips, and she realized he was steadying her, readying her for what was to come. The gentle but firm pressure of his hands kept her still, though her hips wanted to thrust and writhe as though he lay between her legs and moved within her.

With a quick motion, he swept her hair from her neck and returned his hands to her hips. She leaned back against him, feeling the pressure of his mouth at her throat. The two sharp points of his teeth dimpled her skin, and she was afraid for one tiny moment, like the sharp prick of a needle in her heart.

Then his teeth sank in, and a brief moment of pain dampened the fire burning between her legs and raging across her chest. But his lips quickly pressed over the wound, and instantly it faded.

She felt him begin to feed, drawing what he needed from her, and this time it was longer, more drawn out. It was as though the velvet thread within her skin was now a thin rope, coiled throughout her body. As he fed, he drew it out through her neck, and it moved beneath her skin, unspooling and sliding within her. The glorious tension built deep in her belly, between the raging electricity generated by his hands.

The velvet rope grew taut and strong, and still he fed, still she tried to writhe and move, and still he held her tightly, binding her close to him. Her hands moved helplessly on her thighs, and her eyes closed, her mouth open in a meaningless cry.

She wanted him, wanted to turn and take him within her, as though the only release for this great building tension would be to feel him fill her and complete her in open-mouthed, shared ecstasy.

Then the shuddering climax began, low in her abdomen and exploding throughout her body in cascades of vibrating shivers and moaning cries that seemed to come from her very skin as well as from her throat. Her back arched uncontrollably, and she felt his teeth slip and sink in a little deeper. The sudden jolt of pain helped banish the roil of shuddering ecstasy, which in truth was something of a relief. She felt as though she had skated up against something too big for her, something so powerful and huge that she could not take it within herself, could not feel that much without losing herself in it. She recoiled from that feeling, backed away from it in momentary fear.

She was suddenly aware that Ryan's mouth was no longer on her throat, and for that matter, she was not sitting up. She was lying on her side, and Ryan was pressing something against her neck.

"It's all right," she heard herself say, as much to herself as to Ryan.

Ryan was calling out something, and she didn't understand the words. They seemed to be in some other language. But someone must have understood him, because there were suddenly other people in the room. There were voices, and shadows, but the room was so dark…

Chapter Three

Voices. Angry but hushed, intense, as though afraid to wake her. Murmuring to each other beyond the darkness that still held her eyes closed.

"Do you need money?" A woman's voice, cool and crisp.

Ryan's voice responded. Even in a whisper, she would know his deep tones. "I don't want your money."

"You've got to get out of here, Ryan," the woman said. "If they catch you, they will fucking kill you."

"I'm not going anywhere," he replied.

"Ryan, it's your life," the woman argued. "Attacking a human is an automatic death sentence."

"I didn't… I mean, I didn't mean to…" Ryan's voice was unsure, hesitant. Isabel struggled to speak, but it was as though her voice wasn't listening to her brain.

"You think they care?" The woman's voice was rising. "They'll kill you whether you meant to do it or not."

The voices hushed as somewhere a door opened and impatient footsteps approached Isabel. "Has there been any change?" a new voice asked, a lightly accented male.

"No," said Ryan in a normal tone. "No movement."

A harsh fluorescent light pierced through the darkness that surrounded Isabel. Somewhere, she heard bleeps and muted voices that told her she was in a hospital. She struggled to blink, and moved her lips a little. "Hello," said the accented voice, and she focused for a moment on a vague face hovering above her. "There you are."

Ryan appeared next to the other man, and for some reason Ryan seemed clearer, more real to her. His eyes were their normal blue again, full of concern. "Are you okay?" he asked.

"Of course she's not," snapped the other man, whom Isabel now saw wore the white coat of a doctor. "Miss, you're suffering from moderate exsanguinations, otherwise known as blood loss, from a vampire bite gone too far."

"I'm so sorry," Ryan stammered, his face pale even for a vampire. "I didn't…"

Isabel tried to speak, but her voice was still not cooperating.

The doctor shot a glare at Ryan. "Miss, do you want me to send these…people away? Blink once for yes, twice for no."

Isabel carefully blinked twice. The doctor shrugged. "All right," he said. "But I'm leaving the door open." He vanished from Isabel's sight.

The woman's voice came again, cool and controlled. "There, she's alive, you can go now," she said.

"Shut up," Ryan said, turning to the woman. Isabel still couldn't see her. But in a swish of fabric, she sensed the woman leaving.

Ryan turned back to look at her. "I beg your forgiveness," he said formally. "That has never happened to me before. I cannot understand it."

"Neither can I," snapped a new voice, one Isabel recognized as Fiona's. "I cannot fucking believe you, Ryan."

Ryan turned away, and Isabel couldn't see what was happening. She concentrated on lifting her hand, but it wasn't cooperating.

"I lost control," Ryan admitted.

"Damn right you did and I don't need to tell you you're fired," Fiona snapped, all the matronly madam tones gone from her voice. "I haven't had a vampire go ape-shit like this since the sixties! For that matter, if she presses assault charges your ass is grass, so I suggest you hightail it to your little penthouse flat and clear out of town fast."

Ryan's voice was flat and dejected. "I'm sorry, Fiona," he said. "I don't know what happened. It just…got away from me."

"And at the end of the day, she's gonna end up owning my place, so I'm not crying for your problems," Fiona returned.

"She's awake, Fiona," he said dully, and Fiona muttered something in another language.

Isabel finally managed to say something. "Water," she croaked, and Ryan was there, pressing a cup to her cracked lips. She sipped a little, and suddenly her mouth was working again.

"He's not fired," she croaked, trying to lift her head.

Fiona hovered into view, a severe gray business suit masking her generous curves. "I am so sorry, Miss Nelson," she said. "This has not happened…"

"Since the sixties, I heard," Isabel rasped. "He's not fired. It's not his fault."

Fiona shot a look at Ryan.

"I moved," Isabel said. "He didn't mean for it to go that far. I moved, he slipped; it was an accident."

Fiona shook her head, her red hair glinting in the fluorescent lights above her. "I don't allow accidents in my place, Miss Nelson."

Isabel thought for a moment. "If you fire him, I'll sue," she said, smiling a little. "Keep him and I won't."

Ryan gaped at her. Fiona sputtered for a moment, seeming undecided whether to glare at Isabel or at Ryan. "Fine then," she said. "He's on probation. Get better, dear." She swept out of the room as grandly as if she still had the long skirts of her Nocturnal Urges evening gowns.

Ryan held the cup to her lips again, and she drank gratefully. "You didn't have to do that," he murmured.

"Yes, I did," Isabel said, and reached up to his free hand. She felt that electricity again, but muted this time, a vibration beneath the skin rather than thrumming heat.

Ryan shook his head. "I never lost control before, and you barely moved," he murmured. "I can't understand it."

Gently he brushed a lock of her hair away from her face.

"Get the fuck away from her," snapped a voice from the doorway. Ryan's hand jerked away from her face, and when he moved away, she saw Duane in the doorway.

Duane strode across the small room and shoved Ryan hard. Isabel struggled to get up. "Duane, stop it," she tried to shout, but it came out weak and thin.

Ryan backed away, his hands held up to protect but careful not to show any offensive moves, she realized.

"Duane, I'm all right," she said, and Duane stopped moving toward Ryan.

"You're not all right," he said. "This fucking leech…"

Ryan's eyes flashed for a moment, but his hands remained still.

"Stop it, Duane," Isabel said, grateful that some steadiness had returned to her voice. "It was my fault."

"Bullshit," Duane said. "These *things* aren't supposed to bite unwilling women, they're—"

"I paid him," Isabel said.

Duane whirled around, staring at her. "You went back? Alone?"

She nodded, ignoring a twinge of pain from her neck. "I wanted to try it again," she said. "I didn't think you'd mind."

Duane gaped at her. "You can't go alone," he said.

"Why not?" Isabel asked, feeling defensive. "You do, don't you?"

Duane flushed, and she saw she'd hit a nerve. "Not for a while," he said.

"I'm sorry," Ryan said again, and moved toward the door. "I hope you get well quickly, Miss Nelson."

Somehow, hearing her name so formally stung Isabel. She wanted to say something to him, but somehow it was different with Duane in the room. Ryan disappeared through the door.

"Are they going to let you go home?" Duane asked.

Isabel nodded. "I think so, it was just a little accident," she said.

"There are no accidents with those things," Duane growled.

"Stop that," Isabel said. "If you hate them so much, why did you take me there?"

"Hey, I don't hate them," Duane said. "A leech can't help its nature. Use them for what they're good at, but you don't forget what they are."

Isabel shook her head, struggling to sit up. Duane moved to help her. "They're not leeches," she said. "They're people."

Duane shook his head, smiling in that condescending manner that made her want to smack him one. "That's my girl," he said. "Always the bleeding heart."

* * * * *

This time, when Det. Freitas appeared at Isabel's cubicle door, she was holding her badge. "Got a second?"

Isabel automatically touched the bandage at her neck. "You're always checking up on me, Annie."

Freitas grinned. "Comes from a long line of Portuguese grandmothers," she said. "Let's grab some food."

As they walked to the café, Freitas kept sneaking looks at Isabel's neck. "Yes, I feel just fine," Isabel finally said.

"I wasn't going to say anything," Freitas said. "Just wanted to make sure you were in one piece and your teeth were the same length."

"Ha," Isabel said as they reached the café. "I got my shots, there's no problem there."

"Good," Freitas said. "I hate the night shift, myself."

Isabel stared at her for a second before she burst out laughing. "You have the strangest sense of humor, Annie," she said.

"Not laughing much these days," Freitas said, scanning the menu. "I don't know why I look at this; I always order the same thing…"

"What's happening on the police beat?" Isabel said. "You beat up any suspects this week?"

"Nah, they run too fast," Freitas said. "Too many onion omelets, I'm slowin' down…"

"So what's giving you fits?" Isabel asked.

Freitas sighed and closed the menu. "Another dead body at Nocturnal Urges," she said softly. "I gotta say, Isabel. Going back there alone was a really bad idea."

"While we're on the subject, how the hell did you find out about that?" Isabel said.

"I know everything," Freitas said, smiling. "My spies are everywhere."

"I didn't press charges, it wasn't his fault," Isabel said.

The waitress came to take their order, and after she had cleared away the menus, Freitas leveled her cop eyes at Isabel. Sometimes Freitas could be almost a normal person, Isabel thought, and other times the cop in her came out and those laser-like eyes would just bore right through you.

"How did it happen?" Freitas asked.

Isabel frowned. "You asking as my friend or as a cop?"

Freitas shrugged. "How about both?"

"As a cop, I can definitely say it was not his fault, just an accident. He got carried away," Isabel said. "That's why I didn't press any charges."

"Yeah, I saw that," Freitas said. "So explain 'carried away'."

Isabel shrugged. "I, uh, moved too much," she said, her face feeling hot. "His teeth sank in a little too far. He called for help right away," she added.

"Huh." Freitas kept gazing at her with those narrow cop eyes.

"What?" Isabel said. "Why are you asking about this?"

Freitas leaned forward. "Because a vamp doesn't lose control just because you move, Isabel," she said. "A vamp like Ryan bites two or three people a night, only taking a little blood so the human can replenish it easily. A vamp like Ryan has been around the block enough to know how to hold a customer, how to keep the bite shallow. It's natural to them. You don't think they go around ripping throats out, do you?"

Isabel lowered her head. "I don't know how it's supposed to work."

"Vamps live off humans like parasites, that much of what Osborne and his nutbars say is true," Freitas said. "But a good parasite doesn't kill its host. Hell, in order to drink a human dry the vamp would have to swallow something like two gallons of blood. That'd be like you or me sitting down to eat a whole turkey and following it with an Easter ham. It can be done, but why do it? You'd be sick."

"So how come you hear about vamps killing people?" Isabel asked.

Freitas shrugged. "How come you hear about humans killing people?" she said. "It sure isn't for food. Hell, the latest left half the blood on the ground…"

Isabel gaped in sudden understanding. Freitas grabbed her coffee. "That was dumb," she said. "I shouldn't have said that in front of you. Please, Isabel, don't repeat that to anyone."

"You think Ryan's the one killing people around Nocturnal Urges," Isabel said.

Freitas shrugged. "He could be," she said. "He lost control with you, and that just does not happen. He's also been off-duty or at least not with a customer during the approximate time of each murder, he's at maybe two hundred years old but we can't find a background on him in the States and listen to my mouth run."

"So why are you telling me all this?" Isabel said.

Freitas fixed her cop eyes on Isabel, but this time there was the Portuguese grandmother in there as well. "Don't go back to Nocturnal Urges, Isabel," she warned. "Don't go with Caveman the Boyfriend, and certainly don't go alone."

Isabel snickered. "Duane would freak out if he heard you call him that," she said.

"I'm serious, Isabel," Freitas said. "I don't wanna find you in the alley."

"Okay, okay," Isabel said. "I'm off the biting list for a while anyway."

"Good," Freitas said. "I hope you're having red meat."

Isabel burst out laughing again.

* * * * *

Sometimes there were side benefits to Duane's night shifts, Isabel thought. For one thing, it meant she could play classic rock music in her own apartment without getting the standard Duane eyeroll. The Beatles sang out cheerful lyrics as she folded towels in the living room.

She carried the stack of towels down the hallway toward the closet. As she passed the front door, a sharp knock made her jump, and the towels spilled onto the floor.

"Shit," she said, and peered through the peephole.

Ryan's chiseled face appeared in the distorted fisheye view of the peephole.

Isabel's heart started beating fast. Quickly she unlocked the door, and there he was, looking out of place in her ordinary hallway. "Miss Nelson," he said, in that warm baritone voice.

"Hello," she said. "What brings you here?"

Ryan shifted his feet a little. "I just came to see if you were recovering all right," he said.

Isabel stepped back to give him room to enter, but he didn't move. "Oh, of course," she said. "Please come in."

Ryan stared at her a moment, and burst out laughing. It was a rich, rolling laugh, the kind that inspires half-smiles just from hearing it. "Oh, no," he said, as he attempted to hide it behind his hand. "No, Miss Nelson, we don't need to be invited in."

Isabel felt quite silly, and she knew her face was reddening. "I'm sorry, I don't know much about…you," she said, smiling.

Ryan stepped in, and she gratefully closed the door. "It's all right. The movies have done ridiculous things to us, and we have done little to change that," he said.

"When you hesitated out there, I thought—"

Ryan nodded. "I was just wondering if your husband was here, and I didn't want to cause a scene."

This time it was Isabel's turn to laugh. She stifled it as quickly as possible. "Oh no, he's not my husband," she said, giggling. "He's my boyfriend."

"Ah. Forgive me," Ryan said.

Isabel suddenly felt awkward, standing in her entryway with Ryan. "Please, have a seat," she said, gesturing to the living room. Ryan inclined his head in an oddly old-fashioned way and walked over to the large white couch.

Isabel moved over by a huge papasan chair, avoiding sitting on the couch with Ryan. Even in this calm, normal environment, she could feel the electricity around him, as though he were touching her from across the room.

The silence grew slightly awkward. "Can I offer you something to drink?" Isabel asked, and immediately felt like an idiot. "I mean… Oh dear."

Ryan covered his mouth again.

"You're laughing at me," Isabel accused, smiling.

Ryan shrugged. "I would be quite happy with a soda, if you have them," he said.

Isabel quickly retrieved two cans of diet soda and gave him one. "I always seem to be making a fool of myself around you," she said, opening her soda with a slight hiss-pop that seemed unnaturally loud, even over the music.

"I would hardly say so," Ryan said. "Any woman who likes the Beatles cannot be a fool."

Isabel blinked. "You know this music?" she asked.

Ryan nodded. "I saw them in concert, in 1964," he said. "A powerful experience."

Isabel shook her head. "You are always surprising me."

This time, it was Ryan who seemed off-balance. "You are expecting a long black cape and Transylvanian accent," he said. It wasn't a question.

Isabel shrugged. "The décor at Nocturnal Urges, the stories around…your people," she said. "What's real, and what's just from the movies?"

Ryan leaned back a little. "The club plays up the stereotypes of the urban vampire because that's what the marks want," he said. "It is all designed to meet expectations, down to the fingernails."

Isabel instinctively glanced down at Ryan's tapered, carefully manicured nails. "They're not really like that?"

"They grow faster than yours," Ryan said, extending his hand for a better view. "But they can be trimmed, the same as yours. Fiona requests that we keep ours in their 'natural state'."

"I'm being so rude, asking all these questions," Isabel said. "You ask me something so I'll feel like less of an ass."

"Are you truly all right?" Ryan asked immediately. "I have been quite concerned."

She nodded. "I'm recovering nicely. I'll even be bite-worthy in a few weeks."

Ryan shook his head. "That would probably be a bad idea."

Isabel quashed the sudden surge of disappointment. "It's my turn to ask a question," she said, grinning playfully. "What about garlic?"

"My favorite appetizer is garlic bread with cheese," he said, smiling. "I have grown quite fond of Italian food as well."

"Your turn," Isabel said, smiling. She was smiling so much she felt her face begin to grow sore, but she couldn't seem to stop.

"How old are you?" Ryan asked.

"Oh, that's an easy one," Isabel replied. "I'm twenty-five. Which probably sounds very young to you, but I'm starting to feel…not like a teenager again."

Ryan shook his head. "When I was twenty-five, the world was a potato farm four miles from a tiny village in Ireland," he said. "It seems many worlds from where I am now."

There was a sadness to his tone, a solemnity that seemed to settle over him. "I'm sorry," Isabel said softly.

"Don't be," Ryan said. "Sometimes we think we leave our pain behind, and sometimes…it follows us. Either way, it must be borne."

Isabel returned to more casual topics. "Is it true that holy things hurt you? Holy water, crosses?"

"Holy water is meant for reverence, not splashing us. I've never recoiled from a cross in my life," Ryan said. "In my life, I was a devout Catholic. But the church has understandably been reluctant to accept my people."

"You say that like an activist," Isabel said.

"Not like Drew," Ryan said immediately. "I see nothing wrong in the sharing of pleasure without the sharing of souls. But he and I differ."

Isabel flushed a little, remembering that huge sensation she had brushed against, too much, far too much. "And the sun?" Isabel asked, staring at his pale skin.

Ryan inclined his head somberly. "I will not burst into flames in the sun," he said. "However, it is not...recommended."

"What happens?" Isabel asked.

"Sunburn."

The matter-of-fact answer threatened to set off Isabel's giggles again. "Next you'll be telling me you can see yourself in the mirror," she said.

Ryan shook his head. "That is the one aspect that science cannot explain," he said. "All else—the blood cravings, our unusual physical attributes—it can all be deduced from our varied physiology. But why light reflections from us do not appear in mirrors... That science cannot explain."

Isabel cocked an eyebrow skeptically. "You really don't show up in a mirror?"

Ryan glanced around, and stood up. He crossed over to her fireplace, and stood before the beveled mirror above it. Isabel rose and stood next to him. She saw only herself. Still, she was suddenly very conscious of his presence beside her, and she felt a surging in her blood that she quelled with a physical effort.

"Fascinating," she breathed, and turned to see Ryan moving back to the couch. "It's so strange that no one can figure it out."

Ryan shrugged. "They also don't know why a duck's quack doesn't echo," he said.

That did it for Isabel. She giggled again, like a young girl, and suddenly she *felt* young, nervous as a virgin, with the same heat beneath her skin that she first felt as a teenager.

Ryan hid his smile behind his hand again, and she wished he wouldn't. She could tell he had a nice smile.

"It is my turn," Ryan said softly. "Why did you come to me that night?"

Isabel stared at him for a moment, but the honesty in his gaze was too much. She dropped her eyes. "I was alone for the night and I wanted to try it again," she said.

Ryan was silent a moment. "Both true and not true," he said. "You are a complicated people."

"Americans? Humans?" Isabel asked.

"Women."

Isabel giggled again. "Duane would agree with you," she said.

Ryan was silent again, as though he were waiting. She sipped her soda, avoiding his eyes. "Is it so unusual to have repeat customers?" she asked.

"Not at all," Ryan said. "Without regulars, the trade would quickly dry up."

Isabel shrugged. "Then why am I so unusual?"

"You know why," he said, and his voice was more intense, not the soothing warm-flannel voice but a penetrating deep heat that was nearly physical.

"No, I don't," Isabel said. "I wanted it again, I could do it again, why not?"

"Because that's not all it was."

Isabel shook her head, willfully avoiding his eyes. "Yes it was," she said. "It was great, don't get me wrong. But it was…"

"It was more," Ryan insisted. "Something I haven't…"

Isabel stood up quickly. "No, it was just an orgasm, a good come, that's it," she said rapidly. "That's all. I'm sorry if you thought it was something different, truly I am, because you seem very nice and you're very kind to worry about me, but it was just another bite, that's all."

Ryan was standing behind her, she sensed him, and somehow she sensed uncertainty and turmoil as well, as though she were feeling his emotions. Or were those her own?

"I'm Duane's girl," she said desperately.

Ryan's hand was on her arm, not pulling, just touching with that light electricity that sank through her skin. "No woman belongs to a man," he said softly.

"That's not what I meant," she said.

Ryan was standing too close.

"Please go," she said, her voice low.

Ryan hesitated. "Do you want me to go?"

She dipped her head. "No," she said frankly. "I don't, and that's why you should go."

Ryan stood there for another moment, and then his hand was gone. "Forgive me if I overstepped my bounds," he said, and a few agonizing seconds later, she heard her front door close gently.

Only then did she turn back to the empty living room, suddenly devoid of whatever had filled it a few moments ago. Only then did she let herself relax, and realized her hands were shaking.

What is this power he has over me?

She suddenly scrambled to take the soda cans into the kitchen, empty the soda down the sink drain and put the cans in the recycling bin. She looked around for any signs of Ryan's visit, a pillow out of place, a blood smear on the wall… *Oh, very funny, Isabel, you're completely losing it.*

Still, the fact that she was so worried about Duane finding out was a clear sign that Ryan was a lot more than a marital aid with teeth, and if her own confusion wasn't enough of a deterrent, Duane's irritability since the night of her bite should be. He had not been directly cross with her, but he had been jumpy, easily frustrated and sometimes she saw him looking at her in a funny way.

I can't see Ryan again, not for any reason, she thought.

A sharp knock at the door, and she jumped nearly out of her skin. *It's Ryan, he's come back*, she thought, and went to the door, prepared to be firm.

She opened the door, and Duane leaped forward, sweeping her up into his arms. "Duane!" she cried out, half in surprise, half in relief. "You scared me to death!"

"I got the night off," he said, setting her back down.

"I see that," Isabel replied. "Jeez, you know how to give a girl a heart attack. Come in, I should have enough stroganoff for two."

* * * * *

"Mmm," Isabel said.

"That's an encouraging mmm," Duane said. His fingers pressed against the muscles of her shoulders, massaging and relaxing.

"That's an I'm-tired-and-don't-want-to-do-the-dishes mmm," Isabel hinted.

"Don't do them," Duane said. "They'll wait till morning."

"You got a lot to learn about what turns a woman on," she teased.

"Oh yeah?" Duane said, trailing his fingers down her back to the places on either side that tickled. "Rubber gloves, huh? That's what you like?"

Isabel giggled helplessly as he tickled her sides. "Stop, no more," she gasped. "No fair."

"Not my fault I'm not ticklish," Duane said. "Be at my mercy, wench."

"Never," Isabel declared, and he kept tickling her until she scrambled away. "Mitts off, evil one."

"Come now, wench, sit by my foot like a good woman should," Duane said.

Isabel rolled her eyes. "If I wasn't so tired, I'd smack you for that one," she said.

Just as she sat next to him on the couch, the doorbell rang.

"Lord, what now?" Isabel groaned. She got up and walked over to the door, muttering, and "This better be good" to herself.

Freitas was at the door, in her work suit and waving her badge. "Sorry to disturb you, Isabel," she said. "Official stuff."

"Detective," Duane said from behind Isabel, and she made a mental note that this time he'd remembered Anne's rank. "What can we do for you?"

"It's just the two of you?" Freitas asked.

"Yes," Isabel said. "Why? What's going on?"

"Any visitors tonight?" Freitas' eyes were doing the cop stare again, and Isabel felt herself withering.

"No, just Duane here," Isabel lied. She felt the lie as if it pasted a banner over her head, as if neon lie detectors glared over her, and certainly Freitas was picking up on it. *I'll come to your office and tell you all about it tomorrow*, she pleaded mentally with Freitas. But somehow, she knew Duane would go ballistic if he knew Ryan had been there.

"What's going on, Detective?" Duane asked.

Freitas leveled her gaze on him for a moment, and then put away the badge, as though she had forgotten she was holding it. "A man was just found murdered in the alley two blocks from here," she said. "He had been to Nocturnal Urges tonight."

Isabel gasped. "Again," she said. "That's…"

"Five," Freitas said. "You didn't see anything, hear anything?"

"No," Isabel said. "Why me?"

Freitas shook her head. "Two blocks from here, you're patrons of Nocturnal Urges, I took a shot," she said. "If you think of anything, give me a call."

"Of course," Isabel said. "I'll see you later."

Freitas nodded, and suddenly seemed much older in the few seconds before she turned to walk away down the hallway. Isabel closed the door slowly, suddenly saddened for the death of some woman whose name she didn't even know.

"Wow," Duane said. "Some crazy killing people—that shit is nothing to fool with, Isabel. You're not going back there."

"I hadn't planned on it," Isabel said.

"You and the detective are kind of, what, friends now?" Duane asked, but Isabel ignored his question, leaning back against the door. She felt confused, torn, as if nothing was the same and yet everything was the same. Somewhere she realized it wasn't the murder only two blocks away. That it had been building for weeks, something that had unseated her comfortable, ordinary life.

It felt as though the ground underneath her had become untrustworthy, like the floor of her grandmother's attic that was boarded, but not nailed down. The wrong step would send you crashing down into the ceilings below you, and the boards themselves were bowed with age.

She felt alone, and yet her body was filled with need, more hunger than she knew how to satisfy, more desire than simple sex could fulfill.

"Love me, Duane," she said, raising her eyes to his.

Duane blinked. "Wow, are you sure you're up to—"

Isabel pushed herself into his arms, drawing his head down to hers with a nearly frantic need, that hunger that started somewhere in her chest where unshed tears burned. He clasped her tightly and pulled her down the hallway, still kissing her, toward the bedroom. The lamp was on, casting a dim light across her bed.

She tore at his buttons with urgency, pulling his shirt off his broad frame. She pressed kisses and licks across his chest, catching his flat nipple between her lips and sucking it. He kneaded her head between his large hands, drawing her face back up to his. His mouth crushed across hers, hard and strong, his tongue pressing between her teeth to glide against her own.

It seemed she couldn't get enough. She grasped at him, her nails digging into his shoulders, as though by pressing that close to him she could feel again, the turmoil within her would be eased and the confusion would wane.

But Duane stepped back for a moment and she reached out for him.

"Wait," he said, smiling. "Let's try something."

"Duane," she said.

Duane turned to the nightstand and withdrew the silken scarf she had left there weeks ago. "Please," he said.

Isabel would have agreed to anything, if only he would take her in his arms again. She nodded, and he quickly wound the scarf around her head, over her eyes. The darkness swept in, and she felt the scarf's smooth fabric with her fingertips.

"Duane?" she said.

"I'm here," he replied, and she felt his fingers probing between her breasts. It was different, not the usual preamble. This was rougher, more insistent and infinitely exciting. She reached out and found only empty space as he moved away from her. She took a step, and could not find him.

"Duane, where are you?" she said, her heart pounding for reasons that had nothing to do with fear.

Then she felt his hands on her, pulling at her blouse with insistent force, freeing her shoulders and arms and leaving her skin bare above the taut satin of her bra. His hands were already fumbling at her belt, and he was having trouble with it. She tried to help, but he pushed her hands away. She reached up and behind to find his head, bringing it down to the unscathed side of her neck. He nuzzled her, kissing and licking her, and she quelled the image of Ryan that immediately rose to mind.

Duane was still having trouble with the belt, so she turned toward him and unlatched it herself.

"Naughty," he said, clasping her wrists together in one strong hand. He pushed her back on the bed, drawing her hands up over her head. "Stay."

She could not see anything, only feel his hands move down over her body to her waist, where he pulled her slacks away, down her long legs to the floor. She couldn't help it, she reached up toward him, pulling him closer to her.

He responded by pulling her hands back over her head and pinning them there with one rough hand. "Stay," he commanded.

Isabel writhed beneath him, arching her back to bring her breasts closer to him. But he just teased her, his hand smoothing the skin across her abdomen, below the breasts, breathing hard against her chest but refusing to touch it. Her legs pumped beneath him, trying to draw him close.

She lurched her head upward, trying to capture his mouth. But she missed in her darkness, and caught his ear instead. Passionately she sucked at it, and his hand tightened on her hip. He ground his hips against hers, still clad in rough jeans that chafed her tender skin in a delicious friction that went on and on.

"Oh God, Duane, please," she cried out. Her words dissolved into cries as his mouth descended between her breasts, licking and kissing the tender skin as he moved over to suck a hard, taut nipple into his mouth. He molded her nipple through the fabric, and then slipped it free. She felt the moist heat of his mouth take her breast in hard passion.

She struggled against his restraining hand, wanting to reach down where his jeans remained in her way, to tear them apart and take his hardness in her hand, to bring him to her, to feel him within her. But he held her tightly, and the struggle itself was intoxicating and exciting.

Duane's hand slipped downward, beneath the thin nylon of her panties and groped her mercilessly, without preamble or finesse. His rough fingers made her cry out at sharp sensations spearing through her. He pulled and tugged, and her panties were gone.

"God, Isabel, I can't wait," he said, finally releasing her hands as she heard his zipper go.

"Duane, oh God, Duane," she cried in her darkness. His weight pressed down hard on her, driving her into the mattress, and she felt his naked heat settle between her legs. She clutched at the small of his back, heedless of her nails digging into the skin, urging him onward as his breath, fast and hard, came hot on her neck.

He thrust upward, hammering into her with force that made her cry out in mixed pleasure and shock. As always, there was a slight lessening of the passionate madness the moment he entered her, the actual sensation dampening the delicious tension that had built up. But he thrust again, hard and fast, and the tension built again, powerful and strong.

She cried out and held him close, feeling his hard driving thrusts push her deep into the mattress. It seemed she could not get him deep enough into her, as though she would draw his entire body into her skin. Not just the deep hard heat of him penetrating between her thighs, she wanted to envelop all of him into her and fill that horrible emptiness with heat and passion and *feeling*.

"Ryan, oh God," she moaned, feeling him speed up, knowing he was close, that this hard passion could only be brought to explosion soon. She felt it beginning, almost insanely soon, as the frantic clapping beat of his sweat-soaked body slamming against her own skin sped to a pace nearly out of control.

"Isabel," he cried, jerking so hard she had to brace herself on his shoulders.

Only another moment, she thought, and he thrust hard four more times in quick succession, hard fast powerful thrusts and she came, huge bursts of glorious ecstasy radiating out from her very skin, and she cried out again in wordless sounds of release.

Just as she ebbed, Duane sped up again, hard and fast, crying out as he exploded, within her, his hands clutching the blanket on either side of her shoulders. She rode the waves with him, feeling his body begin to relax as his own passion waned within her, and it was almost as good as her own climax, feeling him within her.

He lay there for a moment, and did not withdraw immediately. She started to reach up for the blindfold, and her hand froze in midair as it suddenly struck her.

She had cried out beneath Duane. Cried out in passion.

Cried out another name.

Oh God.

Had he heard? He was still hard inside her, beginning to soften. Was he just now realizing what she had said?

Oh no, oh please don't let him have heard.

She felt him withdraw, and he rolled away from her. She pulled off the blindfold, blinking a little at the sudden light, and glanced over at him. For once he was not asleep. He was staring at the ceiling, slightly out of breath.

She didn't know what to say. Perhaps, if she said nothing, he'd think he imagined—

"I'm Duane, you know," he said, his tone trying to be funny and failing. "In case you were wondering."

For a brief second, Isabel thought of pretending she didn't know what he was talking about. Maybe he'd think she didn't realize what she'd said. Maybe he'd even convince himself he'd heard her wrong.

Jesus, Isabel, who are you?

"I don't know where THAT came from," Isabel said, trying for a light tone herself. "Must be residual from the bite. Sorry about that."

"Yeah," Duane said. "Except he was here, wasn't he." It was a statement, not a question.

"What are you talking about?" Isabel said, immediately falling back on the lie and wishing like mad she had never heard of Ryan, Nocturnal Urges, vampires or sex.

"You went back there alone to see him; you lie to the cops…"

"What?" Isabel tried once more.

Duane rolled on his side. "I know, Isabel," he said, his voice as serious as she'd ever heard it. "You lied to that cop. Someone did come to the apartment, someone you didn't want the cop to know about, and now I know who, don't I?"

Isabel gave it up. "I'm sorry, Duane, I just didn't want to…complicate things," she said. "He just came by to see if I was okay. He had a soda and left. The end."

"Didn't give him a sip or two just for old times' sake?" Duane said, and now his tone was getting harsh. She read the hurt underlying it, and she understood it, but it still pissed her off.

"Of course not," she said, sitting upright and fixing her bra to cover herself again.

"Don't," Duane snapped. "Don't act like I'm being so fucking unreasonable. You lie to the cops, you lie to me, you call out the name of some goddamn leech…"

"Don't say that!" Isabel snapped back.

"What, leech?" Duane yelled.

"Stop it!" Isabel cried.

Duane jumped to his feet and started pulling on his clothes with harsh, jerking motions. "Jesus, I think I could handle it if you were fucking a man behind my back, but to fuck a leech…"

"I'm not fucking him!" Isabel shouted.

"No, you're just thinking about him while you're fucking me!" Duane shouted back. "What are you thinking, Isabel? He's a monster!"

"Stop saying that," Isabel cried, pulling a blanket up against her semi-nude body.

Duane got right in her face, and she saw all the hurt pride and pain come out in fury through his eyes and words.

"He's a fucking vampire, an undead leech, creature, monster demon animal—"

"Get out!" Isabel shouted.

"I'm gone," Duane said, and strode out of the room. A moment later, she heard the front door slam with force enough that somewhere a picture fell off the wall with a crash.

Isabel gathered the blanket around her body, still warm, still full of fizzing endorphins, as though her body didn't realize what had just happened.

She sat there, curling herself smaller and smaller, trying to draw herself into the blanket. Tears tried to come, but it was too much for tears. She squashed them back down her throat like bitter gall.

Chapter Four

❧

"Hey, Fiona, how's tricks?" Freitas called, raising her shield up at eye level as Brent the Bouncer came toward her.

Fiona shook her head vehemently. "It can't be, not tonight," she snapped. "No sirens, no flashing lights, no way there's been another one!"

"Hate to ruin your day, Fiona, but the bastard is branching out," Freitas replied, whipping out the photograph. "His buddies say this one was here last night, and ended up dead a few miles away in Midtown."

Fiona glanced at the photo. "I don't recognize him. He didn't order a special."

"Special?" Freitas asked. "That's what you call it?"

"Give it a try sometime, Detective," Fiona cajoled. "Might loosen you up."

"I'm gonna ignore that," Freitas said. "Hey, Brent!"

The bouncer ambled over in his laid-back manner. Freitas shoved the photo in his face. "Recognize this guy?"

Brent stared at it for a second, and his eyes flicked to Fiona for an instant. "Yeah," he said. "I remember him. He came in with a bunch of frat boys, loud and drunk. I had to kick him out."

Freitas pulled out her notebook. "Now we're getting somewhere. Why'd you boot him?"

"He was bothering one of the girls," Brent said. "Shoving her around, calling her a leech."

"I don't stand for that shit in my place," Fiona said imperiously.

"You know, it's real funny how your language drops out of the nineteenth century when you're talking with me, Fiona," Freitas said, writing quickly. "The vampire girl, was she here with anyone?"

"No, she was one of ours," Brent said. "Rebecca."

"Thank you, Brent," Fiona said, and Brent immediately shut up and moved off.

Freitas continued writing, although at this point she was basically scribbling gibberish to make Fiona nervous. "Once again, Fiona, the city would like you to consider—"

"No," Fiona snapped.

"Voluntarily—"

"No."

Freitas sighed. "It can't be good for business to have your customers eaten, Fiona."

"My customers are not eaten. Someone's killing them, you haven't found out who, and I'm not closing my place until you get a court order," Fiona said, folding her arms.

Freitas gave up. "When's Rebecca come in?"

"Seven," Fiona said. "Until then, she's sleeping."

"I always meant to ask you that, Fiona," Freitas said. "How come you and Brent never sleep during the day?"

"I sleep during the early morning, so I can be awake when the police come for their daily chat," Fiona shot back.

"And poor Brent?" Freitas said.

Fiona glanced over at the hulking bouncer, who was facing away from them, pretending he didn't know what they were talking about.

"Brent does what I tell him to do," Fiona said.

Freitas raised a mental eyebrow at that, but closed her notebook. "Thanks for everything, Fiona," she said. "Of course, if you should think of anything that might help the investigation…"

"Absolutely," Fiona said, and turned to go back inside. Freitas watched her go, and waved with false cheerfulness to Brent before heading back up the street toward her car.

Brent stood under the awning, watching the detective leave. He didn't turn when Ryan came up behind him.

"What did she ask?" Ryan said.

"The same," Brent replied. "This is getting serious."

Ryan stared at the detective's car as it trundled away from the club. "It was always serious, Brent."

* * * * *

Freitas stared at the apartment door. Somehow, it looked exactly like she thought it would—a splintery, peeling wooden door with a lousy lock, covered in bumper stickers.

Vampires: A Grave Problem

Your Civil Rights End At My Throat

Vamps Welcome at Sunrise Services

That one's particularly funny, Freitas thought, and knocked with three short raps.

A few steps, then a male voice. "Whozzit?"

"Memphis P.D., please open the door," Freitas said, holding her badge up to the peephole. Just to be safe, she kept one hand on her holster.

The chain rasped, and Jonathan Osborne opened the door. He was wearing a sweatsuit, no shoes and his eyes weren't focused. "Can I help you?"

"Sorry if I woke you," Freitas said, putting away her badge. "Wanted to chat with you a few minutes."

Osborne blinked a moment, and then stepped aside without a word. Freitas followed him into the apartment.

It was covered in books and stacks of flyers, piled on a sagging couch and a rickety kitchen table. On the walls, she saw several posters, ranging from a giant picture of a movie Count Dracula with a big red X across his face to a stark black square with VAMPS SUCK in large red block letters.

"Nice place," Freitas said.

"Yeah," Osborne said. "It's a real dump."

Freitas couldn't really disagree. "How are things in the protest biz, Jonathan?"

Osborne shrugged. "Can't complain. Saved four souls this week, it's been good."

"Yeah?" Freitas said. "How'd you save 'em?"

"Shared the word of God," Osborne replied, and now he was starting to wake up. "Showed them the power that the vamps can hold over them, and gave them the strength to set themselves free."

Freitas wandered over to the bookshelves, scanning titles like *Vampyre Victims* and *Never Cross a Human*.

"How many people do you have in your group, Jonathan?" Freitas asked.

Osborne shrugged. "I don't know, about fifty or so on the mailing list. Only fifteen that really show up for the protests."

"Any of 'em particularly vocal?" Freitas asked.

"They got reasons to hate the vamps, most of 'em," Osborne said. "Mostly they're God-fearing folk out to save souls."

"I'm sure," Freitas said.

"You a believer?" Osborne asked, a shrewd look in his eyes she didn't like at all.

"I belong to the Church of Law and Order," Freitas replied. "So where were you last night, Jonathan?"

Osborne blinked again. "Protesting, all night," he said. "Ask any of my people, they'll tell you. What, did someone get killed again?"

"I'll need a list of your people who were picketing last night," Freitas said. "Anyone outside your group who can corroborate your whereabouts?"

"I guess that heathen bouncer or the vamps across the street," Osborne said, writing down a few names on a slip of paper. "What, am I in some kind of trouble?"

Freitas leveled her cop eyes at him. "Stay away from the patrons, Jonathan," she said sternly. "You don't want to fuck with me. Wave your signs all you want, but I better not catch you crossing the line."

"Whatever," Osborne said, handing her the list.

Freitas knew when she was being blown off. "Be good," she said, heading out the door.

As she walked down the apartment building stairs, the cell phone rang. Swearing to herself, she fumbled it out of her jacket. "Freitas."

"Hey, Annie," Betschart said. "I finished your vamp-kill."

Freitas opened the exterior door and gratefully stepped out of Osborne's dingy apartment building onto a slightly less dingy street. "Who said it was a vamp?"

"It's a vamp."

Freitas sighed, walking briskly down the street toward her car. Fortunately, it appeared unmolested by the denizens of Osborne's less-than-upscale neighborhood. "That's a problem for me, Joann. I've got a shortage of vamp suspects."

"Okay, there's one way it isn't a vamp."

"Now you're talking." Freitas slid in behind the wheel and started the car, letting it warm up.

"If the human had a set of false teeth made, something custom-designed to resemble vamp teeth, then he could do the job on Hamburger Boy."

"Ugh," Freitas said. "You just ruined my lunch plans."

"Sorry."

"Where does someone get teeth like that made?" Freitas asked.

"I see them from time to time, humans who got the shot as kids but grew up wanting to be vamps. They get the teeth made from the same companies that do custom dentures, sometimes have their own teeth pulled so they can have permanent implants," Betschart said.

"So they're kooks," Freitas said.

"I make no judgments on other people's lifestyles, Annie. That's why I live such a happy, healthy life."

"I thought you lived a happy, healthy life because you spend your work day cutting people open," Freitas shot back.

"Caught me."

The car was warm. "As much fun as this is, I need to drive now."

"I'll have a report on your desk this afternoon. Drive carelessly." Betschart clicked off without saying goodbye. It was one of her many charms.

Freitas rolled into traffic, heading downtown along Union Street. She knew exactly where she was going, and when she pulled into the parking garage of one of the nicest office buildings in downtown Memphis, she flashed her badge and was waved in immediately.

She strode through the lobby to one of the few first-floor suites. VAMP was engraved on a conservative plaque outside the shuttered doors. It was the only suite where the windows were covered.

Freitas knocked, and a tiny camera swiveled toward her face. She held up her badge to it and waited.

A moment later, the door swung inward and she stepped through a pair of black curtains into a quiet reception area, tastefully furnished in hunter green with silk flowers on the coffee table.

The young man working the desk rose to greet her. "Detective, how may I help you?" he asked.

"I'm here to see Drew Sanford," Freitas said.

"Is he expecting you?" the flunky asked.

"Nope."

The flunky stood there, a little nonplussed. He was clearly waiting for her to explain herself, but instead Freitas stood silent. "Well, I'll go see if he's available," the flunky said, and disappeared through the door.

It was strange, Freitas thought. Although the room was carefully shielded from any possible sunlight, it was not dark and moody like Nocturnal Urges. It could have been the office of an investment company or a high-powered law firm.

"Detective," Drew Sanford said, appearing with the flunky. "How nice of you to stop by." He extended a hand, and Freitas shook it politely. "Follow me."

Sanford led Freitas back down the hallway, passing closed office doors marked with signs like RECRUITMENT, PLEDGES and OUTREACH.

"Quite an operation you have here," Freitas said as they reached a plush corporate office. Sanford sat down in a comfy-looking executive chair, and gestured to the guest chair across his mahogany desk. "About how many people in your organization?"

"Thank you," Sanford said.

Freitas pulled out her notebook. "For what?"

"For referring to us as people," Sanford said, leaning forward. "There are approximately two hundred in the local VAMP chapter, who actively participate in our organization and regularly attend events."

"Including the protests," Freitas said.

Sanford nodded. "There are another nine hundred or so on our international mailing list, mostly from the internet."

Freitas paused a moment. "More than eleven hundred?"

"Or so," Sanford said, a small smile creasing his lips. "More every day, and many of them humans. They are coming to believe, as we do, that this abominable practice of selling the bite is perversion, nothing less. We are gaining influence, and we will convince your government to make it illegal."

"My government is your government, the last time I looked," Freitas said.

Sanford leaned back, eyes cool as ice chips on glass. "Of course it is," he said. "I misspoke."

"It's getting dangerous around Nocturnal Urges these days," Freitas said.

"Indeed," Sanford said. "Obviously the wanton disregard for the pure nature of the bite has begun to lead both humans and vampires down the path to madness."

Freitas' pen paused. "Explain that to me, if you would."

"The bite is meant to be shared between a single human and vampire, a most holy and sacred bond that should not be taken lightly," Sanford said. "It is not meant to be merely food or sexual pleasure, and to demean it is to demean us all, to cast mud on the moral center of the vampire existence."

"How do you get your blood?" Freitas asked.

Sanford inclined his head. "I have been with my current consort for twenty-nine years, Detective," he said.

"Consort?" Freitas said.

"Unfortunately a vampire will outlive many life partners over the course of his existence," Sanford said. "I have had nine consorts over the course of my life, and I have been faithful to each of them."

"I thought the law didn't allow you to marry," Freitas said.

Sanford smiled, but there was no humor in it. "It is the term we use for our life partners. Currently we are not allowed the legal protections of marriage, no. I am bound to my consort and share the bite only with her. I supplement with animal blood from the butcher, as do my less fortunate brethren."

"Okay," Freitas said, scribbling. "Your consort is…"

"Beth," Sanford said. "And I was home with her last night when the young man was murdered."

Freitas turned on the cop eyes. "I never asked you about a murder."

"I read the newspapers, Detective," Sanford said.

"You were out with the protesters a couple of weeks ago, bugged a few patrons," Freitas said. "You're the big cheese here. Why were you slumming on the picket lines on a Friday night?"

Sanford steepled his fingers in an oddly religious gesture. "I find it often improves morale among our people on the front lines for me to make an appearance."

"Another young man was murdered that night," Freitas said.

Sanford did not reply.

Freitas stared at him for a moment, and finally asked her real question. "What would you say if I suggested a vamp was killing humans?"

"I would say you were back in the nineteenth century, when you were hunting us openly instead of using courts and harassment to keep my people on the run," Sanford replied. "We do not kill. We survive. We prosper. And for that, we will always be punished."

Freitas grinned humorlessly. "So, were you doing Malcolm X or Jerry Falwell just then?"

Sanford returned her smile, and this time his teeth showed. "Fine gentlemen. I've met them both."

* * * * *

The protesters were gone.

Isabel walked down the alley, drawing her coat closely around her. No one waved a sign or shoved a flyer at her. When she reached the door, she handed Brent her cover fee. "Why is it so quiet?" she asked.

Brent shrugged. "Slow night," he said. "Makes my life easier."

Isabel passed through the doorway into the club. Creatures of the Night was quieter tonight and the crowd was thin. It could be just a standard weeknight, Isabel thought, or maybe the news scared them off.

She slipped into a chair and watched the crowd. The dancers were mostly slow and rhythmic, listening to the music and swaying instead of the frenetic movements she had seen before.

It wasn't long before Fiona showed up. "Oh no, Miss Nelson," she said. "I happen to know you are not safe for a bite tonight."

"Don't worry, I'm not here for a bite," she said. "I just thought I'd...stop by."

"Of course," Fiona said, her matronly smile belying the cold wall in her eyes. "A drink then. On the house."

"Oh, that's not…" Isabel's voice trailed off as Fiona drifted over by the bar. "…necessary."

She watched the crowd a little longer, and couldn't help scanning for faces she knew. Each time a male laugh reached her ears, or she caught sight of dark hair and flashing smile, her heart trilled a little beat.

"Your drink, ma'am," said a female voice, and Isabel looked up to see Elyse, the vampire from her first night at Nocturnal Urges.

"Hello," Isabel said, flushing a little. It seemed strange to be waited on by someone who had watched you make love, she thought. "How are you?"

Elyse froze a second, and then smiled. "Ryan said you were different."

"He did?" Isabel said, trying for a casual tone.

Elyse nodded, her cornsilk hair falling over a little black dress with a low neckline that emphasized her milk-white, translucent skin. "He said you talked to him like a person. That means a lot to us." She placed the drink in front of Isabel.

"Is he…working tonight?" Isabel asked.

Elyse shook her head. "No, it's his night off."

The disappointment must have shown in Isabel's face, because Elyse's eyes suddenly showed understanding. "You were looking for him?"

"No, of course not," Isabel said mechanically.

"Too bad," Elyse said, shrugging. She wrote something on the bill slip and handed it to Isabel. "Have a nice evening."

So much for 'on the house', Isabel thought, and glanced at the bill.

It wasn't a charge. It was an address.

Isabel looked over at the bar, and saw Elyse returning her tray to the bartender. She tried to say *thank you* with her eyes, and Elyse only smiled, looking like nothing more than an innocent farm girl in a dress too grown-up for her, until the ivory-white fangs showed.

Isabel gulped half her drink and got up. She moved in between the dancers, working her way toward the door. Brushing past a pair of laughing girls, she stumbled into a broad chest.

"I'm sorry," she said, and looked up into Duane's face. "Oh."

Duane stared down at her. "Shit," he said. "Didn't take long, did it?"

Isabel's face grew hot. "I'd talk it over with you, but you're sure not listening," she snapped. "Let me by."

Duane stepped aside with an overdramatized courtly gesture, and Isabel strode past him and out into the street.

The address on the card was only a few blocks away, but it didn't take long for the neighborhood to deteriorate. Broken glass and trash in the gutters, a rusty fire escape jutting from the side of old brick buildings. She walked steadily, with a purposeful stride that belied her nervousness.

Turning down the street, she saw the apartment building up ahead. It was in sad shape, and she suddenly realized how upscale her small Midtown apartment must have seemed to him. A torn window screen was the worst damage her apartment had suffered. This building had windowpanes blocked with plywood, and someone had spray-painted VAMPS SUCK on the front door.

Two young men were sitting on the front stoop. Glancing at them quickly, she saw they had the telltale fingernails and pallor of vampires.

"You lost?" one of them asked. Isabel shook her head and stepped past them. She could feel their eyes boring into her as she went into the dark foyer, barely lit by a single bulb that cast strange shadows on industrial-green walls.

The note said apartment 2B, so she climbed the stairs, tripping a little on broken floor tiles. More graffiti was spray-painted on the walls, which would have been a relief from the peeling green paint if it hadn't been such charming homilies as DIE VAMPS DIE and GOD KNOWS WHAT YOU ARE. That last one was particularly uplifting, Isabel thought.

When she reached the second floor, a door opened and a young girl came out. She couldn't have been more than fifteen years old, but she was dressed in a skimpy black vinyl dress cut far too low for her small breasts and hemmed barely below her underwear line. Her red hair was teased up over a young face covered with too much makeup.

The girl brushed past Isabel and slipped on the top step, losing her balance in stiletto-heeled knee boots. Instinctively, Isabel reached out and helped her steady herself. The girl reacted as if Isabel had shocked her with a taser gun, jerking away and nearly falling again.

"I'm sorry, I didn't mean to startle you," Isabel said. "Are you all right?"

The girl nodded, and Isabel saw the young vampire's teeth when she opened her mouth as if to say something. But she must have thought the better of it, because she quickly moved past Isabel and down the stairs.

Just down the hall was the door with 2B painted on it. Isabel stood before it for a moment and felt silly. But she knew what she had to do, and it had to be tonight, before she lost her nerve.

She knocked on the door.

* * * * *

"You look deep in thought," Betschart said, sliding onto the stool next to Freitas.

"Drowning the job in an adult beverage," Freitas said, sipping her whiskey.

Betschart held up a finger to the bartender. "Vamp case?"

"You got another series of murders broiling I don't know about?" Freitas said. "They're one step away from dragging in the feds and putting me back to writing parking tickets."

"Teeth didn't go anywhere, huh?" Betschart asked.

Freitas held up her fingers and started to tick them off. "I'm down to two vampires at Nocturnal Urges who were off-duty or at least not physically in the presence of a mark during each murder," she said.

Betschart handed the bartender some cash and downed half her drink.

"Rough day for you too?" Freitas said.

"Tell me the other suspects," Betschart replied.

Freitas shrugged. "If you ask me, Osborne's too out-of-it to go ripping out people's throats," she said. "His group, if you can call it that, hates vampires like I hate interleague play in baseball. So their only reason would be to frame the vamps. I have trouble envisioning Osborne as the diabolical genius who orders custom-made teeth, stalks the marks, tears out their throats and sets it up to look like vamps did it. Call me crazy."

"Crazy."

Freitas rolled her eyes. "Smartass. Then there's Sanford and his brownshirts."

"That guy gives me the creeps. You ever see his commercials?" Betschart finished her drink and signaled for another one.

"I grew up in the Bible Belt, my dear. The difference between a tent revivalist and a snake-oil salesman has only to do with the quality of his shoes, not the pointiness of his teeth."

Betschart grinned at her. "Pointiness? Is that a word?"

"Shut up." Freitas finished her drink.

"Besides, wouldn't it be kind of against Sanford's mission, protecting the rights of vamps and all that? Making it look like some vamp is eating the marks?"

Freitas considered. "Yeah, but he thinks NU is barely above the vamp pro's, you know? Getting NU shut down would only help his mission to rid the world of impure biting."

Betschart giggled. "Sorry, this conversation is a little surreal. So you're back to square one."

"Not really," Freitas mused. "Number one rule of detective work in multiple-case homicide—what do the victims have in common?"

"They were all NU marks," Betschart said immediately.

"Yeah," Freitas said. "But more than that."

Betschart grinned. "That's a hell of a light bulb going on above your head. Gonna share with the rest of the class?"

"See ya, Joann, I've got work to do," Freitas said, tossing a dollar bill on the bar.

"God, you're a cheap tipper," Betschart said, adding a dollar of her own. "Go get 'em, Annie."

Freitas was already gone.

* * * * *

Isabel felt like a fool, standing in the dingy hallway in the fall of soft light coming from Ryan's open door. He stood framed in the doorway, wearing an ordinary flannel shirt and a pair of jeans. His handsome, chiseled face betrayed absolute shock at seeing her in his doorway.

"Miss Nelson," he finally said.

"Please call me Isabel," she replied. "May I come in?"

Ryan stepped back and held the door for her. She came into his small studio, and it was almost like she had stepped through a portal into some other world than the dingy hallway and siren-filled streets.

Cracked walls had been carefully painted, the worst places covered with framed photographs of lovely natural vistas, rolling hills of green beneath azure skies. The old, splintered wood floor was softened by area rugs of deep green and blue patterns. A huge, deep couch stood before an honest-to-God fireplace, where a warm fire blazed, providing much of the light in the room. The only other light was provided by an old-fashioned gas lamp on a table next to the bed, a large brass antique covered with a wedding-ring quilt that had to be handmade.

Everywhere there were pictures, framed and hanging on the walls or smaller shots on a table or on the mantelpiece. None of them showed people—only landscapes and views of natural beauty. She stopped to look at one, a misty shot across a lazy river toward an ancient stone building that looked like a castle.

"Kylemore Abbey, in Ireland," Ryan said, following her gaze.

"And that one?" Isabel asked, pointing at a dusky picture of a still body of water, reflecting the darkening sky above it. "Loch Ness?"

"Loch Rannoch, actually. Fewer dinosaurs," Ryan said.

Isabel smothered a giggle. "When did you go back?"

Ryan shook his head. "I have not returned since the potato famine," he said. "These are photo prints I have purchased over the years, not photos I have taken myself. They remind me of places I have not seen in many years."

"What is it about you?" Isabel said, and suddenly the words were falling without conscious thought. "You make me laugh, you make me warm, and yet there is so much sadness in you. What are you hiding from, Ryan? Why are you here?"

Ryan looked down at his feet. "I do not believe you came here for my life story."

"What if I did?" Isabel challenged. "I want to hear about you, about the things you've seen and done. I want to understand you."

"Surely your consort would not appreciate your curiosity," he replied.

It was Isabel's turn to look at the floor. "That's…not a factor anymore," she said.

"Indeed."

She looked back at him. "You don't seem surprised."

Ryan kept his distance, hovering near the fireplace. "A man who believes he owns a woman, body, soul and mind, will not keep her long," he said. "Perhaps one must live a few hundred years to understand women, and if so, I have a few more centuries to go." Isabel stifled another smile. "But I know enough to know that women own their own minds, bodies and souls. To take her freedom from her is the one way to lose her. One such as you will not permit yourself to be owned for long."

Isabel stared at him, and despite herself, felt a sting of tears in her eyes. Ryan immediately looked contrite, and withdrew a cloth handkerchief from a nearby chest of drawers. "Forgive me," he said. "It is none of my business."

"I love the way you see me," Isabel said, sitting down on the couch and dabbing the few stray tears away. "It's like you see me as someone other than I am, someone strong and beautiful, more than I am, and I want to be what you see."

Ryan sat beside her and rested a hand on her shoulder. "I see only what you have shown me," he said gently. "You have been kind to others, warm and giving, and it is easy for one like you to be taken advantage of. The night you came to the club, I knew you were not a mark. Those who come to us do so for their own selfish pleasure and it feeds us, so we do not complain. But you are not one to simply take pleasure for yourself and give nothing in return. You share, giving of yourself fully, and that's why…" His voice trailed off.

"Why what?" Isabel said. "Why it went wrong that second time?"

Ryan looked at the fire. She loved the way the warm light danced over the angles of his face, the slight curl of his hair, cut too short for his face. She was reminded again of her thoughts the first time she saw him, that he seemed out of a sepia-toned photograph, something not from this time of ugly sordid fluorescent garishness, but from a time of gentleness and quiet.

"There is more to the bite than the simple pleasure we give," he said slowly. "It is — can be — a melding of minds and souls as well. It is that preciousness that Drew and his people wish to preserve. They forget that a true melding of body, mind and spirit is a brilliant, rare beauty, something that happens only once in a lifetime."

He turned to face her. "Or twice."

Isabel stared up into the dark azure of his eyes, and this time they did not swell black and suck her in. This time they were human eyes, and she had to say what she had come to say. "I love you."

His face was unreadable, and she went on anyway. The words fell out of her mouth in a babbling stream, and she was helpless to stop them. "I'm sorry, I know you must get women stalkers all the time, people who mistake the bite for true love and who come knocking on your door, and I'm so sorry, but I'm in love with you, I know I am because I can't stop thinking about you, not just the bite or the pleasure but when you make me laugh, and mostly I love the way I look to you, the way you see me, and I know I'm just another crazy female mark but I had to tell you."

He was frozen, inches away from her.

"Please say something," Isabel said miserably, and turned to gaze into the fire.

* * * * *

The drunk sprawled into the gutter right at Freitas' feet. Automatically, she extended a hand to help him up. "Easy, fella, better go sleep it off," she said, and froze as she saw Duane's face. "You!"

"Hell with you," Duane said, pushing away from her and stumbling down the street.

Freitas watched him go before she stepped up to the doorway of Nocturnal Urges.

"No charge for servants of the people, Detective," Brent said, bowing low.

"Sorry, Brent, but I'm not a mark," Freitas said. "I wanted to chat with you."

Brent blinked. "I'd better go get the madam," he said.

"Nope," Freitas said. "Just you. What'd you throw him out for?"

Brent folded his arms. "Harassing the working girls. Miss Fiona has strict rules. No one screws with the marks and no one hurts the workers. We're all about mutual pleasure at Nocturnal Urges."

"Thanks for the recruitment poster," Freitas said. "What did Duane do?"

"Him?" Brent indicated the direction Duane had gone. "Feeling up the new girl, Elyse, called her some unsavory names. Leech-bitch was the most creative he could get, I think. Not generally like him."

"A regular, eh?" Freitas pulled out the notebook.

"Yeah." Brent eyed the notebook with some concern. "He was, till about six months ago. Vanished for a while. Then he came here with some pretty little thing for a twosome."

"Isabel," Freitas said. "She came back by herself later, right?"

Brent sighed. "Oh, don't get me started on that shit-storm. Ryan got the mother of all screaming matches from Miss Fiona. I can't believe she didn't fire him—we haven't had a mess like that since 1963."

Freitas shook her head. "I'll never get over the way you guys talk about the past as though it was yesterday. I was born in 1963."

Brent shrugged. "To me, it was yesterday, and you're just a baby."

"Thanks." Freitas scribbled a little. "What about Jim Parker, the frat boy from the other night? He messed with Elyse too?"

Brent shook his head. "No, he tried to rip off Rebecca's corset on the dance floor. Out he goes."

"Not the same girl?" Freitas asked. Brent shook his head. "Then the one before, Mr. Insurance Guy, what's his name, Matthew Cooker? He got kicked out as well."

Brent nodded. "Started a fight with another mark over Marianne. They both wanted her first. Fucking pigs."

Freitas leveled cop eyes at him. "The others too? Every one of them was messing with a vamp and got kicked out?"

Brent nodded, folding his arms and doing his best bouncer stance. "We don't stand for that kind of shit in Miss Fiona's place."

"You'd do just about anything for Miss Fiona, wouldn't you?" Freitas said.

Brent shrugged. "I keep her people safe. That's my job."

"How far does your job go?" She watched him closely.

"To the street, Detective," Brent said, his face impassive. "No farther. Then they're your problem."

* * * * *

The silence had grown dreadful. Isabel felt chilly, and wished she had something to pull around her shoulders, even though she still had her jacket on. Ryan had not spoken in at least three full minutes.

Finally, she decided she had to say something. "Look, I'm going to go now," she said without moving. "I'm sorry if I embarrassed you."

"Hardly." Ryan's voice was back to that warm-flannel comfort. She didn't get up. "But I would be lying if I said I did not have concerns."

Isabel bowed her head. "Go on."

"You are right that sometimes the marks…mistake pleasure for love," Ryan said slowly. "No, they do not come knocking on my door. But they have come to the club seeking something more than the bite."

Isabel felt even more foolish. She looked around for a convenient hole to fall through and disappear, but none appeared.

"But you are not one of them."

Where had her courage gone? She couldn't bring herself to look at him. "How do you know?" she asked quietly.

"I don't," Ryan said slowly. "It is possible that your feelings for me, however strong they may seem, are simply part of the bite."

Isabel wanted to protest, but she knew he was right. There was no way she could be sure. This strange heat, this obsession — it might be perfectly normal for a new mark.

"My feelings for you, however, are a different story."

Isabel audibly gasped. She looked up at him, and his eyes were intense, still blue, still human and full of emotion. "I know why it went wrong that night," he said roughly. "I lost control because something happened I didn't expect; something I have not felt in two centuries. There is a bond between us, something more than simple pleasure. I think you know it, and you are afraid of it, and you would be happy to dismiss this as some infatuation born from physical pleasure, because it will not fit with your life, your friends, your world. But I know better. The love between a man and a woman is holy and beautiful in its strength and power. The love between vampire and human is rare and difficult, but no less holy and beautiful, Isabel."

"What are you saying?" Isabel asked, her heart beating.

Ryan reached out and smoothed a tendril of her hair back from her brow. "I love you, Isabel," he said softly. "Your kindness, your laughter, the strength you have yet to find within yourself. You said I see you differently; I do not. I see you as you are, and I would see you shine as you truly are and not as how others would have you. You do not see me as an animal or a parasite, but as a man. What is love, but seeing the reflection in another's eyes of what we truly wish to be?"

"What if it's all an illusion?" Isabel breathed.

"There is only one way to know," Ryan whispered, leaning forward. "There will be no bite tonight, love."

His lips touched hers, and she forgot to be afraid of his teeth. Gently he molded his lips over hers, barely pressing against her, but the thrumming heat of him sank in, electrifying the nerves of her mouth, parting her lips and letting his tongue slide between them. The kiss deepened, and he skillfully kept her from hurting her tender mouth on his teeth.

Her hands crept up his arms to his shoulders, spare but strong. She slid them up behind his neck, pressing him closer to her on the couch. Her body leaned into his, wanting to be closer, to melt through to him. But he kept a distance, an agonizing space that she longed to fill.

"Slowly, love," he breathed against her mouth. She shivered, and pressed light kisses along his face to his ear. She caught his earlobe between her lips and nibbled it, feeling his hands tighten on her shoulders.

"Slow enough for you?" she whispered into his ear, dancing the tip of her tongue along the rim of his ear. She kissed downward a bit, lightly kissing the side of his neck. She playfully pressed her teeth against the place where a pulse beat, warm beneath the pale skin. A low chuckle was her reward, and she felt his hand slide down her back and under her jacket, sending shooting bolts of shivery pleasure from the electric heat of his skin. A quick shrug and her jacket fell to the floor. His hands moved across her back, still covered in a light mauve peasant blouse. Even through the thin fabric, she felt the controlled passion of his touch, and it fired heat in her stomach as though stoking a furnace that needed little more fuel to blaze.

Ryan guided her mouth back up to his, pressing her closer to him as she kissed him again, running her fingers through his black hair. She felt his hands moving over her and shifted to allow him access to her front.

He hesitated a moment. "Touch me, Ryan," she whispered.

Gently, he brushed the backs of his fingers over the soft, tender skin above her breasts, bared by the peasant blouse. He slid his fingers, full of electric warmth, slowly down toward the tie that hid her breasts from view. She arched her back, trying to bring her body closer to him. But he seemed determined to go as slowly as possible.

He slid two fingers into the space between her breasts, as though testing the tender, soft skin. The heat of his hand sped her heartbeat, pounding just beneath his fingers. His lips grazed hers again, just as he gently moved his hand over her silken bra, dipping to take the weight of her breast in his hand. She murmured something even she didn't recognize to him, pushing her breast into his palm, feeling the nipple tighten beneath the fabric. The feeling was comforting, an embrace, even as it made her arch her back toward him.

He pressed against the hidden bud, thumbing it lightly, feeling it harden beneath his fingers. Still he molded her breast in his hand, without pushing the bra aside or moving on to the other one. Over and over he rolled her nipple in his fingers, lightly, never too hard, listening to her quickening breath as broken storms of sensation rolled through her from the motions of his hand.

"Oh Ryan, please," she said, and he hushed her with a swift kiss. Only then did he gently push the bra aside, lifting the weight of her breast free of its confines and touching the bare nipple. The electric thrumming heat of him sank through to her breast, filling her with a twisting, groaning tension that begged to be released.

Then he stopped, and her body cried out in dismay even before she spoke. "Ryan," she began, and he dipped his head to her neck, carefully avoiding the still-healing wound at her throat. Instead, he kissed and nuzzled along her collarbone, sliding his hands under her blouse and helping her lift it over her head.

A moment of sanity returned, and Isabel pushed his hands back. "My turn," she said, and began to unbutton his shirt. He waited patiently, but his hands kept creeping up along her jean-clad leg or over her bare shoulder. After each button, she leaned forward to kiss his chest, lick a short line here, nibble a touch there. A moment later, his shirt was gone, and in the flickering light of the fireplace, his skin seemed to shine like pale burnished gold, untouched by the sun.

He leaned over her, and she dipped her head to capture a flat nipple in her teeth. He groaned a little, and she felt his response hardening against her thigh. Isabel slid a hand down between his legs, but he guided her away again, though she felt the tight heat of him through the coarse fabric.

Ryan moved off the couch and spread a thick blanket on top of the rugs already before the fireplace. "Come here, love," he said, his voice roughened with arousal.

Isabel slid down to the floor with him, entwining her arms around his bare shoulders. For a moment, she simply enjoyed the press of skin on warm skin, feeling his heat and electricity sink through her, setting fire to her senses. She sensed that huge feeling again, the nearly frightening mass that she had barely brushed against before, something they seemed to make between them.

"Ryan—" she began.

"I know, love," he said, then his mouth was on her, moving down to her breast, and she forgot what she was going to say. He was so careful, keeping the sharp points of his teeth away from her tender skin. Yet, she could feel their presence, a hardness behind soft, tender lips and skillful tongue, a danger just beyond the passion. He swirled his tongue around the hard nipple and she moaned just a little.

He turned his head, sliding his tongue between the taut silk of her bra and the other nipple. It hardened in his mouth, sensitive beyond belief, and she cried out again, her hands moving over his neck and shoulders, wanting to draw him nearer to her.

Ryan moved back up, his hands quickly unclasping her bra and pulling it free. His warm chest pressed against her bare breasts, thrumming that strange, otherworldly electricity directly through her skin into her body. She felt it fire through her chest, down her back and through her arms and legs, until it seemed it must shoot out her fingers and toes and eyes and mouth. But instead it was contained, a heat and power that seemed partly him and partly her, something shared and built together.

His eyes were still blue.

"Love," she murmured, reaching up to touch his face.

He ran his hand through her hair. "Such beauty," he said, and in that moment, she felt beautiful. Not because he had said so, because words were cheap. Because she saw through his eyes in that moment, saw that he found her beautiful, and that beauty had nothing to do with her face, hair and skin, but what he found within her heart.

He slid downward, caressing her skin with hands, lips and tongue. She felt his fingers grasping at her jeans, and lifted her hips as he pulled them free. His hand wandered down the outside of her thigh, moved over her knee and slid, very slowly, up between her thighs.

Then he stopped, just a bare space away from the edge of her panties, and moved to the other thigh. He stroked downward, away from her, and she moaned in frustration.

His hand swept back up again, stopping just short, then he brushed his fingers against her, still covered by the fabric. The sensation sank in for just that brief second, like a thunderbolt of pleasure shooting up from between her legs all the way up her spine to be let out in a cry from her mouth. Then he did it again, and it was nearly as sharp, nearly as powerful.

"Oh love," she cried out, reaching down to make him stay there, make him touch her. Instead, he teased her, touching her one moment, and leaving her tense and unfilled the next. Gently he tugged at her panties, and she helped him remove them. The touch of his fingers parting the soft folds, finding the hard bud of her arousal and stroking it gently, sent a raging storm of excitement and thunderclaps of pleasure through her body. His finger penetrated her, and its thrumming heat filled her from within, tightening the tension coiled throughout her body.

"Ryan," she murmured, and pulled at his jeans. Her hands were shaking and she could not get the buttons undone. He helped her, sliding them off. He was glorious in the firelight, full and hard, and she took him in her hand, feeling the shudders cascade throughout his body. She stroked him gently, as he had touched her, teasing him one moment, leaving him the next. With one hand she explored him, seeking out the textures of his skin, while she let the other hand wander over his body, seeking out and finding pressure points that made him jerk and gasp above her.

Ryan moved over her, his eyes intense. She slid her legs up on either side of him, urging him closer. Her hands wound behind his neck, and she reached up for his kiss. He complied, lowering down to her while keeping balanced above her, between her thighs. First his tongue penetrated her mouth, gliding through her lips in the mating dance of the kiss. Then his hand swept her body in one long caress, from her knee up the side of her thigh, over her hip and up to her breast, where a hardened nipple pressed against the light mat of hair on his muscled chest.

Isabel felt him press against her, sliding just a bit into her, and then withdraw. Just that one touch was electric, a bolt of pure pleasure rocketing through her body.

Then he slid a bit more into her, just past her entrance, and slid back out, waiting.

"Oh, Ryan," she moaned.

He slid in a bit more and only the trembling in his arms showed the strength with which he was controlling himself. Isabel cried out beneath him, urging him onward, but he slid back out again.

He hovered above her and she cried wordlessly to him, reaching down to grasp his buttocks and urge him into her.

He slid in again, this time burying himself deeply within her. The thrumming heat of him sank in and she cried out, grasping at his shoulders and drawing him close. He did not move for a moment, letting the sensation fade. Then he moved and she instinctively moved with him.

She met each gentle thrust with a thrust of her own, in perfect harmony. It built between them, that huge feeling she had sensed, that great mountain of glorious pleasure that seemed too big to take within herself. It was, she realized. It was too big for one person alone. It was something they shared, something they could feel only together.

He moved faster, and she moved with him. Not only where he filled her, hard and full of heat within her, but in his skin, his eyes, the sounds of pleasure coming from his hoarse, broken voice. It grew between them, not as something being taken from her or drawn from him, but something they created in a tapestry of sounds and sensations that seemed to fill the room, the world beyond completely forgotten.

"Isabel," he cried, and she felt him begin, his hands tightening on her body, and she felt it too. For an instant she was afraid again, afraid of that feeling that was too big for her, afraid it would overwhelm her. *Too much, it's too much*, she thought, but Ryan was there with her, feeling it with her, and she joined him completely. It washed over them, wave after wave, a shattering, crystal feeling that filled every empty place within her and had to be let out in hoarse cries and shuddering thrusts.

The heat exploded between them, not within one or the other, but shared and multiplied with each other, a mutual joy that did not fade, but slowed to a rapid heartbeat as he shuddered to a stop. He did not withdraw, but remained within her, and she relished the feel of him, spent inside her, as her contractions slowed to a stop.

Gently he withdrew from her, shifting his weight to his side. Then he drew her close again, as though he could not get enough of his body close to her. She pressed against him, her body warm and satiated. She wanted every inch of her skin pressed against his.

His arms encircled her, and he drew down a blanket from the couch over them, enveloping their bodies in its cocoon.

"Love," he breathed, pressing gentle kisses against her face. Isabel lay within his arms, and the last of the emptiness, the lonely void waiting to be filled, dissipated away, floating up through the chimney and out into the cool dark night.

* * * * *

He stumbled in the darkness. The world seemed to spin a little, faint and whirling just beyond his sight.

Man, I'm wasted, he thought, and tried to remember how many drinks he had had that night. At some point, there had been a dark-skinned beauty with flashing white teeth, but then hard pavement beneath his hands and the laughter of drunk college students jeering at him.

He tried to remember where he was, blinking in the darkness. Some alley, somewhere in the back streets, but nothing seemed familiar.

He stumbled toward the street, but the opening was blocked by a cloaked figure. With the streetlights, it seemed as though rays of light flowed from it, some magical creature to guide him.

"Hey," he said, aware on some level that his words were slurring. "Can you help me? I'm lost." But it seemed to come out *canoo hep ee, im losht.*

"Shhh," said the voice, and he shushed. It drew close, faceless and shadowed.

He looked up at it, and screamed.

Teeth.

Chapter Five

ஐ

Isabel gazed out her bedroom window, wrapped in her favorite robe. She should have been bone-tired, even exhausted from almost no sleep. But instead, the light seemed to have a different cast to it, as though it had been specially filtered just for her, and she felt only calmed and at peace as she combed out her wet, tangled hair.

A memory tried to invade her mind, of Ryan's smiling face pressed against her chest, of murmurs between kisses buried beneath the wedding-ring quilt, of a shared cup of water dribbled onto her breasts and carefully removed by his eager tongue. Shivers still tickled her spine, and she couldn't seem to stop smiling.

It had never been like this, not with Duane or the lovers she had had before him. Sometimes it was love, sometimes, just sex. In the cool morning light, she was forced to admit with Duane it had mostly been sex, though he had made her laugh.

Ryan had not wanted her to go. He wanted her to stay and spend the day with him. But Isabel had to go to work, and as much as she wanted to play hooky, she knew she had to see Duane. He obviously knew it was over—his hurt and anger at Nocturnal Urges had not exactly been a sign toward reconciliation. But she owed him a real explanation.

Isabel shivered, her hair still wet and cooling from the shower. She felt as though Ryan's kisses were imprinted on her skin and longed to feel them again. She laid down her comb and went into the kitchen to make some coffee.

The doorbell rang.

Frowning, Isabel went to the door as the coffee perked and gurgled in the pot. Duane stood in the doorway, haggard, and smelling like beer.

"Oh Lord," Isabel said, pulling him inside. "You look like hell, Duane. Go, sit down."

Duane stumbled over to the table, sprawling into a chair. Isabel poured a quick cup of coffee for him, which he sipped unmindful of the heat. It must have burned his tongue.

"Duane, are you all right?" Isabel asked, and then mentally kicked herself for such a stupid question.

"Think it'll snow?" Duane asked, staring at the television.

Isabel sat opposite him. "What happened to you?"

"Drunk," Duane said.

"I can see that," Isabel said. "This isn't like you."

"Wasn't feeling myself. Someone broke my heart."

Isabel cast her eyes down. "Oh, Duane," she said softly. "I'm sorry. I wasn't trying to lie to you before, truly I wasn't. I was lying to myself about how I felt. I-I'm in love with someone else, Duane. It's over with us. I hope…I hope we can still be friends."

The words hung in the air between them, and Isabel wished she could mitigate them with some kindness, some softening that would ease the blow. She glanced up at Duane, and he was staring at her.

"The leech? You'd really leave me for…"

"Don't call him that," Isabel snapped. "I'll be as gracious as I can, Duane, but there I draw the line."

Duane shook his head. "I'm sorry, Isabel." He walked over to the television and turned it on.

"Duane, I—" Isabel's voice trailed off as Duane switched the TV to the early morning news.

"Finally, a break in the case of the vampire murders in downtown Memphis," said a chirpy female anchor voice faking sincerity. *"Police sources report they have a suspect in the killings, a rogue vampire with a history of violence who works at the club Nocturnal Urges, near which most of the victims were killed."*

The image switched to a live shot of Freitas leading a suspect through a gaggle of television cameras up the steps of the main police station. The crowds parted for a moment, and Isabel saw Ryan's angled face just before he disappeared from view.

"Oh no," Isabel cried. "No, it's not possible."

"He did another one last night," Duane said. "I really am sorry, Isabel. I know you don't like to be fooled."

Isabel felt as though the world were spinning beneath her. "But he didn't," she said. "He couldn't."

Duane slid an arm around her shoulder, and to his credit, it felt like an attempt to comfort, not to cajole.

"Last night?" Isabel asked.

"I'm sorry, baby," Duane said, and the nickname grated on her as it never really had before.

"Last night? But he was with me last night!" she exclaimed, and almost didn't notice the way Duane flinched. "He was with me; he couldn't have hurt anyone last night!"

"With you?" Duane said.

"I have to tell Annie," Isabel said, walking quickly back toward her bedroom. "I have to hurry!"

She reached for her clothes, and realized that Duane had followed her into her bedroom. "Duane, I'm sorry, I have to go."

"You can't," Duane said hoarsely. "You're going to tell the world you shacked up with a vampire?"

Isabel was suddenly furious. "What's bothering you more, Duane? That I'm leaving you, or that our friends will find out I'm leaving you, or that they'll find out I'm leaving you for a vampire?"

"You can't do this to me," Duane pleaded.

Isabel pulled on her clothes quickly—heaven knows he'd seen her bare skin before. "I'm sorry, Duane. I'm going."

Duane stepped in front of her. "I won't let you. You can't humiliate me like this."

Isabel suddenly was not afraid. "You can't stop me, Duane. I have to help him. I love him. I'm sorry it will hurt you; I wish I could do something about that, but I can't. The only way you can stop me is by hurting me, and we both know you're not going to do that."

She stood face-to-face with him, and he stared down at her. Then he seemed to shrink a little, saddened with an enormous weight that broke her heart a little to see. He stepped back into the hallway, letting her pass.

She stopped beside him, and put her hand on his for a moment. "You know what? You're going to be fine without me, Duane," she said, not looking at him, just squeezing his hand. "You always were. It's your pride that's been hurt, not your heart. I was never the center of your world, Duane, and you were never the center of mine. I hope...I hope only good things for you."

Isabel let go of his hand and walked away, down the hallway and out the door. Somehow, she knew the key would be on the kitchen table when she came back.

* * * * *

Isabel went through the metal detectors, trying to hide her nervousness. But it must have showed anyway, because an officer came over to her in the main hall as she stared at the directory.

"Can I help you?" said the officer, whose nametag identified him as Patrolman Wyben.

"I'm looking for Detective Freitas," Isabel said.

"Homicide," Wyben said, pointing to the stairs on the far side of the lobby. "Up two flights, ask the desk sergeant."

"Thank you," Isabel said, heading across the lobby with more bravery than she felt. Just being in this building made her feel guilty of something.

Climbing the steps, she approached a man at a desk helpfully labeled DESK SERGEANT. "Excuse me, could you tell me where I can find Detective Freitas?" Isabel asked.

"Sit down," Desk Sergeant said without looking up. "I'll tell her you're here."

Unnerved by his brusque tone, Isabel sat down. Desk Sergeant kept writing on his forms. He didn't pick up the phone or get up to go speak to anyone. Unless he was communicating psychically, Isabel thought, he wasn't letting anyone know she was here.

Isabel waited, feeling more foolish by the moment. She watched the clock tick by, and when ten minutes had passed, she got up and stood before Desk Sergeant again.

"Excuse me," she said. "If you could just direct me to—"

"The detectives are very busy," Desk Sergeant snapped. "Just leave a message."

Isabel's face flushed. "I can't, I need to see Detective Freitas."

"Leave a message," he insisted.

Isabel's face grew hot, and she was suddenly angry. "Fine," she snapped. "The message is, 'Dear Detective, you've got the wrong man, Ryan was with me all night and could not possibly have murdered anyone. Love, Isabel Nelson.'"

The desk sergeant's head shot up. "This isn't funny, miss."

"Absolutely right!" Isabel said. "So, can I please see…"

"Just a minute," the desk sergeant said, and got up to disappear back through a door locked with a keypad. Isabel waited, growing more irritated by the moment.

A taller, younger man stepped out of the door with Desk Sergeant. "Hi, Miss Nelson, I'm Sergeant Ken Henry," he said, holding out his hand. Isabel shook it perfunctorily. "Would you come with me?"

Isabel followed Henry though the hallways, past rows of desks with men talking on phones. Somehow, she'd expected a police station to be dingy and scary, but this looked like an insurance office, she thought.

Henry led her into a smaller room with a table and two chairs. She sat down, suddenly nervous again. Henry sat opposite her. "So you told the desk sergeant you know something about the vampire cases?"

"Yes," Isabel said. "I saw you arrested Ryan. He could not have killed anyone last night. He was with me."

"This is Ryan…" Henry popped open a pen and held it above a pad of paper.

Isabel's face suddenly grew warm. She realized she didn't know Ryan's last name. She had never asked him.

"This is really embarrassing," she said. "I guess his last name… It never came up."

"But you spent the night with him," Henry said.

Isabel blushed even harder. She made a mental note of questions she was going to ask Ryan as soon as they got out of here, beginning with his last name.

"What time did you see him, and where?" Henry asked.

"It was about ten o'clock," Isabel said. "First I went to Nocturnal Urges…"

"But Ryan Callahan didn't work last night," Henry said.

Callahan. Isabel nodded. "He wasn't there. So I went to his apartment."

"Where is that?" Henry asked.

Isabel gave him the address. "It's a fairly nasty place, but his apartment is very nice, kind of a warm cabin-style with pictures of Ireland and maybe the last functioning fireplace on that city block. That ought to convince you I'm not making this up."

"Sorry," Henry said, not sounding the least bit apologetic. "How did you know where he lived?"

"Elyse told me," Isabel said. "She works at Nocturnal Urges."

"Elyse is a vampire?" Henry said, and Isabel nodded. "Callahan, too. Did you know that?"

"Of course I knew that," Isabel said.

"Nasty bite you've got there," Henry said, pointing at her half-healed wound. "Callahan?"

"Yes, but—"

"Did you report it?" he pressed.

"It wasn't like that!" Isabel protested. "He didn't mean it…"

"But you knew he was a vampire," Henry pressed.

"So what?" Isabel said. "That doesn't make him…"

"The sort who might bite?" Henry said.

Isabel stared at him. "He was with me all night, that's all you really need to know, isn't it?"

Henry glanced down at his pad of paper. "What time did you leave Callahan's apartment?"

Isabel thought fast. "About three a.m., I think. I got home about three-thirty, so that would seem about right."

"So how did you know he'd been arrested?" Henry asked.

"TV," Isabel said. "Now you'll have to let him go, right? He hasn't hurt anyone."

Henry stood up. "Thanks for giving us your statement, Miss Nelson. I'll see it gets to Detective Freitas."

"Wait," Isabel said. "You have to let him go, he didn't hurt anyone!"

"Sorry, that's not up to me," Henry said, opening the door.

Isabel stood up. "Can I please see Detective Freitas?"

"Detective Freitas is…"

"Very busy, I heard," Isabel said. "Does she even know I'm here?"

"That's really — "

"Annie!" Isabel shouted out into the hallway. "Anne Freitas! Can you hear me?"

Henry reacted instantly, placing a restraining hand on her arm. "Ma'am, I have to ask you to lower your voice or — "

"ANNE FREITAS! ANNE FREITAS!" Isabel shouted, and other detectives started to get out of their chairs. Isabel kept shouting, and soon there were more hands on her, roughly pushing her down the hallway, more voices telling her to be quiet or she'd be put under arrest, and she kept shouting louder and louder until a voice cut through like a hot knife through butter: "All of you shut up and let her go!"

The crowd parted, and Isabel shook off Henry's hand as Freitas came through the group. "What the bloody hell is going on here?" Freitas snapped. "Isabel, have you gone nuts?"

"Not yet, give me another half-hour of this," Isabel replied.

Henry glared at Isabel. "Sorry, Detective, I was trying to—"

"Can it, Ken," Freitas snapped. "I think I'll re-interview this witness, if you don't mind."

Henry shrugged, and handed over his pad of paper with obvious contempt. Freitas took it, and led Isabel back into an interrogation room.

"Well, you sure know how to get attention," Freitas said.

Isabel ducked her head. "Sorry."

Freitas sat down and scanned Henry's notes. Then she blinked, and glanced up at Isabel. "Look, I'm not really interviewing you here. I know you, I consider you a friend, and that pretty much puts me out of the running," she said. "But I had to get you away from those bozos long enough to ask you something, right here, right now."

"I'm telling the truth," Isabel said.

Freitas held up a hand. "Listen to me, Isabel. If you're fibbing, it's going to go very badly for you. If you're not, it's going to go very badly for you and Ryan both."

Isabel gaped at her. "What do you mean? How could it be worse than being charged with murder?"

"First of all, Ryan Callahan's not charged yet," Freitas said. "We picked him up for questioning, but we have not arrested him, we have not charged him. TV jumped to their own damned conclusions, color me shocked, and now I've got a city screaming for vampire blood."

Isabel shook her head. "I still don't see…"

"Wake up, Isabel," Freitas snapped. "If you go public, you're admitting to having an affair with a vamp. Not just using them for the bite, not just employing them as night workers, but actually consorting with them. "

"What, you think I'm worried that my country-club membership will be cancelled?" Isabel cried.

Freitas turned off the cop eyes and looked honestly concerned. "I'm worried you're going to lose your job, Isabel. I'm worried that you'll get kicked out of your apartment if Ryan tries to move in, and that you'll get killed by his neighbors if you move in with him. I'm worried your family and friends will be horrified and shun you. I'm worried that those kooks in SAV will harass you as a very public example of 'mixing'. I'm worried that you're going to throw away your whole life because of one roll in the hay, when it may not even exonerate him, because frankly, I think he did it."

Isabel sat in stunned silence. She wasn't sure which shocked her more—Freitas' recitation of horrors that she had not considered, or the flat conviction in her voice.

"Why?" Isabel said. "Why do you think he did it?"

"I'm not at liberty to say," Freitas said formally.

"Give me a break, Annie, it's me!" Isabel cried. "You've got him locked up on more than being off-duty last night, I'm not asking for forensics reports, why do you think the man I love murdered five men?"

Freitas leaned forward. "Let me tell you a little bit about your lover, Isabel. He's the only one who has no alibi for each murder. When we asked him about last night, he said he was home alone. He didn't tell us about this little rendezvous."

"He was trying to protect me," Isabel murmured.

"He also has a history of violence, especially protecting other vamps, and all the victims had harassed the vamps in some way," Freitas went on. "The attack on you was certainly unprovoked, and he's been known to throw around abusive patrons…"

"He's supposed to just stand there while drunken fools hurt his friends?" Isabel cried.

"He's killed before, Isabel," Freitas said softly. "Interpol has a file on him. He was tried and convicted in Ireland, but fled before execution."

Isabel gaped at her. "It's not possible," she whispered. "When was that?"

Freitas gave a sad smile. "1838. I'm still getting through the file, and it's not very complete. They vacated his sentence in the 1920s. But it's a record, and it's not going to look good in court."

"Who?" Isabel breathed.

"Who'd he kill?" Freitas replied. "His wife. Hell, given the times, he's lucky they didn't just set him on fire. Vamps usually didn't get a trial then."

"Seems they barely get one now," Isabel shot back, hiding her churning emotions behind ersatz anger.

"Isabel, I'm your friend, and that's the only reason I'm talking to you now. I have to turn over this statement you gave Henry. But if it's not true, if you're trying to protect him, you're only buying yourself trouble, hon. Yeah, we're probably going to release Ryan—but your life is ruined and he may be charged anyway. If you walk out now, recant the statement, it'll be over. You'll be safe from the press, from Osborne's kooks and from Ryan Callahan."

Isabel's head lifted up. "I don't need protection from Ryan," she declared. "Let me write the statement."

"Isabel—"

"That's my decision, Annie," Isabel said. "Let me do it."

Freitas stared at her. Then she slowly pushed a legal pad toward Isabel.

* * * * *

It was hours before they let her see Ryan. Desk Sergeant led him into the interview room, still handcuffed, and shoved him into a chair.

"Can't you take off the handcuffs?" Isabel cried, but Ryan shook his head mutely even as Desk Sergeant stomped out without a word.

"Isabel, you shouldn't have done this," he began, but she shushed him with a kiss.

"Nonsense," she said. "You should have told them you were with me last night, saved yourself this whole mess."

Ryan looked up at her with eyes that suddenly reminded her how very old he was. The weight of centuries lay in his gaze. "It is futile, love," he said.

"Did you kill those men?" Isabel asked with the surety of one who knows the answer.

Ryan lowered his head. "No."

"Well then," she said. "You've got nothing to worry about." Even as she said it, she felt naïve. *Well, someone has to be upbeat here*, she thought.

"Isabel, there's something you should know," he began.

Isabel looked over at the mirrored wall, wondering if they were watching. "Careful, love," she said.

"It's nothing they don't know," Ryan said. "About Ireland, my wife…"

"You don't have to tell me," she replied, though her heart was pounding.

"Yes, I do," Ryan said. "She was human. We were married in 1831, lived on my family's farm outside the village. We had to have a traveling cleric marry us, a man who didn't know what I was, because the church would not recognize the union. We thought that would be the end of it.

But naturally, the villagers didn't like the idea of a mixed couple. They threw rocks at her when she came to town for market day. Mysterious things would happen on the farm, dead chickens, so on.

"One day, a couple of men in a wagon chased her down a dirt road. They didn't mean for it to go so far, but it didn't matter. They ran her over, and instead of taking her for help, they left her to die in a ditch."

"You found her there," Isabel said.

Ryan nodded. "She was dying. I couldn't bear it, I wanted her with me. So I turned her. No vaccine in those days, of course. I shared my blood with her and she was reborn."

Isabel frowned. "I don't understand. She became a vampire?"

"Making a human into a vampire against their will was considered murder back then," Ryan said. "They held a trial, dragged her before the authorities to prove she was a vampire. She didn't believe it herself, you see—despite the craving, the physical changes, she couldn't believe what had happened until the trial. They condemned me to death, but I escaped."

"How?" Isabel breathed.

Ryan shrugged. "It wasn't exactly Attica," he said. "I knew my life was over. I fled the village, joined with thousands of other immigrants and came to the United States. Ireland changed the law in 1925, which is why my sentence was commuted."

"They can't possibly hold this against you," Isabel said. "It was a hundred and seventy years ago, and it was an act of love!"

Ryan smiled sadly. "Have you ever noticed that it is acts of love that so often become mortal crimes in the eyes of men?"

Isabel leaned against him, resting her head against his shoulder. "We'll work this out," she declared.

From the hallway beyond the room, a commotion was building, voices raised and the occasional thump. Isabel rose to her feet. "I'll be just a moment," she said.

"Be careful," Ryan said.

Isabel opened the door and peered out into the squad room. A number of officers were wrestling a shouting, twisting man down into a chair.

"Let go of me!" the man shouted, and as an officer moved out of the way, Isabel recognized him as Jonathan Osborne, the protester from outside Nocturnal Urges.

Freitas was standing over him, reading what Isabel recognized as the Miranda warning off a small index card. Osborne kept shouting, demanding to be freed, as Freitas continued impassively. He spat at her and it landed on her jacket. Freitas didn't even flinch, just finished reading. "Toss him in holding," she told Henry. Looking over her shoulder, Freitas saw Isabel watching and crossed the room.

"What's going on?" Isabel asked.

Freitas went into the room and unlocked Ryan's handcuffs. "My apologies, Mr. Callahan," Freitas said. "We've got the killer."

Ryan jumped to his feet. "How? When?"

Freitas inclined her head at the squad room. "There was another murder just before dawn, while you were with us. We found him at the scene, staggering around in the mess, high as the proverbial kite," she said. "Had a pair of false vampire teeth, do you believe it?"

Ryan stared at her. "Him? It was a man?"

"Yeah," Freitas said.

"Listen, the circus is gathered out front. Let me drive you two home."

Ryan offered his hand to Freitas. "Thank you, Detective."

Freitas snorted. "For what, dragging you in here? Letting the cameras get a good look at you?"

Ryan shook his head. "For treating me as an ordinary suspect," he said with a touch of wry amusement. "Many detectives would not have bothered to cover the windows."

Freitas glanced away. "Well, don't go spreading it around," she said gruffly.

Isabel and Ryan followed Freitas through the squad room, where Isabel sensed every eye upon them. Sgt. Henry was openly glaring from across the room as Osborne babbled incoherently to him.

On the ride down the elevator to the parking garage, none of them spoke. It wasn't until they got in Freitas' car that Ryan spoke up. "Don't take us home, Detective. Take us to Nocturnal Urges."

"Okay," Freitas said. "But the press will probably be camped out there, too."

Isabel stared at him, and wanted to know everything at once. She wanted to ask him more about Ireland, why he worked at Nocturnal Urges, all about his life in America. It seemed so strange to be in love with a man whose last name she hadn't known until this morning.

But his hand stole over to squeeze hers, and she buried her questions. *There will be many nights to ask them*, she thought.

Freitas pulled into the lot a block away from Nocturnal Urges. "Should I come with you?" she asked.

"Perhaps," Ryan said.

They walked up the sidewalk toward the club. The protesters were back in full force, and as they passed between the shouting groups, Isabel saw Drew Sanford being interviewed by television crews. Ryan ducked his head a bit, and the protesters were too busy shouting and the television crews too busy filming to notice the prime suspect walking by.

"Thank God," Brent said at the door. "You okay, Ryan?"

Ryan nodded. "Come in with us, okay?"

"Miss Fiona said to keep the riffraff out," Brent said, indicating the crowds on the sidewalks.

Ryan grinned. "One day you're gonna tell her off, Brent," he said.

Brent shrugged. "Not today."

"Come in with us," Ryan said, and Brent followed them into Nocturnal Urges.

There was almost no crowd, which made sense for the early hour, Isabel supposed. Besides, most of the attention seemed to be in the street outside tonight.

The Creatures of the Night were just setting up onstage. There were almost no patrons in the club, just Fiona behind the bar dipping margarita glasses in salt and glaring at a guy nursing a beer—Isabel gasped. It was Duane, she'd recognize him anywhere. *Surely, he hasn't been drinking here all day*, she thought.

"Isabel, what's going on?" Freitas whispered.

"I have no idea," she replied, as Elyse came into the room and took over the margarita glasses from Fiona.

"Ryan!" Fiona called out, crossing the room in yet another of her grand gowns. This one was a luxurious purple, sweeping to the floor, with a plunging neckline that would make a lesser woman blush. "You're released, I see. Is it all over with?"

"Almost." Ryan turned to Freitas. "Detective, you had several suspects to choose from, yet you zeroed in on me. I have a great respect for your deductive capabilities, and so I assume it was not just because I was a vampire. Something told you to look at vampires."

"I really can't discuss the case with you," Freitas said.

"Oh, for pity's sake..." Isabel groaned.

"It was a vampire," Ryan said. "But I had the advantage, because I know I didn't do it. You crossed off Drew and his people, presumably because they have alibis."

Freitas folded her arms. "Did you notice we got the guy?"

"Just listen, detective, and if you're so inclined to tell me when I'm wrong, I'd be grateful," Ryan said. "Since I knew I didn't do it, and I trust that you properly vetted Drew's people, that left either someone none of us knows about...or one of the vampires at Nocturnal Urges."

"Like a nutbar anti-vamp protester with fake vampire teeth," Freitas said.

Isabel ignored her. "But most of the Nocturnal Urges vampires probably had alibis too," Isabel mused.

"Just being at work wasn't enough, because I was working on one of the nights that someone was killed," Ryan said. "The night Isabel came to Nocturnal Urges for the first time."

Duane's head lifted and Isabel saw him staring at Ryan.

"So it must have been possible, at least, for the killer to sneak out," Ryan continued.

"Osborne. Caught him. Watch the news," Freitas said.

"But does it make any sense?" Ryan asked. "What good does it do to frame vampires for murders? We are already hated, already suspicious in the eyes of the humans."

"He's a few sandwiches short of a picnic, Callahan," Freitas said.

"Did he drink the blood?" Ryan asked.

Freitas stared at him. "That doesn't prove Osborne didn't do it," she said, but the protest in her voice was weak.

"This is crazy," Fiona protested. "None of my people would hurt a mark. Why would we? It only hurts business!"

"But these weren't ordinary marks," Isabel said. "They were jerks, men who messed around with the vampires. Someone was…protecting them?"

Isabel turned to look at Brent, who immediately grew pale. *Well, pale for a vampire*, Isabel thought.

"Not me, no way!" Brent said, holding up his hands. "I told the detective, it goes as far as the street, no farther!"

"He kicks them out, he doesn't kill them," Fiona said.

"True," Ryan said. "I know Brent, he couldn't hurt a fly. He drinks cow's blood from the butcher. He can't bite a human, even a willing one."

Brent looked down at his feet in embarrassment. Ryan put a hand on his shoulder. "Nothing to be ashamed of, man."

Duane downed his drink and stumbled past the bar, toward the door. But Ryan called out after him. "Please, sir, don't move."

Isabel stared at Duane. "Ryan, what are you doing?"

"Mr. Russell," Ryan called, and his voice was more insistent.

"Fuck you," Duane growled, and kept moving.

"Duane!" Ryan shouted, running toward the door. Duane turned on him and swung a drunken punch, his face contorted with fury. Freitas was already moving to separate them, with Brent right behind her. Isabel shouted something—she wasn't sure what—but suddenly everyone was still.

Duane stood alone in front of the bar.

Elyse held his neck between her hands.

"Elyse, please," Ryan pleaded, his voice trying for that calm tone Isabel loved so much, but there was a ragged edge to it she had never heard. "Let him go."

Elyse's nails dug into the skin on either side of Duane's neck. Isabel clapped her hand over her mouth, horrified at the look of stupefied terror on Duane's face.

"He's evil, Ryan," Elyse spat. "He's just like the others. He's a bastard and he deserves whatever he gets."

Freitas had drawn her gun, but held it carefully down by her side. "Miss, let's talk this out, okay?"

Elyse hissed at Freitas, her pretty face contorted into a rictus of hate. Freitas stepped back, her free hand held out in a calming gesture.

"Elyse, this isn't the way," Ryan said. "You can't get your revenge by killing him."

"Don't pretend you care," Elyse snapped. "When he's gone, you can be with your pretty little human. No messy entanglements."

Isabel felt as though she were still a few pages behind. "You wanted Ryan?" she said. "Then why did you help me find him?"

"Stupid girl!" Elyse growled. "He can have you. He can have any human he wants. I don't care."

"She doesn't love me," Ryan said dully. "She hates me. She's killed all these people, oh God, those poor men, because she can't kill me."

"Why?" Isabel asked.

"He made me into this!" Elyse hissed, baring her teeth an inch from Duane's throat. Duane was too petrified to move. "He turned me into this thing, forced me to live an eternity like this!"

Ryan stepped forward. "Elyse, I can never get your forgiveness," he said, his voice broken. "But this man has done nothing to you."

"Do you think that matters?" Elyse spat.

Ryan took another step. "He's not me, Elyse. If you want me, come for me."

Elyse grinned, a horrible, sadistic smile that bared her white teeth. "First him. Then her. Then you," she cackled.

"Not happening, hon," Freitas said, edging closer.

Elyse hissed again.

"Please, Elyse," Ryan said. "This can still end well."

Elyse smiled, and for a bare instant, Isabel caught a glimpse of the sane woman still inside her, a woman filled with despair. "No, it won't," she said, and lowered her teeth to Duane's throat.

Duane screamed. Ryan leapt forward, pulling Duane away just as Elyse's teeth grazed into his throat. As Ryan and Duane fell away from the bar, Elyse leapt up onto the bar, still hissing.

Freitas shot Elyse twice, and still she held on, screeching out her hate as she tried to jump down toward Ryan. Freitas shot her a third time, and Elyse tumbled to the floor.

Isabel ran over to Ryan and Duane. "I thought bullets don't kill them," she said breathlessly.

"They don't," Freitas said, training her pistol on Elyse's bloodied, twisting form. "It just slows them down."

Brent knelt beside Duane, pressing a handkerchief against the bloody wound. Duane was conscious, staring at Elyse.

Ryan crawled over to Elyse, kneeling beside her. "What would you have?" he asked, his voice filled with a terrible sadness.

"You know," Elyse whispered.

Ryan glanced up at Freitas, who stepped back. Then he turned to Elyse, and lowering his head, sank his teeth into her ivory-pale neck.

Elyse cried out, a terrible wail of misery, horror and sadness. It seemed to fill the room, echoing beyond its walls, a sound that brought tears to Isabel's eyes and echoed inside her chest, where she was conscious of her heartbeat as never before.

Ryan drank, and Elyse's voice began to fade. Slowly, it disappeared, and her shaking ceased.

Ryan lifted his head, and turning away, wiped the blood from his mouth. Then his shoulders began to shake and Isabel went to him, drawing him into her arms with all the strength she could muster. She held him, let him grieve, and because he mourned, she mourned with him.

* * * * *

If Isabel never saw the inside of the police station again, it would be too soon.

"You might have shared all this stuff with me before, you know," Freitas said.

"Turn in someone who might be innocent, just to save my own skin?" Ryan said. "Not very gentlemanly. I suspected Elyse, but suspicion is a long way from proof. And I did not want to believe her capable of such horrors."

"A few things I don't understand," Isabel said to Freitas. "You knew Elyse worked the same schedule as Ryan. Why arrest him and not Elyse?"

Freitas rolled her eyes. "As I will no doubt be explaining at my next personnel review, for the fiftieth time, I did not arrest Ryan. I brought him in for questioning at an ungodly hour because I thought it would be quiet that way. And yes, that means someone in my department tipped the TV news crews, and yes, that's a conversation I'll be having with my higher-ups."

"But why Ryan?" Isabel pressed.

"History," Ryan said. "My murder conviction."

"Elyse," Freitas said, nodding. "I apologize, Mr. Callahan. Your file wasn't entirely clear on that point."

"She came across in the mid-1950s, but we did not see each other again until she came to Nocturnal Urges two months ago," Ryan said. "She told me my sentence had been commuted. But she had never forgiven me. She hated what she was, and hated me for making her into a monster. I tried to help her, wanted to help her, to atone. She took out her fury on all men for the sins of one."

Isabel placed her hand on Ryan's. "You are not a monster," she said softly. "You loved her, and that's all that matters."

Freitas stood up. "If you don't mind, I have about a year's worth of paperwork to file," she said.

Ryan stood as well. "Will you get into trouble for allowing the bite?"

Freitas smiled, a tired, sad smile that mitigated her cop's eyes. "What bite?"

Isabel took Ryan's hand, and smiled at Freitas. She walked through the police station at Ryan's side, and when they stepped out into the faint pearl-pink rays of the rising sun, she stepped close to him and leaned her head on his shoulder.

Together they walked away from the sunlight, into the shadows between brick and stone, disappearing into the darkness together.

A MORE PERFECT UNION

ॐ

Prologue

ℰ

It really was a dark and stormy night.

Samantha stepped out of the ramshackle hotel building she laughingly called "home". The flickering yellow streetlights cast a waxy, anemic glow into the Memphis alley. Her black heels clicked unevenly on the broken, wet pavement as the rain pattered against her umbrella, the cloth flapping away from one of the thin metal ribs in the wind.

Samantha stayed to the side of the alley until the smell of the trash bins, full of rotting seafood from the restaurant next door, forced her to move into the middle of the trash-strewn alley. It was a rancid, sour-sweet smell, sickening and dead, but still powerful.

Suddenly a young man lunged from behind the trash bin, his torn shirt soaked to the skin. He was thin, with sandy-brown hair and the haunted eyes of someone who had spent too much time crying of late. He held up a wooden cross with a shaking hand. "Back, you fiend!" he shouted. "You will not harm any soul tonight!"

"Oh, please." Samantha rolled her eyes. "Not again."

The young man was resolute. He held the cross in one hand and a long wooden stake in the other. It still had some varnish and a bit of scrollwork from the chair leg from which it was made.

Samantha trudged forward slowly, her umbrella flapping badly in the wind. The young man held the cross out in front of him like a shield before his widening eyes as Samantha walked directly up to him.

Samantha reached out and wrapped her fingers harmlessly around the cross. "See?" she said wearily. She yanked it away, letting it clatter to the ground.

The young man stumbled backward, reaching inside his coat. He came out with a small flask of water, which he threw in Samantha's face.

She started a moment, water running into her eyes. "You ruined my makeup," she grumbled, wiping the holy water from her face. Then she continued her slow walk forward.

The young man retreated farther up the alley, still facing her.

"Are you going to go away?" Samantha asked.

"You…you are a spawn of Satan, and you must be destroyed," the young man said in a thin, frightened voice.

"Grr. Argh." Samantha made her hands into claws and scratched at the air in front of her. "Now go away."

The young man looked down at the stake in his hand and raised it half-heartedly.

Samantha stared into his red-rimmed, terrified eyes and reached inside him. She knew his name was Richard and a thin blonde girl had left him two weeks before. She rolled him under easily, letting her calm fill his troubled mind. His frightened eyes grew cool and his trembling fingers stilled. Samantha stepped closer and easily took the stake from his nerveless fingers.

For a moment, he tempted her. She leaned toward his neck where the blood flowed warm and thick beneath the tender skin. She smelled the thin spice-scent of his fear and the roiling salty warmth of his blood…and planted a light kiss on his cheek.

Samantha snapped the stake in two and walked past Richard down the alley to the stage door of Nocturnal Urges. When she looked back over her shoulder, he was still standing there, frozen in the rain. She broke the link gently, and he fell to his knees in the water. After a long moment, he looked over at her.

"Mwah!" she called, waving and making a kiss-kiss face at him from the stage door. He stared at her, then scrambled to his feet and ran away into the rain.

Samantha smiled and went to work.

Chapter One

ഔ

7:04 p.m.

"We live in troubling times," the deep, male voice intoned over a swirling background of fluttering newspaper headlines against dark, ominous smoke.

"There are some who think the American dream is for sale. That tolerance means accepting any behavior, any lifestyle. That the actions of a few must dictate our beliefs."

A flag appeared, veiled far away in the smoky dust, growing closer.

"They think that public schools are a place for our children to learn depravity. That libraries should be a haven for pornography. That faith is something to be quashed instead of celebrated in our town square."

The flag filled the screen, waving in the unseen breeze. A face began to materialize in front of it, and the voice-over changed to the voice of the man himself, a man somewhere in the gray years between youth and middle age, his hair cut painfully short around his otherwise handsome face. His eyes were serious and penetrating.

"There's a reason we call them 'human rights'," he said gravely. "I'm Joe Renfrow, and I approved this message."

"Oh, for God's sake, Andi, turn that shit off," griped the lanky black man, lounging on the couch.

"No need to get testy, David, I didn't write the damn thing," replied the slender blonde curled up in the armchair. She reached forward to turn off the TV.

"I hate that motherfucker," David sighed.

"He's gonna win," Andi said distractedly, returning to her novel. "No way what's-his-name has a chance."

"His name is Robert Carton," Samantha said, stepping through the greenroom door. Unlike most theater greenrooms, Nocturnal Urges' waiting area was actually painted green—deep hunter green with a burgundy paisley border carefully applied at waist level. The couches and chairs were tastefully antique, with a television discreetly placed inside a huge oak armoire. *No one could ever accuse Fiona of bad taste*, Samantha thought.

"You're not still volunteering for him, are you?" Andi asked.

"Stuffing envelopes is all," Samantha said, shaking out her umbrella.

David sat upright, staring at her. "Girl, what have you done to your face?"

"Is it that bad?" Samantha asked.

David peered at her eyes. "It depends. Are you planning to perform in 'The Life and Times of Tammy Faye'?"

Samantha groaned and went over to the vanity. Like everything else backstage at Nocturnal Urges, it was an antique, all heavy glass and gilt edges.

"You ever want to go back in time and smack the shit out of Bram Stoker?" Samantha asked, grabbing a tissue and dabbing at the trails of mascara down her cheeks.

Andi raised her eyes from her novel. "Not again."

Samantha nodded, sitting down at the vanity. "Third Van Helsing wannabe this month. I swear, I'm going to insist Fiona hire somebody for the back door. This is getting ridiculous."

"Uh, darling," David said, sliding to his feet and strolling across the room toward her. His motions were those of the dancer he once had been, smooth and feline without a hint of a flounce. His skin was the color of dark chocolate, cocoa without milk, smooth and warm. His hair was shorn close to his head above cheerful eyes and, of course, the gleaming white fangs of a vampire. "Another bouncer at the back door equals another salary to pay. And in case you've forgotten, Fiona is cheap."

Samantha sighed, trying to clean the mascara trails off her cheeks. "How am I doing?" she asked, turning to David.

David knelt beside her. "Honey, you're just smearing it," he said, taking the tissues away.

Samantha sighed as David began to clean her face. "I miss mirrors."

"Not me," Andi said, back in her novel. "I don't want to know when I'm having a bad hair day."

"I barely remember what I look like," Samantha said.

David grabbed a second tissue, dabbing at Samantha's face. "Trust me, baby. You look *mahvelous*—underneath all this crap you trowel on."

"The marks like it when I look trashy," Samantha said. "Turns 'em on."

"Uh-huh," David said. He opened a drawer in the vanity and pulled out a tray of makeup supplies. "Sit still. This is my chance to make you beautiful."

"Do your worst, Michelangelo," Samantha said.

David gently touched up the eyeliner around Samantha's crystal blue eyes and dabbed a light coating of mascara on her already thick lashes. "Honey, you know you don't need any of this shit," he said, swiping a little at the thick blue eye shadow layered above her eyelids.

"I like it," Samantha said.

David pulled out a brush and stroked it through Samantha's honey-blonde waves. "I'd love to explore why you think painting yourself like a whore makes you a better biter, but I don't have time to psychoanalyze you tonight, honey," he said. "I'm expecting at least two horny college boys."

"It really doesn't bother you?" Samantha asked. "Both of you—you do the whole thing…and it doesn't bother you?"

"Baby, I have the best job in the world," David said, brushing her hair until it crackled. "I get fed, get laid and get paid."

Andi giggled. "You should really try it, Sam," she said. "It's a lot easier once you give up the voyeur thing. You get a whole lot more clients, too."

"I'm thinking about it, but I wonder if it'll bother me. You know, having sex with strangers?" Samantha asked.

"And exactly what else am I supposed to do?" David said. "Write the great American novel? Spin off a few divisions of my computer software empire?"

"I don't know if I could go through with it," Samantha said, patting down her hair.

"Boy, are you in the wrong line of work," Andi said from her chair. "You give suckjobs all night."

"That's not the same," Samantha said. "Taking blood is just…food. They enjoy it and we get fed."

Andi raised her head above the chair. "Don't tell me you don't enjoy it, too," she said. "If you're rolling them like you're supposed to, you should feel everything they feel."

"I am," Samantha said defensively. "Of course, I am."

David put away his tray. "You're still thinking like a human, sweetie," he said. He turned her chair toward the vanity. "But you're not. And you never will be again."

Samantha faced the mirror and saw nothing. The reflection showed only an empty room—tastefully appointed, but empty. "I know," she said listlessly.

The door opened and Fiona swept in. Fiona always seemed to sweep across a floor, as though she wore ice skates beneath her voluminous skirts and all the world was a frozen lake for her to command. Or more than that—as though she were a force of nature, not bound by such silly things as gravity. She was easily one of the oldest vampires Samantha had ever met—at least three hundred years, maybe more. As always, she bound her plentiful breasts into an uplifting corset beneath her green silk gown, her fiery red hair cascading in ringlets over her shoulders. "David, your frat kids are here."

"God bless those horny closet boys," David said. "Level?"

"Bite and touch," Fiona said. "They must have had their allowances cut off."

"Rats," David said. "I was looking forward to an orgy." He straightened his sleeves and moved past Fiona into the dark hallway.

"Sam," Fiona said. "Got one for you. Husband and wife, names Steve and Ellen. Or so they say. Newbies."

Samantha stood up and took off her coat. Beneath it, she wore a sleeveless white dress, tight across the breasts and below to her waist, then loose and filmy to her calves. "Which one gets bitten?"

"The husband," Fiona said. "Roll and bite him while he's doing the wife. Light touch, nothing too intrusive. Just the way you like it."

"Fiona, there was another nut in the alley tonight," Samantha said.

Fiona peered at her. "He hurt you?"

"No," Samantha said. "Splashed me with holy water is all. I rolled him and got away. But they're stepping up."

"It's those damn commercials," Fiona said, glaring at the

television as if it could wither under her gaze. "Fucking politicians. It's only a month to the election then it'll all die down. No worries, dear."

Samantha shot a glance at Andi, who grinned.

Fiona turned back to Samantha. "Go, girl," she said. "Customers waiting. Room four."

Each room had a hidden entrance. Room four's was behind a pillar and could be seen in good lighting if one were really looking for it. It helped preserve the ambience Fiona had designed for the rooms.

Samantha stepped out from behind the pillar, shadowed in dancing candlelight. Steve and Ellen were already engaged, writhing together on the four-poster bed. A sheet was thankfully lying over their nether regions as Steve thrust forward and Ellen cried out beneath him. He was a balding man beginning to run to fat and Ellen was a thin, mousy woman with straight, colorless hair. They were an ordinary-looking couple, the sort that lived in a suburb with neatly tended lawns and clean, well-kept cars and only experimented in secret.

Quietly Samantha moved to the bed. She slid onto the mattress beside them and they slowed to look at her.

Steve's eyes roved over Samantha, full of a raging hunger. His gaze took in the curves of her breasts swelling above her neckline. Samantha gave him the vampire smile, seductive and innocent at the same time, baring the tips of her fangs where they protruded ever so slightly below the rest of her teeth.

"Hello," Samantha said, using the husky, seductive voice Fiona had taught her. They all thought it was a vampire trick, to arouse the mark with voice alone but, in fact, any human could do it—with practice. "My name is Miranda."

Steve stared at her, motionless. Samantha spared a quick glance down at Ellen and was instantly sorry she had. Ellen was simply waiting, pinned beneath her husband, with no interest in Samantha whatsoever. In that instant, Samantha knew it was Steve's wish to be here, not Ellen's.

Samantha looked back up at Steve, her eyes carefully neutral. She reached out toward him, hovering her hand just above his bare shoulder. She let the energy flow from within her heart outward, and the tingle of it touched Steve's bare skin. He cried out and thrust into Ellen again. Samantha continued to stroke the air just above Steve's arm and shoulder, then down his back, letting the energy grow into him, exciting him as he moved faster and faster.

Ellen's arms crept up Steve's back. Samantha let her energy flow into Ellen's hands, creeping down through her arms and into the older woman's torso. Ellen moaned a little, flushed and panting heavily.

Samantha lowered herself beside Ellen and looked up at Steve. "Look at me," she murmured. Steve looked down at her, still pushing himself into his wife.

Samantha reached inside and rolled him. It was a gentle thing, a casual touch of her mind to his. She let calm and peace flow through her eyes into his mind, and stilled the last few coherent thoughts within it. In that moment, she knew Steve was imagining Samantha beneath him instead of Ellen. She saw little in the way of love and devotion to his wife, only a vague selfishness born of a dull life, craving the excitement of youth, enhanced by the passing of years.

Samantha rose up again and moved behind Steve. She straddled behind his ass, rising and falling faster now. She slid her body over Steve's, allowing the energy to flow between them.

She saw Ellen's face beneath them, composed and ready, flushed with passion, but afraid. "Ellen," Samantha whispered, and Ellen looked up.

Quickly, Samantha rolled her as well. She reached inside

and let the calm flow over Ellen's small, rabbity mind. She saw an endless parade of days, dull and dry, a house empty of long-gone children's voices, fears of her husband's waning affection livened by pinpricks of terror born of Nocturnal Urges, of Fiona…and of Samantha herself. She saw herself through Ellen's eyes, a beautiful creature of danger and lust that Ellen feared more than her husband's disinterest.

Samantha rode Steve's body up and down, her arms running down his shoulders and breasts pressed against his back. She lowered her mouth to his shoulder, carefully placed away from the major arteries. The raw smell of his lust rose up, and she could sense the blood pumping fast and hot beneath the skin. He was food, and he smelled like food. Her stomach growled, and her lips parted, letting her fangs press against the skin.

With practiced strength she struck, sinking her fangs into the meat of his shoulder. Blood welled up in her mouth, warm and salty, and she swallowed it down. She latched her mouth over the small wound and sucked gently, drawing more blood out through the two small holes with a smooth suction. Through her link to him, she felt him begin to explode, shuddering and crying out, thrusting hard into Ellen with his head thrown back and his eyes closed. She rode him as his body staggered beneath her, swallowing mouthful after mouthful of his hot, pumping blood.

Then Ellen cried out in a reedy voice made hoarse with pleasure, and Samantha felt a new wave of ecstasy course through her, rising up through the invisible thread that connected her to Ellen. She felt a surge of joy and a hot, bitter pleasure shoot from Ellen through her and into Steve who jolted beneath her into a second, smaller explosion. He opened his eyes and stared at his wife who was clawing at his back and weeping with overwhelming sensation. Gently, Samantha disengaged her mouth from Steve's shoulder as they ground to a halt beneath her. She began to move away, but saw a thin line of blood trickle down Steve's back from where Ellen had clawed it. She smelled it, hot and coppery against his skin, and the hunger rose up. She licked it, catching every drop, feeding from him again, sucking down every tiny bit of blood until the wound was clean.

They weren't looking at her. They lay together, staring at each other as if they had never seen one another before.

Slowly, Samantha eased off them and slid from the bed. She was too embarrassed by her own loss of control to look back as she slipped into the door behind the pillar.

7:48 p.m.

Detective Anne Freitas felt distinctly like a horse's ass.

She stepped carefully around the clanking weights, keeping out of the way of her fellow officers. The dank basement room was packed with after-shift workouts, mostly younger ones in sweats and sneakers, toning muscles they'd likely never use in the line of duty. Stupid rock music was playing from a radio somewhere and the running hum of the treadmills nearly drowned it out.

Freitas was wearing jeans, sturdy shoes, a button-down shirt and a suit jacket. She felt more than a little out of place.

The basement workout room had no windows, but stretched half the length of the building. Freitas wandered about, ignoring the funny looks that the nearly all-male officers gave her, and finally gave up, going over to the desk.

"Jimmy," she said.

Jimmy looked up from the stack of coarse white towels he was folding, his thin, liver-spotted hands still firm and sure. "Annie!" he said. "It's been way too long."

"Thanks for reminding me, Jimbo," Freitas said. "I'm looking for Parker."

Jimmy scratched his narrow, pointed chin with an

obnoxious smirk on his face. "Well now, you're the hotshot detective," he said lazily. "Where do you think you might find Parker?"

Freitas rolled her eyes. "I don't know Parker," she said. "All I've got is a name, so how about giving me a break, old man?"

"Parker, Parker…" Jimmy grinned, pretending to mull it over. "Don't know'm."

"Spare me, Jimbo, you know everybody," Freitas said. "Ought to after the umpteen years you've been here. Now you gonna help me or should I haul your skinny ass upstairs for obstruction?"

Jimmy sat down on his stool. "Seen 'em come and I've seen 'em go. Ain't never seen a right hook that come near yours, Annie."

"Thanks," Freitas said tiredly.

"'Cept maybe Parker's."

Freitas glanced at him, and he pointed over toward the threadbare boxing ring. "Thanks, Jimbo," Freitas said, and walked over to the ring.

Two men were bashing away at each other, slamming meaty fists into protective gear with ugly thuds. Freitas watched for a minute, and her opinion of Jimmy's eyesight dropped with each thud-thud-thud of the gloves. The tall one was quick but untrained, missing openings left and right. The shorter one was all muscle, no brains. Freitas amused herself for a few minutes, trying to guess which one was Parker.

The spotter blew a whistle, and the men retreated to their corners, grinning through their sweat.

Freitas gave up trying to be clever. "Parker!" she called out.

Both of them looked at her. *Well, that doesn't help,* she thought.

"Yeah?"

Freitas turned around to see a young woman stepping out from behind a training bag. She was a little taller than Freitas, which still put her a few inches shorter than the average woman. She had straight hair pulled back behind her ears, a dark red, just short of being unnatural. A small, nasty-looking burn scar showed on her muscled arm, disappearing under the strap of her tank top.

"Wanted to see your moves," Freitas improvised. "Jimbo said you're pretty quick."

"Am," Parker said. "Hey, Chapman! Wanna get your ass kicked by a girl?"

The taller one leaned over the rope. "Don't see no girls around here, Parker."

Parker pulled herself up to the ring easily. "You got that right," she said, pulling on a helmet.

The shorter one hopped down and took off his helmet. Now Freitas recognized him. Lieutenant Chris Cox was a hatchet-faced man who still bore his Marine haircut of twenty years ago and a nasty puckered scar at the side of his neck he refused to discuss. "Cox," she said, "how's things on the Chain Gang?"

"Toothsome," Cox snickered.

"Wow, that's funny," Freitas said. "Bet you never used that one before."

Up in the ring, Parker and Chapman circled around each other for a few moments. Then Chapman struck first, punching out much too slowly as Parker dodged easily to the left and jabbed a quick one into Chapman's side. He turned toward her, but she was already dodging out of the way and rocketing a gloved fist into the side of his helmet.

Good, but it isn't mine, Freitas thought.

"So, you still hanging out with the leeches?" Cox asked

"Talk like that's gonna get you in front of a review board," Freitas said absently.

"Yeah, they might make me watch a video," Cox said. "Never found out why you didn't call us for that vamp-grab last fall."

"I've seen your deft touch," Freitas said.

"Hey, you're a good cop," Cox said, and the patronizing tone in his voice was probably meant to be flattering. "You get sick of helping the leeches and you could be on my team."

"I'll keep it in mind," Freitas replied.

Chapman stumbled a bit. Parker backed off a moment to allow him to get his bearings. He came back at her, not really seeing now, just blindly swinging. Quickly, she grabbed his overextended arm and bent it up behind his back, sweeping a foot between his legs and dropping him hard and fast face-first onto the mat.

"I surrender," he croaked. "You feel better now?"

Parker let him up. "Yep," she said cheerfully, stripping off her helmet and gloves.

Freitas began to clap slowly. "Nice moves," she said as Parker jumped down. "Where'd you study?"

"Tae Kwon Do World," Parker replied. Freitas smirked. "What?"

Freitas shook her head. "You're a natural talent and your training comes from a storefront sensei?"

Parker folded her arms defensively in front of her chest. "So who the hell are you?"

"Didn't mean to offend," Freitas said.

Parker didn't relax. "Sensei is a hell of a man. Might even teach you a thing or two," she replied.

"Let's start over. Good fight," Freitas said.

"Let's not. Bite me," Parker replied, and walked over to

the other side of the ring. She gathered up a gym bag and hoisted it onto her shoulder. As she started to walk past, Freitas reached out and touched her shoulder.

Parker slammed a hand up and Freitas automatically reacted, blocking the blow and twisting Parker's arm in an aikido move, forcing the younger woman down onto the floor in one blow. Parker's leg swung up toward Freitas and she rolled with it, dodging the blow's main force and pressing down on Parker's arm, pinning her to the floor.

Parker stared up, breathing heavily. "Who the hell are you?"

"Anne Freitas," she replied. "Your new partner."

9:12 p.m.

The young man sobbed against Samantha's shoulder, his thin shoulders shaking. She patted his arm gently. "It's okay, Kyle," she said.

"It's not okay," he whimpered, sniffling. "I'll never feel like this again. Ever."

"Sure you will," she said kindly. "You're young. There are many years ahead of you. It doesn't feel like it now, but your heart will heal."

"But—"

"No buts," Samantha said firmly. "Repeat after me—I am a good guy."

Kyle looked at her, his face miserable and young, so very young. "I am a good guy."

Samantha shook her head. "I don't believe you."

"I am a good guy." He lowered his eyes.

Samantha leaned forward, tipped up his face and kissed him. She molded her mouth to his, smooth and sure, and let a touch of power flow from her to him through her hand on the underside of his jaw. Then she released him gently.

"Now say, I am worthy of being loved," she murmured.

Kyle smiled a little. "Oh, come on, Miranda."

Samantha met his gaze and reached inside, just a little touch, tasting the bitter tang of his pain and a sudden image of an anonymous dorm room, a nowhere space with no posters on the walls or books on the shelves.

She slid a hand down the back of his neck, letting more power flow through his skin. His entire body jumped, and she leaned him back onto the pillows, keeping her eyes focused on his. She breathed calm into him and lowered her mouth to his neck.

Kyle clutched at her shoulder, moaning just a bit as she struck, sinking her fangs into him. She drew the rich, warm blood from him, swallowing it down as she felt his body convulse beside her. His voice cried out, harsh and hoarse, a shadow of the man he was slowly becoming. She felt the sudden explosion of pleasure leap from his cry to her torso, gripping her in its energy for a moment before it faded. His grasping hands tightened almost painfully on her shoulders then relaxed.

Samantha lifted her head and whispered in his ear. "I am worthy of being loved," she said, keeping her voice low but with an undercurrent of power in it.

"I am worthy of being loved," Kyle said sleepily.

"All right." Samantha slipped away from him and stood up. "You take care now, okay?"

Kyle nodded, his breathing calming down. "Thanks, Miranda."

"Anytime," she said, and slipped behind the pillar and into the access hallway. She walked toward the greenroom, ignoring the sounds coming from room nine. Someone was having a moaning, thrashing good time.

Samantha went into the greenroom and plopped onto a chair. "I don't know which is worse," she began. "When they treat you like meat or when—"

"The talker was back, huh?" David said, lounging on a couch.

Samantha smiled. "Poor kid. He always buys a bite then ends up crying on my shoulder about the girl who just dumped him. This is the third girlfriend this fall."

"Damn," David said, flipping channels on the television. "Boy gets around."

Samantha waggled her eyebrows. "Not that I can tell."

David grinned. "Maybe you should educate him in the ways of the flesh."

Samantha thought for a moment then shook her head. "He's too young."

"Gotta be eighteen to get in the door," David said.

"Not what I meant," Samantha said. "He's about twenty, I think. That definitely involves robbing the cradle."

David glanced up at her. "I didn't say marry him, I said fuck him, darlin'."

Samantha didn't answer.

David sat up, suddenly serious. "Honey, why don't you just take the leap? You'll make three times the money, enough to get out of that fleabag hotel. It's just tricks, babe. It's nothing."

Samantha shook her head. "It's not nothing."

David shrugged. "You get used to it. It's a job, like any other."

"We steal their souls," Samantha said quietly.

David burst out laughing. "Have you been listening to those idiots out front again?"

"I know we don't actually steal the souls," Samantha

said. "But drawing them in for a false shot of pleasure? Faking intimacy, passion… Isn't that deception? When we roll them and we get a glimpse of their minds, isn't that stealing their souls? Exerting power over them?"

"Hell no," David said. "The people who come here are broken in some way. They're missing something or searching for something. We give them what they want and hold nothing back."

"They should find it with each other," Samantha said.

David laughed quietly. "We should all be so lucky, honey," he said. "Me, I gave up on Prince Charming a few decades ago."

Samantha stared at the flapping flag on the television. "Me too."

10:23 p.m.

Freitas and Parker stepped through the maze of card tables and phone banks in the campaign office. Formerly a car dealership, the room was silent and dark, the volunteers having gone home hours before. Although the door had been unlocked, the only light came from a glassed-in office on the far side of the room marked JEFF MORRIS, CAMPAIGN MANAGER on a hand-lettered sign. Freitas stopped just out of sight, beyond the light shining from the office, with Parker behind her.

"There's a reason we call them human rights."

Beyond the glass, a short, red-faced man with a beard beginning to go gray paused the screen. "There. Right there is our problem."

A tawny-haired young man lay on an old, burnt-orange couch beside the desk, resting his arm across his eyes. "Tell me something I don't know, Jeff," he said in a weary voice.

Jeff Morris stood up, pointing at the television. "That

tagline is undercutting everything we've done. Nobody's talking about health care or highway construction or education funding initiatives. No, it's the goddamn vamps."

"They're calling us wishy-washy on vamp rights," said a tall, willowy blonde, leaning against the wall. She had unbuttoned her gray suit coat at the end of a long day and was rubbing the bridge of her nose.

"We are wishy-washy on vamp rights," said the young man on the couch.

"Do you mind, Danny?" Morris snapped. "I'd rather not lose this election until we've well and truly screwed it, if it's okay with you."

"We should be coming out in favor of vamp rights," Danny said neutrally.

The woman shook her head. "We've been over this," she said. "The country isn't ready for vamp rights. We say vamps should be allowed to marry and we're dead. This is, after all, the South."

"Last I looked, South didn't mean stupid, Meredith," Danny said.

Morris stomped over to the TV and shut it off. "Goddammit, Danny, you start in with this every time we try to come up with a strategy," he snapped. "We have to find a way to counter these attacks, not feed them. The councilman—"

"The councilman will be better served by having a real agenda that provides an alternative to Joe Renfrow's Hate-O-Wagon," Danny said without heat.

"Right now, the Hate-O-Wagon is rolling over us and gaining speed," Meredith said. "The press is using reactive language again—we're 'reacting to attacks', we're 'issuing a response'. We haven't done anything substantive in two weeks."

"We announced the child care initiative three days ago!" Morris shouted.

"Did we?" Meredith asked, faking wide eyes. "I didn't know that. I didn't see it on TV."

In the shadows outside Morris's office, Parker leaned over to Freitas and whispered, "How long are we going to hover here?"

"Shh," Freitas replied.

Morris glared at Danny. "You gonna say something useful?"

"I already did and you ignored it," Danny said without looking up. "It's your campaign. You're in charge. Give us orders."

Morris wandered over to his desk. "What if we find some aspect of vamp life to condemn?"

Meredith blinked. "Like the sex trade?"

"Yeah," Morris said. "The bite-selling near Beale and the vamp hookers."

"It's legal," Danny interjected.

"So are plaid bellbottoms, but I can still be strongly against them," Morris returned. "We come out against the sex trade and we separate ourselves from the vamps without backing off on our current stance on vamp marriage."

"We have no stance on vamp marriage," Danny said.

"Sure we do," Meredith said, reciting as if from a press release. "'The councilman believes that while human rights must apply to all people, the nation as a whole is not ready to embrace the idea of vampires gaining full equality under the law, and that must include the right to marry humans. Until the hearts and minds of the American people are open to the idea, the councilman cannot in good conscience support ideas that the majority of his constituents oppose.'"

"Thanks, it sounds just as weaselly as the first fifteen times I heard it," Danny said.

Freitas stepped out of the shadows and into the office doorway with Parker close behind her. "Hello, I'm looking for Jeff Morris?"

"That's me," Morris said. "What can I do for you?"

Freitas pulled out her badge and Parker followed suit. "Detectives Freitas and Parker," she said. "Understand you've got a bit of a problem."

Morris reached out his hand. Freitas hesitated for a moment before handing him her badge to examine. "You're Freitas and she's Parker?"

"The same," Parker said, and her tone was snotty enough for Freitas to shoot her a quick look.

"I'm Meredith Schwartz, campaign spokesman," the woman said, reaching out to shake Freitas' hand. She had the professional woman's double pump, just enough pressure not to be threatening.

Parker inclined her head toward the young man on the couch. "He got a name?"

"Danny Carton," the young man said, waving without lifting his arm from his face.

"Councilman's son. What do you do around here?" Parker asked.

Danny lifted his arm for a moment to look at her. "Whatever I'm told," he replied.

Morris handed Freitas back her badge. "Forgive the paranoia, Detective, but politics is a paranoid business," he said. "Yes, we do have a problem. Meredith, do you have the letters?"

Meredith walked over to a soft leather briefcase sitting on the desk and rifled through it. She pulled out a file folder and handed it to Freitas. "There's been six of them within the last two weeks, all vague, nonspecific threats," she said. "We don't qualify for Secret Service protection so we put in a few discreet inquiries to your lieutenant."

"Yes, he impressed upon me the need for discretion," Freitas said absently, flipping through the letters. "'Die, vamp-lover?'"

"They lack in creativity and panache," Danny said.

Freitas handed the folder to Parker who took it without comment. "We can look into who might be sending them, but it'll help if you can give us a few ideas," she said. "Anyone spring to mind as a serious Carton-hater?"

"Anyone with an IQ under seventy," muttered Danny.

Morris shot him a look before responding. "It wouldn't necessarily help our opponent, and I doubt he'd risk a stunt like this anyway," he said. "There's the standard hate groups, the far right—anyone who hates vamps is probably high on the list. We're highly visible public officials, and with the TV commercials, it brings out the crazies."

"Wouldn't hurt you if it got out, though, would it?" Parker said.

Freitas shot her a warning look, which Parker disregarded. "I mean, if you wanted to let the voters know you were pro-vamp without actually saying it, the letters would help. You could deny them and still separate yourself from the pro-vamp movement."

"Damn, why didn't I think of that?" Danny asked sarcastically.

"Detective Parker, I assure you we have no such intentions," Morris snapped. "I trust such speculations won't interfere in your attempts to find the real threat."

"Of course not," Freitas said hastily. "Here's my card, and if you think of anything that might help, give us a call."

"We'll be in touch," Parker added. Morris glared at her.

As quickly as dignity allowed, Freitas walked out of the campaign office with Parker behind her. She waited until they were in the parking lot before she turned toward her. "Are you out of your mind?"

Parker crossed her arms defensively. "I didn't take this job to kiss ass."

"No, you took it to catch the bad guys, I assume?" Freitas snapped. "And if you really think these guys were pulling a publicity stunt, why the hell did you say it to their faces?"

"To gauge their reactions," Parker replied.

"Oh sure!" Freitas said. "They'll just fall down and confess to a hoax within thirty seconds because of your brilliance!"

Parker shrugged. "I didn't see it hurting anything."

"Kid, you've been a detective about fourteen hours. Why don't you let me do the talking until you grow up?" Freitas returned.

Parker shook her head. "This is not going to work out," she said. "I don't need a baby-sitter."

Freitas laughed without humor. "And I'm not gonna baby-sit you. But you are gonna shut up until I tell you to talk, at least until you install some filters between your brain and your mouth, you hear me?"

"You don't outrank me," Parker shot back.

"I have seniority," Freitas replied. "Got a problem with it? Take it to the lieutenant. But he's gonna tell you to shut up and learn."

Parker stared at her. "On one condition."

"What?" Freitas snapped.

"Don't call me 'kid'."

11:58 p.m.

Danny Carton walked down the dark alley alone.

The shadows were deep between the flickering streetlights. Far away, he heard the faint sounds of the jazz clubs on Beale Street. In the building to his left, he heard the thumping bass of the vampire club Nocturnal Urges. The rain had stopped, pooling in the potholes with rainbow slicks of oil shimmering in the streetlights.

"Hey, mister, lookin' for a date?" The girl stepped out of a recessed doorway in an abandoned building. Small and slender, she had close-cropped black hair and large gray eyes. She wore a red fake leather miniskirt and a black tank top with a rip in the side. She teetered on stiletto heels as she stalked toward him.

"What's your name?" Danny asked.

"Celia," the girl said, smiling with red-smeared lips in what was supposed to be a seductive grin. "Fifty bucks for anything you want."

Danny stared at her. "You're not a vamp."

She grinned widely, baring pointed fangs. "We prefer undead-American."

"They're fake," Danny said.

The girl grinned wider, and thrust her small breasts forward. "I'm all real, honey," she said.

Danny shook his head sadly and pointed behind her. The girl turned and saw her reflection in what remained of a glass door. "Shit," she breathed, and turned back to him. "I'm not a vamp, I'm better," she said desperately. "I can do things they can't. Anything you want. I'm the real thing."

"You're illegal," Danny said. "How old are you?"

"Old enough," she replied.

Danny stared at her. "I'm guessing fifteen at the most,"

he said.

"Fuck you!" the girl cried, fear and panic in her voice. "I'm eighteen, and you're an asshole!" She turned and wobbled back toward her doorway.

"Wait, kid!" Danny called, following her.

Celia turned back, instantly switching the faltering seductress back on. "You still wanna party?"

Danny shoved a handful of bills at her. She took it and grabbed his hand, dragging him toward the shadows of the abandoned building. "No!" he cried, pulling back from her in the shadows of the piss-smelling hallway.

The girl stared down at the wad of money then looked back up at him, cold darkness falling across her face. "What do you want me to do?" she asked, and to Danny's horror, she started peeling down the straps of her tank top.

He retreated immediately, stumbling back out into the relative sanity of the streetlights. "Just go eat something."

The girl stood in the doorway, confusion and suspicion warring on her face. "Mister, this is enough for anything you want," she said, clutching the crumpled money.

Danny shook his head. "Go home tonight," he said softly. "Don't…don't do it tonight. Go home and eat something, get some sleep. It's on me."

The girl stood frozen, still staring at him, the wad of bills in her hand. Danny turned and fled, nearly running down the alley.

The rain was falling again.

Chapter Two

ໜ

1992

Memphis

"So they found you out?"

The woman's deep voice surprised Samantha, nearly making her drop the file box in her arms. She looked around the parking lot and saw no one. "Hello?" she said.

"They found you out." The woman was right behind her, suddenly very close. Samantha jumped again, startling backward against her car door.

The woman reached out her hand. "Easy, Miranda."

"That's not my name anymore," Samantha returned, fear clutching her chest. "Dear God, tell me you're alone."

"Entirely, my dear," Fiona said, smiling without caring to cover her gleaming white fangs. Her red hair stood as a shocking contrast to her sensible gray suit. "I'm my own master now."

Samantha laughed, a dry, sardonic sound. "I can't believe he let you go," she said. "What did you have to give him? To do for him?"

"Nothing," Fiona said, her smile fading. "Cristoval is dead, Miranda."

Samantha stared at Fiona and ever so gently tried to reach inside through her eyes. Instantly she was met with the cool steel wall of Fiona's power, rebuffing her without effort.

"That was rude, my dear," Fiona said without heat.

"Forgive me. It would be just like him to send you to me

like this," Samantha said, glancing around the parking lot again in the cool glare of the streetlights. Most of the cars were gone, the sun long since set. "How do I know he's really dead?"

Fiona shrugged. "I have no way to prove it, my dear, except that I am my own master now and determine my own destiny. Could that be possible if Cristoval were still alive?"

Samantha shook her head. "How did it… I don't want to know," she amended quickly. "I have to go, Fiona."

"They found you out?" Fiona asked again.

Samantha hung her head. "Yes," she said quietly. "It never lasts long. This was better than most—an office job, entirely indoors, no chance of the sun being a problem."

"How did they discover you?" she asked.

"The bathroom," Samantha said. "I got careless, and came out of the stall while a woman was washing her hands. The mirror."

"Careless indeed," Fiona said. "Now what will you do, Miranda?"

"That's not my name!" Samantha shouted with all the fury and emotion of the day driving out of her toward Fiona. The bland, manicured secretary's shocked face, her fast recoil to Samantha's pleadings, her running footsteps down the hall to the office manager's desk, the hastily convened meeting, cleaning out her desk while everyone—people she thought were her friends—stared and whispered. This, coupled with the stunning news that Cristoval was dead, a tectonic shift in her universe that was impossible to comprehend—the emotions hadn't had a chance to settle in yet. It all flew out from her heart toward Fiona who recoiled just a step.

Fiona stared at her. "Whatever you call yourself, I can help you," she said softly. "Come work for me."

Samantha laughed bitterly. "Doing what?"

Fiona told her.

Samantha lowered her eyes. "I haven't…not since…"

"No wonder you look so dreadful," Fiona said without a shred of diplomacy. "Honestly, my dear, I was tempted to call a healer the instant I saw you. Your face, your hair…you're skin and bones. You can't possibly subside only on animal blood. You know that."

"I've managed, with a few supplements, nothing like…" Samantha's voice trailed off.

"Come with me," Fiona said. "It's food, company and most of all, safety. The club is all mine now, and you need not hide what you are, Mir—my dear. It is nothing to be ashamed of."

"Samantha," she replied. "My name is Samantha."

* * * * *

11:12 a.m.

"Coffee?" Lieutenant Frank Fradella poured a second cup without waiting for Freitas' response.

"Black," Freitas replied.

"I remember," Fradella said, handing her the cup. "Too harsh for me."

Freitas accepted the cup without comment. "I don't suppose I can talk you out of this."

"Nope," Fradella replied, sitting behind his desk. "Monroe's been gone for nearly a year. Time for a new partner, Annie."

"It's not," she replied. "I don't need a partner, and besides, the kid's a pain in the ass."

"Just like you were a hundred years ago," Fradella smirked. "Don't get riled up about this. Parker's bright and committed, resourceful and doesn't mind working the long hours. She'll be a good detective when she gets a little ugliness under her belt."

"Great." Freitas sipped her coffee. "Did I ever tell you I flunked my baby-sitting course in junior high?"

"I don't doubt it," Fradella said. "Parker's not gonna need you standing over her shoulder, Annie. Just a little seasoning."

Freitas rolled her eyes. "Semantics," she said. "And it's Detective Freitas, Lieutenant."

Fradella stared at her a moment. "This isn't going to be uncomfortable for us, is it?"

"No problem here," Freitas said smoothly.

Fradella met her eyes then turned and opened his office door. "Parker!"

A moment later, Parker came in. Her hands were folded in front of her, as though she were trying to look tough but secretly afraid of her hands trembling, Freitas thought. "You rang?" she said.

"What did you make of the letters?" Fradella asked.

Parker glanced at Freitas for a moment then spoke. "All from the same guy—he used the same kind of language, same typeface and generally same printer style. He's not highly educated—no more than high school, maybe a dropout."

"He. You think it's a man?" Fradella asked.

Parker nodded. "Very aggressive language—implies fear of the vamps and what they represent. Men tend to react more aggressively to what they perceive as sexual deviance while women tend to merely disdain it. Women are rarely driven to violence when exposed to homosexual behavior, for example, while heterosexual men can respond with great violence, particularly if they feel their own sexuality is threatened."

"So you think he is going to become violent?" Fradella asked.

Parker nodded. "I could be wrong, but I think he's working himself up to confronting the congressman directly. The letters are more impersonal, sent to the campaign and its more visible members. Councilman Carton is a public authority figure, not easily challenged. But I think he's escalating up to it."

Freitas grinned. "See? My work is done. She's brilliant."

"Nice try," Fradella said. "You two are going to get real close."

Parker shot Freitas a look. "Okay," she said without enthusiasm.

"I don't want the Feds in on this one." Fradella clapped a hand on Freitas' shoulder. "I'm assigning you two to watch over the campaign. Follow Carton around for a bit—join his private security at his public events. Watch the crowds and see if we can catch this asshole before somebody gets hurt."

"I hate you," Freitas said cheerfully to Fradella. Parker blinked.

Fradella shrugged. "I care?"

3:35 p.m.

Samantha stepped into the campaign office and unwound her scarf. No one was looking at her. The room was filled with volunteers carrying boxes or answering ringing phones. Cable news blared from a corner television set. Samantha quickly stepped over to the coat rack and took off her wide-brimmed hat and coat. She stuffed her gloves into the coat pocket and glanced quickly around to see if anyone had noticed her clothing, definitely inappropriate for a Memphis September. She ran her hands lightly over her skin, feeling for heat and tight, dry skin.

No sunburn. Good.

She moved over to her usual station, sorting the mail. Some of it was hate mail, blasting Robert Carton as a "weak-ass liberal". Some of it was friendly, giving him noncommittal, useless advice on how to beat his opponents.

The ones with money went straight to Mr. Morris. Usually there were checks, but on a few occasions, they sent cash. On one heartrending occasion, a poorly spelled letter spilled change out across her card table.

The volunteers were a little more subdued today, and Samantha realized why as she heard raised voices from behind Mr. Morris' closed door. They were shouting again. There had been a lot of shouting this week. The staff was rarely seen at the campaign office. Instead, they were usually out on the stump with Mr. Carton, who had been seen at the office exactly once. Samantha answered to a large, domineering woman named Frances who thwapped the volunteers with her cardboard fan, omnipresent in her hand with GOOD SHEPHERD FUNERAL HOME lettered across it in large, block letters. Frances was nowhere to be seen at the moment, and Samantha breathed a sigh of relief.

The door to Mr. Morris' office banged open and Meredith Schwartz stepped out. A cool and lovely blonde, she had a kind way of speaking to people that felt both professional and friendly at the same time. Samantha secretly admired her poise, always looking fresh and lovely in gray or blue suits and heels, no matter the hour.

"Excuse me?" Meredith said, an uncharacteristic hesitancy in her tone. "Could I borrow a few volunteers?"

The room fell silent and the volunteers looked at each other. Meredith glanced around. "You," she said, pointing to a young black woman Samantha knew as Nikki who was picking up buttons from a box she had spilled on the floor. Then she pointed at Frances, just returning from the bathroom, funeral home fan in hand. Meredith glanced around the room and pointed to a pair of young women by the photocopier. Then she looked at Samantha. "You too," she said.

Samantha glanced at the others and followed them hesitantly into the office. She stood quietly by the door as Frances and the two young women settled onto the couch. Nikki remained standing by Samantha.

"Your focus group, Jeff," Meredith said. Her voice had a tinge of annoyance to it.

"Hardly scientific," snarked a voice, and Samantha looked past Mr. Morris to see a young man sitting behind the desk. He was no more than thirty years old, but his eyes looked older. His tawny blond hair was cut conservatively short, but his light blue shirt was unbuttoned with a plain striped tie at half-mast. His feet were propped up on Morris' desk, making it impossible to see how tall he was. But his hands were slightly worn, not carefully manicured like Mr. Morris', as they clasped on top of his head.

"Best I could do," Meredith returned, leaning against the wall.

"All right," Morris said, and put up a large color photograph on the wall. Robert Carton stood at a podium, imposing and strong in traditional navy-blue suit uniform with a red power tie, ostensibly speaking to an unseen crowd about some very serious topic. An American flag hung from a short flagpole on the dais behind him. Consciously or not, Carton's suit and tie matched the flag.

Morris put up another photo beside it. Now Robert Carton leaned against a fence post in a field somewhere with waving stalks of ripe corn stretching behind him under an azure blue sky. He wore a red plaid shirt open at the throat and jeans with a small belt buckle. His arms were folded casually and he had a Robert Redford smile on his face, comfortable wrinkles around his eyes and the corners of his mouth.

"Which do you find more attractive?" Morris asked.

"Second one, no question," Frances responded immediately, and the girls on the couch with her nodded in agreement.

Morris looked at Nikki who nodded slowly. "The first looks like a strong leader, but the second is more approachable," she said thoughtfully. "I suppose it depends what the context is."

"There you go," the young man behind the desk said, his voice irritated.

Meredith looked at Samantha. "What do you think?"

Samantha glanced at Meredith then looked down shyly. "I don't really think it's my place to say," she said hesitantly.

"Sure it is," the young man behind the desk said. "That's why we brought you in here."

Samantha looked at him full-on for the first time—his eyes were blank and casually disinterested. She found herself suddenly reaching toward him with her mind, as though to roll him. She let the barest touch skate across him and was met with a bored curiosity, mild annoyance and an undercurrent of sadness—profound and bitter. It tasted like lemon juice without sugar to soften its tartness, and it reminded her she was invading his privacy. She mentally recoiled, and the touch fell silent.

But she knew his name was Danny Carton and, under the boredom, he really did want to hear what she had to say.

"Well, I think you're underestimating women voters," she said quietly. "You're grading these pictures on how attractive they will be, assuming that women vote their hearts and not their heads. Men aren't assumed to vote for candidates they find physically attractive. They respond to the same traits women do—a sense of strong leadership, of responsibility and experience, but most of all, a detailed outline of what the person wants to do."

"I think you're taking this in the wrong spirit," Morris began.

"Let her finish, Jeff," Danny said, swinging his legs down off the desk and sitting up.

"If you want to attract women voters, don't annoy them with glamour shots that insult their intelligence," Samantha said. "Talk about the issues they care about. Health care, education, child care, the economy. Impress them with your priorities. Then they'll vote for you."

Meredith grinned while Mr. Morris glared at her. "Thanks, girls, we're done with you now," Morris said. Frances hauled herself to her feet and shooed the women back into the outer office. Samantha followed meekly, worried she had overstepped her bounds.

"Boy, you made us all look so dumb!" Nikki said.

"I'm sorry," Samantha said quickly.

"No way, don't be!" Nikki said. "I wish I'd had the guts to say that."

Samantha smiled at her, the careful smile of closed lips that showed no teeth. She was about to say something, perhaps to ask Nikki some meaningless friendly question, when the door opened again behind them. Meredith and Mr. Morris came out, Meredith already on a cell phone as they headed for the door.

"You," Danny said, beckoning to Samantha. "Come in here."

Samantha blinked. Fear jumped in her chest—*He knows. He knows what I am.* Then she followed him back into the room. "Yes?"

Danny sat down behind the desk. "What's your name?"

"Samantha, sir," she said. "Samantha Crews."

"Have a seat, Samantha Crews," Danny said.

Samantha sat down, nervously rubbing her hands together. *Stupid, that was stupid, now they'll send you away.*

Danny was staring at her. "Where did you go to school?" he asked.

Mulanne Finishing School, class of 1912, she thought. "I never did," she said. "Not past h-high school, anyway."

Danny blinked. "You never went to college?"

"No, sir," Samantha said.

Danny laughed, a cheerful, throaty sound that made little goose bumps jump up on her arms. "Samantha, you don't have to call me 'sir'. I'm maybe two years older than you are."

Samantha didn't laugh, but it was a near thing. She ducked her head and smiled behind her hand.

Danny was staring at her again, his gaze intense.

"Can I ask what this is about?" Samantha said. "Did I speak out of turn earlier?"

"No, not at all," Danny said. "You articulated in ten seconds what I spent an hour yelling at the top of my lungs. You've got a clear mind for politics, Samantha, and I'm wondering why someone as bright as you never went to college."

Somehow Samantha knew that wasn't quite true, and she knew instinctively he would appreciate bluntness more than game-playing. "That's not what you're worried about," she said. "You're afraid I'm a plant from the other side, working for Joe Renfrow."

Danny's smile faded a little. "Yeah, I am," he said seriously. "Though I can't imagine anyone with your brains working for Renfrow."

Samantha had to smile again, bringing up her hand to hide it. "True," she said. "I'm not a Renfrow supporter, sir—Mr. Carton."

"Danny," he interjected.

"Danny," she said uncomfortably. "Renfrow spreads fear. That's all he can sell. He's no leader."

Danny sprang to his feet. "You like ice cream, Samantha Crews?"

Samantha rose slowly. "Is there anyone who doesn't?"

Danny came around the desk. "Let's go get ice cream."

"Uh, okay," Samantha said. "Are you nuts?"

"Quite possibly," Danny said, shrugging. "Let's go to that parlor down the street, and you tell me all about what women voters are really interested in. The ice cream's on me."

Samantha smiled again, remembering at the last second to keep her lips closed over her teeth. She had a sudden image of Danny with ice cream smeared on his chest, and that made her snicker, until she imagined licking it off the line that ran down the middle of his chest, and she ducked her head in embarrassment, heat rising in her cheeks.

"Hey," Danny said, starting to reach out toward her then thinking better of it and letting his hands drop down. "No funny business. Honest. I'd just like to hear what you think, away from this sensory deprivation chamber." He pitched his voice low. "This place has all the character and atmosphere of a giant ant farm."

"Okay," Samantha said, hoping the blush had faded. "You're on."

Danny walked out of the office and Samantha followed him. Without comment to anyone, Danny grabbed his jacket and walked out the door, Samantha at his side and very self-conscious of the looks they were getting. The afternoon light was bright, and she was suddenly aware she had left her hat and glasses at the office. She walked a little behind Danny, trying to stay in his shadow without being obvious about it.

"So tell me about vampires," Danny said.

Samantha froze. "What?"

Danny pointed toward the ice cream parlor and they walked over to the sunny patio. "Inside or outside?"

"Inside," Samantha said quickly. They stepped into the cool marble shop and Danny bought them cones—his pistachio, hers chocolate mocha.

"Why did you ask me about vampires?" Samantha asked, carefully licking her ice cream.

"That's why you joined us, right?" Danny asked. "Most young people are with us because of the vamp issue. The soccer moms are with us for education, and the moneymen for our plans to bring more federal dollars to the city. For the idealists, it's the vamps."

"What makes you think I'm an idealist?" Samantha asked.

Danny shrugged. "You talk like one," he said. "Like the pictures. You see it the way it should be, about ideas and plans and promises, instead of appearances."

"And what about you?" Samantha asked. "I don't get you as an appearance kind of guy."

Danny grinned. "I guess that means I'm in the wrong business." He took a couple more licks on his cone.

Samantha smiled, keeping her lips closed over her teeth. "It was you," she said. "You were the one who wrote the speech at the park two months ago."

Danny glanced down. "Bad form to say who wrote what. The councilman approved everything."

Samantha shook her head. "But the councilman is your

father, and you wrote that speech about bringing fairness and equality to all sentient beings, not just the ones who can walk in the daylight. 'If a society is to be judged by how it treats its least powerful members, so we will be judged on how we treat our brothers and sisters of the night.'"

Danny shrugged and ate his ice cream.

Samantha directed her attention to her cone. "That speech was what made me join the campaign," she said.

"I'm glad," Danny said softly.

She glanced up at him, and he was looking at her with the strangest expression. "What?" she asked.

He seemed to cover instantly. "You eat your ice cream funny," he said, grinning. "Those little licks. You'll be here all day." Samantha ducked her head, smiling. Then she coyly took a long, luxurious lick that went twice around the cone, disappearing into her mouth without showing her teeth.

Danny suddenly seemed a little flustered, glancing around with a little blush to his cheeks. "I guess I deserved that," he said, smiling.

Samantha met his eyes again and felt that driving need to touch his mind, sink into his thoughts and never come out.

What is the matter with me? she thought.

6:58 p.m.

Samantha opened the stage door and nearly tripped over the small form hiding in the shadows. She let out a gasp of surprise.

"Shh," the girl said. "I'm avoiding Fiona."

"Celia, what are you doing?" Samantha said. "Fiona's going to feed you to Brent if you don't quit sneaking in here."

"Oh, like I'm scared of Brent," Celia snarked, following Samantha down the narrow hallway toward the Nocturnal

Urges greenroom. "He doesn't even drink human blood."

"He does too," Samantha said. "Fiona gets it for him. You can't live too long on animal blood. It's a good weight-loss plan, though."

Celia snickered, dropping into an armchair as Samantha walked over to an armoire, moving dresses out of the way as she searched for something to wear. Celia's bony shoulders showed through the straps of her ripped black tank top where a few finger-sized bruises were fading against her young skin. "Where's the rest of 'em?"

"Probably getting ready for work," Samantha said absently, staring at a green silk chemise. "I'm early."

"Don't wear the green, it's not good with your complexion. Try red," Celia said, smacking her gum.

Samantha stared at Celia, lounging ungracefully in her bright red, faux leather miniskirt. "You always wear red," she said.

"It suits me," Celia said, ruffling her hand through her spiky black hair. "Suits you too."

Samantha kept staring at her. "You okay, Celia? You need anything?"

Celia's smile faded. "Yeah, same as always," she said.

"No," Samantha said, her voice firm. "Not in a hundred years, so quit asking."

"Fiona won't hire me without it," Celia pleaded.

Samantha shook her head. "And that's such a tragedy? God, Celia, you could do so many things if you tried. There's programs, plenty of people willing to help you, but you've got to actually seek them out and ask for it."

"Sure!" Celia snapped, her young voice sarcastic and bitter. "I can get all cleaned up so I can flip burgers and live in a rathole until some asshole knocks me up and I spend the rest of my life waiting tables by day and getting beat-up by my loving whatever at night. No way."

Samantha sighed. "You know, Celia, some day I'm afraid that you're going to find someone to take you up on the offer you keep making, and you're going to find out exactly why none of us will turn you."

"Doesn't seem such a bad deal," Celia said, shrugging. "I'm never out during the day anyway. Work for Fiona, guaranteed disease-free, and as a weekend bonus, I never die."

Samantha turned to face her, dropping the green chemise. She advanced slowly on Celia, letting her lips curl back from her fangs. She caught the girl's widening eyes and reached inside. But instead of letting peace and calm flow through, she projected images of pain and screaming, monstrous faces contorted with hate, terror spiking through a swirl of dark nightmares toward Celia's cringing mind.

"This is what we are," she hissed, intentionally letting her voice darken to a feral snarl. "This is what you invite in."

Celia's eyes were wide, cringing down in the chair. A tear escaped her eye, but she was helpless to move. The nightmare played inside her mind, reflected in her large gray eyes. Samantha saw herself through Celia's mind—saw a darkly glowing blonde monster, beautiful horror and gleaming death.

Samantha blinked and let the connection lapse. She was suddenly ashamed of herself and tried to withdraw the images. But it was too late.

"I'm sorry, Celia," she stammered. "I didn't mean—"

"No, it's okay," Celia said in a high, frightened voice. "I didn't...when was that...?"

"A long time ago, much before you were born and, no, I didn't do it," Samantha whispered. "I got there just as he was...finishing." She sat in the chair opposite Celia. "Don't try to get turned anymore, honey. Go get the shot. Make yourself safe. Get out of this horrible place and live your life in the light."

Celia looked down at her shoes. "I'll think about it, okay?"

"Okay," Samantha said, and reached out to touch the girl's shoulder. Celia automatically flinched, and Samantha felt tears prick behind her eyes. Celia was only a kid, but she felt as though they were friends. Until today.

The door opened and Andi came in. "Hey, Sam," she said. "We're on for a threesome tonight, Fiona says."

Samantha sighed. "Matching black?"

Andi nodded. "You bite, I ride." She glanced at Celia, still curled in the chair. "Honey, better scram or Fiona'll flip out. But there's sandwiches in the fridge for the janitors—you're welcome to grab a couple."

"Thanks," Celia said, and scrambled out the door.

8:24 p.m.

The campaign office door creaked open and Freitas glanced up from her handheld computer. A tall redhead stood in the doorway, her hair still in its perfect coif above her classy dark-blue suit.

"Shit," Freitas muttered. Parker stood up, arms folded in her best bad-cop posture.

Freitas got up and walked over toward the woman. "Out, Franks," she ordered.

"Moonlighting, Detective?" Dana Franks asked. "That's very interesting."

"Skip it," Freitas returned.

Dana extended a hand toward Parker. "I'm Dana Franks, from WBYS Channel 13," she said. "And you are?"

"Parker, and scram," Parker replied curtly. Freitas grinned just a bit.

"Awfully late to be hanging around the campaign office," Dana said. "Something afoot in Cartonville?"

Freitas smiled humorlessly. "Please direct all your questions to the campaign staff," she said. "Police policy is 'no comment'."

Dana dropped the smooth act. "Detective, what have I done to piss you off?"

Freitas folded her arms. "I believe we had our last on-the-record chat ten months ago, Miss Franks."

"What, that?" Dana said, incredulous. "You have to be kidding. Every station in town ran that story!"

Freitas leaned forward. "They ran it after you blasted it everywhere."

"By an hour!" Dana protested. "We led for an hour!"

"Enough time to screw over an innocent man," Freitas said.

"Vampire," Dana replied.

"I'm not arguing this with you," Freitas said. "Direct your questions to the campaign staff. Office opens at nine a.m., if I remember correctly. Now get out. We're busy."

"I can tell," Dana said, glancing over at the table where Freitas' handheld computer and Parker's paperback novel sat.

Parker stepped over and opened the door wordlessly. Dana grinned and turned on her heel. "Have a nice evening, Detectives," she shot back as she stalked out.

"I hate reporters," Freitas breathed, returning to their table.

"Are you sure we shouldn't have talked to the campaign folks before we sent her packing? They might be pissed,"

Parker asked, sitting back down.

"They told us to leave them alone. I'm not in the business of playing doorkeeper and I don't work for them," Freitas said, picking up her handheld.

"What do you think they keep shouting about in there?" Parker asked.

"None of my business," Freitas replied, tapping the tiny screen with her stylus. "None of yours, either."

Parker read a couple more paragraphs before she tossed the book down. "How much longer do we get to sit here like a couple of idiots?"

Freitas shrugged. "It's a bullshit detail, Parker. Get used to it. You need patience."

Parker got up and paced back and forth like a restless animal, rubbing her elbows nervously. "Hell, I'd rather be on a street detail than this," she said.

Freitas sighed. "Go home."

Parker stopped pacing. "No, I'm just bitching. I'll be fine."

Freitas shook her head. "No, I mean your shift's over. So's mine. Go home. I'll hang around here until the Three Stooges in there give up on Magic Man and go the hell home."

Parker glanced outside. The street beyond the tinted car-dealership windows was deserted, with a few cars parked beneath the circle of streetlight. "I don't need to go home," she said.

"Then go out," Freitas said. "Go to a bar, get a drink, go dancing, go to your sewing circle, whatever the hell it is you do to unwind. You seriously need some unwinding."

"Really?" Parker asked. "You're not testing me or something?"

Freitas laughed. "It's a shit detail, Parker, get out of here before I draw my gun."

Parker almost smiled. It was a near thing. She grabbed her paperback and leather jacket. "Thanks," she said, and bolted.

Freitas resumed tapping on the word-scramble game on her handheld…and listening to the raised voices in the glassed-in room behind her.

9:15 p.m.

"I'm Miranda," Samantha said.

"Whatever," the man replied. His name was… Samantha couldn't remember.

Andi helped Samantha up onto the bed. They faced him, both lovely blondes in matching black merry widows. He laid back on the pillows, completely naked and already aroused.

Andi turned toward Samantha and pulled her close. They knelt facing each other on the bed and Andi leaned forward, kissing Samantha full on the mouth. Samantha played along, faking the kiss and running her nails through Andi's hair. Samantha didn't mind playing lesbian games for the marks, but it just didn't do anything for her to play with Andi.

Andi, however, ran her hands over Samantha's torso with excitement. She moved her fingers along Samantha's bare back, fingering the laces on her merry widow.

Andi lowered her head to the curves of Samantha's breasts, exposed above the merry widow's tightly laced bodice. She danced her tongue around the curves of Samantha's cleavage, licking and sucking harder at the tender skin right above the hidden nipples.

Then Andi explored the straps on Samantha's knee-high stockings, darting her fingers in between Samantha's legs.

185

Andi didn't actually touch her, but Samantha cried out in false ecstasy as though Andi were stroking her, even penetrating her.

Andi raised her head and caught Samantha's mouth again. The key to the act was closing her eyes and using her imagination, Samantha knew. But when she did, she suddenly saw Danny's face. It was Danny's lips she felt, and when she slid her tongue into Andi's mouth, startling her partner for a split second, it was Danny she kissed in her mind's eye. Andi gripped her shoulders more tightly, her tongue playing against Samantha's with a gentle moan purring in her throat. Samantha let the fantasy take her over completely, imagining Danny's warm body against her, his mouth pressing harder on her, his tongue penetrating her in a moist, sliding friction that warmed her to her center. It was Danny's hand that cupped her lace-bound breast, rubbing the nipple to make it stand out beneath the fabric.

Andi's hand drifted higher on Samantha's thigh, gently touching her through the fabric, but it was Danny who made her cry out against Andi's lips, her eyes still tightly closed. A shudder of sensation rocketed through her from the gentle rub of Andi's fingertips against her. Samantha's hips rocked hard, a moan escaping her.

A moment of sanity intervened and Samantha chanced a glance over at the mark. He was entranced, clutching a pillow and so aroused it seemed he might go any second. She looked back at Andi, who had hidden her surprise. Samantha felt a sudden flush of embarrassment, but in Andi's eyes she read an amused delight and a kind understanding, something entirely female and empathic.

In one motion, they turned their heads toward the mark and smiled, showing the points of their teeth in perfect harmony. They both dropped to their hands and knees and crawled toward him very slowly, going on either side of his stretched-out body. Samantha pressed the full length of her body against his left side, and Andi against his right.

Samantha let the power flow through her hand and drifted her fingers down his side to his thigh. She let the heat sink through his skin, dancing her hand around his groin but never quite touching him. His muscles spasmed and he gasped out a name that was neither Andi nor Miranda.

His hands wandered across their skin, delving between Andi's legs as she nibbled along his chest. He pinched Samantha's breast through her merry widow. It hurt, and the pain calmed some of the confused storm in Samantha's mind.

Andi and Samantha's eyes met over his chest, and Andi slid her leg up over his groin. Samantha moved out of the way, letting Andi sink down onto him. He thrust up into her and Andi gasped, gripping his hips with her thighs and moving up and down with him. Samantha shifted upward, catching his eyes and reaching inside. She touched him and knew he was empty, cold and alone, and the fire burning through him from Andi was very close to burning him up. She soothed him with a touch and lowered her head to his chest.

Samantha struck just above the flat nipple, a quick bite that sank in through the skin to let the blood well up on his muscled chest. She latched onto it and sucked, drawing blood close to his heart, warm and fresh. He gripped her hair hard and shoved her face against him, and she sucked harder, drawing it up into her mouth as Andi rode his bucking hips faster, crying out and kneading her own breasts, gently pinching her own nipples as he stared into her and screamed out his pleasure, writhing beneath them as he shoved into Andi and clutched Samantha's head with taut, powerful force. The power of it flowed through her, filling her torso with his hot pleasure.

His wild, bucking motions slowed, and Andi carefully

withdrew. Samantha licked the last of the blood and slid away into the shadows with her.

Andi grinned at her in the hallway. "And who were YOU thinking of?" she asked.

"Oh, shut up," Samantha said.

10:03 p.m.

Parker slammed a fist into the man-shaped dummy's head. Then she turned and kicked, turned and kicked, her breathing controlled and strong.

"A lot of power tonight," Sensei said. "But very little control."

Parker stopped, stretching out her arms. "I'm frustrated," she admitted. "I know, I'm not approaching it right."

"No, sometimes it's necessary to burn off a little energy," Sensei said. Sensei — that was always how Parker thought of him, although she knew his name from the checks she had written him for her lessons all these years. He was exactly the opposite of what one would expect from a master of martial arts. He was a nondescript Caucasian man with blond hair beginning to gray, small of frame, on the south side of forty years old and no taller than five-foot-nine. If he walked down the street, Parker often thought, he would be a prime target for a mugger. Small, spare and unassuming, he projected no danger vibes whatsoever.

But that mythical mugger would get a huge surprise, Parker thought.

"I need some meditation, I guess," Parker said.

"I have a better idea," Sensei said, and beckoned to her. She followed him back into his office, beyond the lightly padded dojo where she had learned so much. Sensei stepped behind his beaten-metal desk and retrieved a bottle of bourbon.

Parker grinned, dropping into a chair. "Perfect," she said, as he poured a splash of amber-colored liquid into two glasses. "Cheers."

Sensei sat in the other chair, still in his uniform. Parker was in loose-fitting workout clothes from the bag she kept in the trunk of her car, not having expected to get any time in the dojo tonight.

"What's so frustrating?" Sensei asked.

"Honestly?" Parker said. "I think I made a huge mistake."

"The promotion?" Sensei asked.

"Yeah." Parker took a sip. "It's all bullshit. Baby-sitting a politician, arguing with this stick-up-her-ass old fart of a partner. I'd rather be out on the street, doing my job."

"No, you'd rather be out confronting who you think of as 'the bad guys'," Sensei said. "You're never quite happy unless you're standing in someone's face, Kelly. You liked working the street because it was confrontational. Being a detective requires more nuances and personal skills. It's only natural to feel out of your depth."

"I have never had a force complaint," Parker insisted.

"I didn't say you were a bully," Sensei replied. "You don't use force unless it is necessary. But when it is necessary, you delight in it. You attack with all that anger you have never fully faced or sublimated."

"Teacher or shrink?" Parker shot back, taking another sip.

"Both," Sensei said, smiling. "I was glad you took the promotion. You have burned with only one kind of energy for so long, Kelly. It has left you alone too long. You search for something you won't find, not on these streets."

"I might," Parker said quietly.

Sensei shook his head. "You don't believe that," he replied. "You tell yourself that, but you know better."

Parker shrugged. "It may be useless, but it beats sitting around an empty office, waiting for a fight that won't come," she said.

"Ah," Sensei replied. "You're still waiting for the fight."

"Oh, shut up," Parker grinned.

11:43 p.m.

"Samantha, got a bite-only for you, room six," Fiona said, marking on her clipboard in the greenroom doorway.

Samantha looked up from the sink where she was washing the last of Andi's lipstick off her face. "Just me, right?"

Fiona grinned. "You should really go bi, Sam, you'd enjoy the job so much more."

Samantha rolled her eyes and grabbed her usual white dress. "Give me five minutes and I'm there."

"He's not a newbie, but he's nervous, so go easy on him. Name's Bob," Fiona said, heading back out the greenroom door.

"Bob, right, sure it is," Samantha muttered. She sighed and slid the white dress over her head. She cinched her breasts into its tight-fitting bodice and carefully checked herself over for any signs of her session with Andi. Then she walked down the hall and slipped into room six.

Bob was sitting in the middle of the bed, a middle-aged man with distinguished silver hair who seemed massively uncomfortable, hiding in the shadows of the curtains hanging off the four-poster bed. He wore only a pair of boxers, and when Samantha came in, he pulled the blanket up over them. "I'm just here for a bite, nothing more," he said quickly.

"You don't need to be afraid of me," Samantha said in her low, sultry voice, with an undercurrent of calming power in it. "My name is Miranda."

Bob turned away from her. "That's nice," he said quickly, facing the opposite wall.

Samantha slid up onto the bed, crawling toward him. She knelt on the bed behind his bare back, and let power flow outward from her chest to her hands. Gently she hovered her hands over his skin, letting the power flow into his shoulders and the sensitive skin at the back of his neck. Bob shivered, his body starting beneath her.

Samantha slid closer to him, pressing the full front of her body against his back. She kept herself mostly out of his line of sight, letting his fantasy take hold of him while her power soaked into him through their skin. She rocked her pelvis gently against him, accustoming him to the motions of her body, sliding her hands up and down his arms and letting the power envelop him.

His whole body stuttered beneath her. The nerve endings would be tingling by now, the blood racing beneath his skin. She could smell it, the hot, rich salt of his blood so close beneath the tender skin of his neck. Samantha had fed well tonight and would not take much from him. But the smell of him was intoxicating, strangely familiar and made her want to take more in her mouth. She moved faster against him, a warmth filling her that she hadn't experienced in a long time.

Suddenly eager, Samantha began to push him down on the bed. He resisted for a second, but she let a jolt of the sexual energy she felt leap through to him. He groaned and fell backward onto the pillow.

She stared straight into his eyes and froze.

Ten whole seconds passed, his body still caught in the grip of her power. Then she started breathing again. She reached inside, touching him lightly, keeping as much of her shield in place as possible. She let the calm fill him, the calm that kept the pain of the bite from interfering with pleasure.

Then she lowered her head to his arm and struck, a small bite on the inner arm. The skin was tougher, the blood harder to suck out. It took longer, but Bob didn't mind. The pressure within built, up through the long, drawn-out caress of her mouth on him, a slow draught between her lips. She felt the glorious tension build up inside him, higher and stronger. Despite her racing thoughts and conflicted feelings, she felt it too, that tightening deep in her abdomen, the panting breath in her chest.

He cried out, his entire body spasming, and she felt it burst through her, unstoppable and overwhelming. Everything in her mind screamed as her body reacted involuntarily, shuddering against him.

Gently, Samantha disengaged. He collapsed backward, already drifting sleepily. She slid off the bed and retreated into the shadows, reaching for the door.

Leaving Robert Carton asleep on the bed.

Chapter Three

ഔ

1976

Chicago

Samantha looked over her shoulder in the alley. No one was there. The silence filled the streets with a tinny radio tinkling through someone's window.

"Did he see you?" Todd whispered from the shadows.

"Shh!" Samantha murmured, sliding into the shadows with him. "One of these nights, he's going to see you."

"I have a wooden stake with his name on it," Todd replied, pulling her close into his arms. He kissed her, slow and thorough, careful to avoid her fangs.

Samantha pulled away for a second. "Don't joke like that," she said. "If he finds out…"

"He doesn't know I exist, Miranda," Todd said. "I'm just the rookie on the beat, someone to ignore. No threat. Stop worrying so much."

"I do worry," Samantha said, dropping her eyes.

Todd kissed her forehead. "Then come away with me," he said. "Leave Cristoval, Chicago, everything. We'll go live in Kansas, raise chickens. I'll be the sheriff of Podunk County."

She laughed. "You'd go crazy in a week."

Todd sobered, staring at her. "I'd brave Podunk County for you, Miranda."

Samantha melted into him, drawing him close and feeling him through his dark uniform. Playfully, she pulled off his hat and slipped it on her own head.

Todd dipped his head down to nuzzle her neck. "Careful, you're impersonating a police officer," he whispered, kissing the line along her shoulder.

"And what's the penalty for that?" Samantha breathed, stilling her impulse to moan at the gentle kisses raising a line of fire along her skin. His mouth was so warm, it seemed he could light a fire within her just by pressing his lips to her skin.

"I can come up with something," Todd said, sliding his hands up and down her back, dropping lower to cup her buttocks and pull her close against him. She gasped against his chest at the feel of him, hard beneath his uniform pants. He pressed tight against her simple shift dress, and she grabbed at his belt buckle, suddenly eager and wanting.

"Not here," he said, his voice husky and slightly broken. "Come to my place."

"Not enough time," she whispered.

"I don't want to make love to you in an alley," he protested.

"Close your eyes," Samantha said. "Imagine we're somewhere else." She slid her hand inside his pants and freed him, her hand sliding and caressing, bringing him to heated life with just a touch of power flowing through to him. His entire body clenched, his face contorted with pleasure above her. "Pretend we're on a beach with no one for miles but the starfish and the seagulls."

Samantha leaned back on the old wooden crate behind her, grabbing his hands and forcing them along her thighs, pushing her skirt up and sliding her panties away. "We're in a hammock," she whispered. "The sun is warming our skin."

Todd moved between her legs, and she freed him of the last restraining barrier of cloth. "The waves," he murmured, pushing against her with insistent strength. She held his face between her hands and reached his mind, letting a touch of calm and her own excitement flow to him. In a bare second, she let him feel what she felt, the hot excitement between her legs and the tingle of her skin, the racing desire that filled her body. In a flash, she felt what he felt—a heated desire that was nearly pain, a fire that could not be quenched anywhere but inside her.

Todd slid into her, hard and full, and Samantha lost her voice. His hands gripped her hips, holding her still while he moved within her. His gentle thrusts pushed her against the brick wall behind them, and she held him close against her. His neck was close, smelling of salt and sex, and the hunger rose, welling up inside her chest even as he drove himself deeper within her. She deepened the link between them, letting him feel what she felt, and sensing his pleasure at being sheathed within her.

His excitement grew, his youth overpowering him. He began to speed up inside her, jerking harder. He was close, riding her harder. She pressed her lips against his throat, but a tiny thread of sanity reminded her of the danger—mustn't mark his skin where it shows. She scrabbled at his collar with her nails, popping a button as she exposed skin farther along his shoulder. A few marks were still fading in the smooth muscle past his neck.

Todd cried out, driving hard into her, and she struck. His blood pooled in her mouth and she drank him. A long draught, warm and rich and tasting of him, the essential sandalwood spice of his skin and the salt of his heart's blood filled her even as he pushed deeply into her, his body clenched hard against her. She was pinned hard against the rough brick wall, feeling him explode as his hands tightened almost painfully on her buttocks. The shuddering pleasure began somewhere in her abdomen and flowed through her body, vibrating outward through her skin until she cried out, unable to contain it within herself.

He was breathing hard, wobbly in the legs, as he withdrew from her. Quickly he tucked himself away, but he remained standing there, holding her close as she moved her skirt into place. "Wow," he said. "I think that was the best ever."

"Yes," Samantha breathed. "Think what it'll be when we're really there."

Todd buried his face in her neck, breathing her scent as if he still couldn't get enough of her. "Where?"

"That beach," she said. "Of course, I'd have to wait until night to go out, if that's all right with you."

He pulled away and stared at her. "You mean it? We'll go?"

"Yes," she said, smiling. "I'll go with you." His eyes met hers, and smiled with her.

"Touching," Cristoval said from the shadows.

Todd wrenched away from Samantha in a single movement, going for his service pistol with the reflexes of a cop. He drew his weapon and leveled it at the looming shapes appearing out of the shadows. It was the kiss, Cristoval's vampires seeming to coalesce out of darkness.

"Back down," Todd warned in his best cop voice, pulling Samantha behind him.

"Todd, get out of here," Samantha pleaded, pulling at his free arm. "Run, now."

"No way," Todd said, aiming the gun at Cristoval.

Dark and grim, Cristoval appeared the perfect vampire out of the movies. His hair was dark and glossy, his eyes a depthless black in the dim light of the streetlights. His smile was charming and chilling at the same time as he glided forward toward Todd.

"Fiona!" Samantha cried out toward the kiss.

"She's not….heeere," giggled Diego, a thin vampire with dancing madness in his eyes, already licking his lips suggestively from behind Cristoval. Samantha averted her eyes from him. She had forgotten, Fiona was away on one of the mysterious missions Cristoval ordered, Fiona was gone…

The rest of the kiss was only steps behind him, at least thirteen vampires waiting to do Cristoval's bidding. Fiona was not there to be the voice of practicality and calm.

Samantha tried to step in front of Todd, but he kept trying to push her back behind him in a useless display of human chivalry.

"Cristoval, please," Samantha begged, though she knew it was useless.

"Cristoval, please," Diego mocked in a high voice, his smile widening to a bloody grin. He had fed recently.

Cristoval held up a hand, and Diego froze instantly. "You have been disloyal, my beloved Miranda," Cristoval said in his smooth, reasonable voice. "Do you want his heart?"

"Oh, please, no," Samantha cried, and stepped in front of Todd, pushing aside his attempt to restrain her. *Please run, run away, please leave me, leave me now!* she cried along the mental link that was fading from their lovemaking. The wonderful endorphins were still flowing through her skin, tingling with the adrenaline that fed her fear. "Cristoval—"

Cristoval gazed into Samantha's eyes, and he caught her unprepared. *Too late, my love*, he said, reaching into her and feeding her the image of what he intended to do.

Samantha screamed, a high, miserable sound that echoed in the alley, as Cristoval gestured to Diego and the vampires flowed forward as one body. Todd fired at them, the bullets knocking them down but not killing them. Three loud reports deafened Samantha before one of them took away his gun. His screams echoed down the alley as Diego bore him to the ground behind her. Grisly ripping sounds and guttural moans echoed over his weakening cries.

Samantha fought Cristoval's mind, fought his control. It was like a padded vise gripping her and holding her still, but she wiggled a little here, a little there and suddenly it began to loosen.

She felt Cristoval's surprise, and shoved back at him with the passion and strength she had felt just a few moments ago in Todd's arms. It broke that vise in a sudden snap, and she flew at the kiss.

Diego was hunched over Todd, making grotesque sounds as he fed. Samantha pulled Diego off him in one desperate pull and kicked another vampire into the wall. The others backed off in surprise, and Cristoval allowed them.

Samantha looked down at Todd.

She knelt beside him, and smoothed some of the blood off his face. She couldn't bear to look at the rest of him. She laid her head against his heart, listening, and heard the last thump before it stopped.

The sobs tried to rise up but she quelled them, pouring them down her throat and back inside the prison of her chest. She sealed up the tears and poured concrete over her aching heart, turning cold as she gently removed the silver badge from what remained of Todd's chest. She wiped the blood off it, knowing how proud he was — had been — of that badge.

Samantha rose to face Cristoval, and in his surprise, she caught him with her eyes. She reached inside the black emptiness of his mind and poured her anger, the white heat of her hate, into him. The force of it flung him backward into the kiss members still standing, and they caught him. But he stood straight again with five hundred years of fury rising up and lashing out through his mind into hers.

It overwhelmed her, driving her down to her knees in Todd's blood. The cascade of images poured through her mind, a torn-out throat, maggots in the stump of a living woman's arm, a child's insane screaming in a windowless room. Samantha clutched hard to the badge, its sharp edge digging into her palm and keeping her centered in reality as the images Cristoval forced through her mind tore at her sanity.

Cristoval stood over her, imposing and cold. "I will not force you to eat his heart, Miranda," he said calmly. "Not if you come with us now, without complaint."

He pushed just a touch harder at her mind, enough for Samantha to know he could make her do it, if he chose.

"Reach out to me," Cristoval said, and his voice did not brook a hesitation. Samantha reached upward without looking, and Cristoval bore her up to her feet. He leaned close to her ear and whispered, "You will be with me tonight, Miranda."

And she knew he was right.

* * * * *

3:23 p.m.

In the daylight, the downtown Memphis streets lose their magic. Somehow, the neon lights and sultry music shield nighttime visitors from broken pavement and chain-link fences topped with razor wire. The windows mended with cardboard and spray-painted wooden doors were fewer in recent years, as the renovations of downtown swept outward. But the farther one got from the tourists, the more dilapidated the buildings became.

Robert Carton stood in front of Nocturnal Urges, surrounded by the press and more than a few passersby. The exterior of the club was painted as though it were built of masonry, with the club's name in huge, dripping red letters.

In the daylight, it was robbed of its mystery and power, seeming only a cheap sideshow attraction between the boarded-up storefronts and aging warehouses.

Back behind a cordon of police officers, a small group of people led by a bushy-haired, bearded young man waved signs with pleasant homilies such as VAMPS WELCOME AT SUNRISE SERVICES and YOUR CIVIL RIGHTS END AT MY THROAT.

"It is a sad thing for vampires today that a place like this exists," Carton said gravely, staring at the closed doors of the club. "Most vampires are ordinary folk, harming no one as they go about their business. It's the few depraved individuals who seek to lower the morality of our entire community who make it so hard for the ones who want to, pardon the expression, walk in the daylight."

Meredith Schwartz stepped in, cool as usual in the afternoon sunlight. "We have with us today a friend to both the councilman and the vampires of Memphis," she said. "A leader in the vampire community and a spokesman for morality and the judicious advancement of vampire rights, it is my great honor and privilege to introduce Drew Sanford, president of Vampires Against Moral Perversion."

A tall, spare vampire stepped forward from the small group of campaign workers at the side of the crowd. Meredith led the applause, kick-started at the back by Jeff Morris. Danny half-heartedly joined in.

"Will you quit pouting? People are watching," Morris said.

Danny clapped harder. "This was a bad idea," he said quietly.

"Shut. Up." Morris snapped.

Drew Sanford stood before them, wearing an old-fashioned three-piece suit and fedora. "You must forgive me for not doffing my hat in the presence of ladies," Sanford said in his polite southern drawl. "Unfortunately, I am somewhat prone to sunburn."

The press sent up a dutiful laugh.

"It is my honor to appear with Councilman Carton," Sanford said. "Like him, my organization has sought neither to vilify our kind nor to deify us. We cannot be expected to retain more rights than are permitted ordinary humans. Nor should we be permitted an exemption from the rules of character and virtue that govern humans. The rampant disregard for morality and the sanctity of the bite at Nocturnal Urges and similar…places…has done more to set back the cause of vampire rights than any human-rights group ever could. That is why we hope Councilman Carton will take up our cause in Washington and support the laws to make all of us equal, and equally responsible, in this community."

Robert Carton began to applaud, and Meredith quickly picked it up. "We'll take some questions now," she said.

A chorus of boos came at Meredith from the placard-waving crowd. "Why don't you go get bitten!" shouted the bearded man. Meredith ignored them, and an officer went over to speak heatedly with the bearded man.

As usual, Dana Franks was the first to ask a question. "Mr. Sanford," she began. "Do you support the right of vampires to marry humans?"

Morris froze. "Told you," Danny muttered.

Sanford seemed to weigh his words carefully. "I have been lucky enough to be partnered to the same wonderful woman for many years," he said. "In my time on this earth, I have had nine women gracious enough to share their lives, and their blood, with me. Unfortunately, we have never been allowed the covenant of marriage. Should the day ever come when it is permitted, I will welcome it. However, I believe the human population is not yet ready for this institution to progress further than the legitimate partnerships we now enjoy. I would rather wait until we can all celebrate together, than push forward with something that not everyone is ready to embrace."

The protesters emitted another round of boos and hisses as the cop pointed at them and snapped words Danny couldn't hear.

"Sanford's good," Morris whispered.

"Yep," Danny replied. "We should be running his candidacy."

Morris shot him a glare. "Anytime you want to go home, Danny, just say the word."

Robert Carton stepped forward. "I could hardly top Mr. Sanford's eloquent statement, so I won't try," he said. "But I agree with him, and look forward to working with him and all the other law-abiding vampires to bring us closer together, not farther apart."

Dana Franks wouldn't let go. "What about the vampires who work in these clubs?" she asked. "After all, what they're doing is legal, isn't it?"

"What they are doing is legal, Miss Franks," Carton replied sternly. "That doesn't make it right."

"Bingo," Morris said, rubbing his hands together. "That's tonight's sound bite."

Another reporter picked up Dana Franks' cues. "There are those, Councilman, who argue that the vampires work in these clubs because the stigma attached to them keeps them out of other lines of work, that unless a job requires physical strength or imperviousness to certain hazards, they are discriminated against." He poised his pen over his notebook, waiting.

"Well, I've heard those arguments, sir, and I look forward to examining cases of real discrimination in the future and closing any loopholes that might keep vampires out of legitimate work," Carton said.

"Uh-oh," Morris said. "It's getting away from them."

Sanford spoke up. "I should add that in many cases, those 'discrimination' complaints are brought about by advocates of the club lifestyle as excuses for not seeking more mundane lines of work," he said.

Danny nudged Morris, who caught Meredith's eye.

A third reporter waved his hand. "What about Tunstall's Law, which would make vampirism a legitimate cause for firing from police and fire departments, human hospitals and public schools? Is that something you're willing to oppose, Councilman?"

Carton blinked for half a second while Morris swore quietly next to Danny. "Well, it's difficult to speculate on what I will or will not vote on a law half a year from now," he said. "I will say that Tunstall's Law brings up specific concerns about the rights of parents to keep their children away from vampires if they choose, and there are constitutional issues that have to be explored. Of course, the discussion on these very important issues continues."

Sanford glanced at Carton, looking ill for a moment. Then he caught himself as Meredith stepped in front of them, thanking the press and clapping for both of them. The flashbulbs went off again, catching a few more shots as she led them, still waving, back toward the campaign van.

"Well, that was nicely weaselly," Danny muttered, clapping away.

"Shut up, we got the sound bite," Morris replied.

Morris went over toward the van, thanking Sanford and his cadre of well-dressed vampires, all in hats and sunglasses. The protesters resumed their catcalls and chants from their spot by the sidewalk, and Dana Franks went over to speak to them. The rest of the reporters quickly dispersed to their cars, eager to be away from the neighborhood.

Danny started to follow the campaign people toward the van. But there at the edge of the crowd, he saw Samantha Crews, standing quietly in the shadow of the Nocturnal Urges awning in a baseball cap and sunglasses. He shouldn't have been able to recognize her that far away, but she caught his eye, even in the shade. She was the only one brave enough to stand directly on the club's property—the owner had understandably refused the congressman permission, so he had stood on the sidewalk nearby.

Danny switched directions and walked over toward her. Samantha saw him coming and started—as if to run away. "Wait, where are you going?" he called out, running after her.

She stopped. "Home," she replied, taking off her sunglasses. "I just…wanted to see the speech."

"What did you think?" Danny asked.

Samantha cast her eyes down.

"No, really," Danny said, trying to catch her gaze. "What did you think?"

She looked back up at him. "I know he's your father," she said quietly. "But why are you working for him?"

Danny froze. No one had ever asked him the question point-blank. They made all manner of assumptions. But the last time he had faced the question Samantha posed to him, he was staring himself in the mirror.

"That's a very long conversation," he said.

Samantha stared at the campaign van, workers loading back onto it to head back to their world, away from broken streets and razor wire. "I've got time," she said.

"Danny!" Meredith called. "We've got to go!"

Danny turned back toward her. "I'm going to stay here a

while," he said. "I'll catch a taxi back."

Meredith blinked, but stepped back into the van. Morris stared at him for more than a minute as Danny walked away from them with Samantha, slinging his coat over his shoulder and loosening his tie.

They walked through the streets in silence for a while. The silence lay entirely between them—the neighborhood was anything but silent. Music thumped a pounding bass beat from passing cars, interspersed with faraway sirens squealing through the air. There were a few shouts behind the beaten doors of the low-rent housing they passed. Long boxlike apartment buildings of darkened brick were littered with trash and broken glass. Their dull façades were peppered with windowpanes mended with rough boards and duct tape, caged behind slumping chain-link fences topped with rusty razor wire.

"Do you live here?" Danny said incredulously, stepping around an ancient, rusted dumpster on the broken sidewalk.

"A few blocks from here," Samantha said. "It's cheap and no one bothers me." She stopped to point at an expanse of scraggly, unkempt grass at a corner. "That used to be a corner market. It was the place where the young people gathered. The old fellow who used to run it was friendly to all of them, always hired the kids from the poorest families to stock the shelves and run the register." Her face grew sad. "He was shot by a robber, killed instantly. He had no children of his own. No one took over the store and the city had it torn down."

"I think I read about that in *City Magazine*," Danny said thoughtfully, staring at the vacant lot. It was scattered with broken bottles and a few strewn pieces of ragged, muddy clothing.

"He was a kind man," Samantha said softly. "When he died, the last kindness went out of this neighborhood."

They walked on another block into rows of sagging frame houses, duct-taped air conditioners hanging out of splintered window frames and broken panes covered with cardboard and thick plastic. There were young people sitting on the steps listening to music on a portable CD player and riding skateboards on the blacktop.

Danny looked at his watch.

"School's out, but it doesn't matter—they don't go," Samantha said. "None of them bother. Their parents are working two jobs each, they'll never know. The school doesn't send anyone out after them. They're afraid to come here."

"Hey, Sam!" one of them called out. "You lookin' sexy, girl!"

Samantha flipped him off, and they all oohed together. Danny was suddenly nervous.

The one who had called out after her sauntered over. He was taller than Danny and at least ten years younger, with shining black skin and prominent muscles. "Who's this?" he said, pointing at Danny.

"He's cool, Red, he's with me," Samantha said. "I'm taking him to meet Sensei."

Red—and Danny could see no earthly reason why he'd have that name—lowered his sunglasses. "Sensei don't see the suits," he said. "It's gettin' so he won't see my boys neither."

"Your boys have been doing some bad shit," Samantha chided. "You got to keep a better hand on 'em, Red."

Red shrugged. "What am I supposed to be upholdin'? My civic leadership? Get all city council and shit? That's your bag, Sam. I'm just tryin' to keep my ass in one piece."

"Do that," Samantha said. "But don't expect Sensei to treat you like a leader if you won't be one."

Red mulled that and glanced back at the young men lounging on the stoops. To Danny, they seemed like sleek, dangerous panthers, never entirely at rest, coiled and ready to strike.

"You really gonna see Sensei with the suit here?" Red asked, pitching his voice low.

"For me, he'll see him," Samantha said.

"He don't look bad." Red shot out a fist at Danny who stumbled backward. Samantha instantly deflected Red's fist up toward the sky and held it tight, twisting it fast behind his back. She had moved so fast Danny wasn't sure he actually saw her hit him. Just a blink and Red was immobilized.

"Damn, girl, you didn't have to go all bitch on me," he protested.

"Hands off the boy, he's with me," Samantha said, and this time there was a warning to her voice.

"Got it, lemme go," Red said, and Samantha let him go.

"Behave yourself, Red, and I'll put in a word for you with Sensei," Samantha said.

Red nodded, tipped an invisible hat to Danny and scrambled back to his group who immediately started catcalling him.

Danny started breathing again. "Damn," he said. "Who are you?"

"Just a neighborhood girl," Samantha said, walking farther. "Red isn't dealing yet, and he doesn't let his boys do it. But it's only a matter of time."

"Seems like he can stand up for himself," Danny said, glancing over his shoulder. "Why do you think he'll end up dealing?"

Samantha indicated the street filled with broken glass and trash. "The only operational businesses in a five-block radius are the clubs, the liquor stores, one plate-glass shop and that gas station up at the corner," she said. "Just blocks and blocks of empty warehouses. The guys don't exactly clean up enough for the retail shops in the tourist sector. What else are they going to do?"

"They could learn," Danny said.

Samantha smiled beneath the brim of her baseball cap. "No one ever told them that," she said sadly. "I've seen it a hundred times."

Danny gazed down at her. "My God, you have old eyes," he said.

Samantha blinked.

"Wait! Let me rephrase," Danny said. "I just meant that there is so much sadness, so much living behind your eyes. Your face isn't old at all. How old are you, twenty-eight?"

Samantha looked downward. "A little older than that," she said. "You never answered my question. About your father."

Danny followed her around the corner, back onto a busier street. "I'm working for him because he's my father and because I believe in him," he said.

"That's half true," she said.

"What? You want me to say I believe in everything my father says?" Danny said, suddenly annoyed. "I don't. But he'll do great things in Washington."

"You mean you'll do great things," Samantha said. "You want to influence him, guide him toward the things you want."

"Yeah, I guess," Danny said as they walked past the gas station and convenience store she'd mentioned earlier. "Is that so bad? What if we could clean up this place? Fix those apartments? How about a community center where the market used to be, a place where those kids could go—"

"To deal or fight," Samantha said. "They've got places to

go."

"Fine," Danny replied. "How about a one-stop center for social services? Job training, welfare assistance, GED classes, licensed child care, a food pantry? Set that up on that corner, and organize volunteers to help clean up the streets and repair the houses of people who can't afford to do it themselves."

Samantha laughed, a bitter sound that held little joy. "You are such a dreamer, Danny Carton," she said. "I bet they're all your ideas, aren't they? Councilman Carton's proposal to link drug treatment and vocational training centers to the homeless shelters, a cigarette-and-liquor tax to repair inner-city schools…all of that's you, isn't it?"

Danny didn't answer.

"But what about the vamps?" Samantha asked. "That doesn't seem like you."

"It isn't," Danny admitted, looking up at the sky. "I wanted us to come out full-force in favor of vamp rights. Equal treatment under the law, vamp marriage, stop Tunstall's Law in its tracks."

"So what happened today?" Samantha asked.

Danny shrugged. "I'm one voice in the campaign. Hell, they were probably right. Can't win on a platform of vamp rights and bleeding-heart social programs. The suits, as your buddy Red calls them, will eat us for lunch."

"What about the folks down here?" Samantha said. "I bet there's a few votes to be had in this neighborhood. And young people—they'll find it quite appealing."

Danny smiled a sardonic grin. "They don't vote," he said quietly. "It's only the little gray-haired ladies and businessmen who bother to vote anymore. That's why they rule the world."

Samantha shook her head. "Once your father may have

been a leader, but now he's a stuffed shirt, spouting other people's ideas," she said. "They're your ideas. Why don't you fight for them? Why don't you run?"

Danny burst out laughing. "I'm nobody!" he said. "I'm a city councilman's son by his ex-wife! I've never held so much as a seat on a commission! I have no backing from any of the political heavyweights in this town. All I can do is give advice and hope to gain enough respect that my ideas might carry some weight."

"You could do it," she said. "But nobody's ever told you that."

Danny opened his mouth to reply, but noticed they were standing in front of a storefront karate studio. "Is this where you were taking me?"

"I expect so," said a small, slim man with graying blond hair, appearing in the doorway, a slight smile on his face. He extended a hand. "Pleased to meet you. Any friend of Samantha's, and all that."

Danny shook his hand, and was surprised at the strength in the older man's grip. "A pleasure, sir. Danny Carton, with Carton for Congress."

"But you are not the Carton who's running for Congress," the man replied.

"Good to know the commercials are working," Danny said.

"Sensei, I thought you and Danny here would like to get to know each other," Samantha said. "I think he could use some direction."

Danny shot her a look.

"Of course," Sensei said. He started to lead Danny into the dojo. Danny stopped at the doorway. "Aren't you coming?" he asked.

Samantha shook her head, sitting down on the curb in

the shade of the awning. Danny followed Sensei, mystified.

"Samantha does not like my dojo," Sensei said, leading him toward the main practice area, entirely lined with mirrors.

Danny stopped at the edge of the dojo, taking off his shoes.

Sensei turned to watch him. "Thank you for your respect," he said. "Now, shall we see what has brought you here?"

"To tell you the truth, I don't know," Danny said. "Samantha, she keeps asking me about my work, encouraging me to…I don't know. Break with the campaign or something."

"I imagine Samantha has said no such thing," Sensei said. "It is something you have thought of, and Samantha makes you think that it is possible."

"How does she live down here? How do you?" Danny said incredulously. "It's very different from my world."

"Different, yes, but no harder," Sensei said. "One adapts to one's environment. If one is told one must fight or be killed—one will fight. If one is told one must lie or be destroyed—one will lie. That is the way of survival."

"So Samantha's buddies will eventually sell drugs and shoot each other because that's what society expects of them? That's not the way it's supposed to be," Danny said.

Sensei steepled his fingers in front of his chest. "And you will lead a man to Congress despite your reservations about his worthiness because it is what is expected of you? How is that different?"

"I'm not expected to do anything but hang around and show support," Danny said.

Sensei turned Danny toward the mirrored wall. "He wasn't there when you grew up, was he?" Sensei said, standing behind Danny.

"Doesn't matter, he was doing important things," Danny said, staring at himself. "He took care of this town."

"But now he does what he is told, bends with the wind," Sensei said, an unseen voice behind him. "He is doing what is expected of him, so that he may survive."

"That is the way of survival, at least in politics," Danny said.

"You thought he would be different," Sensei replied.

"Yes," Danny said.

"You thought he would be a leader."

"Yes."

"A pity." Sensei pushed him forward gently, hidden almost entirely behind him, so Danny could look himself in the face. "You want to make this a better place for the people who live here. Do you think you have chosen the path that will succeed? Or the path of mere survival?"

Danny stared at himself in the darkening room. "I don't know," he admitted.

"Close your eyes," Sensei said.

Danny felt silly but he closed his eyes. Darkness swept over his mind and he saw the sunlight, the way it reflected onto his father this afternoon, leaving Sanford in shadow, and Samantha standing by the sidelines, watching.

"What do you see?" Sensei asked.

"My father, at his speech this morning," Danny said. "You should have heard him."

"What is the most striking thing that you see?" Sensei asked.

"Samantha," Danny said instantly. "I can see her even though she's kind of hiding in the shadow."

"What is so striking about Samantha?" Sensei asked.

Danny was barely aware that he was smiling. "Her hair," he said. "It's like this fine-spun gold, but she's hiding it under a hat. You can barely see it, but I remember what it looked like in the sun when we went for ice cream that time."

"What are you doing there?" Sensei continued, his voice seeming to float.

Danny stopped smiling. "Standing at the back with Jeff, showing my support," he said.

"What do you want to do?"

Danny shrugged. "Charge up to the front. Tell the people my father will fight for the vamps, give them every right that humans have, save them from being treated as second-class citizens. Tell them a vote for him is a vote for equality under the law."

"Why don't you?"

Danny laughed out loud, a bitter sound. "Because someone would club me over the head before I finished the first sentence."

"Then why do you want to do it?"

Danny's mind flashed on an image but he dismissed it. "Because it's the right thing to do."

"Wrong," Sensei said. "That is not what you wanted to say."

Danny shook his head. "It's crazy, stupid. I barely—"

"Answer."

Danny sighed. "For Samantha," he said. "To show her what we're fighting for. To make her proud of our campaign."

"Proud of you."

Danny opened his eyes. "This is crazy," he said. "What the hell am I doing here?"

Sensei was still standing behind him, even though his

Elizabeth Donald

voice had traveled all around the room. "Learning, perhaps."

5:03 p.m.

"Thank God you're here," Morris snapped as Freitas and Parker entered the campaign office. "We got another one."

Freitas hustled through the campaign office, now silent and empty of workers. Robert Carton and Meredith Schwartz were staring at a poster on the table. "This was tacked on the door when we got back from a campaign stop downtown, by that sex club near Beale," Meredith said.

It was a blown-up photograph of several campaign workers, standing in a crowd near a van. The faces of Meredith Schwartz, Jeff Morris and Danny Carton were marked out in red Xs.

"That's not so good," Freitas muttered, bending close to the picture. "Very fresh."

"That's today," Robert Carton said. "That looks like the club in the background where we were this morning. How the hell did they get this so fast?"

"Are you sure it's from today?" Freitas asked.

"I think so," Meredith said. "I was wearing that blue scarf this morning. I dropped it somewhere today. But there it is, in the photo."

"Who has touched the poster?" Parker said.

"Me," Morris said. "And Meredith. I don't think you did, did you, Mr. Carton?"

"I don't think so, but it's possible," Carton said. "Look, can you get on the horn and get some officers to cruise that neighborhood?"

Freitas frowned. "I kind of doubt the guy will still be there," she said.

Carton shook his head. "You don't understand, Danny is

214

there," he said, his voice a little ragged. "He stayed behind to canvass the neighborhood when we left this morning. We haven't heard from him and he's not answering his cell phone. Please, send someone down there and look for my son."

Freitas reached out and touched Carton's shoulder. "We'll get someone down there right away," she said. "You keep trying his cell phone. Did he have a car or anyone with him?"

"Not that I saw," Carton replied.

"Yes," Morris said. "He was with one of the volunteers. That young blonde girl, Serena something. The one that mouthed off to us when we were testing photos for the mailers, remember?" He looked to Meredith for confirmation and she nodded.

"With all due discretion, I think Danny may have had his eye on her," Morris said. "At any rate, I think they were going to knock on doors this afternoon."

"In that neighborhood?" Freitas said. "Excuse me." She led Parker a bit away from them. "Okay, I'm going. You stay with them and get a team to examine that poster."

"I should go," Parker said. "I'm familiar with the neighborhood. My dojo is right near there."

"And I'm familiar with the vamp clubs, so if little Danny's gone for a walk on the wild side, I can find him and make sure he's in one piece," Freitas said.

"I can do this," Parker insisted.

Freitas stared at her. "It's rough down there," she said.

Parker folded her arms, glaring.

Freitas shrugged. "All right. Find the kid. Don't get hurt."

6:23 p.m.

Danny stepped out of the dojo into the warm rosy light of the sunset. Samantha was sitting on the sidewalk, leaning back against the smoky glass with her baseball cap in her hands. "Have you been waiting all this time?" he asked.

"Like I was going to leave you alone in this neighborhood?" she said, rising to her feet.

"Want to grab a bite?" Danny said.

She stared at him. "What's the matter?" he asked.

"Nothing," Samantha said, smiling. "Some food would be nice."

They walked for a few moments in a comfortable silence. Danny gently reached out and took her hand. She clasped it gently and couldn't keep from stroking her fingers along his. The sliding motion of their hands made the surge of excitement in her chest grow larger, a swelling feeling that would not retreat back into her heart. The silence lay between them but, oddly, Samantha did not feel the need to fill it with conversation. It seemed natural, comfortable, and she was content to hold his hand.

They crossed the street and began passing a small, unkempt park with a low, black metal fence separating it from the broken sidewalk. Unseen birds chirped a twilight song in harmony with the fading light, and Danny suddenly pulled her through the gate into the park. She stumbled after him as he drew her up the hill toward a scraggly old tree shading the walkway.

Samantha didn't know what to say. She stared at him, a combination of fear and desire swirling inside her chest that kept her frozen. She wanted to lean forward, to kiss him, to enfold herself in his arms. At the same time her heart screamed to run away, to flee into the safety of the anonymous night and leave this strange, confusing moment behind her.

Danny leaned over her, sliding a warm hand against the side of her face, keeping her still. Gently his lips brushed hers, a bare touch that sent an electric shock through her as though he had power over her, as though she were a helpless human. He kissed her again, so lightly, and she knew she wanted more.

His arms stole around her back, drawing her closer. His mouth opened and she felt the hot intrusion of his tongue between her lips.

Instantly Samantha wrenched away from him, her hand flying up involuntarily to cover her mouth.

"I'm sorry," Danny said immediately, holding out his hands in a calming gesture. "I'm so sorry. I thought…I thought you wanted…"

"I did," Samantha stuttered, the fear and wanting circling each other inside her like a pair of birds in an eternal battle around her heart.

Danny stared at her. "I'm gonna go out on a limb here," he said, the words falling over themselves. "There's something about you…I don't know what, and I know that doesn't exactly ring as the most romantic sentiment in the world, but that something is just intoxicating to me. You are an incredible woman and I want you. I think you want me too, and if you don't, now is a good time to tell me to go to hell, and I'll go, I swear it."

Samantha stared up at him, her eyes growing wider in the fading light.

Danny plunged on. "But if you don't want me to go…be with me, Samantha. I feel like you're hiding from something. I want to help you. Talk to me."

Samantha turned away, hiding her face from his earnest eyes. "You can't help me," she said. "No one can."

Danny came up behind her, respecting a small distance.

"Someone hurt you," he said. "Is he…still hurting you?"

Samantha bowed her head. "He's dead."

Awkwardly Danny touched her shoulders and she didn't want to run away. She didn't want to flinch and hide and cover her smile with her hand. Her heart pounded as she stared into the fading orange-red sun, and all she wanted was to lean back against his chest and tell him everything.

But she couldn't. Something inside her simply rose up as a wall, blocking her from speaking. She fought herself, her mind warring with her heart, now free of its concrete prison and rising through her body toward him.

Danny stroked her hair, a gesture meant to calm instead of inflame her. "You're safe now," he murmured. Samantha almost laughed at the incongruity of it, standing in a park at dusk in the middle of the city, feeling safe.

"Do you want to tell me?" he asked uncertainly.

Samantha turned to face him. She stared up at his eyes, so sad and earnest, so kind and willing. She reached inside, caressed the surface of his mind just a little, and an image rose back to her.

Celia standing in an alley. Peeling down the straps of her shirt. Her eyes tired and old in her too-young face.

Samantha backed away, horrified. She covered her mouth with her hand. "No, not you. Not…no."

Danny shook his head, confused. "What…what happened to your eyes?" He stared at her. "What did you do to me?"

Samantha turned to flee then, unable to face the rest of that memory. Her imagination put them up against the wall, Danny using that poor child cruelly, without care. She wanted to run, to keep running until she reached open water, wade out into it until she didn't have to see Celia in the alley anymore.

She stopped still.

There at the gate to the park stood a man in a dark cloak. The hood hid his face from view, but Samantha felt the aura of power coming off him and knew he was a vampire.

Danny came up beside her, whispering urgently. "We'll back out the other way."

"We're surrounded," Samantha said dully. "They're all around us."

Danny looked wildly about them and saw only shadows growing between the lackluster trees. The street was still in sight, anonymous cars whizzing past on their way to somewhere else.

The cloaked man walked forward slowly. "Miran-da," he singsonged.

Samantha froze. "No," she whispered. "It's not possible."

He pulled back the cloak. Diego hadn't aged a day.

Chapter Four

ဆာ

1945

San Francisco

Samantha sat in the window, watching the last few rays smoke the clouds to a lovely orange-scarlet. She smoked a cigarette, tapping the ashes into a jar lid sitting beside her on the fire escape.

The streets were ringing with the news—the war was over. Somewhere overseas the humans had decided to stop killing each other. Music was playing from a dozen open windows in the apartment buildings, and people had been randomly hugging each other on the street for hours.

Behind her, she heard mutterings muffled by a closed door. Diego was locked in the closet again. He had been bad. Cristoval did not condone Diego's games with young girls. This time Diego had chosen a nice suburban girl instead of his usual street urchins. This time there were newspaper stories and parents' pleas and police knocking on doors.

Samantha took a long drag on her cigarette.

"That's an unladylike habit, Miranda," Fiona said, sitting beside her.

"Come into the modern era, Fiona," Samantha said. "A lady can smoke on the street if she wishes."

"Some things do not change over time," Fiona said imperiously.

Samantha smiled and stubbed out her cigarette on the jar lid. "Does that make me a lady again?"

"You're always a lady," Fiona said, smiling.

Behind them, Diego started singsonging again. He never actually sang a tune, but he would make up his own words and sing them in an odd, toneless cadence that gave Samantha chills. The closet door muffled his voice enough that she was spared the words.

"Cristoval should kill him," Samantha said, pitching her voice low.

Fiona lowered her head. "I have asked him to do so."

Samantha stared at Fiona. "You've never asked anything of him," she said, incredulous.

"I have asked this," Fiona replied.

Samantha shook her head. "A ritual favor? That would extend your time of service another decade, wouldn't it?"

Fiona nodded, staring out at the sunset. "I have no great love for the humans," she said calmly. "They shoot at us for sport. Their men make free with our women and call it fun. But I have no wish to see them…it is evil what Diego does. It was a mistake to bring him over, and it is more of a mistake to let him live."

Samantha shivered. "I didn't see what he—"

"And that is good," Fiona interrupted. "It was unimaginable."

Behind them, Diego fell silent. Samantha sneaked a peek into the bedroom again—just to make sure the door was still closed. It was bolted, mute and blank. Somewhere behind it, there was movement, slight shifting sounds in the shadows.

"Will he do it?" Samantha whispered.

Fiona shook her head. "Cristoval would never destroy one he created," she said. "He will punish him instead."

"A week in the closet won't do anything," Samantha said, frustrated.

Fiona looked at her. "Cristoval has other ways of punishing, Miranda," she said sternly. "You would do well not to explore them."

Samantha blinked. "I haven't done anything wrong, have I?" she asked, worried.

Fiona shook her head. "You are his favorite, his plaything," she said. "As long as you please him and do as he says, you are safe." She stood up and placed a hand on Samantha's shoulder. "But never test him, my dear. I would not see harm come to you."

The hallway door opened and Cristoval glided in. He kissed Fiona's hand like a courtly gentleman of a bygone era. Samantha had no idea how old he was, but his manners were those of another time. "Fiona, my dear," he said.

"Cristoval," she replied, and bowing slightly, swept out of the room, closing the door behind her.

Cristoval came over to Samantha, gliding his fingertips up her arm. The barest touch sent shivers through her, his power strong and forceful as it sank through her skin. "My beloved Miranda," he said, using his voice in that low, seductive huskiness. "Whatever are you looking at?"

"The humans," Samantha said. "The celebrations."

Cristoval knelt beside her, his voice whispering in her ear. "They are nothing, their wars are nothing," he said softly. "We are above their petty torments, Miranda. We are superior to them in every way."

"They breathe and their hearts beat," Samantha said.

"But they die," Cristoval said, kissing her shoulder.

She felt the electricity of his touch and shivered. "Wait," she murmured. "Diego."

Diego was singsonging again behind the closet door, something about a river and a young girl's hair.

Cristoval grew more insistent. His hand slipped up her

thigh to cup a breast, kneading the nipple to a hardened point as he nibbled at her neck. Samantha sighed, shifting uncomfortably on the windowsill.

Still, she found the strength to speak again. "I can't," she whispered. "Not with Diego in the closet."

"Yes, you can," Cristoval murmured, sliding his hand to her other breast, kneading it until it, too, was hard and exquisitely sensitive to his touch. He molded her flesh through the fabric of her dress and she cried out softly.

Cristoval kissed her, his mouth rough and hard, barely keeping his teeth away from her tender lips and tongue. His hand tightened on her breast until a sharp pinch of pain dampened the fire in her blood.

She broke the kiss. "Diego," she insisted.

"Diiii-eh-go," Diego singsonged.

"He can hear us," Samantha warned.

Cristoval stared at her and the heat in his gaze shifted to anger. She flinched away from the hot flash of fury in his eyes. Cristoval captured her eyes then, and his displeasure flowed over her. A few images flashed across her mind, shading from wanton sexuality to darker places, things that had more to do with pain and humiliation than pleasure.

He grabbed her wrist, and Samantha immediately came to him, submissive and yielding in his arms. "Forgive me," she said quickly, and began to kiss his neck the way he liked.

Cristoval's tension eased and he drew her onto the bed. A few practiced motions and her dress and shift were gone. She lay in the dying sunlight, her skin golden and smooth. Shedding his clothes quickly, he slid between her legs without further preamble and thrust upward into her. It was rough and it hurt a little. He took her cry for pleasure and began to move harder, pounding into her.

Samantha grasped at his shoulders, wrapping her legs

around him as he pushed hard into her. The pain faded as she relaxed, warming to him and feeling the surge of pleasure grow between them. He twined his fingers in her hair, holding her down as he pounded harder and faster, his breath coming hard now.

In the closet, Diego was skittering about, panting on his own. Samantha closed her eyes and tried to ignore it, letting the pleasure build…

But her mind flashed on Diego again, imagining that it was he who buried himself deep within her, that Diego filled her with his screaming laughter and his seed. Her eyes flew open and she reassured herself that it was Cristoval, staring at the wall over her head as he cried out, thrusting hard into her, his hands clenching in her hair as he exploded within her. The thrill of his climax shot through the mental link and fought with her adrenaline surge, dampening her excitement until it faded to an unfulfilled ache within her. Cristoval withdrew from her and immediately got up, moving to the bathroom.

She lay in the last breaths of sunlight for a moment, the fluttering of her muscles returning to normal, the sweat drying on her skin.

From the closet, Diego's voice came softly. "My turn?"

A shiver crawled over her bare skin in the shadows. "Never," Samantha breathed, shuddering.

и и и и и

6:30 p.m.

Sunset

Danny tried to step in front of Samantha. She grabbed his arm and pulled him back as hard as she could. He stumbled to the ground at the foot of the tree, surprised. "Samantha—"

"When I tell you, run," Samantha murmured, stepping forward toward Diego.

"The hell you say," Danny snapped, standing up behind her.

Diego grinned, the last of the light dancing in his eyes. "Sooo much prettier than the last one, Miranda," he said.

"Fiona said you died with Cristoval," Samantha replied, her calm tone belying the panic in her chest.

"Poor Cristoval, he never knew what hit him," Diego sighed, a wistful tone in his voice. "They thought we all died when those dreadful people set fire to our lovely house. Fire, fire, burning bright."

Samantha steeled herself to sound strong and unafraid. "Tell them to come out, Diego. I'm not in the mood to play with shadows."

Diego waved a hand, and a full kiss of vampires coalesced out of the shadows between the trees. Samantha shivered. That was Cristoval's trick, and Diego had mastered it to a level unmatched by anyone except their old master. "You've improved your act since the old days," she said, buying time. She took a few small steps to the left where only one vampire stood between Danny and the street. Danny followed her, and she sent a silent prayer of thanks to any god who would listen for his willingness to play along.

"Do you want his heart, Miranda?" Diego said, smiling insanely.

Samantha stilled the fear again, circling in this ballast of power growing between them. "You'll have to take my heart first," she said.

Diego licked his lips and started forward.

Danny had had enough. "Samantha," he breathed behind her.

Samantha cast a glance to the left, gauging how far

Danny would have to run. *He'll never make it past the big guy by the fence without me, but if I move, Diego will be on him in a second,* she thought.

"Did you kill Cristoval?" Samantha shouted.

It was purely a bluff, something to distract Diego for a moment. But Diego froze in mid-stride, shock and fear glittering in his eyes. It was the first real emotion she had ever seen in Diego, apart from his insanity and lust. "My God, you did," Samantha said, more quietly.

Our chance, Samantha thought, and sent an image to Danny through their tenuous link as hard as she could. *RUN,* she thought to him, and showed him the low fence past the big vampire, staring at Diego in confusion.

But... Danny's mind was protesting, and she sensed real fear and concern for her in his heart. Somehow, the idea of something happening to her in this park was more frightening to him than his own death. She felt a sudden surge of warmth mixed with fear from him, and it threw her concentration for just a second.

Diego hissed and lunged forward, his eyes lit with a dancing mad glee. Samantha moved ahead of him, standing between him and Danny.

"Freeze!" shouted a female voice. Diego turned around in mid-stride and Samantha looked past him to see a police officer standing at the gate of the park, her weapon drawn. She seemed very young, Samantha thought, with fiery red hair drawn back in a sensible ponytail. She was not in uniform, but she held up a badge next to her service pistol.

The officer stepped forward slowly. "You," she said to Diego. "Let's see the hands, asshole."

Diego grinned and held up his hands. "To whom do I owe the pleasure?" he smirked.

The cop wasn't having it. Her eyes were moving very

quickly, gauging the scene. "Detective Kelly Parker, and shut the hell up," she snapped. "Danny Carton, you okay?"

"Yes," Danny replied, coming up beside Samantha.

Parker stepped forward slowly. "Been looking for you," she said, keeping her attention on Diego. "Okay, buddy, clasp your hands on top of your head. Kneel and cross your ankles."

Diego's grin grew wider. He clasped his hands on his head and dropped to one knee. "But, officer—"

"Shut the fuck up and do what I say, now!" Parker snapped at him.

But it was too late. Samantha saw Diego capture Parker's eyes, and the hand holding the gun faltered. In that second, he lunged for her. Samantha moved a split second later, but she was too slow. The gun spun away into the shadows and Diego had Parker by the throat.

"Diego, you can't hurt her," Samantha said, pleading. "It's not like old days. They will tear the town apart looking for you. You'll never be safe."

Diego leaned close to Parker's neck, grinning. He sniffed her skin, and Samantha could sense the fear running through her. God knew what images Diego was sending her through their link, she thought. Parker's eyes were wide and terrified, her body was frozen under his command.

Danny lunged for the gun, searching through the shadows between the bushes.

"So pretty," Diego whispered, just as he struck. Parker screamed, and he bit harder into her neck, blood streaming past his mouth and down onto her shirt.

"Diego!" Samantha shouted, and for a bare second he looked up, Parker's blood smearing his face.

It was all she needed. Samantha caught Diego with her eyes, sinking fast into his crazed mirror-maze of a mind, her shields full and strong. She fed him images she knew he would like—the girls selling themselves on the back alley, the dead college boy in the alley who was murdered by a rogue vampire last year.

Diego wilted in front of her, his gaze held captive to her. Samantha gave him the sensation of burning on the palms of his hands, as though Parker were made of fire. Diego's hands flexed and dropped away from the officer's neck, and Parker fell to the ground. Danny ran to her side, pulling out a handkerchief and pressing it against the wound in her neck.

Samantha stepped forward again, and this time she hurt Diego, driving him to his knees under the thrall of her power. Diego whimpered aloud, but his mind spoke through the link. *Let me go,* he said.

No, Samantha replied.

Diego still managed to smirk, even while pressed to the ground before her. From the shadows, his kiss emerged again. They growled as they closed in, and Samantha could sense their hunger. Diego had forged them into one mind much more closely than even Cristoval had managed. If he hadn't been insane, he might have made an excellent master vampire, Samantha thought.

Let me go and I will not harm them, Diego said.

Neither will your kiss, Samantha replied. *These people are mine to protect, and you will not touch them.*

Agreed. For tonight.

"Pick her up," Samantha said to Danny who had located Parker's gun and held it in his left hand while his right still pressed against Parker's wound. He cast a glance at the kiss of vampires then tried to pick up Detective Parker.

"I can walk," Parker whispered, but her legs were wobbly. Danny settled for sliding an arm around her waist and helping her past Diego's kneeling form to the gate of the park.

Samantha stepped around Diego carefully. Without the eye contact, she felt his struggles strengthen. She gripped his mind harder as they walked away toward Parker's car. Just before they reached it, as Parker handed the keys to Danny, Samantha felt Diego break free.

But he kept his bargain. He stood up with his kiss, drawing the cloak back over his head as the last of the shadows grew to cover the ground and the sun finally set.

6:39 p.m.

"I don't need a damn hospital," Parker insisted, holding the soaked handkerchief against her neck.

Danny shook his head. "I'm driving, so I say you do," he said.

"Asshole kid, don't you tell me…" Parker reached out toward the wheel.

Samantha leaned forward from the backseat. "Go to Sensei," she said.

Danny glanced in the rearview mirror. "She needs stitches at least," he said.

"Sensei has patched up the neighborhood kids quite a few times," Samantha said. "And if she does need a hospital, he'll convince her."

"Fuck that," Parker said, and winced. "Damn, I thought the bite was supposed to feel good."

"Only through the mind-touch," Samantha said absently. "Through the touch, he can make it be anything he wants. Pleasure, pain or worse."

"Well, that's good to know," Parker said sarcastically.

Up ahead, Danny saw the dojo, its lights still shining serenely onto the sidewalk in the twilight. He screeched a fast turn off the street into the small parking lot just up from the dojo and pulled into a space. Samantha got out and ran toward the door while Danny came around to help Detective Parker. "Is there someone we can call for you?" Danny asked.

"Shut up," Parker breathed. Her face was pale.

Sensei was standing at the doorway with Samantha when they got to the door. He slid his arm around Parker on the other side and they helped her into the dojo. "Kelly, you have been misbehaving," he said.

"Would you believe I didn't start it this time?" Parker said, grinning weakly.

They half-carried her through the dojo to a mirrored panel on the far side of the room. Sensei pressed a small switch that Danny hadn't even noticed, and with a click, the panel swung open a bit. Sensei pushed it farther open and switched on a light.

It was a small room, but brightly lit. Wire shelving against the far wall held medical supplies, food packs and bottled water. It stood next to a small sink and toilet. In the middle of the room was a cot, directly under the light. Danny carefully helped Parker lie down on the cot, and Sensei immediately crossed to the shelf, pulling out several packs of gauze.

Parker glanced up at Danny. "We were trying to find you," she said. "Another threat against your father…he was worried about you."

Danny blinked. "He was? I mean…what threat?"

Samantha stared at him. "What's going on?"

"Someone's been sending us hate mail at the campaign," Danny said. "We figured it was just a garden-variety crazy."

Samantha shook her head. "Doesn't sound like Diego."

Parker looked over at her. "The vamp at the park. Tell me."

Samantha lowered her eyes. "Diego. Particularly violent, has a predilection for young girls."

Danny made a sickened noise, and Samantha cast a quick glance at him. His face was twisted in disgust.

Samantha went on. "I'd heard he was dead, but clearly I was misinformed. He's got a full kiss, at least twelve of them, and they're devoted. Oh, and he's insane."

"Kiss?" Danny asked.

"A group of vampires, melded together under one master," Sensei said, peering closely at the seeping bite wound on Parker's neck. "A master with sufficient mental control can bind other vampires to his will. They retain individual personalities and mental capacity, but they are literally incapable of denying his wishes. It's like an extended form of the vampire touch, which temporarily links the human's mind to the vampire and makes them susceptible to suggestion. But the mind-touch can be broken. The kiss cannot."

"Wrong," Samantha said. "The kiss can be broken. But it's very rare. And it's incredibly hard."

Sensei glanced up at her. Danny was staring at her. Samantha chose to look at Detective Parker who was fully awake and absorbing every word.

"The point is, it's not Diego's style to send threats to people he doesn't get to torture in person," Samantha said. "First of all, his focus is games with young girls. Second, he has no interest in human politics. Third, killing isn't what he's after. It's just a side effect of his lust."

"Not enough 'ew' in the world," Parker muttered. "Am I gonna need stitches?"

"Oh, yes," Sensei said. "You could probably do with a blood transfusion, but you're too stubborn."

"Detective, you should document these injuries," Danny

insisted. "Attacking a human, particularly a police officer, is an automatic death sentence for a vampire."

"I wouldn't shed any tears for Diego," Samantha said. "But I'd be afraid for the officers who tried to arrest him."

Parker's gaze shifted back to Samantha. "Is he really that tough?"

"It's not like that," Samantha replied. "He has the most tightly bound kiss I've ever seen. He has the ability to make them appear like shadows, misdirecting human eyesight so you couldn't see them until they were on you. And did I mention the part where he's insane?"

"Mr. Carton does have a point, Kelly," Sensei said.

"Wait," Samantha said. "What happens if this goes to a report? If everyone gets involved, the press and the Chain Gang—I mean, the rest of the police—and everybody? It'll be a nightmare."

"We weren't doing anything wrong," Danny insisted.

Samantha sighed in frustration. "No, but think about it," she said. "Councilman's son attacked by rogue vampires. Big headlines. Police cracking down on any vampire skull they can find. It'll be a witch hunt, with vampires playing the part of the witches."

"And what happens if your friend goes and kills a busload of schoolchildren? What then?" Danny said.

"He is not my friend," Samantha retorted.

Sensei injected a local anesthetic at the site of Parker's wound. Parker gritted her teeth for a second. "Eventually, I'm going to get around to asking the hard questions, miss," Parker said.

Samantha nodded. "I understand," she said softly.

"Stop talking, Kelly," Sensei said. "Could you two give us a moment?"

Samantha turned and walked out into the dojo. She stood in the middle of the darkened room, her arms folded under her breasts, hugging herself. Behind her, she heard Danny follow her. He tried to touch her arms and she flinched away, a few traitorous tears escaping from behind her eyes.

"Samantha," Danny began, but didn't seem to know what to say.

She turned to face him then, the tears spilling down her cheeks. "So you know, and now it's different," she said, her voice hurt and angry and sad all at once.

"I'd rather you just told me," Danny said quietly.

Samantha looked at the mirrored walls, surrounding her with empty reflections. "Then look," she said.

Danny looked, and saw himself standing alone in an empty room. He slowly raised a hand behind Samantha's back, and saw only himself, waving at thin air. "My God," he murmured.

Samantha's voice kept faltering, but she spoke anyway. "I was born in 1894 in Baltimore," she said. "I was made a vampire at age eighteen. I've lived a very long time hiding what I am from people who don't understand me. Yes, I lied to the people at the campaign, I lied to you, and if you hate me for it, I wouldn't blame you."

Danny circled around her, but she turned away and wouldn't look at him. "Did you think we'd send you away if we knew?" he asked, puzzled.

"Wouldn't you?" she cried. "I've lost jobs without number when they found out. I've been denied jobs because I wouldn't pass the mirror test. No decent apartment building will rent to me, so I live in a pay-by-the-hour hotel. If I'm accused of biting someone without their permission, I'll be locked in a cage for a matter of weeks before they cut off my head, whether or not they have proof. And your father stood in the street today and denounced me."

"That's not what he did," Danny said, grasping at the one thing he could understand. "He wanted to…to help people. That's all we want to do. To help you, too."

"You can't help me," she cried, and now the tears were streaming. "No one can help me. You're like some beautiful spotlight, shining into this place and thinking you'll make everything better, for me, for everyone. But you'll burn out and disappear, they all do, and nothing ever changes—ever."

Danny took another step toward her. "That's not true," he said quietly. "Sometimes things change. It can get better. You can be safe."

Samantha shook her head. "The last person who promised me I'd be safe was murdered," she said flatly. "Diego tore his throat out, dug through his chest with his claws and drank him in front of me. It took less than a minute."

Danny recoiled for just a second, horror in his eyes. But it was not horror of her, she saw—it was horror at what she had said, and a sadness falling over him born purely of compassion, regret for what she had experienced. It was like nothing she had ever sensed.

"Samantha," Danny said, reaching toward her. "It doesn't matter. It doesn't make a difference to me."

"But it will," Samantha said harshly. "Wouldn't it kill your father's campaign for you to have dinner with a street vampire?"

The word made Danny flinch, and Samantha seized on that as well. "Vampire!" she cried. "See, it's a dirty word! But it's what I am, and I can't change it. I can't change it!"

She wept in earnest then, digging her nails into her arms and dropping down to her knees. She had not filed her nails today, and they drew blood from the tender skin inside her forearms.

"I can't," she whispered.

Danny knelt beside her, wrapping his arms around her shoulders. She wanted to flinch away again, but the strength in his arms and warmth of his skin drew her closer to him. She found herself leaning into his chest, his arms comforting her, his hand stroking her hair and his soft voice whispering things to her that she didn't understand.

Celia, she thought, and looked up at him. "Let me touch your mind," she whispered. "Please."

Danny looked back at her. "Like the park?"

"Deeper," Samantha said. "I need…to know something. Do you trust me?"

Danny nodded, and she felt his own surprise at how easily his trust had grown. She reached into him and touched his mind.

It was like falling into a well, but slowly, as though a curtain of air and light held her softly in its grip. She saw through the eyes of a small boy, holding his mother's hand as they took the boxes out of his sunny bedroom, all his toys packed up to move away from the big house where he had always lived.

Then he was older, fighting off a bully on the playground. But the bully hadn't been after him, she saw—he'd been beating up a smaller kid who was still on all fours, clutching his stomach. Danny took the rest of the beating in the smaller boy's stead.

Now she stood in his place under a tree on a sunny May day with birds chirping and a breeze lifting the hair from his forehead as he laid a white rose on his mother's coffin. The councilman was not there. No one was there except Danny and two young men—

Jon and Dave, my roommates. Danny was there with her in

this memory lane, somehow watching and reliving with her. *They were the only ones who cared.*

She sat in a classroom, arguing with a professor about some political issue while the rest of the students took notes or looked bored. Then she sat in a small office with Mr. Morris and Meredith Schwartz, barely listening as they argued.

Celia, Samantha whispered. But the name meant nothing to his memories.

She pushed the image forward, and the memory opened before her—Celia standing in the hallway, peeling her tank top down, and Danny running away, telling her to eat something, take the night off and rest. The relief welled up in her mind, and he caught a glimpse of what she had thought when she first saw Celia in his mind. His repulsion and saddened horror was real, and more—a wish to find Celia and help her.

Is that all you do, rescue the downtrodden? Samantha asked.

It's a living, Danny replied, and a bubble of humor passed between them.

Samantha relaxed, and began to withdraw through his mind, letting the images fly past. But one leapt out at her, pushed by Danny's mind. A woman whose hair shone like burnished gold in the fading sun, whose pale skin seemed like creamy silk, a woman who shone like an angel. She looked at this woman, and Danny reached back to her.

This is you, he said.

No, Samantha replied. *This is me.* She showed him a pale, twisted wretch, dull yellow hair hiding an over-made face and a body that stank of sullen lust. A sharp-toothed harridan, a lowly parasite, ice-cold misery and ancient sadness.

But Danny let his picture flow over her, the feel of her

lips on his as they stood under the tree, her saucy smile as she talked back to Red, her fierce resolve before Diego. *I didn't know until now,* he said.

Samantha felt it, sure and strong within him, and a surge of guilt struck her as an image rose from her own mind. In a panic, she broke the link, a sudden move like hacking through a gossamer thread with a sword. But it kept the picture of Robert Carton asleep on her bed at Nocturnal Urges away from Danny.

Danny looked at her, his eyes full of a thousand emotions, and leaned forward to kiss her. She let him, and allowed the power to sink through her arms and hands as well as her mouth, filling him with electric heat and tingling power. This time when his tongue pressed against her lips, she allowed it, carefully sliding her tongue against his, away from her teeth. She felt his body against hers, so warm and alive, and he held her as though she were something precious to him, something to keep close and warm.

Parker's voice was growing louder in the hidden room, and Danny broke the kiss. He gently wiped the tears away from her face, and Samantha smiled at him.

"Just one question," Danny said. "Who was Cristoval?"

Samantha's smile faded. "That is a much longer story."

"Someday I'll ask you to tell me," Danny said. "But for now…"

"Now we should see what Detective Parker is yelling about," Samantha said, smiling. It felt good to smile without hiding it behind her hand or curling her lips over her teeth. It felt natural, almost…human.

Danny helped her to her feet. "You're an amazing woman, Samantha," he said.

"I love you too," she replied, and the look on his face was enough to make her brave a hundred Diegos.

8:42 p.m.

"Jesus God, where the hell have you been?" Morris shouted, striding across the campaign office.

"Busy," Danny replied, walking through the doorway with Parker.

Freitas barreled out of the office. "Dammit, Parker, there's such a thing as answering your goddamn cell phone," she snapped, then froze when she saw the bandages on Parker's neck. "The hell? What happened to you?"

Parker touched her neck gently. "Mr. Carton ran into a little trouble," she said. "Sorry about the phone. I was busy getting hurt."

"Just like I told you not to," Freitas said, peering closer at the wound. "Jesus, is that a bite?"

"Relax, I had my shots in first grade like everybody else," Parker said. "Detective, could I speak to you alone for a moment?"

Morris hauled Danny into his office, practically by the scruff of his neck, leaving the detectives alone in the outer office. Robert Carton shot to his feet from the chair behind Morris' desk. "Danny," he said. "Are you all right?"

"Yeah," Danny said, unconsciously standing at attention. "Just got a little lost. Detective Parker was kind enough to help me out."

"Hero cop saves councilman's son from rogue vampire," Morris recited, grinning.

"Not a good idea," Danny said. "I don't think we should make this public."

"Why not?" Morris asked.

"I was...not on campaign business." Danny said, looking away from his father.

"Shit, the blonde chick?" Morris snapped. "God, are you that fucking stupid? Rule number one—Hands off the volunteers! Especially the pretty girls with wide eyes and big tits!"

"Jeff, shut your mouth before you fall into it," Meredith said, disgusted. "Is she all right, Danny? Did she get hurt?"

"She's fine," Danny replied. "We dropped her off at her place. But they're going to wonder what we were doing there after dark, and the answers aren't kosher."

"All right," Carton said. "Jeff, we'll keep this in-house for now. Danny, have you made a complete statement to the detectives?"

"Yes," he said. "We received another threat, I take it?"

Morris pointed to a photocopy of the picture, sitting on the desk. "Can we all agree not to go traipsing off into dark alleys for a little while? Danny?"

"No problem," Danny replied.

"I suggest we all get some sleep and start fresh in the morning," Carton said. "Danny, can I give you a lift to your house?"

"No thanks," Danny said. "My car is here."

Carton grasped his shoulder. "I'm glad you're safe, Dan," he said, and left the room. Danny stared after him, thoughtful.

9:23 p.m.

"Okay, two questions," Freitas said, driving through the cold, dark drizzle. "Why the hell aren't we calling the Chain Gang in on a vampire attack, against a police officer no less? And why the royal fuck aren't you in a hospital?"

"Second question first," Parker said, leaning back against her shoulder belt. "I got my stitches and I'll heal up fine.

Nothing else needed."

"Says you and Doctor Back-Alley," Freitas returned. "You look pale as hell, Parker."

"Thanks, I'll schedule some tanning time," Parker shot back. "You want to talk or you want to bust my ass?"

"Talk now. Bust later."

Parker pressed her hand gently against her neck and winced. "There's more going on here than a rogue vamp, Detective. You said you know the vamps pretty well. I don't. But I know what'll happen if this gets out. Big headlines, burning vamps on Beale Street. I'm taking a risk that I can trust you, okay?"

"Got it," Freitas said. "Now spill it, or I'm turning this car toward the station."

"His name is Diego," Parker said. "Not from around here. My source says he's at least ninety, so he's got high survival skills. He's got a kiss."

"Oh, shit," Freitas breathed, and turned onto Poplar toward Midtown.

"You know what those are?" Parker said.

"Hell yes," Freitas said. "We've had the odd rogue from time to time, but a rogue kiss hasn't been seen in Memphis since before you were born. Think a street gang on crack, but of one single, controlling mind and practically impervious to anything."

"That's what we've got," Parker said.

Freitas shot a look at the younger woman. "Then why the fuck aren't you dead, Parker? A rogue kiss should have made hamburger out of you and Sonny Boy."

"We had help," Parker said. "The source."

"Spill it."

Parker shook her head. "Do you know what could

happen to her if I—"

"Her, the chippie that Junior was chatting up?" Freitas interrupted. "Serena something? She's a vampire and she protected you?"

"Shit," Parker said.

"Yeah, I do this for a living," Freitas said, rolling her eyes.

"She's in hiding," Parker said. "She's got some history with this Diego guy, and he's after her but good. Plus being outed as a vampire is like getting a big, old target sign strapped to her back, you know?"

Freitas didn't answer.

"I owe her," Parker said.

"Parker, I get it, I do," Freitas said. "But a rogue kiss is bad news. We've got to talk to Fradella, get a task force on this. When we take them, it's going to be a tactical Chain Gang operation, not the shootout at the OK Corral, unless you plan on being lunch again."

"My first bite and it hurts like a motherfucker," Parker said. "And…"

Freitas glanced at her. "And what?"

"Is it supposed…" Parker's voice trailed off. "Never mind."

"Hell with that, what's the deal?" Freitas asked.

Parker didn't answer. She stared out the window at the passing traffic.

"Look, uh, Parker," Freitas said hesitantly. "If it felt good, there's no shame, you know. It's supposed to. That's, uh, how those places like Nocturnal Urges stay in business."

"No," Parker said. "It didn't. Not in any way. But it was like…like he fed some pictures in my mind. Rough stuff."

"Jesus," Freitas said. "I never heard of that."

Parker shook her head. "It doesn't matter. We've got to find the kiss."

"No way," Freitas said. "Sorry, Parker. The lieutenant gets in on this now. No delays."

"He'll tell everyone."

"No," Freitas said, smiling grimly as she pulled into an apartment parking lot not far from the university. "I'll call in a favor."

9:41 p.m.

"So?" David was leaning forward over the back of the camelback couch, grinning.

"So nothing," Samantha said. "We…went home. To our separate homes."

David shook his head. "I don't believe you. Hot guy, romantic kiss in the moonlight and you…go to work?"

Samantha sighed. "I didn't want to. But sitting in my room for ten minutes convinced me it was better to come in."

David rolled his eyes. "It doesn't have to be hearts and flowers, hon. Just enjoy yourself. God knows you deserve it."

"It's…complicated," Samantha said. "He doesn't know about this place."

"Ahh," David said. "The plot sickens."

Samantha fluffed her hair, shaping it by feel. "It was just a kiss, David. Nothing."

"Suuuure," David said. "How many years have we been friends, honey?"

Samantha shrugged. "I've lost count."

David turned serious for a moment. "In all that time, I've never seen you happy," he said. "When you came in here, all nervous and high-strung, at first I thought you'd been attacked again. But when you started talking about this what's-his-name…you glowed."

Samantha burst out laughing. "Oh, please," she said. "That's the silliest thing I've ever heard. Nobody ever really glows."

"I could read a book by your light," David said. "Whatever he did, whoever he is, honey…you're happy."

"Just a dream," Samantha said, sitting down in a chair. "A pleasant little fantasy to occupy me. Nothing real."

David leaned back against the pillows. "Because of him or because of you?"

"Yes," she replied.

10:01 p.m.

Fradella was blinking hard as he answered his apartment door. "God, Annie, this better be good."

Parker glanced at Freitas. "Annie?" she said.

"Shuddup," Freitas muttered. "Let us in, Lieutenant. I'd rather not shout in the hallway."

Fradella unchained the door and let them in, bleary-eyed. He wore a blue bathrobe over pajama bottoms and a plain white T-shirt. The butt of his service revolver protruded from the pocket of his robe.

"Expecting a gang attack?" Freitas asked.

"No, I save the good weapons for you," Fradella said, yawning. "Why the hell are you waking me up?"

"Christ, Frank, it's not even eleven," Freitas retorted. "When did you turn into such a wuss?"

"When I started showing up for work at eight a.m., Annie my dear," Fradella returned.

"This is really entertaining, but can we get back to business?" Parker said, wavering a little on her feet.

"Sit down, Parker," Freitas ordered.

"I don't—"

"Sit down and quit being a fucking hero." Freitas rolled her eyes.

Fradella focused on Parker for the first time. "Detective, you look like shit. What the hell happened to your neck?"

"Well, that's a long story," Freitas said. "We're going to tell you, and you're going to want to tell people farther up the ladder. I'm going to ask you not to, and see if we can't handle this without literally making a federal case out of it, in the interests of not burning the city to the ground."

"Okay, I'm sufficiently intrigued," Fradella said. "Will coffee be required?"

"Absolutely," Freitas said.

Chapter Five

ॐ

1935

New Orleans

Samantha sat across from the young woman who lolled in a chair, drowsy with wine.

"It's like the power, only without skin," Cristoval whispered in her ear. As always, his voice sent a thrill of fear and excitement through her. She often wondered if that was a vampire trick or merely her own attraction to him.

"Attraction, Miranda," Cristoval said.

Can you always read my mind? Samantha thought.

"Only when you leave yourself so open, my dear," Cristoval said. "You have more power in the mind-touch than even you realize. Go on, touch this young woman."

Samantha shifted her gaze, catching the young woman's face. She reached out, as though throwing a lasso made of gossamer thread around a rose petal. She skated lightly over the woman's thoughts, which were muddled with wine and glowing with satisfaction from the bite she had received from Cristoval.

"Now deepen it," Cristoval said. "Push harder."

Samantha sank deeper into the young woman's mind, like pushing her finger through jelly. Suddenly she knew the young woman's name was Maude, but she hated it and insisted everyone call her Melissa. But behind Melissa's fun-loving, wanton embraces and fondness for wine, Maude remained, crying out for sanity and safety. While Melissa writhed beneath Cristoval's hungry mouth, Maude wept for a picture she barely remembered from childhood—a home with a fence and flowers by the mailbox.

Samantha pushed harder and Melissa jerked, muttering something.

"Easy," Cristoval said, and Samantha backed off, waiting. "Now feed her something."

"What?" Samantha asked.

"Anything," Cristoval said.

Samantha searched her mind for an image. She selected one, and played it for Melissa as though the inside of Melissa's mind were a picture show. It was Cristoval, dashing in a formal suit and top hat. They were dancing at the governor's ball on stolen invitations, the entire room murmuring about the strangely handsome young couple that swept across the ballroom floor in mysterious beauty.

Then Samantha's memory turned traitor, moving forward to that night in the hotel, when Cristoval had doffed the top hat and her burgundy gown fell to the floor...

She felt the heat rising in her cheeks. Melissa moaned softly, but not in pain.

"Now make her do something," Cristoval said. "Use the memory. Make her into you, make her act as you."

Samantha slid deeper into the memory. She let Melissa feel her way into it, the sensation of the corset being unlaced behind her back, the tight bodice releasing her soft breasts into Cristoval's warm, grasping fingers. Melissa sat more upright, running her own hands over her body as if she could feel Cristoval touching her.

Then Samantha let it move on, to when she pushed Cristoval into a chair. Melissa rose to her feet, somewhat shaky, and pressed herself forward into the real Cristoval. She unbuttoned his shirt one button at a time, stopping to kiss and lick her way down his chest.

"Amazing," Cristoval said, a smile gracing his face. "She feels almost like you, my dear. Quite an accomplishment."

Samantha felt a surge of power, using her control to manipulate Melissa as though she were a doll. Through the link, she felt everything Melissa felt, as though she were running her hands over Cristoval's chest, thrusting her breasts at him, begging him to touch her.

Somewhere inside, Maude cried out in pain.

Samantha broke the link, withdrawing quickly. Melissa's hands faltered, gazing up at Cristoval as though she didn't know how she'd gotten there.

"Is it always that easy?" Samantha asked.

"Only if they're befuddled or weak in some way," Cristoval said. "A strong mind is not so easily bent. How did she break the link?"

"I did," Samantha said. "She didn't want to do what she was doing."

Cristoval laughed out loud, pushing a confused Melissa out of his way as he stood up. "You have far too much compassion for the sheep, my love," he said. "They are food. They are playthings. Don't confuse them with Chosen Ones."

"Isn't that what they say about us?" Samantha asked.

Cristoval shook his head. "You are but young," he replied. "You will understand someday."

Samantha looked over at Melissa, torn. Then she felt Cristoval sliding into her mind again. She was part of the kiss, and he needed no eye contact to be inside her consciousness. He slid into her as easily as he moved within her body when they made love. But inside her mind, he gave her images, feelings, the sensation of true ecstasy, the raw surge of power over the kiss, stimulating her from within until she cried out and reached for him.

But somewhere inside, Samantha wept.

* * * * *

10:22 p.m.

The door swung open and Fiona glided in. Tonight's gown was black velvet, unusually dark for her. "Got a repeater for you, Samantha," she said, checking her clipboard.

Samantha sighed, rising up from the greenroom couch.

"Duty calls," Andi said. "Sure you don't need any help?"

"You shush," Fiona said.

Samantha straightened her hair and walked down to room four. It was a busy night at Nocturnal Urges with some vocal enthusiasm behind several of the doors. She slipped through the door, around the pillar and approached the bed.

"My name is Miranda," she said, pitching her voice low.

"I remember," Robert Carton said. He sat on the bed, sitting upright with the sheet pooled around his waist.

Samantha froze. "I am flattered that you have returned so soon," she murmured, falling back on her training. "But I fear it is far too soon. You must wait two weeks to regain your strength."

Carton smiled. "Nice try, Miranda," he said. "We both know you barely took any the other night."

Samantha sidled around the bed, keeping up the act while her mind raced. "You are experienced in the ways of the dark ones," she said, going for sultry and mysterious while she tried to think of a way out of this room.

"Come here," Carton said, reaching for her hand.

Samantha allowed him to draw her onto the bed, facing him on her knees.

"Give me what I want, Miranda," Carton whispered, reaching for her.

"I can't," she whispered. "It's wrong."

Carton laughed out loud. "Wrong game, lovely miss," he said. "I didn't sign up for this show."

Samantha shook her head. "If you keep this up, you'll be caught, Councilman," she said.

Carton froze. Then he grabbed her by the hair and pulled her face into the light. "Who are you?" he demanded.

"It doesn't matter," Samantha said, her heart racing. "But if I recognize you, others will too. You must stop coming here."

Carton's face was filled with panic, but he was very close to her skin. She had stilled the power so as to not inflame him further, but he refused to let her go. He pressed his face into the silken curtain of her hair. "One last bite then," he said. "One more, and I swear I'll never return."

"I shouldn't," Samantha protested.

"Please," Carton said. "I'll never return."

Samantha pulled back and stared into his eyes. She dove into his mind, skating through nervousness and a high-strung panic over the campaign and the threats against his staff, confusion about his work and a quiet loneliness that made her feel pity for him. Beneath it was the hunger, the driving lust that brought him here, that had brought him to vampires again and again, a need so great it made him shake.

She guarded her thoughts, leaving him with only the river flowing through his mind. Then she dipped her head to his shoulder, away from the collarbone, and struck. As before, she took only a little blood, swallowing its rich warmth as the pleasure welled up and burst inside him, clutching her hair and drawing her closer to him against his chest.

Carton sagged back against the mound of pillows, drawing her with him. Samantha carefully licked the wound clean, but in her heart a terrible sadness and apprehension grew. Somehow it seemed so wrong, in a way it hadn't the other night. She lifted her head and wiped her lip clean of his blood. As she broke the link, she sensed the peace filling him.

At that moment, the door burst open, letting in a cacophony of pounding music from the club's dance floor. Through the open door, Samantha caught a glimpse of gyrating humans under the black-iron chandeliers as the house band Creatures of the Night rolled on. But she recoiled back in an instant as Meredith Schwartz charged into the room, stopping just a few steps past the door.

"Oh, my God," Meredith whispered.

Samantha sat in the middle of the bed, frozen. Carton scrambled for a shirt to cover his bare chest and the fresh bite on his shoulder. "Meredith, what the hell are you doing?"

"I thought I was wrong. I hoped I was wrong," Meredith said, her voice stunned and bleak. "That you could come here, to… Oh, God."

A huge form appeared in the doorway. Brent, the vampire bouncer for Nocturnal Urges, charged in and grabbed Meredith's arm.

"Brent, it's okay," Samantha said, rising from the bed.

"The hell it is," Brent replied.

Samantha crossed over to him. "Special case, Brent. I'll take responsibility. Just give them a minute."

Brent glanced over at Meredith and Robert Carton. "Okay, but you get to explain to Miss Fiona," he said, and left the room.

"Explain," Meredith said bitterly. "Today we stood in front of this building and condemned it. Now you sneak off to get your jollies with these…"

"Hey," Samantha said.

Meredith stared at her. "I know you," she said. "That girl at the… Oh, my God, Robert, you've got your vampire mistress working at the campaign?"

"What?" Carton said, nonplussed. "I don't…"

Samantha sighed. "Meredith, it's not—"

"What it seems?" Meredith fairly shouted. Her calm demeanor had completely shattered, her lovely face crumpling. "Of course, it is! I left a good job to guide the campaign of a man I believed in, causes I felt were just! What did I do that for, Robert? Why did I follow you? So you could stand for truth and justice by day and get suckjobs by night?"

"Meredith, please calm down," Carton said, still scrambling around for his shirt.

"I tell the truth, first and foremost," Meredith said, her voice breaking. "You made me into a liar, Robert."

Carton reached out for her arm, and Meredith jerked it away. "Don't touch me," she snapped. "Don't ever touch me again."

Meredith turned and ran from the room. Carton stood frozen. Samantha lowered her head, her stomach roiling. "You should go after her," she said. "Talk to her before she does something you'll both regret."

"Do you really work for the campaign?" Carton said.

Samantha blinked. "I volunteer," she said. "Please, don't tell them. I didn't mean any harm. I wanted to be part of something. I wanted to do something that mattered."

Carton stared at her for one long moment, and his face reflected her own fear and sadness. "Me too," he said, and followed Meredith out the door.

12:12 a.m.

Fradella sipped from his third cup of coffee. This late at night, he'd be up for hours, Freitas thought.

"This is one fucked-up situation, Detectives," he said.

"Shh." Freitas indicated the couch. Parker had drifted off to sleep as Freitas had talked, her face pale and looking younger by the moment. Fradella cocked his head toward the balcony door and they stepped out into the cool night air for a moment.

"What exactly do you propose?" Fradella asked. "Ignore this Diego guy and maybe he'll go away?"

"Two days," Freitas said. "Give me and Sleeping Beauty in there two days to find out what we're dealing with. The vamp world has its own way of dealing with rogues. Give them a chance before we tear the city apart."

"Do you think there's any connection between the rogue kiss and the threats against the campaign?" Fradella sipped his coffee.

Freitas thought before she answered. "No," she said. "Doesn't jibe with what Parker says. This guy's nuts but he's not that brand of nuts."

"So just your garden-variety homicidal maniac running amok in my town, and you want to face him down with the kid?"

Freitas shrugged. "Well, when you put it that way…"

"Dammit, Annie," Fradella began.

"You're not supposed to call me Annie anymore," she said stolidly.

"Right," Fradella said, staring out at the faint glimmers of stars above the Memphis city lights. "And what if I don't like that arrangement?"

"Tough," Freitas said, but her voice was quiet, almost sad.

Fradella seemed about to say something else, but Freitas' pager went off. "Shit," she said, checking it. "I'm not catching."

"I'll tell them to find someone else," Fradella said,

stepping back inside for his phone. "Don't worry, I won't tell them you're here. I'll just say you called me or some such bullshit."

Freitas shot him a look, then went over to the couch and shook Parker's shoulder while Fradella talked to the desk sergeant. "Hey, sleepyhead," she said. "C'mon, I'm taking you home."

"Got work to do," Parker said sleepily, struggling to sit up.

"You've got the brains of a lobotomized flea, you know that?" Freitas said. "Get some rest tonight and tomorrow you'll be ready to face down the bad guys."

"Sorry, Detectives, you're working," Fradella said, hanging up the phone. "You'll never guess what just came in."

12:35 a.m.

Samantha walked along the street, her shoes clicking on the sidewalk. She didn't know why she'd taken the Midtown bus instead of walking one block up the alley to her hotel. Somehow, she just didn't want to go home.

She should have been exhausted. The day had been unbelievably long. She should be collapsing with mental and physical overload. But, somehow, there was a budding joy inside her, the sense that somewhere, someone was thinking of her. Someone's heart was filled with her, as her heart was filled with him.

Samantha stood across the street from the campaign office. Its windows were dark and empty. It was the middle of the night, after all.

She kept walking, passing bookstores and restaurants and the ice cream parlor where she and Danny had talked, now dark and cold. The streets of Memphis were never exactly empty, but in the wee hours of the morning, they were quiet with only the occasional passing car.

Up ahead, the waning lights of the business district gave way to houses, set back behind hedges and fences constructed to block the busy street from the high-rent homes. The shadows of older trees fell across her as she walked beneath them.

Behind her, a car pulled over to a stop. She started, imagining Diego breaking his word to come after her.

"Hey, miss, need a ride?" came Danny's amused voice.

Samantha turned, smiling. "How did you just happen to be here?"

"I was going to say the same thing," Danny said, climbing out of his car door. "I was just driving around, trying to think."

"Me too," Samantha said. "But you shouldn't be running around alone after dark."

"You either," Danny returned.

Samantha shrugged. "I can take care of myself."

Danny came around the car and opened the passenger door. "Your chariot, milady," he said with an exaggerated bow.

Samantha giggled and slipped into the car. He closed the door, came around and started driving again.

"So what were you thinking about?" Samantha asked.

"You," Danny said, his honest smile causing little flip-flops in her stomach.

"I'm not that interesting," Samantha said.

Danny laughed. "Sure," he said. "You're more than a hundred years old. I try to imagine the things you've seen, the history you've experienced and I'm overwhelmed by it."

"It's not that much," Samantha said.

Danny reached over and held her hand in his. The feel of his hand sent shivers through her in a way no one's touch ever had—not Todd's, not Cristoval's. He squeezed it gently, an expression of support and comfort. Then his fingers began to stroke the back of her hand, tantalizing the tender skin with featherlight touches. Goose bumps rose on her arm as he lightly teased the thin web of flesh between her index and middle fingers, pressing it as though he pressed inside her.

"Wow," she said, instantly feeling silly. Yet the feelings he created in her didn't feel silly at all—they surged deep within her, a tumult of heat and ache that was nearly painful between her legs, and she shifted in her seat, suddenly uncomfortable.

"Samantha," Danny said, his voice hesitant.

"Yes," she said, ignoring the surge of nervousness that welled up inside her, warring with the excited heat the continued caress of his hand gave her.

Danny made a left turn, hard enough that centrifugal force pressed her for a moment against the door. She laughed, nervous and excited at the same time. "Don't kill us," she said, giggling.

Danny drove a little more carefully up the narrow side street flanked with small, older houses. "Sorry," he said.

Samantha reached out this time, laying her hand gently against his thigh. Danny swerved for a second, and she giggled again. She seemed helpless to stop giggling, as though everything were wonderful and silly and magical all at once.

"Just don't get too creative over there," Danny said, his voice a little rougher.

Samantha didn't move her hand. She just let it lie against the warm strength of his leg, with a low current of power running through her to him. It grew slowly, like the sun's rays warming the earth, as the power sank through her arm and into him. She felt him harden beneath the denim, and slid her hand a little higher to touch him with just a bit of power. Danny's breathing was coming a little harder now, and he brought the car to a stop in front of a small brick house.

"Where are we?" she asked.

"My house," Danny said, turning to face her. His eyes were full of questions, and Samantha leaned forward to answer them.

Her lips pressed against his with a gentle intensity she had not known before. It was as though he had the power, letting his own electric warmth sink into her through the sliding motion of tongues, the dance of lips and teeth, careful to keep away from her sharp incisors. Danny's hand cradled under her chin, and she felt it as strongly as if he had the power to stimulate her nerve endings, to make her glow with his warmth. Her very skin tingled with the penetration of his tongue, sliding in the moist warmth of her mouth.

Then Danny broke the kiss, and she felt suddenly bereft, empty, as though the brief interruption of touch were too much to handle. He got out of the car, catching his foot a bit on the doorframe. She giggled and got out, still smiling. There he stood in the circle of streetlights, as though all the lights on the street encircled his head in a glowing halo. She knew his heart in a way humans never know each other, knew his innate kindness and love waiting to be shown. She knew he would never harm her, and she wanted only to protect him and keep him from the ugliness that lay in the shadows.

She went to him then, and he took her hand in his to lead her up the steps. There were no flowers along the walkway, but the hedges were well-trimmed. He unlocked the door and led her into a darkened foyer, dropping his keys in a ceramic dish on a short table.

Suddenly uncertain, he stood in the shadows as she hovered in the doorway. "I, uh, invite you in," he said.

Samantha burst out laughing. "Not necessary, but thank you," she said, following him into the house.

"Another movie myth shattered," Danny said, smiling.

Samantha let the front door close. She still felt that strange nervousness, a sense of unreality pervading the entire moment. It wasn't like the tricks at the club, or like it had been with Cristoval or even Todd. It was as though she were a young human woman again, untouched and pure, waiting for her bridegroom to take her.

Danny started to reach for the light switch, but Samantha reached out to stop him. Her hand touched his arm and the power suddenly shot out of control, a flash of tingling pleasure that rocketed through her into him, staggering him a bit on his feet. The ache wasn't just inside her anymore — it was everywhere, all through her, wanting him with an intensity she had never felt.

She didn't want to wait any longer. She stepped into his arms, pulling him down toward her. His taut muscles, slim and strong beneath his shirt, pressed warm against her chest, and she felt him press hard against the softness of her stomach. She felt his hands clasp at the small of her back, drawing her close. In his eagerness, he slid his hand inside her shirt, running his hands over the smooth skin of her back. She kissed along his jaw to lick gently at his ear, then down to his neck to where the pulse beat faster beneath the skin. She could smell his desire, nearly taste it in the blood moving just beyond her reach, and she fought with herself to keep from tasting him. Just a little, so hot and flavorful, so close…

Suddenly Danny stiffened, and Samantha pulled back. "I'm sorry," he said immediately. "I just, I wasn't…"

"It's okay," Samantha said. "I don't bite unless asked."

Danny seemed to relax again, but Samantha felt the

hunger rising up like a traitorous beast within her. His neck was very close and he smelled like food. It was the sudden jolt of adrenaline that made him smell so good, the fear that made her want to do more than feel him. She wanted to taste him, to roll his blood in her mouth and drink him down.

Resolutely she quashed the hunger, shoving it back inside the mental cage in which she kept it imprisoned, ashamed of herself. Instead, she thought about the feel of his hands on her bare skin, and what his whole body would feel like against hers. She nestled close to him, gentling his muscles with smooth strokes of her hands over his clothes.

Danny still seemed tense, despite her calming efforts. "What's wrong?" she whispered, almost afraid to hear the answer. *Gee, maybe the idea that your lover thinks of you as a bedtime snack is a turnoff,* she thought.

"It's stupid," Danny said.

Samantha smiled, being sure to hide her fangs this time. "Tell me."

"Well, you're…a bit older than me," Danny said hesitantly. "And you must have…you know, been with…"

"With…who?" Samantha asked, quashing the image that rose to her mind.

"Vampires," Danny said. "They're supposed to be…impressive."

Samantha giggled again, and then the giggles turned to real laughter and she kissed Danny with all her heart. "Don't believe everything you read," she said, still smiling.

Danny smiled, but she could still see the uncertainty in his eyes. "What could I give you that you haven't had?" he murmured.

Samantha's giggles softened and she stroked the tawny hair away from his dear, kind face. His eyes met hers, those warm eyes so full of life and love, not just for her, but for life itself. "You," she said. "I've never been with anyone like you."

She reached up and pulled him back to her, and this time he met her with equal abandon, clutching her close to him and burying his hands in her hair. The smell of his passion struck her, and the ache grew to an almost unbearable level, pervading her entire body. He moved forward with her, toward the stairwell behind them, and pressed her down onto it. The stair risers pressed against her back as he lowered himself against her, sliding his still clothed body against hers in a gentle but insistent motion. He rocked against her, his weight pinning her beneath him.

His hands slid upward from her waist, up her sides to cup her breasts in his warm, strong hands. Samantha arched her back into him, sudden cascades of sensation tingling outward from her heart to her breasts, stimulated by the gliding motions of his hands over her. Danny pulled at her tank top and she obliged, helping him pull it over her head, vanishing into the shadows of the foyer below. The cool wash of air touched her bare skin, gentle washes over her in the places where he wasn't pressed against her.

His fingers skated over the smooth alabaster skin of her breasts—half covered by a thin, lacy bra—and lightly tweaked the nipples to make them stand out, hard and sensitive beneath the fabric. The sensation speared through her torso and she shifted beneath him, suddenly eager and aching.

Samantha reached upward, grasping for him. Danny lowered his head to her breasts, flicking his tongue between them for a hot jolt of electricity before capturing a nipple in his mouth, rolling it and rubbing his tongue across it over the lace. He sucked her nipple between his teeth—lace and all— and she wound her fingers into his hair, holding his head to her breast, keeping him prisoner against her with her firm strength. When his mouth moved, she begged him with her body to keep touching her, keep the flame flickering beneath her skin, keep her warm against the cool night. He devoured her breast, taking more and more of her into his mouth. He flicked his tongue inside the lace, freeing the rock-hard nipple to his greedy mouth. He sucked harder, kneading her breast with his fingers, and she cried out in a hoarse voice at the heat flowing freely beneath her skin.

Danny shifted again, sliding his groin up between her legs in a gentle rocking motion that sent heat flaring up through her body. "Danny," she breathed, pulling him closer to herself, as though she could sink her body into his — as she wanted him to sink into her. The ache was strong and painful now. She pushed herself up against him in a rhythmic motion, rubbing her clit against the rough denim of his jeans, with bursts of sensation ripping through her. He shoved hard against her, as if trying to push inside her through the fabric, and she dug her nails into his shoulders in sudden passion.

"Upstairs," Danny murmured urgently.

Samantha ran her arms over his shoulders, banded with light muscles beneath his thin cotton T-shirt and warm, so warm against her cool, bare skin. "I'm not sure I can walk," she whispered, only half joking. Her hands trembled and her muscles leaped in places she didn't know she had.

It was Danny's turn to laugh. He supported her in his arms, his strong hands keeping her centered against him as he half walked, half carried her up the stairs. She barely noticed the hallway before he pulled her into the bedroom, all shadows and darkness, and a large mirror over a low wooden dresser before the bed.

Danny pressed her down onto the bed and Samantha pulled at his shirt. "No fair," she said, tugging at the cloth.

Danny smiled and raised his arms, pulling the shirt off and letting it vanish to the floor. He was wonderful, and not in the ways she expected—not as muscled and firm as Todd, not as lithe and graceful as Cristoval, but something in the way she felt for him colored her view of his bare torso, making him more delectable and attractive than any man she had ever seen. She dipped her head down his chest, licking along the centerline, before she found a flat nipple and teased it into life. His fingers kneaded her scalp, entwining within her hair, as she gently sucked his nipple, smoothing her hands over his skin with the power flowing freely between them.

His hands swept over her body again, inflaming her skin as though her blood could still pump beneath the surface. His hands moved down along the length of her thighs, gripping her tightly against him. He pushed between her legs, and the sudden excitement flared through her with nearly painful strength. She could smell her own scent now, the smell of lust and excitement, musky and strong in the dark bedroom.

She helped as much as she could, raising herself to him and letting her jeans and panties vanish into the darkness. The cool air drifted over her body again, this time touching her along the insides of her thighs where he hovered over her.

Samantha reached for Danny's belt buckle, grasping with an eagerness she could scarcely believe. But he shoved against her again, the rough denim abrading her sensitive skin and making her cry out beneath him. "Danny," she breathed, and his fingers found her breasts, reducing her to gasps and cries as he rubbed against her and over her, raising the tension within her to an almost unbearable level. He tweaked both nipples as he rocked between her thighs, and the words kept breaking as she tried to plead with him.

"Danny, please," she nearly begged, grabbing for his belt buckle again. His own hands shook as he undid the clasp, and she pulled the belt free, dropping it on the bed. She unbuttoned his jeans and he let them fall, kicking them away into the shadows. He pressed against her full and hot and close, so close she could barely stand the roiling pressure within her body. She could feel him pressing against her, shooting new sensations through her body.

She looked up at him, and his eyes were focused on her and only her. There was more than passion in his eyes, more than the heat and driving need that pressed between her thighs.

"Samantha," he murmured, and lowered himself to kiss her. Gently, his mouth moved over hers, his tongue sliding into her mouth. She welcomed his tongue, the gliding motion of his mouth against hers, drinking his passion like blood. She slid her legs up his sides, drawing him against her.

Still he did not enter her. She reached down to urge him on, wrapping her hand around him, feeling him swell and pulse beneath her hand. She traced downward to the heavy sac beneath, teasing it with fingertips, feeling him swell and pulse beneath her hand.

She felt him slip down, so close, and still he waited, teasing her with gentle motion that drove the frenzy within her to its breaking point.

"Danny!" she pleaded, and he pushed himself into her. He had to work his way into her, almost too large for her and pressing against her on all sides. He filled her, and she could not help but groan in pleasure as he moved slowly, so slowly, within her. The heat did not lessen, but grew outward and flowed through her, driving her onward with a frenzy she could not control.

He murmured something against her neck, sliding with agonizing restraint as she urged him on with her hips and the driving fury in her blood.

"My God," Danny said, and she looked up at him. He was staring at the mirror above the vanity. Danny was alone in the mirror, his body bent over nothing at all, a mere impression in the coverlet. Slowly, he drew out of her.

Samantha moved backward, sitting up before him. "I'm here," she whispered.

Danny walked around the bed to the mirror, standing nude before it, glancing back at the room, to Samantha kneeling in the middle of the bed—and he didn't need to worry about being "impressive", Samantha thought with another roil of eagerness. She slid off the bed to stand beside him, pressing her body against his, feeling him hard and eager against the curve of her stomach.

Danny looked down at her, his hand rising to stroke the silken skin of her breasts again, drawing her closer and feeling her as though testing the pliability of her skin. He moved behind her, turning her to face the mirror. In its reflection, she saw only him, naked and rampant before the bed.

Behind her, she felt him stroke her body with long, gentle sliding motions, up and down her sides and over the flat plane of her stomach, the curve of her hip, the tender skin of her thigh, the swell of her breast still encased in the bra. He pressed hard against her ass from behind her, but when she looked in the mirror, she saw only him, touching the air. It was a strange vertigo, watching him touching nothing while feeling his hands on her, inflaming her in broad, sweeping caresses over her body. His fingers slid downward again, slipping between her thighs to touch her clit ever so softly, in a rubbing motion that made her groan and lean back against him, suddenly dizzy. His fingers circled it over and over, a rhythmic friction that sent sensations shooting through her.

"Samantha," he murmured, lowering his mouth to her shoulder blade and kissing lightly toward her spine. Tingling shivers shot down the long muscles of her back and she arched forward, bracing herself on the dresser. His warm hands slid around her waist, sliding down over the tops of her thighs and parting them with a gentle, insistent force that reminded her of his strength.

Behind her, she felt him lower between her thighs, pressing against her. She clutched the edge of the dresser as his hands drifted back up to her breasts for a moment, tweaking the nipples one more time before he settled his hands on her hips, bracing her.

He slid upward slowly, so slowly she nearly begged him aloud to fill her, make her whole again. His breathing was harsh and jagged, his hands clutching into the soft skin of her hips. She glanced back up at the mirror and saw only him, his head thrown back in pleasure, before he withdrew and plunged forward again.

She cried out in earnest this time, braced against the dresser, feeling him press into her slowly. He filled her again and again, gliding into her more easily now, but holding back, seemingly afraid he would break her. The tension built within her, a delicious and frustrating pleasure that hovered within her skin, crying out for more. He reached places inside her that made her cry out for more, always more, but he was so slow and smooth, teasing her from the inside out.

When he slid out again, Samantha let go of the dresser and turned to him. His eyes were hard and glittering, filled with the heat and wanton strength that comes from something entirely animal and instinctive and sexual and male. She pushed him back onto the bed, and he slid backward to give her room.

She crawled above him on all fours, and he tore at her bra, his trembling fingers mangling the clasp as it released her breasts into his grasping hands. He raised his head to suck on them and she threw back her head, moaning aloud with her own instinctive passion. She reached down and found him still warm from her, stroking him with her hand.

She let the power flow from her hand into him with full force, and he gasped against her breast, suddenly wordless. She moved her hand up and down, repeating his rhythm when he had touched her, but with the power flowing into him. Her hand rose and fell with a quickening beat. Danny's hands clenched on the coverlet, his head thrown back in gasps.

Then Samantha backed off, letting him regain his composure for a bare moment. She slid her legs down, gripping him with her thigh muscles, and settled on him. For a moment, she simply leaned back, rocked upright on him, letting him penetrate into her as deeply as he could go. She leaned forward and pressed her breasts against him, clasping his hips with her thighs and moving back and forth above him. He thrust upward, and it was all she could do not to sink teeth into him, to draw his blood into her mouth as he slid inside her.

They rode together, finding the rhythm between their bodies that seemed to match. Her hands roved over his chest, flowing power to him as he filled her deep within, sliding against her inner walls with a glorious friction that continued to grow. Samantha met each of Danny's thrusts with one of her own, pressing and releasing, riding over and over as their breaths began to come in shorter bursts, still together. She wound her fingers in his, clutching tightly to him, and their eyes met.

Without meaning to, she rolled him, sinking into his mind as he thrust into her body. She felt a sudden sliding pleasure, felt what she must feel like to him and opened her own mind to him so he could feel her as well. She felt his roiling emotions and driving lust, and wanted to sink her whole body into him, be one person, entirely joined in every way.

I was wrong, she thought. *This is truly what it means to be one.*

She felt his pleasure rising, so close, and gripped him more urgently as his hands tightened hard in hers and his voice broke beneath her, wordless cries of hoarse pleasure. He erupted within her, and she felt his mind blank under a white void of exploding joy and shuddering delight. She felt it, rode it hard and drank it into her mind and body like blood flowing from his veins. It was a mental pleasure, filling her with joy and satisfaction.

He slowed beneath her, but he did not withdraw. *You're not done,* he thought through their mental link.

He was still hard and strong, and he moved ever so gently within her. He pressed against her and relaxed in a slow motion, seeming to find just the right place to send a bolt of pleasure through her. She slid her hands against the sides of his head, kissing him gently as he moved within her, softer now, but still sliding inside her in a delicious friction that grew — warm and wet and full of life. She felt it rise within her, felt the joy she had experienced vicariously from so many others, felt it burning within her and rising up, faster and stronger. Through the link, he seemed to know exactly what to do, how to move, his hands gliding over the sensitive nubs of her nipples.

It suddenly began to bloom within her, and sensing it, he thrust upward hard and fast. It jolted her into a climax that shot outward through her body, head thrown back and voice crying out, his hands roaming over her and his own voice matching her cries as he felt her contract around him, shuddering as tears filled her eyes.

"Wow," he murmured, stroking her face as he gently withdrew from her. She remained on top of him for a moment, and he kissed her softly.

Then she slid to his side, and he drew her against him. The cool air from the vent washed over their bodies, and

Samantha laid her head on his shoulder. Danny's arm around her seemed the strongest comfort she had ever known, his embrace a safe haven she had never even imagined. He kept stroking her hair and kissing her forehead—unable to stop touching and caressing her even as the splendid pleasure ebbed. She was about to break the link but, on impulse, she let it fade to a gossamer thread, a connection that continued to pulse quietly between them. He stroked her bare arm as it lay across her chest.

There was an energy between them, something that felt like the power she could generate with her hand, but not quite the same. It wasn't like the power Cristoval had exercised over her, because Danny didn't take her over or control her in any way. Nor did she control him, as some vampires could do with their human companions. It was more like the energy was borne of the two of them together, forged somewhere halfway between his heart and hers, something they shared interlocked and impossible to sever.

When the panic struck him, she felt it a second before he jerked upright. "Oh, my God," he said.

"It's okay," she soothed.

"We didn't use anything, I didn't even think…" Danny said.

Samantha smiled. "You don't have to, not with me," she said. "I can't carry disease, I can't get pregnant. It's okay. Lie down."

Danny relaxed, lying back down on his side, facing her. "I forgot, I'm sorry," he said. "I think I read that somewhere, but I didn't connect… I don't usually… I mean, I never…"

"That was absolutely not your first time," Samantha teased.

Danny grinned. "No," he said. "But it was my first time with you."

She kissed him, gently and thoroughly. He leaned his head back against the pillow, his hand wandering over her cool skin like a warm ember against her. "You said, 'I don't usually…'" Samantha said. "You don't usually what?"

"Take beautiful women into my bed on short notice," Danny said, smiling.

"You usually prefer an appointment?" Samantha returned.

"Well, I have to warn the rest of my harem, just to be a gentleman," Danny said.

Samantha tickled the spot right under his belly button, making his whole body jump.

"Hey, no fair!" Danny said. "How'd you know—"

Samantha ducked her head down and gently tugged at a flat nipple, catching it between her lips and rolling her tongue over it.

"Whoa," Danny said, his voice a little rougher. "A few more minutes and that sort of thing could get you into trouble."

Samantha snickered. "I like trouble," she said, grinning.

Danny reached his hand toward her face, touching it gently, seeming to explore the contours and planes of her face with his fingertips. He slipped a finger into her mouth, lightly touching one of her fangs, almost testing it.

Samantha slid her tongue along his finger, drawing it into her mouth between her fangs. She danced her tongue against the sensitive web between his fingers, and increased the pressure to suck on his finger more tightly. She tasted herself and smelled his lust rising up again.

Danny exhaled.

Slowly, Samantha let his finger go, running her hands over his chest with a light, dextrous touch. "Danny, do you want me to…"

Danny slid his own hand against the curve of her breast, and Samantha lost her words for a moment. "Yes?" he asked, molding her soft flesh against his palm.

"Oh, now you're getting in trouble," she breathed, shifting her hips. Suddenly it was warmer in the room.

Danny lowered his head to her breast, catching her nipple between his flat, even teeth and teasing it with ever-so-soft nibbles that never came close to breaking skin. Samantha felt a sudden release that had nothing to do with the surging feeling he created in her skin and everything to do with the sure knowledge that Danny would never turn to her with a snarl, never sink his teeth into her, never twist her arm or breast to hurt her and watch her beg for release. She felt utterly safe entwined with him, knowing his touch would bring only pleasure, not pain.

"Danny," she murmured, drawing his head away from her breast with a twinge of regret. "Do you want me to give you the bite?"

His eyes were suddenly confused, and she felt a swirl of conflicting emotions in him. Fear and uncertainty damped his growing passion, and overriding it all was a concern for what she would feel when he said…

"No," she answered for him. "You'd rather I didn't."

His face was filled with worry, entirely about her, about hurting her feelings. It made her want to kiss him again. "Not yet," he said. "I'm…not quite ready for that. It's not that I don't trust you, it's—"

"It's all right," Samantha reassured him. "The bite is something very different, something you haven't done before. It is a special bond between human and vampire, and one I'd like to share with you. When you're comfortable, we can give it a try. Until then—" she slid her hand down his side, onto his thigh, teasing him by dancing her hand everywhere but where he wanted her to touch him "—we can play," she whispered.

Danny pushed his leg between her thighs, raising it up until it rocked against her, warm and strong. She tightened her thighs around his leg, rolling her hips against him as she took hold of him in her hand, letting the power seep through. His whole body jerked, his hands clutching her closer to him as a few sounds escaped him.

Then Samantha rolled away, playfully wrapping herself in a sheet. Danny groaned and reached toward her. "No fair, no fair!" he cried.

Samantha stuck out her tongue at him and scampered toward the foot of the bed, just out of reach. Danny buried his face in the pillow and moaned. "Devil woman!" he complained.

Samantha reached out and tickled the underside of his foot, and he jerked it away, exploding out of the covers toward her. "Come here!" he said, and she jumped off the bed onto the floor, crawling around to the other side, giggling.

Danny reached down toward her, and Samantha darted back the other way, vampire reflexes keeping her just a second ahead of him. She popped up on the other side of the bed, and when he lunged toward her, she dropped back down and scampered to the other side. His growls of frustration made her giggle, and a second later something looped around her waist and physically hauled her back up onto the bed in a tangle of sheets. It was his discarded belt, now wrapped around her waist with the end looped around his hand.

"Stay," he said.

Samantha giggled again. "I'm really bad with taking orders," she said, and tried to squirm away. Danny grabbed hold of the sheet entwined around her and hauled her back beneath him, cinching the belt tighter around her waist. He lowered his mouth onto hers. Warm and full, his tongue slid against hers and she wrapped her arms around his shoulders, pulling him closer. She tried to free herself of the tangle of sheets, but he mistook her movements for another attempt at silliness and wound the belt more tightly in his hand, rendering her immobile beneath him.

"Stay," he repeated in a lower voice, and she pressed her hips against him through the sheet that entwined her legs.

"Okay," she murmured.

"Will you behave?" he grinned.

Samantha slid her hand over his backside, down his hip and took him in her hand. "Never," she said softly, caressing him. He was hard again, hot and urgent within her hand.

Danny closed his eyes, his whole body shuddering. Then he was the one pulling at the sheets, trying to free her legs.

"Forget it," she whispered, and Danny gave up on the sheets and slid between her legs, up into her in one powerful thrust. Her voice made sounds with no words in them, crying out against his shoulder, her legs struggling against the twined sheets that held her immobile as he pushed within her.

Danny's hands were clenched tight—one on the belt and the other on the pillow beside her head. He thrust into her over and over, his eyes closed, but the sensations ripping through him soared through the link into her, and she fed him as well in a building whirlpool of pleasure. The bed seemed to rotate in the room, the very moonlight streaming through the window seemed to swirl around them.

Her breath caught in her chest as she urged him onward, straining against the pressure of the belt around her waist, her hands moving helplessly up and down his flexing back. The sheet and belt tied her down, kept her trapped beneath him as though he had complete control of her body. He quickened the pace, thrusting harder, his heart hammering inside his chest with a power she could feel through his skin and through the link, as though her own heart were beating again with the power of his. It was fierce, relentless and animalistic, with an intensity even the last time had lacked.

Danny's face was suddenly directly above hers, his eyes boring into hers with fiery intensity. It was as though he rolled her—impossible as that could be—sinking his mind and heart and soul into her as deeply as he sank his body into her. She met his gaze with her own strength, her own passion. Somewhere inside a part of her cried out to keep something separate, keep something to herself, or he would end up possessing all of her.

But then his mouth pressed down on hers as he bucked twice more into her, a shuddering explosion ripping through him that made him cry out in a hoarse voice against her mouth. As he burst through her, she felt the wave begin inside her, rolling outward and washing over her in a sudden white void of thought and feeling, tying her more tightly than the belt and sheets that still bound her down, filling and consuming her completely and binding her to the man still inside her, the man to whom she cried out, a tear escaping her eye as the wave ebbed and came again, almost too much to bear. He stayed within her, feeling what she felt, until his clenched muscles finally relaxed and he sagged onto her.

Samantha slid her arms up around him, stroking his hair as he rested his head on her breast, almost in comfort. She felt him grow soft and withdraw, yet he remained on top of her, warm and heavy and slightly out of breath.

"Beloved," she whispered, too softly for him to hear.

12:59 a.m.

"Oh, bloody hell," Freitas said, shining her flashlight around the alley.

Fradella wasn't far away. He was only over by the

corner, under the streetlights, talking to the uniforms who had responded to the scene. Somehow, it was both comforting and unnerving that he was there. It had been many years since she and Fradella had done a late-night crime scene, Freitas thought.

The car was startlingly clean, a glistening pattern of dew forming on its green hood in the cooling night air. Shining her flashlight around it, Freitas saw no marks whatsoever, save for a tiny dimple on the passenger front door that had been painstakingly repainted and sealed. The interior was thankfully dark.

Parker was talking to the vampires crowded by the back door of Nocturnal Urges. Tall and short, slim and voluptuous, they suited every fantasy in their dark-pale beauty. Most were still dressed for work, in various stages of gothic dress, tightly bound lingerie or black leather. Freitas could not hear what they were saying, but their blank faces and Parker's annoyed body language already told her they had seen nothing, heard nothing, knew nothing.

A strident voice cut through from behind the vampires and they parted as though a physical force propelled them. Fiona strode out into the alley, Brent the bouncer hovering behind her like the great monolith he was.

"No, not again, I will not go through this again!" Fiona shouted, pointing at Freitas and the green car under the streetlight.

Fradella was already walking to intercept her. Freitas was too tired and cranky to take Fiona's bitchery tonight. "Not everything is about you, Fiona," she snapped.

Fiona glared at her.

"Ms. Knight, no one is suggesting that this had anything to do with your club," Fradella said in his best calm-the-civilians tone. "We just need to know if anyone saw anything tonight."

"No one saw anything," Fiona said imperiously. "Lieutenant, I'm sure you're well aware of the hits my club took in the press after last year's...unfortunate occurrences."

"Unfortunate?" Freitas said, incredulous. "One of your employees went nuts and started killing the patrons."

"We've tightened our hiring practices since then," Fiona replied.

The sheer absurdity of it washed over Freitas and she laughed, a tired, humorless sound that caught her a look from Fradella. Her laughter dried up fast, however, when she saw Brent's face.

He was staring into the car as the crime-scene photographers' flashbulbs briefly lit the interior, a frozen look of recognition on his bland face.

"Brent?" Freitas said. "What do you see?"

"He sees nothing," Fiona said.

"Fiona, with all due respect, shut up," Freitas said. "Talk to me, Brent."

"Nothing," Brent whispered, still staring at the car.

Fradella glared at Fiona. "Ms. Knight, you will order your people to cooperate fully or you will see the full weight of my department on your establishment."

Fiona smiled, showing the full sharpness of her gleaming white fangs. "I would have weathered your grandfather's threats, Lieutenant," she said. "Do you think you can scare me?"

Fradella leveled his best cop look at her and Fiona stared right back. Meanwhile, Freitas kept her eyes on Brent. His face registered sadness and worry, a nervous tic at the corner of his eye.

"IRS," Fradella shot back.

Fiona didn't exactly flinch, but she sighed. "Talk to

them, Brent," she said, shooting a look of venom at Freitas. "Leave me out of the papers this time, Detective."

Fiona turned and swept away.

"Brent, what do you see?" Freitas said.

Brent the vampire bouncer was an unexpectedly tall man, his bulk shown through his shoulders and muscled arms. He did not exactly slouch, but something in the way he held himself made him seem smaller than his actual size. Freitas knew he had been with Fiona for decades, intimidating the unruly marks with his size and fangs. She also knew he couldn't even bring himself to bite a willing human, and had subsisted on animal blood with donated human supplements since the mid-1960s.

Brent circled slowly around the back of the car, the light mist falling on his worried face. Freitas and Fradella followed him around to the driver's side, the place where the car wasn't so clean.

Freitas shined her flashlight at the driver. The shattered window gleamed in the beam of light, its sharp edges glinting red. There was a tangle of bloodstained hair visible, however, much of the rest was hidden by the shadows.

Freitas stepped around Brent and shined the light full into Meredith Schwartz's face. Her tangled blonde hair fell away from her still face, matted with blood.

"I know her," Brent said. "She barged into one of the rooms tonight."

"Oh, shit," Freitas said. "Her name was Meredith Schwartz. That mean anything to you?"

Brent shook his head. "But the client was a newbie. Only been here a couple of times before, I think. Alone. There was shouting, but the vamp told me to leave, she'd handle it."

"Not policy, is it?" Freitas asked.

"No," Brent replied. "Miss Fiona says they can work out

their disagreements in the street. But Miranda knows how to handle herself."

Freitas glanced up at Fradella. "Who was the client?" she asked Brent.

Brent shrugged. "Like I said, a newbie."

Freitas' worried eyes focused on Fradella's. He motioned to Parker who loped over. "Take Brent's full statement," Fradella said. "Detective Freitas and I have to talk to the campaign folks."

Parker shrugged, and Fradella and Freitas strode quickly away, talking in a low voice. She turned back to interview Brent and saw that he was pale—paler than the usual vampire, at least. "You okay, buddy?"

"Could we...maybe talk somewhere else?" Brent said. "I'd rather not look at that." He pointed at Meredith's mangled face and winced as the scene photographers took another picture.

Parker led him back down the block toward the club. "Kinda squeamish for a vampire, aren't you?"

Brent didn't answer.

Parker pulled her pen back out. "Okay, walk me through it."

"The lady in the car—she came in alone," Brent said. "I was on the door, so I don't know how she got back there. But I got a radio call from Andi, one of the girls. She said a crazed woman had burst into room four. I got back there fast, and the lady..."

"Meredith Schwartz," Parker prompted.

"Her," Brent said, pointing at the car. "She was shouting something at the client, who was sitting on the bed. Something like, 'I thought I was wrong'. I went to haul her ass out of there but Miranda stopped me."

"Miranda? She new?" Parker asked.

"No, she's been around for a long time," Brent said. "She shooed me out of there, said she'd handle it. Miss Fiona tells us not to be marriage counselors, let them work it out in the street. But I trusted her judgment. Besides, like I want to get mixed up in something like that?"

"What happened next?" Parker said.

"A minute later, the lady comes out and the client follows right after. The end, right?" Brent wiped off his brow.

"Right," Parker muttered. "And Miranda?"

"She called off the rest of the night," Brent said. "Went home, I guess."

"Where does she live?" Parker asked.

Brent pointed up the alley. "That hotel on the corner, over the seafood place," he said.

Parker stared up the street. "Right past the murder scene," she muttered, as another flashbulb went off. In its glare, she saw a frightened face in a doorway. She was young, with spiky black hair and a face much too thin for her age. Parker started to walk toward her and the girl vanished, the clicking of her heels scattering unevenly into the abandoned building. "Shit! Who was that?"

"Who?" Brent said, craning his thick neck over Parker's diminutive frame.

"Girl, young, looks like street, spiky black hair, thin," Parker rattled off.

"Celia," Brent said immediately. "Human pro, works this alley. Don't bother, you won't find her. She's hidden from cops in these warehouses and alleyways since she was ten."

"That wasn't too long ago, by my measure," Parker said absently. "You see her, tell her to talk to me, okay?"

"She won't," Brent said. "She wants to be a vamp. None of the vamps will turn her, of course, but she keeps trying.

Perfect cure-all for a human hooker—live forever and never catch anything."

Parker blinked. "The vaccination—"

"You only get the shots if your parents take you to the clinics," Brent said. "There's still a few who fall through the cracks. They don't get the measles shot either."

"Unbelievable," Parker muttered, and walked toward the car. "Hey, Chapman!"

Chapman loped over to her, all lanky muscle and smiles. The smile faded when he saw the bandage on her neck. "Shit, Parker, you okay?"

Parker indicated the warehouse. "Got a search to do. You game?"

Chapman indicated the street. "Uh, don't we have plenty to do around here?"

Parker rolled her eyes. "Crime scene and forensics, they have plenty to do. We have to find some witnesses and one of them is hiding in that building."

"Then we circle it and proceed floor by floor," Chapman said.

Parker laughed humorlessly. "Brilliant. She'll vanish. Let's do this all friendly-like. Got me?"

"Aye, ma'am," Chapman said, and grinned again.

Parker stepped into the warehouse, pulling up her flashlight to eye level. Broken windows could not provide enough ventilation to make the smell of urine dissipate. The rusted skeletons of long-dead machinery cast strange shadows on the splintered wooden floor.

"Celia!" Parker called out. "It's safe to come out. We're not after you."

Nothing answered but the creaks of the building and murmured voices in the alley behind them. Chapman stood behind her, his own flashlight sweeping across the floor. Parker saw scuff marks in the thick layers of dust, and followed them as though tracking a wild animal. Chapman followed behind her, one hand resting lightly on the butt of his gun.

"Just like old times," he murmured, looking around the building. "Quiet, soft light, just the two of us."

"You're damn funny tonight," Parker replied. "If we were still partners, that could qualify as harassment."

"Now you're my boss, so I can say anything I want," Chapman said, grinning.

The scuffmarks led through the main room into a narrow hallway, its plaster walls deeply scored and cracked. Some indefinable brown material was smeared on the floor. Parker pretended not to notice.

"Remind me why you wanted the glamour of investigations," Chapman muttered.

"Shut up," Parker replied. "Celia!"

Footsteps pattered behind them and Chapman whirled back out of the hallway into the main room, his weapon drawn. "Freeze!"

"Shit, you'll scare her!" Parker shouted, scrambling after him. "Celia, it's okay!"

"Fuck you!" came a thin voice from somewhere in the shadows.

Parker swept the room with her flashlight. The eldritch shapes of the rusted machinery made it impossible to see anything clearly. "Chapman, freeze," she said.

"What?" he asked.

"We're between her and the escape route, and she can't go back into the alley," Parker said. "Celia, I just want to talk to you."

"The hell you do." Something in the echoes made it impossible to tell where she was.

Parker took a deep breath. "I think you saw something," she said. "The lady who was killed out there, she was a nice lady. She needs your help."

"That's it, appeal to her civic pride," Chapman muttered.

"Michael, I'm going to tell you one more time to shut the fuck up," Parker said, her teeth gritting. "Please, Celia. I'll give you my card. A get-out-of-jail-free card the next time you get busted. Just for talking to me."

"No way."

"Shit," Parker said, thinking fast. "Okay! You know the vamps in this neighborhood, right. You must know Samantha?"

Silence greeted her.

"Samantha knows me. I'm Detective Kelly Parker. She knows me, and she can get a message to me. Tell her when you want to talk to me, and I'm there. No tricks, no games. I just want to help."

The silence fell again, and Chapman was staring at Parker. "We should seal the building and bag her," he said.

"And what, sweat her? Shut up and trust me." Parker raised her voice. "We're leaving now. Remember what I said. Talk to Samantha."

Chapman was still sweeping the room with his flashlight, but he followed Parker out into the street. "That was really dumb, Kelly," he said, shaking his head. "You've got a material witness in there."

"When I want your opinion, Officer, I'll ask for it," she replied.

"Oh, we're back to 'officer' and 'detective', are we?" he snapped. "God, Kelly…"

"Get a grip, *Michael*," Parker said.

Chapman didn't look at her as he hooked his flashlight onto his belt. "Fine. Good luck on your investigation, ma'am."

He stalked off, and Parker watched him go. The mist was turning into a light rain, drizzling over the green car and mixing with the blood pooled on the sidewalk, just as the flashbulbs popped one more time, banishing the shadows for an instant.

Chapter Six

๛

1929

Atlanta

Something was stirring in the streets. There were shouts and whispers in every house Samantha passed. She was trying to get back to the house the kiss had taken from the old woman now buried in the garden she had tended for forty-six years. Sirens blared too often, unseen in nearby streets. The air was thick with unrelieved tension, like humidity turgid before a storm.

It was a bad night for a vampire to be out. They already suspected the kiss, and Fiona had told Cristoval they would have to move on soon.

A thin young man with tousled dark hair stumbled away from an apartment building doorway. His eyes were wild, yet somehow blank. He saw Samantha on the other side of the street and ran over toward her. Samantha recoiled instinctively.

"Help me," he cried. "Please."

There were shouts in the building he had just escaped, punctuated by the sounds of breaking glass.

"What—" Samantha began.

"Where did he go?" hoarse voices cried from within the building.

"They'll kill me," the young man pleaded, and Samantha believed him. As the thundering footsteps grew louder from the building, she grabbed his hand and led him down an alley away from them. Together they raced, sirens squealing again, coming out a few blocks away. Samantha cut through a few backyards, still pulling the young man with her.

"You'll be safe here, trust me," she said, opening the back gate. The young man looked around curiously, but she pulled at his arm and drew him up onto the back porch and into the kitchen, bolting the door.

"Miranda?" Cristoval said, gliding in from the parlor. "What have you brought us?"

Samantha turned to face him, suddenly afraid. "No, he's not…that," she said. "He's being chased. The humans are in a killing mood today."

Cristoval regarded the young man thoughtfully. "They so often are," he said, and Samantha felt the slight ripple of power from him as he rolled the young man easily. A thoughtful frown creased Cristoval's smooth face, surprising her. "Interesting," he said.

"Please, Cristoval, I told him he'd be safe here," Samantha said.

Cristoval raised an eyebrow without looking at her. "Are you making a request, love?"

Samantha froze. A formal request of the one who had made her could extend her service for a decade. But she had told the young man to trust her. Ten minutes ago it was an ordinary evening. How could it have gotten so far out of hand so quickly?

"Never mind, love," Cristoval said. "I will offer him the choice."

"No, he doesn't understand," Samantha said.

"I think he does," Cristoval said, and Samantha sensed him break the link gently. "Don't you?"

"Yes," the young man breathed. "I understand."

"Do you accept?"

The young man nodded, and Samantha felt despair well up in her chest. "Wait, you don't know what you're saying," she cried. "It's not what it seems, it's—"

"Silence," Cristoval commanded, and Samantha felt the weight of the kiss clamp down on her, stilling her voice. It was always like that, a tether around her mind and body, only allowing her so much movement before forcing her back into line.

Cristoval glanced out the window. The sun had just set, the last rosy tinges fading from the clouds. He looked back at the young man, his eyes penetrating deep, boring into him, rolling him more deeply than before.

Samantha cringed away, horrified.

Cristoval lowered his head to the young man's neck. He stood unresisting as Cristoval struck, drinking deeply. The young man's hands crept up and clutched at Cristoval's shoulders, his face contorted and grimacing.

Cristoval raised his bloodstained face. "I cannot drink it all, Miranda," he said. "Assist."

Samantha felt the kiss propelling her forward. "Forgive me," she murmured, and lowered her mouth to the other side of the young man's neck. She drank, draining him more than she ever had a living person. She felt life seeping out of him, as he sagged to his knees in the small, dingy kitchen, in shadows growing long and dark. She felt overly full, her body heavy and still. Behind them, she sensed the rest of the kiss gathering in the small kitchen's two doorways, drawn by the dance of power.

Cristoval stood before the young man and carefully exposed his wrist. "Drink," he commanded.

The young man's head lolled, and Samantha caught him as he sagged, a tear rolling down her cheek. Cristoval sliced his own wrist with a sharpened fingernail and dark blood welled up. "Drink," he repeated.

The young man latched on to Cristoval's wrist and he drank.

Almost immediately, his sagging body grew stronger, rising up before them. He drank deeply as Samantha crawled away, curling into the corner. She had condemned the young man to her own fate, saving his life by killing him. When the shakes came, throwing him onto the floor in twisting agony, she forced herself to watch. She could not help him now, but she could bear witness to his pain. As his body went through its final spasms, she felt the surge of power rise from him through Cristoval into the rest of the kiss, and the blood she had consumed filled her with a powerful, almost sexual energy. The essence of him had increased the power of the kiss, drawing them more closely together. She no longer felt heavy and full, but strong and potent, rising back to her feet.

"Do not blame yourself, love," Cristoval said, standing beside her. "He is a Chosen One. It is the blessing of eternal life."

"I've heard that before," Samantha said, watching the change take place.

It took a long time for the young man to stop twitching. When he rose, it was smooth and elegant. His wild eyes were now chilling and dark, his gleaming white fangs sharp and untested as he faced the kiss.

"Welcome, my son," Cristoval said, reaching out to the young man. "Give us your name."

"Diego," he said. "I'm hungry, Father."

* * * * *

9:23 a.m.

Samantha let the water cascade over her shoulders. Its gentle warmth soothed her muscles and sank through her skin, letting her relax. The light film of perspiration washed away and she leaned against the wall, her eyes closed.

A hand snaked around her waist, warm and firm. She jumped, a small squeal escaping from her.

"It's just me," Danny said, grinning as he slid into the water behind her.

"It better be," she replied, turning to lean her head against his chest. The water flowed over him and down onto her, warming them both and molding them together. He kissed her slowly, thoroughly, and she couldn't help grinning against his mouth.

"What?" he asked, smiling back at her.

"I feel so silly," she said.

"Just the words I want to hear," he said, nibbling at her ear. "Now say I've got a great sense of humor and a good personality. Tell me I remind you of Jerry Lewis. C'mon, gimme the sexy stuff."

"Oh, shush," she said, wrapping her arms around his chest. "I liked Jerry Lewis."

Danny groaned and buried his head in her hair. "I had such high hopes for us."

Samantha giggled, and couldn't help tickling him in a few sensitive spots. He jerked away and the water hit her full-blast in the face.

Danny laughed a bit as she gasped, wiping water out of her eyes. "That's what you get!" he said, smiling.

Samantha let her hand drift lower, sliding in the warm water. "Now do I have your attention?" she murmured.

Danny groaned. "Undivided," he said, his own hands sliding over her skin.

Samantha opened her mouth to reply, but the doorbell interrupted them. It sent a chill through the cheerful morning. Though the water was still warm, Samantha felt as if someone had just dumped ice water on her.

"Shhh," Danny said, his smile gone. "I'll answer it."

"Don't tell them I'm here," she said urgently.

"Why?" he asked, slipping out of the shower and groping about for a pair of drawstring sweatpants lying on the counter.

Samantha shut off the shower. "You can't go public now, not during the campaign," she said.

"Screw the campaign, I'm not ashamed of you," Danny said stubbornly.

The doorbell pealed again.

"We'll figure it out later, now answer the door!" Samantha whispered, wrapping a towel around herself.

Danny shot her a look then vanished through the bathroom door. She heard his feet padding down the stairs and to the door. Carefully, she inched to the landing, listening to hear when it might be safe to make a dash for the bedroom where her clothes lay.

"I'm afraid we have some bad news." It was a woman, her voice clipped and official sounding.

Samantha edged out onto the landing. The turn of the stairwell protected her from view, but she could hear the voices in the living room below as she moved toward the bedroom. Danny's responses were muffled, but the other two were clear.

"I'm sorry to say we found Meredith Schwartz in her car downtown late last night," said a man's unfamiliar voice. "She was murdered."

Samantha froze in the bedroom doorway. The water from the shower seemed suddenly chilly on her skin. She saw Meredith's face in the back room of Nocturnal Urges, so confused and betrayed. And Robert Carton's face, horrified and numb at the same time.

Danny hadn't said anything. The woman said something Samantha couldn't quite catch, and Danny said more loudly, "I'm all right."

"Do you mind telling us where you were last night?" the man asked.

"I was here," Danny said. "I got home around twelve-thirty, maybe."

"Anyone who can vouch for that?" the woman asked.

"No."

Samantha yanked on her jeans, searching about for her shirt. Then she remembered — it was downstairs, at the foot of the stairwell. How had the detectives missed it?

"I think you're lying to us, Mr. Carton," the woman said.

Oh, shit, Samantha thought, searching about for one of Danny's shirts.

"We know Miss Schwartz interrupted a session at Nocturnal Urges last night. She seemed quite upset about a man visiting a vampire. We know your predilection for the vamps, Mr. Carton. Your colleagues suspect you of having an affair with a vamp volunteer on the campaign. Someone named…Serena. Or perhaps Miranda? A vamp who works at Nocturnal Urges?"

"That's…that's crazy!" Danny snapped.

"Look, Mr. Carton, we don't think you hurt Miss Schwartz," the man said soothingly. "But we've got to find the vamp. The way Miss Schwartz was killed — it says vampire to us."

Samantha froze, Danny's shirt unheeded in her hand.

Danny's voice was strong and earnest. "Believe me when I say, I have no idea what you're talking about. I don't know anyone named Miranda or Serena, and I've never been in Nocturnal Urges in my life. The closest I came was standing at the front door with my father and a dozen reporters yesterday morning. I don't know who killed Meredith, but she was a close friend. I-I want to you to leave. Now."

The police were silent for a moment then the front door opened. "Mr. Carton, we really need to—"

"Go!" Danny's voice was close to breaking. "Go find who really killed her. Please."

The door closed and Samantha stepped onto the landing. *I can't wait any longer, I have to tell him the truth,* she thought. She stepped out onto the landing and started to come down the stairs.

Danny was sitting at the bottom landing, his face buried in his hands. His bare shoulders were shaking, and realized he was crying.

"Danny?" she said, her voice hesitant. He didn't move.

Slowly, Samantha came down the stairs. As she drew closer, the waves of sadness came off Danny in physical force through the still fading link from the night before. She drew closer to him. "I'm so sorry, Danny."

"She wasn't just a friend," Danny said. "My father…she and my father were…"

Samantha shivered. Meredith's horrified face grew large in her mind, the look of betrayal…

Clad only in her thin bra, Samantha knelt beside him, sliding her arms over his bare shoulders. Danny turned and buried his head against her. But there was nothing of heat or passion in this embrace, only his sadness, and her heartfelt desire to comfort him.

I can't tell him. Not now. There'll be time later.

"She was the first woman…the first he really cared about since my mother," Danny said. "He wouldn't say it, but I knew…she wasn't just an office fling…"

Danny straightened up. "I have to find him," he said suddenly. "And this Miranda. She'll know—"

Danny stopped then, a sudden fear blooming like nightshade in his face. "My father…" he said.

Tell him, she told herself. But the words wouldn't come. The look on his face, the look on Meredith's face…she couldn't stand to see that horrified betrayal, that sickened hurt and despair on Danny's kind and loving face.

The words wouldn't come.

10:45 a.m.

"So you had a potential suspect, and you just let her go?" Freitas snapped.

Parker leaned forward against Fradella's desk. "I didn't just let her go. I gave a potential *witness* my contact information in case she decided to cooperate."

"As opposed to bringing in the fifteen cops right outside the door and arresting her ass," Freitas said.

"Is there any good reason to think she might be the killer?" Fradella asked wearily.

"No," Parker said vehemently. "I don't even know that she saw anything."

"At the very least, she's a teen hooker and we need to get her off the street," Freitas shot back.

"Okay, both of you sit down and shut up," Fradella said. "This is a grade-A mess we have, and I need you two working together. Medical examiner should have some results later today. You two need to find this Celia and the mysterious Miranda. Either one is a likely witness or the killer herself."

"Celia's human," Parker objected.

"Humans cut throats," Freitas returned.

"Meredith Schwartz's throat was ripped open, not cut, and why are you so hot to pin this on some teenager?" Parker snapped.

"Why are you so hot to protect her?" Freitas retorted.

Fradella slammed a phone book on his desk. "You two sound like a bickering old couple," he snapped. "Find these girls, get some answers and get them fast."

11:34 a.m.

"On me in three…two…" Dana Franks straightened up as the camera light went green, a light mist of rain falling to the sidewalk.

"The campaign office is open today, but all the volunteers have been sent home," she said. "As you can see behind me, several members of the staff have come together to remember spokesman Meredith Schwartz who was found murdered downtown early this morning. Although an official statement has not been made, sources close to the campaign say the councilman is devastated by the loss of a long-time friend and an important part of his campaign."

Franks walked a bit along the sidewalk, her cameraman following her in the gloomy morning light. "Meanwhile, police have continued to question members of the campaign staff and bystanders in the downtown area, searching for any clues to find Meredith Schwartz's killer. Across town, district attorney Joe Renfrow issued a statement that he is 'shocked and saddened by this brutal killing, and will do all in his power to see that Ms. Schwartz's killer is brought to swift justice'.

"Renfrow and Councilman Carton have been locked in a contentious race for Congress. Much of the race has centered on the issue of vampire rights, and it is worth noting that Meredith Schwartz's body was found not far from the infamous vampire club Nocturnal Urges. Police have not said anything about what might have been the motive in this killing, however. For Channel 13, I'm Dana Franks."

The cameraman gave her a thumbs-up, and skittered off to the van for a fast uplink. Franks turned back toward the campaign office where shadowy figures were moving within the glass-walled building but stayed out of easy camera range.

Nearby, a black car pulled up and Councilman Carton stepped out of it. "Shit!" Franks muttered under her breath, waving at the van, although she knew the cameraman wouldn't see her. She ran after Carton anyway. "Councilman!"

Carton moved faster, stalking toward the door quickly. From inside, Franks saw a flunky moving to intercept her, and she called out, "Councilman, is there anything you'd like to say?"

Carton turned toward her. In that instant, his face made her falter. His eyes were deeply socketed, haunted in misery. He looked at least ten years older than he had in front of the vampire club. His pale face froze her in her tracks, even as he shook his head indicating that, no, he did not want to make a statement.

Her training failed her, stopping the follow-up questions in her throat, frozen by the misery in his face. She took a step backward and said, "I understand. My apologies, sir."

Carton blinked, a bit of surprise fighting the dull unhappiness, and then he was gone, vanishing into the glass building. Franks was already walking away when the flunky reached the doorway to shoo away the other reporters drawn by the sight of the councilman.

I must be going soft, Franks thought. But that look…she suddenly thought a quick prayer for him, and walked back toward her news van.

12:28 p.m.

Samantha trudged up the stairs, her weary feet making the stained wooden boards creak. She slipped off the hat and scarf that had partially protected her from the sun, though she knew she'd be facing a pretty bad sunburn tomorrow. She really shouldn't be tired, she thought — she'd had several hours of sleep, though it had been interrupted a few times.

As if it was happening again, she remembered his hands on her skin, a whispered word in the dark and she smiled a little. When she reached the third floor, she barely saw the filthy walls and flickering light in the airless hallway as she walked toward her door.

But as she reached for the doorknob, she saw new scratches around the lock. They were deep scores, revealing fresh, light-colored wood splinters around the old lock.

Samantha backed away from the door. She glanced up and down the hallway but, of course, no one was there. She briefly considered finding a phone and calling Danny then chided herself for being panicky. Surely, it was just another junkie looking for valuables, long since departed. They hit her place every once in a while, and since she had nothing to steal, they moved on.

Samantha edged the door open a bit, and saw nothing out of place. She shouldered it open fast, moving around in circles, trying to see the whole room at once. The narrow bed with a thirty-year-old quilt folded over the end, the ancient sink scrubbed within an inch of its life, the peeling wallpaper carefully glued back into place, the fading plant sitting on the dingy windowsill. Everything seemed in order.

Samantha stood still in the middle of the room and listened. There was the chirp of a bird outside, a television on somewhere below them…and breathing coming from the closet. She inhaled and smelled the stink of human fear, sharp and rancid.

Striding across the room, Samantha yanked open the

closet door and was greeted with a half-swallowed scream. A small form tried to dash past her toward the open door, but Samantha caught her in her arms and held her still easily. "Calm down, Celia!" she said. "Relax."

Celia's struggles eased. Samantha let her go, and the girl edged away, sitting down on the edge of the bed. She seemed thinner than she had only a few days ago, her red skirt and black shirt faded and tattered in the sunlight.

Samantha closed the door and sat down in the easy chair opposite the bed. "Okay, what's going on?" she asked.

Celia ran a hand through her spiky black hair, glancing around the room. "I needed a place to hide. I didn't think you'd be back for a while. Sorry," she added in an awkward, off-hand manner.

Samantha waved her hand dismissively. "Who are you hiding from? Red? Is he giving you a hard time?"

"No, Red's a good guy," Celia insisted. "He never tried nothing bad with me, and he kept what's-his-name off me that time. No, the cops is looking for me and I gotta hide."

"Did you get busted?" Samantha asked.

Celia shook her head and started shaking a cigarette out of a battered pack. "Mind if I smoke?"

Samantha shook her head. "I'll share one, but you should quit," she said.

"Right, because it could really shorten my lifespan," Celia returned.

Samantha took the cigarette and inhaled as Celia lit it. "Thanks."

"I saw that lady get killed," Celia said, rather matter-of-fact. "I saw who did it."

"Uh-huh," Samantha said, not looking at Celia as her mind raced. "Do you want to tell me?"

"No way, you'll end up in an alley too," Celia said. "I just gotta, you know, think things through. Try to come up with someplace to go."

"What about the police?" Samantha asked.

"That's the other reason I come to you," Celia said. "The lady cop, the one I got away from, she said she knew you. Parker, her name was."

"Yeah," Samantha said. "Parker. She's cool, you can trust her."

"I don't trust nobody," Celia said stubbornly. "Before I decide anything, I got to know what's really going on with this thing. I don't have an eternal life, Samantha. I've got to do what I can with just this miserable one I got."

Samantha sighed. "Eternal life isn't everything it's cracked up to be, Celia. What I'm really afraid of is that someday someone's going to take you up on that, and then it'll be too late for you to know what a horrible, dreadful mistake it was."

"Says you," Celia said. "I wouldn't be scared out of my mind that some guy's gonna rip my throat out in the alley, or that the next trick has some godawful disease, or—"

"I'm not going through this again," Samantha cut her off. "I'll find out what's going on with the investigation. If Parker agrees, will you meet her and tell her what you know?"

Celia took a drag on her cigarette. "I'll tell her, but I ain't hanging around to testify or nothing," she said. "You tell her that."

"Got it," Samantha said. "You want to lie low here for a while?"

Celia looked around. "Okay," she said. "But would it kill you to buy a TV?"

1:39 p.m.

Samantha sneaked around to the back door of campaign headquarters. A small army of news vans was parked in front of the building where a few private security guards kept them at bay. At the back door, another guard stopped her. "Senior staff only, miss," he said.

"I'm Samantha Crews," she said. "Please tell Danny Carton I'm here. He'll vouch for me."

The man raised an eyebrow and stepped inside for a moment. Samantha felt odd, waiting at the back door. She hadn't expected the guards—they must have been added since Meredith was found. When the door opened again, the guard was accompanied by Parker and a petite older woman with short-cropped reddish hair and a severe expression.

"Samantha," Parker said. "What's going on?"

Samantha shifted her weight from foot to foot, thinking fast. This suddenly seemed like a very bad idea. "I came to see Danny Carton," she said. "Is he here?"

Parker wasn't buying. "You know Miranda, don't you? We've got to talk to her."

"Can I possibly get in out of the rain first?" Samantha asked, stalling for time.

The older woman nodded to the security guard, and he let her in. The normally bustling office was dark and silent, stacks of campaign literature lying in undisturbed piles on the tables. Somehow, Samantha had expected it to be a mess, papers lying everywhere, police tape across the doorways. It was silly, really—Meredith hadn't been killed at headquarters. But somehow, it seemed wrong for the office to look so normal, so sane, when Meredith was dead. She fought the irrational urge to knock over the piles.

"All right, miss, let's talk about Miranda," the older woman said.

Samantha tried her best cool stare, borrowed from Cristoval. "I don't know you," she said.

"Detective Anne Freitas, and don't change the subject," the older woman replied. "Where is Miranda, and what do you know about Meredith Schwartz's death?"

"Samantha, would you like a cup of coffee?" Parker asked politely.

Freitas shot Parker a look. Parker shot one right back, and replied to a question that hadn't been asked. "Samantha's done nothing wrong. So let's all sit down and talk about this."

Freitas glared at her partner, and Samantha started to laugh. Both of them turned to look at her. "May I ask what's so funny?" Freitas asked.

"This," Samantha said. "Hundreds of years of police tactics in this country, and you still resort to 'good cop, bad cop'?"

Freitas and Parker stared at each other. "Was that what we were doing?" Parker asked.

The door to Morris' office opened and Danny Carton came storming out. "What the hell is going on here?"

"Interrogating a witness," Freitas said.

Danny took Samantha's arm. "She's not answering questions right now."

"Young Mr. Carton, you are a breath away from a charge of obstructing justice," Freitas warned.

"God, you people," Danny retorted. "We just lost a close friend and an important part of this campaign. Can you possibly allow us a little time to deal with it before you start hammering away at us?"

"Deal with it? Or get your stories straight?" Freitas challenged him.

Danny stared at her, frost in his gaze. "I know very well what often happens to vampires who are 'just brought in for a few questions', Detective," he said. "You will not interrogate Ms. Crews today."

"Danny," Parker said. "You know us. Nothing will happen to her."

"I'm grateful for what you did at the park," Danny said to Parker. "But I don't know Detective Freitas very well, and neither of you can control your superiors. I don't fancy Samantha being locked in an interrogation room with an east window at sunrise, because someone 'forgot' it might burn her so badly she'd say anything to get out of that room. Or are you going to tell me those rooms don't exist anymore?"

Parker opened her mouth to reply then turned to Freitas who suddenly found her shoes quite interesting.

"Uh-huh," Danny said.

"You have my word nothing happens to her," Freitas said, dropping the bullish act. Samantha suddenly realized that's all it was—an act. Freitas had played 'bad cop' for so long, she'd forgotten it wasn't always necessary. Samantha opened her mouth to tell Danny it was okay, she'd talk to the detectives right now in his presence.

At that moment, however, Jeff Morris barreled out of his office. "That's it, detectives," he said. "Robert Carton, Danny Carton and I are all represented by counsel. You may not interrogate us without our lawyers present."

Danny pointed to Samantha. "As of now, my lawyer also represents Ms. Crews," he said.

Samantha blinked.

"That's a serious conflict of interest," Freitas said, rallying for one last try.

Danny smiled without humor. "We'll let the lawyers figure that out," he said. "As of right now, this is over."

Freitas nodded. "Have it your way, Mr. Carton. But I assure you, one way or the other you will be speaking with us again."

Samantha stayed quiet as Freitas and Parker walked out the rear door. Then Danny turned to her. "Are you all right?" he asked.

Danny and Samantha stared at each other. It took a monumental effort for Samantha to keep from laughing. It was inappropriate, it was disrespectful to Meredith…but somehow hysterical laughter was all she could feel. The absurdity of it, arguing over lawyers and legalities when a real-life monster roamed the streets…

Samantha waited until she had control of herself to speak. "You didn't have to get me a lawyer," she told Danny.

"The hell he didn't," Morris said firmly. "You're part of the campaign, and your involvement with Danny makes you a key part of their investigation. We're going to protect you, Serena."

"Samantha," Danny said.

"Indeed," said Robert Carton from the door to Morris' office. Samantha turned to face him and if she could still blush, her⁻ cheeks would have reddened immediately. "Samantha, may I speak with you alone?"

Samantha nodded and left a nonplussed Danny to talk with Morris. She went into Morris' glass-walled office and only flinched a little when Carton closed the door. She felt uncomfortable, as though she had been exposed in the act of doing something unnatural. But she watched Danny through the glass, his earnest face just short of classic beauty, and felt better.

"So it's not Miranda after all?" Carton said. "Or is Samantha your day name?"

"My name is Samantha Crews," she said. "Most of the

vampires at Nocturnal Urges use a pseudonym. It keeps away the crazies."

Carton sat down in the large chair next to Morris' whiteboard, covered with meaningless strategies. "I hope you don't consider me one of them."

Samantha shook her head. "Sir, I'm so very sorry for your loss. Danny told me what Meredith meant to you."

Carton looked away, and Samantha felt the wave of grief coming from him. He seemed slightly smaller now, sitting alone in a shadowy office as rain fell outside and made patterns refracted through the glass on his face. "I'm an imperfect man, Samantha," he said. "My interests run to the…exotic. I don't believe this makes me any less of a man or of a public figure. But it is…compromising."

"I understand," Samantha said.

Carton looked at her. "I did not kill Meredith," he said.

Samantha lowered her eyes. It was tempting to roll him, to reach into his mind and test the truth of his words. But something made her shy away from it. She didn't want to roll him without his permission, not for something so important. But part of her didn't want to know if he was telling the truth.

Carton stood up and walked over to the glass wall. Danny was talking to Morris, pretending not to watch them. "It's important to me that you know that," he said.

"Why?" Samantha asked.

Carton didn't look at her. He stood straight and watched the rain fall. "I intend to offer you a permanent position in my staff," he said. "Personal aide, I guess we'd call you."

Samantha's eyes flicked to Danny. "And what would my job really be?"

Carton didn't turn around. "I think it's clear that I have certain…wants," he said. "If I had not gone to Nocturnal

Urges, Meredith would never have been there and nothing would have happened to her. You were right, last night. If I keep it up, I will be caught. And yet…"

He turned then, and his face was honestly pained. "And yet it is the only time I feel alive," he said. "With you on my staff, available to me…I would have no need to seek out the clubs, praying no one will recognize me."

Samantha clasped her hands in front of her, trying to think. A day ago, it would have been perfect. One client, one she liked and respected, instead of the anonymous hundreds at the club. No more silly sex games and play-acting. A chance to be a part of something—to make a difference—to feed without painting herself as a streetwalker. To be Samantha and leave Miranda behind forever…

"I can't," she whispered.

Carton tilted his head. "Why not?" he asked. "You give the bite to strangers every night at Nocturnal Urges. Wouldn't it be better to drink from only one man?"

Samantha nodded. "But I can't do it," she said. "I…sir, I'm in love with your son."

Carton gaped at her. His head shot back toward Danny, who thankfully was not watching them. "I thought he was just another customer," he said quietly.

"No," Samantha said, and now she found her voice, firm and strong. "I love him, sir. He doesn't know about the club. He doesn't know about…you. I can't hide in the background as your secret vampire and be with him. I've spent too long trying to live two lives. One in the daylight and one in the night. I can't do it anymore."

Carton shook his head. "You're so young," he murmured.

Samantha drew herself up. "I'm at least forty years older than you are, sir," she said.

Carton laughed a little. "Perhaps, but you are as naïve as your face is young," he said. "True love conquers all, eh? You'll tell Danny about your nighttime job and you think he'll shrug and take it without a hitch? Danny, the single most idealistic young man I've ever known?"

"He knows I'm a vampire," Samantha said in a small voice.

"Will you think, Samantha?" Carton snapped, striding across the room to stare straight into her face. "Danny is a bright young man on his way up. He's going to play a major part in my work in Washington. After a few years working for me, he's going to move up the food chain. Sooner or later, you're going to see Danny Carton's name on a ballot. He's going to do great things for humans and for vampires, young lady."

"Yes, he will," Samantha said with conviction.

"Not with you."

Samantha stared up at him and saw the absolute certainty in Robert Carton's face, so careworn and tired.

"He will become a national joke," Carton said. "The best he could hope for is aide to some senator, maybe a mid-level appointment at the national party. Someplace where he could push papers, levy some small influence and not embarrass anyone. The people of this country will not entrust their futures to a man who consorts with a vampire, and they are not ready to see their sons and daughters marry the undead."

Samantha's voice faltered. "We're ready for all that," she said desperately. "He says he's not ashamed of me."

Carton's eyes were sad. "Of course, he's not," he said softly. "Danny is the original idealist. He sees the world as it should be and treats everyone as if they lived in that perfect world. He doesn't know how much ugliness and stupidity and hatred and ignorance walk the streets on two legs. But you do, don't you, Samantha?"

A myriad of images flashed across her mind. The mobs that came after Cristoval's kiss and drove them from city to city. The widened eyes of the secretary who failed to see Samantha in the bathroom mirror. The signs held up by protesters outside Nocturnal Urges every day. VAMPS WELCOME AT SUNRISE SERVICES.

She dropped her eyes.

"Don't you see?" Carton said. "If you stay with him openly, you'll kill his career. He'd happily throw it away, because he's enough of an idealist to believe that love lasts forever, and true love can overcome any obstacle. But you and I know better, don't we?"

"Yes," Samantha whispered. "I gave up on Prince Charming a long time ago."

Carton raised her chin with light fingers. "Let Danny go, for his own sake," he said. "Whether you work for me or not, don't destroy him. Hurt him, if you must, to save him."

Samantha's eyes filled with tears. The words sank in and she knew them to be true. Through the glass wall, she saw Danny standing by the front door, watching the rain come down. She wanted to run to him, to hide in his comforting arms, hear his laughter and feel his passion again.

But the glass between them was cold and hard, and gave no quarter.

Chapter Seven

ഔ

1922

Boston

Samantha lay beneath the shady tree, her hand crawling lazily out between the roots to touch the drift of bright sunlight that had found its way between the leaves.

"Quit tempting fate, Miss Miranda," said Fiona, resting against the trunk.

"It won't burn that easily," Samantha said.

Fiona shook her head. "Wait until you get stuck outside without a hat in June. See how eager you are to test the sun then."

Samantha sighed, rolling onto her back and staring up at the patterns the leaves made against the sky. "It is awfully bright today."

"It was silly to come out here," Fiona said. "As soon as the clouds roll in, we must hurry back indoors."

"Yes," Samantha said, with the breathy voice of a smitten youth. "Cristoval will be worried."

Fiona looked at her.

Samantha sat up quickly. "Do you believe in love at first sight?"

"No," Fiona said immediately. "There is lust and there is attraction. There is no love at first sight. Frankly, I begin to doubt there is such a thing as love."

"Oh, nonsense," Samantha said, plucking a dandelion. "Of course, there's such a thing as love. You just haven't experienced it."

"Indeed," Fiona said dryly. "And you have?"

Samantha giggled, lying back down and playing with the dandelion. Its canary yellow tuft tickled her fingertips. "Of course. Cristoval."

Fiona sighed. "Cristoval. He is dashing, mysterious and handsome. But, Miranda, you mustn't be fooled. The kiss—"

"Bother the kiss," Samantha said. "It doesn't change how we feel."

"Of course, it does," Fiona said. "That's all love is—power over another. You love Cristoval and, therefore, he has power over you. The kiss makes you see him as more than he is, and his power over you controls you, dominates you. Don't you see? Your 'love' for Cristoval is…"

Fiona suddenly stopped, as though some invisible hand had clapped over her mouth.

"Is what?" Samantha asked, sitting up. "Is what, Fiona?"

"Is like…" Fiona seemed to be fighting to speak. "Like a dog…for its master. Not a woman for a man."

Samantha thought about that for a moment then dismissed it. "Nonsense," she said. "Cristoval is my soul mate."

"And what does that mean?" Fiona asked.

Samantha opened her mouth but didn't speak.

"Yes, that clears it up," Fiona said. "Soul mate. Honestly, there is no such thing. There are people who match us more closely than others, but there is no perfect match for two people in this world. People are not so easily bound to each other."

"Cristoval is my soul mate," Samantha repeated stubbornly. "We are bound together for all eternity."

Fiona laughed and the tension that had gripped her

seemed to ease. "You are so young, Miranda," she said. "So young. You have no idea what eternity is."

* * * * *

4:24 p.m.

"And whom may it be graces my underworld?" Joann Betschart backed through her office door, her bloodstained gloves still held upright in front of her. "Annie! How nice to see you. Who's the kid?"

Freitas stood up wearily. "Cut the banter, Joann, I'm tired."

"And cranky too, I see. Frank being an ass?" Betschart said, moving over to the sink.

"Ancient history."

Betschart shot Freitas a quick look. "Give me a second to get this crap off me. And who might you be?"

"Parker, temporarily assigned to Detective Freitas here," Parker replied.

"Nice to meetcha," Betschart said. "Don't let Annie here give you any guff. She barks a lot but we all know she's a marshmallow."

"Thanks, Joann, you got anything helpful to say?" Freitas said.

"Tsk, tsk. No fun," Betschart said. "And after I spent much of my day poking around your Ms. Schwartz. Kept herself up, no tattoos, piercings, scars, bite marks, nothing remarkable at all."

"Well, except the part where someone tore out her throat," Parker interjected.

Betschart turned back around, dumping her gloves into a trash can marked "Hazardous Waste." "Shows what you know," she said.

Freitas closed her eyes. "Joann, I'm dead serious. Tell me what's going on."

Betschart dropped into the chair behind her desk. "Took a while. But your Ms. Schwartz wasn't killed by a vampire. Most likely."

Parker frowned. "Who else tears out throats?"

"Leprechauns," Betschart said.

Parker stared at her.

"I'm kidding," the medical examiner said, grinning. "It was a vamp who tore out Meredith Schwartz's throat, all right. But she was already dead."

Freitas pulled out a notebook. "Now you've got my attention," she said. "Drugs?"

"Not a user, no regular track marks," Betschart said. "It'll be at least a week for the tox screen. No, the remaining tissue around the throat and the broken capillaries in the eyes make it clear. Ms. Schwartz was strangled before her throat was torn out. I think she was dead before anyone took a bite."

"So our theory is someone strangled Meredith then a vamp came along and tore her throat out for fun? Does that seem likely?" Freitas asked, writing furiously.

"Or the vamp and the killer are working together, and the vamp tore out her throat to lead us off-track," Parker said.

"Then why go to the trouble of strangling her?" Freitas asked.

Betschart shrugged. "That's your department. I found scrapings of tissue under her nails, and it'll be a day or two before I can tell you if it's vampire or human. I will say, though, that if there's a vamp wandering around just tearing out the throats of dead or nearly dead women sitting in cars, I'd feel a lot happier if he was in your chains."

5:10 p.m.

The car rolled to a stop about two blocks from Nocturnal Urges. Parker was out of the car and walking down the street before Freitas had the doors locked. "Dammit, Parker, quit running off!" she snapped, hustling to catch up.

Parker turned around and walked backward while shouting. "I am going to find Celia. If you want to help, shut the fuck up and stay out of my way. I am through taking your orders."

"Goddammit, Parker, your missing hooker is not the issue here!" Freitas snapped. "Where are you going?"

"I'm going to talk to Red," Parker said. "If you're smart, you'll shut up."

Freitas gave up and walked with her up to the Johnson Street project, where a group of young black men lounged on the front steps. A radio in front of them blared unidentifiable music.

One of them stepped down to the sidewalk. "Officer Parker, I be damned," he said, grinning. "They told us you was going big-time."

"Am," Parker said, reaching out her fist to press the flat knuckles against Red's in a quasi-ritual greeting. "Back here kicking over some rocks for what happened to the nice lady in the good car over by the club."

Red shook his head. "Damn, you guys have been crawling around here all day," he said. "We don't know nothing."

Parker grinned. "That don't sound like the Red I know," she said. "Didn't do nothing—maybe. Don't know nothing—my ass."

Red shrugged. "I put feelers out. Wasn't none of my guys nor Celia, and you can take that to the bank."

"Gotcha," Parker said. "What about the vamps?"

Red held up his hands. "The vamps keep their business, I keep to mine," he said. "What I hear, they scared shitless that they gonna see white folks with torches and pitchforks. They get all the blood and fuckin' they want in the club, Parker. Why'd they need to go after some rich white chick who got herself lost in the ass-end of town for?"

Parker lowered her voice. "We hear talk about some new vamps in town. Rough vamps."

Red glanced over his shoulder at the young men, silent and still, watching the exchange. "Man, that's some scary shit," Red said, pitching his voice low. "I ain't seen 'em, but word is we better stay out of their way. When a vamp goes round the bend, ain't nothing to mess with."

Freitas stepped away from Red and Parker, watching them talk. Stepping back a few steps, she saw the neighborhood as if she hadn't been there before—the faded plastic toys in the yards, rusted razor wire atop sagging chain-link fences protecting an empty parking lot.

"She's from here, you know," said a quiet voice behind her. Freitas jumped, but the small, spare blond man beside her stood harmless and still in the doorway of a project rowhouse.

"You know Detective Parker?" Freitas asked.

The man nodded. "I am her sensei," he said, stepping out onto the small concrete stoop. "She grew up here, and spent the last few years walking the beat here. They know her not just as a police officer but a neighborhood girl."

Freitas tried to think of a question to ask but the sensei kept talking.

"She had a sister. Aileen was troubled, got into drugs and the gang life. Kelly tried to help her but she kept vanishing. I think her failure with her sister still haunts her, Detective Freitas. You are in a unique position to guide Kelly in her new life. She is like a blunt instrument, strong and powerful, but without finesse or shape. She needs your help, whether she admits it or not."

"She doesn't exactly welcome my advice," Freitas said wryly.

Sensei smiled. "Does any child seem to listen to its parent?" he said.

Freitas rolled her eyes. "Damn, that made me feel old. I am in no way old enough to be Parker's..." she looked around and saw that Sensei was gone. "Well, shit," she muttered.

"Motherfuck!" Parker shouted. "Freitas, get over here!"

Freitas hurried over to Parker and Red. "You got something?"

"Damn straight," Parker said. "Thanks, Red." She slapped hands with him, and they hurried back toward the car. "Wanna know who Miranda really is?"

6:44 p.m.

Samantha sat on the couch in Morris' office, watching the rain come down at twilight on the news vans still parked outside. When the office door opened, she sensed Danny's presence before he actually slipped onto the couch beside her. His arms crept around her and she fought the urge to relax against him, to draw strength from his warm body.

"Are you okay?" Danny asked quietly, stroking her hair.

"No," Samantha said honestly. "This has all been...too much."

Danny leaned against her. "Yeah," he said. "But don't worry. The campaign is behind you one-hundred percent. You are not alone in this. I won't let them turn you into some kind of scapegoat."

"Danny," Samantha began, her stomach clenching with

uncertain fear. "We should talk."

"About what?" he asked, holding her closer.

Samantha eased away from him. It was as though her conscious mind couldn't quite function when he was that close to her and she needed a little air space in order to think.

"About us," she said, steeling herself. "Maybe…maybe this isn't such a good idea."

Danny stared at her, and the crestfallen look on his earnest face stabbed her in her heart like an ice pick. Immediately she wanted to take it back, make the words disappear, tell him anything to make that hurt look vanish from his face. *No, this is wrong, this is the wrong thing to do…*

"Can you tell me why?" he asked, his voice stiff.

"Think about it," Samantha said. "I'm a vampire. You're a human."

"Happens every day." Danny's voice was neutral.

Samantha blew out her breath in frustration. "Not for you. Your very job depends on public opinion. Being with me could kill your career."

"Fuck it," Danny said, standing up quickly. "You think I want to live some kind of double life? Living one way in the public's eye, meeting the lowest common denominator of their expectations while secretly yearning for something else that I don't believe is wrong? That's exactly the kind of hypocritical bullshit I've been trying to end!"

"Danny, that hypocritical bullshit is never going to end!" Samantha cried. "It's been that way since the Crucifixion, for God's sake! Since before! You think by standing up and saying you love a vampire, you can single-handedly end prejudice? Some shining example for the rest of the world?"

"Of course not," Danny said, but she saw the truth in his eyes.

"That's why you wanted me in the first place," she said

quietly. "It wasn't me. It was the idea of me. Some perfect image you could hold up as the embodiment of your ideals. Not a real, flesh-and-blood woman."

"Bull," Danny snapped. "I love you. The whole you. Not some picture of you, some image on a pedestal. You're just trying to shove me away with psychological crap."

"No, I'm not," Samantha said sadly. "I'm trying to keep you from killing your career."

Danny pointed at her, honestly angry for the first time since she'd met him. "This is my father," he said. "Dammit. My father put you up to this."

"No," Samantha protested, but it was too late. Danny strode past her to the door and slammed it open. He stalked out into the lobby area where Robert Carton and Jeff Morris were going over the schedule for the rest of the week.

"Damn you!" Danny yelled, shoving the schedules off the table and letting them flutter to the floor. Robert Carton stayed in his chair, surprised into silence. "You couldn't stay out of it, could you? Had to ruin this too?"

"Danny—" Robert began, as Samantha came running after them.

"Don't try to pretend you did it for me!" Danny shouted into his father's shocked face. "This is about you, about your career, about me embarrassing you by being less than perfect! I'm not interested in your definition of perfection!"

"Danny, be reasonable," Morris interjected. "We've already got enough scandal on our hands—"

"Jeff, you can take this whole campaign and shove it up your ass," Danny shot back.

"Danny, no one put me up to it," Samantha pleaded. "Your father only told me things I already knew to be true."

"Bullshit!" Danny snapped at her, his eyes a little too bright in the dim lighting. "You only have to tell me one true thing, Samantha. Do you love me?"

Samantha suddenly felt very self-conscious with Robert Carton and Jeff Morris both staring at her. "Danny, I hardly think—"

"Do you?" Danny shouted again.

"Did we come at a bad time?" asked Detective Freitas, standing at the back door.

"Sorry, just let ourselves in," Parker said beside her.

"God!" Danny shouted, and walked away a few steps to face the window.

Morris stood up. "This is a very bad time, Detectives," he said.

"Sorry, this time we must insist," Parker said. "Samantha Crews, you're coming with us, and I hope you'll do it quietly."

"She's not coming with you, she's represented by counsel," Robert said, standing up. "Unless you're here to arrest her, she's not going anywhere."

Freitas folded her arms in tough-cop stance. "Under the Constitution of the State of Tennessee and the Constitution of the United States, nonhumans are not guaranteed the right to representation and you know that, Councilman. Until now, we've respected Samantha's rights as if she were a human, but we all know she is no human."

Freitas turned to Samantha. "The gloves are off, Miss Crews. You come with us to answer questions or we will send the Chain Gang to pick you up."

"Chain Gang?" Danny asked, turning around.

Parker studied her shoes as Freitas responded. "Special task force for dealing with vamps. So-called because they use specially forged silver chains to restrain vampires. Vamps can break ordinary shackles—"

"But we're allergic to silver," Samantha finished. "It's like metal coated with acid, abrading the skin. We can't fight it. There's no need for the chains, Detective. I'm coming with you."

"This isn't right, Detective, and you know it," Robert protested.

"I don't know," Parker snapped. "Why don't you ask Miranda?"

Suddenly it was Robert Carton who found his shoes very interesting. Samantha closed her eyes.

"What?" Danny asked. "Miranda—the vampire you were looking for? From last night? What does she have to—"

Parker pointed at Samantha.

Danny stared at her. It took all of Samantha's willpower, but she raised her eyes to meet his. Confusion and suspicion warred in his face, the dark blooms of that horrible betrayal she had seen in Meredith's eyes the night before.

"You're Miranda," Danny said softly. "Diego, he called you that, didn't he? I didn't... So you work at that club, at Nocturnal Urges? You're one of their..." His voice trailed off.

"Say it," Samantha said quietly.

"No, I don't think I will," Danny said coldly, and that stiff chill in his voice hurt more than the words would have.

Samantha was suddenly, unreasonably angry. "What did you think I did for a living, Danny?" she said. "Waited tables? Taught school? Worked in a hospital? I'm not *allowed* to do any of those things, remember? Oh, I can pick up trash or work in a factory on the night shift, or I can give suckjobs all night in a vampire club and that's a lot more pleasant than feeding sheets into an industrial washer all night and hoping to God I don't get caught in the machinery, because no one will care if a few vamps get killed on duty!"

"I thought the bite was supposed to be this great

spiritual thing, right? A special bond between human and vampire? But you do it all night, every night, with strangers! How could it be anything special between us?" Danny yelled.

Tears welled up in Samantha's eyes. "You knew what I was and where I live, and you're telling me you didn't wonder how I paid my rent?" she shouted. "Suddenly it makes a difference. I'm not on that pedestal anymore, am I, Danny? Not something you can hold up to admire?"

Parker stepped in. "While it's clear you two have plenty of things to discuss, we have a more pressing question," she said. "You were there when Meredith Schwartz burst in, weren't you, Samantha?"

"This is quite enough," Robert Carton interjected. "I don't care what the law says, you're not interrogating this young woman any further."

"Want me to charge you with obstruction, Councilman?" Freitas challenged. "Think that'll help your campaign?"

"This is blackmail!" Morris yelled.

Samantha held up her hand. "I'll talk to you, Detectives, but we'll talk privately," she said, pointing toward the office door.

"Hell with that," Danny snapped. "I'll hear it all. All of us will. Meredith was my friend too, and I want to know what happened."

"No, you don't," Samantha said, but she already knew she had lost. Danny's face was impenetrable.

"Last chance, Ms. Crews," Freitas said. "I've got the Chain Gang on speed-dial. Answer the questions."

Samantha hugged herself, trying to make herself smaller. There was no one whose eyes she could meet. "I was there," she said quietly.

"Meredith burst in," Parker said. "You were with a client and Meredith was upset about it."

"Yes," Samantha said.

"Was it Danny?" Freitas asked.

"Are you deaf? I didn't even know she worked at the club!" Danny snapped.

"I'm asking Ms. Crews," Freitas shot back.

Samantha shook her head.

"Who was it?" Freitas asked.

There was silence for a moment. Samantha took one last, desperate look at the office door, wishing she could drag the detectives through it, or that perhaps a portal to Hell itself would open up and swallow her, saving her from this last revelation.

"It was me," Robert Carton said quietly. "I was Samantha's client last night."

Parker and Freitas exchanged glances. Somewhere, Samantha heard Robert continuing to talk, telling Freitas about Meredith's shock, about following her out into the parking lot, but she was gone. *I went home and tried to call her apartment,* she heard him say as if from a great distance.

"And you?" Freitas asked Samantha.

"I went for a walk," Samantha said in a small voice. "Danny came along. We went to his house. I was upstairs in the shower when you came this morning. I was with him all night."

She looked up at Danny.

Danny looked brutally shocked, as though someone had jammed a knife into his chest and he couldn't quite grasp it to pull it out. His whole body seemed to sag on his bones, somehow frail and shattered. His face seemed suddenly older, aged and careworn. In a cruel twist of irony, he looked much more like his father.

Danny didn't seem to know who to look at first. He

stared at Samantha then at Robert, then back at Samantha.

Robert held out his hands. "Son, I'm sorry," he began.

"No," Danny said, stumbling backward. "I can't know this. I don't want to… Last night…"

"Danny," Samantha began.

"My father!" Danny nearly screamed, tripping over the pile of papers on the floor. He stumbled around for a moment, and then ran past the detectives toward the back door, his hand over his mouth as though he were about to throw up.

Samantha started to run after him and Freitas caught her arm. "Not a good idea, hon," she said, and her voice was not unkind. She inclined her head toward Parker. As the back door swung open in the rain, Parker went after Danny, who had vanished out into the alley.

"Are you happy now, Detective?" Robert Carton asked wearily. "We've got our own little Greek tragedy, and we're no closer to figuring out who killed Meredith."

There was a knock at the door. "Goddammit, what now?" Morris snapped, walking over to the front door. He opened it, and Dana Franks came in quickly, streaming rainwater from her hair.

"No interviews today," Morris snapped.

"No shit," Franks shot back. "I've got something for you."

Freitas stepped forward. "Make it good, Franks."

Franks handed Freitas an envelope. "Some vamp just appeared out of nowhere, handed this to me and said, 'Give this to the lovely Miranda inside the office, please'. Like I know who the hell that is."

Freitas held the ordinary business-size envelope up to the light. "Looks okay," she told Samantha. "You want to open it?"

Samantha wearily took the envelope and loosened the flap. She pulled out a sheet of typing paper. On it was handwritten a short note in a script she recognized at once.

Dearest Miranda,
I went to call upon you, but you were not at home.
Thank you for leaving me such a pretty little snack.
Shall we talk?
Diego.

Chapter Eight

ΕΟ

1912

Baltimore

Samantha adjusted the trail of pearls in her coiffed hair before the mirror. "I think it's tonight," she told Katherine, smiling.

"Well, if he's going to propose tonight, I think he should present himself like a gentleman and make introductions," Katherine said.

"He's foreign," Samantha said. "I imagine he's afraid of being rejected by the matron."

Katherine shook her head. "Making you sneak out of school is simply not proper."

"Maybe I'm not proper," Samantha said. "I don't care about being proper, or living by the rules. I want to have adventures, like they do in the books. Don't you?"

"No," Katherine said honestly. "What will your parents think?"

Samantha shrugged. "They won't care what I do, as long as I marry money," she said. "Cristoval will please them… How do I look?" She twirled slowly before the mirror, and did not look out the window as the sun set beneath the city skyline, its last golden hues dying against the clouds.

Katherine looked over Samantha's gleaming blonde hair and the sapphire blue velvet dress, adjusting a few of the seed pearls. "You look lovely, Samantha."

The last shadows finally fell across the windowsill.

"Time to go," Samantha said. "Wish me luck!"

"Luck," Katherine said, and hugged her.

Samantha sneaked out into the hallway and down the back steps past the kitchen where the maids were still cleaning up from dinner. Until she began sneaking out to meet Cristoval, she'd had no idea how late the maids had to work to care for the girls at Mulanne Finishing School.

Slipping through the streets, Samantha made her way toward the harbor. She had met Cristoval there a month ago, a grown man skipping rocks along the water surface as though he were a little boy. She had been lost on the harbor front the first time, but her clandestine trips to meet Cristoval had been worth it over the ensuing months. He was exciting, romantic, mysterious and handsome.

"My dear." Cristoval stood before her under the streetlight, impeccably dressed as always. His darkly handsome face smiled gently when he saw her. "You would tempt a saint, and I am no saint."

Samantha smiled and rested a hand on his arm. "I have missed you," she said.

They walked for a bit, talked for a bit and when they came to Cristoval's house, Samantha was disappointed. This was the point where they usually turned back for him to escort her back to the school.

But this time, he led her up the steps. No one seemed to be home—he lived with a group of European businessmen and their wives, colleagues with whom he traveled.

Cristoval held out a hand. "Come inside, love."

Samantha hesitated, her heart speeding up. It was not proper. But hadn't she just told Katherine how little she cared for propriety? Still, it felt wrong somehow.

"Please, dear," Cristoval said. "I have something to ask you."

Now Samantha's heart really was pounding. She took a quick look at the street, and then put her hand in his.

He drew her into the house and through it to a small library in the back. The walls were lined with books she had never heard of and the house seemed ominously empty, filled only with shadows.

"Cristoval, what is it?" Samantha asked.

"This," he said, and leaned over to kiss her. His lips grazed hers gently, but the fire leapt through her, making her heart pound and her body warm.

"Oh, Cristoval," she whispered.

Cristoval kissed her again, and this time his hands wandered to her creamy white shoulders, bared by the dress. The unfamiliar touch of his skin on hers made her start as though he had burned her, although his hand was quite cool.

"Cristoval, I don't know about this," Samantha said.

"It is marriage for which you wait, is it not?" Cristoval said, smiling a little. "A proper lady would wait for the marriage bed."

"Yes," Samantha breathed, barely aware of his words as his hand drifted across the slender column of her neck, touching the sensitive skin and teasing it into life.

Cristoval leaned close to whisper in her ear, his breath brushing lightly on her bared skin. "I offer you more than marriage," he said. "More than a lifetime together, love. All eternity."

"Eternity," Samantha said, unable to think properly. Somewhere, an alarm bell was ringing in her mind, but she ignored it. He was proposing to her, just as she had thought. "Yes, my love. Yes."

Cristoval smiled against her neck and she felt his lips curve against her. His hands drifted up, brushing against the front of her dress, and she felt it through the layers of fabric.

He moved behind her, skillfully unfastening the blue velvet dress until she felt it fall in a crumpled heap to the floor. She resisted the urge to bring her arms up, to cover herself.

His hands stole in front of her, sliding over the ties of her corset. Then they drifted up, gently cupping her tightly bound breasts. She felt the pressure against them, and cried out at the unfamiliar sensations shooting through her. It felt so good and yet so wrong. She did not have to be proper, she reminded herself. They would be married. He would be her husband. He…was touching her, squeezing her breasts through the corset, and the pleasure was close to pain, strong and powerful within her skin.

He led her to the chaise beneath the library window, pressing her back upon the pillows. She lay beneath the moonlight, nervous butterflies warring with surges of delicious excitement within her torso. He had removed his shirt and she let her hands dance across his chest, testing the unfamiliar texture of his skin.

Cristoval pressed hard against her, his fingers quickly untying the petticoats that fell away from her legs. The stockings followed, though his hands moved more slowly, exposing tender skin that had never been touched by a man. Each sensation he explored made her grow more excited until she wanted to beg him to do whatever it was he intended to do, anything to relieve the electric tension within her.

His hand moved up and touched her, a sudden move that both excited and scared her. "Wait, too much," she whispered, but he didn't listen, sliding his fingers back and forth as unfamiliar and powerful sensations shot through her with dizzying speed. She arched her back and his mouth found the mounds of her breasts pressed above the corset's confines. She usually hated the constrictions of the corset, but suddenly its pressure was exciting instead of binding, a delicious contrast to the free sensations he generated with his hand.

His mouth traveled up, licking along her neck until he kissed her. When his tongue slid between her lips, she was shocked enough to gasp. He took advantage of her surprise and thrust his tongue inside, licking and rubbing inside her mouth. A sharp touch of pain hit her lip as she nicked herself on his tooth, and she began to struggle a bit, suddenly more afraid than aroused.

His eyes opened above hers. The pupils expanded through the dark chocolate brown, turning black, and it was as though he sank into her mind. A sense of peace and acceptance flowed through her and her fears stilled. He kissed her again, and her arms crept over his shoulders, open and warm to him. She felt him slip off his trousers, and when he pressed hard and hot against her, she was not afraid.

It was not slow or gentle. In a moment, he was inside her, hard and full, and there was a quicksilver pain that shot through the pleasure and dampened it. The panic tried to rise again, but his hands were sliding over her breasts, still bound in the corset. His mind was still part of hers, and she felt his rising excitement, the slippery pleasure he felt within her.

This must be it, she thought. *This is what it means to truly be one.*

He began to move faster, and the pain faded a little. She tried to match his movements, but felt clumsy and out of rhythm with him. He stilled her with his hands, holding her down beneath him. His hips began to move again, thrusting harder, and the pain was back for a moment. She held onto his shoulders, and his head dipped down to her neck, kissing until she felt the sharp press of his teeth against her skin.

The pain was sudden and vanished just as quickly. His mouth latched onto her neck and she felt him drawing something from her, as though a thick velvet rope were coiled within her body and he was drawing it out from beneath her skin. Everything was moving, the world was turning around the chaise, his body was moving within her and all she could do was cling to him and feel the rush inside her body.

The shuddering pleasure began low in her body where he thrust within her, and shattered outward in an ever-expanding cascade. She cried out, holding tight to him, the corset still binding her down and his body pressing her against the chaise.

Even as it ebbed, he lowered his head again, and she felt that velvet rope moving again inside her skin. She didn't know if she could stand it again, but it rose within her, shuddering pleasure rising from between her legs and exploding outward through her limbs. She screamed this time, crying out for mercy from whatever might be listening.

She caught her breath, and the room was spinning. She was dizzy and weak, her limbs heavy. She became aware that something wet and warm was flowing down her shoulder and over her breasts, dampening the top of her corset. Cristoval lowered his head to lick it, suck the liquid from her skin, and even as it tingled, she looked down and saw it was blood.

"Cristoval," she murmured.

"Shh," he said, and slid up to her neck a third time.

No, she tried to say, she couldn't stand it again. But his mouth clamped onto her neck once more, pulling that velvet rope through her body, and she screamed in a strange mix of fear and ecstasy, pain and joy, as it drew out of her yet another shattering climax. He was drinking from her, she sensed, drawing vital fluid from her body even as he shoved himself into her.

The walls seemed to move and she opened her eyes to stare at the moon thought the window.

It hovered above her, cold and silvery-pale. She stared at

it, round and full, and felt her heart fluttering in her chest. Cristoval was still inside her, rocking between her legs, but it wasn't her any more. Her heart was fluttering harder, as though it were skittering about in her chest, and then the pain came, thunderbolts of tight, clenching pain across her rib cage.

His arm was suddenly up over her face, an open wound in his forearm. "Drink," he commanded. Her mind was fading and she barely felt him lift her head up to press it against his arm. Warm, salty blood filled her mouth and, by reflex, she swallowed.

Cristoval held her tight as her body jumped and convulsed beneath him. Her arms and legs jerked as though someone had tied strings to them and yanked each one randomly. He kept her pinned, the corset still constricting her chest, and she stared at the moon until her vision faded.

The moonlight rewoke her, and she was still in his arms. He was still inside her, still moving slowly, his hands and mouth caressing her with a tenderness that had not been there before. She lay beneath him, unresisting, as the rhythm of his hips sped up, harder and faster within her. His hands finally tore at the corset, suddenly freeing her of its constrictions, loosening the fullness of her young breasts to his fingers' caress. He touched the nipples and they hardened into sensitive buds beneath his hands.

Her arms crept up to his shoulders, pulling him to her, and he pressed his face against her cheek. She felt him arch forward and utter a hoarse cry, his own explosion going off inside her, his breath teasing her ear. She felt his pleasure and a hot, powerful joy filled her. She drank down his passion within her and stared up at the moon as his movements finally slowed.

Then she tested her sharp new fangs with her tongue.

* * * * *

9:32 p.m.

Detective Freitas didn't like TV lights. They made her squint, which made her face harsher than it really was. Parker hovered behind her, equally uncomfortable. She had never been in the spotlight before and found she didn't like it.

"About thirty minutes ago, we conducted a search of a room in the hotel behind us, with the permission of the room's tenant," Freitas told Dana Franks on camera. "We found evidence of a struggle, and a young woman who had been residing there is missing."

"This is what led you to issue a Jennifer Alert?" Dana asked.

"This, combined with other evidence in our possession," Freitas said.

"This is an unusual Jennifer Alert, isn't it?" Dana pressed.

Fradella stepped forward. "Contrary to popular belief, we don't issue Jennifer Alerts only for cute blonde girls who belong to rich suburban families," he said. "We have reason to believe the girl has been kidnapped by an extraordinarily dangerous vampire and several accomplices. We are mobilizing the Vampire Task Force and asking the public to come forward with their information."

"That is the task force often referred to as the Chain Gang, correct?" Dana asked.

Fradella leveled his cop stare at her. "An unfortunate nickname, and one we prefer not to use. The important thing here is the missing girl and getting her back safely."

Dana turned to the camera. "And here is the information again—A Jennifer Alert has been issued for Celia, no last name, age estimated at fifteen. Short, black hair, gray eyes, last seen wearing a black shirt and red skirt in downtown Memphis. Police warn that the alleged kidnappers are extremely dangerous. If you see them, do not approach. Call the police immediately."

Dana tilted her head a bit as the unseen anchor asked her a question. "No, Jim, it's not believed the missing girl had anything to do with the vampires in question before this incident. However, police are keeping fairly quiet about their evidence."

A moment later, the lights switched off. "Idiot," Dana muttered, removing her earpiece.

"I'm pretty sure he heard you," the cameraman said.

"Fuck him, that was a dumb question, and so was 'an unusual Jennifer Alert'," Dana replied. "We don't question Jennifer Alerts when they're issued on the cute little suburban girls. That was a question my supervisor ordered me to ask, Lieutenant, and I apologize."

Fradella shrugged. "Off the record, there's usually no one reporting a kidnapped street kid, Miss Franks. That's why they rarely get an alert. It's a fair question though."

"Still, I'm sorry," Dana said, shaking his hand. "I hope you find the kid."

Freitas gave Dana a stiff nod before the three officers walked back toward the task force van. On the other side of the van, Samantha was arguing with Lieutenant Cox, leader of the Vampire Task Force. Danny Carton was standing nearby, drinking a cup of coffee.

When Samantha saw Parker, she waved her arms. "Thank God, someone sane to talk to this man," she said.

"What's the problem?" Fradella asked.

Lieutenant Cox folded his arms. "Miss Crews thinks she knows more about anti-vampire reconnaissance than my people."

"She probably does," Freitas said. "How old are you, Samantha?"

Samantha had to think for a minute. "A hundred and ten—no, eleven? I think. Who cares? Kicking down the doors of vampire hangouts will guarantee that anyone associated with Diego will be as far underground as they can manage without actually digging a hole to China. And Diego wouldn't be in the usual hangouts, anyway. He's playing a game with his own rules, and unless we figure it out ahead of him, Celia is dead and a lot of others besides."

"I tend to be wary of strangers who offer eternal life, and I am not inclined to take advice on finding this leech from his ex-girlfriend," Cox snapped.

Fradella's gaze leveled on Cox. "That's the last time I hear you use that word, mister."

Cox stared back at him. "I believe you called us in, Lieutenant, and you don't outrank me," he returned. "I'll use any language I damn well please. I've got a vamp to find and your pet leeches had better stay the hell out of my way."

Cox stalked off toward his van. Fradella sighed. "I apologize, Miss Crews."

Samantha shrugged. "I've heard worse. He can call me anything he wants if he gets Celia back in one piece. But I don't think he will. And that's not the worst of it."

"What could be worse?" Danny asked.

Samantha started a bit at Danny's hollow voice. Parker answered for her. "Celia hasn't had the shot. That's what Brent the bouncer told me."

"Shit," Fradella said. "Can you make someone a vampire against their will? Don't they have to drink the vamp's blood or something?"

"Yes, but it's not hard to coerce that," Samantha said. "Also, Celia's got this romantic idea that being a vamp is something glamorous. She's talked about getting turned so she can work at the club."

Parker swore and kicked at the van. Freitas gave her a look.

"If Diego turns her, she'll owe him a hundred years of service," Samantha said. "He'll also tie her into the kiss, which will take over her free will for as long as he wishes, unless she manages to break free."

Samantha wavered a moment, and leaned against the van. Parker caught her arm. "Hell, Samantha, if I didn't know better I'd say you were looking pale."

Samantha shrugged. "I haven't fed in a while. Just got a little dizzy. It's okay."

"Well, I'm not standing around here waiting for Rambo there to kick down the right door," Parker said. "Downtown for me."

Danny pushed away from the van. "I'm there."

Freitas rolled her eyes. "As long as you guys are charging in where angels fear to tread, I'm in. Samantha, what say we drop by Fiona's place? I bet the vamps would like to help find the guy giving them a bad name."

Samantha nodded. "And if Fiona won't help, I've got a few friends."

Fradella held up his cell phone. "I expect this to ring regularly, got me?"

"Aye, sir," Freitas said.

10:01 p.m.

Sensei sipped from a cup of green tea. "Of course, I will help," he said. "I believe Red still answers my calls. No one knows these streets better."

"Did you know Celia at all?" Danny asked.

"No," Sensei said. "Unfortunately, she did not cross my path."

Parker paced the dojo like a caged tiger. "There has to be someone she talked to. Someone who might know—"

"It seems to me that knowing her captors might be more helpful," Sensei interrupted. "The vampire who has her is likely to take her to places comfortable to him. And, Kelly, you must prepare yourself—it seems likely he will kill her, if he hasn't already."

"Goddammit!" Parker shouted, and took a hard swing at the practice dummy in the corner of the dojo.

"Easy, Parker," Danny said. "How do you know this girl?"

"I don't."

Danny glanced over at Sensei. "It just seems like you're...taking this personally."

"I take it personally," she said, and there was something in her voice that told Danny he'd hit a serious nerve.

Parker stalked about the room, still talking as though she didn't quite remember the two men were in the room. "My sister Aileen. She got into drugs in a big way, and it was a short step from sleeping with her dealer to letting him pimp her out. When I was new on the job, I helped clean out a bad crack house not too far from here. Aileen was one of the hookers we caught in the back room."

Her voice faltered, and Danny caught Sensei's impassive gaze.

"I looked the other way and let her slip out the back," Parker said. "I let her go. One free pass, you know? Just one. Only I never saw her again."

Sensei spoke then, his voice calming and serene. "You know Celia is not your sister, Kelly." It was not a question.

"Yeah, it isn't likely, is it?" Parker said. "Fuck it. Call

Red, get his ass out on the street. This one we're gonna find."

10:23 p.m.

Dana Franks turned to face the camera. "An unprecedented citizen search is taking place downtown. Shop owners and street people, vampires and humans are taking to the streets to find this one lost girl. Even Councilman Robert Carton is part of the search. He has declined to appear on camera, but here with me now is his campaign director Jeff Morris."

Morris faced the camera. "The councilman didn't want to publicize his part in this search, but I felt the public should know that he is volunteering his own time and that of several members of the campaign to help find this missing girl. Robert Carton is very concerned about public safety, and—"

Dana interrupted him. "Is there some connection between this kidnapped girl and the murder of Meredith Schwartz, the councilman's press secretary?"

"If there is, the police have not informed us," Morris said without missing a beat. "The tragedy that has struck our campaign family has only strengthened Robert Carton's resolve to stop another tragedy from taking place."

"Thank you, Mr. Morris," Dana said, turning back to the camera. "Behind me, you see Nocturnal Urges, the vampire club behind which Meredith Schwartz was found last night. It is currently closed and owner Fiona Knight has told me she has sent her entire staff out for the search. Gang members, a city councilman and vampires are working together in one cause.

"It's a strange night downtown, Jim."

11:43 p.m.

Samantha got out of the car, running straight down the

street where Parker was waving her arms. "I'm here! I'm here!" she called. Freitas jogged after her, a little more slowly.

"We found him in the alley," Parker said, falling into step with Samantha. "He won't go to a hospital or talk to anyone but you."

"Shit," Samantha breathed.

They reached the alley, where Red was slumped against the brick wall. Blood coated the front of his shirt, and at least two bite marks showed on his neck. Danny had wrapped a bloodstained handkerchief around Red's hand and was holding it tight. Danny looked up at Samantha, his face pale.

Samantha knelt beside Red. "God, I'm sorry," she said.

"Motherfucker bit off my finger," Red said, gritting his teeth. "Gave me a message for you. He's got your girl, and he's gonna do her. You meet him at the park where he met you and your boy, and he'll leave her alone. No harm, no vamp. He says you come alone, no one except your boy. Midnight."

"Shit, that's seventeen minutes from now," Parker said.

"Red, I gotta go. I owe you one," Samantha said.

"Glad to lend a hand," he grinned weakly.

Freitas hovered over them. "There is no fucking way, Miss Crews. You are not doing this."

"Like we have a choice?" Samantha said.

Parker tilted her head toward Freitas. "As much as I hate to agree with her…"

"We don't have time for this!" Danny snapped. "Samantha and I will go to the meeting point. You guys get Cox and his commandos down here. They'll take enough time finding their car keys that we can get Diego and his psychos there, and then all we have to do is keep them there long enough for you guys to do your thing."

Freitas rolled her eyes. "That's an excellent way to get your stupid ass killed, Mr. Carton, and I have no intention of getting fired over your idiotic corpse."

"Arrest me then, because I'm going," Samantha said. "Danny, you stay here with Red."

"Fuck that," Danny said.

"I can take care of myself," Samantha replied.

"I have no doubt," Danny muttered. Samantha flinched.

Parker sighed. "All right. I'm going with you two. I'll hide, so Psycho-Boy won't freak out. But if things get nasty, I can protect you."

"You can get killed," Samantha shot back. "Can I point out that minutes are ticking by?"

"Then let's haul ass," Parker said.

Freitas grabbed Parker's arm as the other two started toward the cars. "Try not to get dead, kid. It's still your first week."

12:00 a.m.

Someone had actually bothered to lock the waist-high gate that surrounded the nameless park. Samantha climbed over it easily and Danny followed, a little more clumsily.

Darkness lay between the unkempt shrubs as they made their way back up to the twisted tree, made into something eldritch and silvery in the moonlight. Samantha shivered, remembering their kiss under the tree—had it only been a day ago?

Danny leaned against the tree, his arms folded. He was striving for a tough look, Samantha could tell, but the hurt was still stamped on his face.

"It was only twice," she said.

Danny averted his eyes. "We have other things to deal

with right now, Samantha. Miranda. Whatever the hell your name is."

"My name is Samantha Crews," she said desperately, looking around at the shadows. "Miranda was a name Cristoval gave me. He was the vampire who made me, and later Diego. He said in my new life I should have a new name, like a baptism. When I left Cristoval I gave up that name, that life. I only used it at Nocturnal Urges to keep away the crazies."

"How many men have you bitten?" Danny asked, the bitterness still strong in the gossamer thread that still bound them.

Samantha folded her arms. "Should I ask you how many cheeseburgers you've had, or how many women you've slept with? Because they aren't really the same thing, and I still wouldn't ask because—"

"Four." Danny stared past her into the darkness and flickering streetlights.

This close to him, she could feel his sadness warring with anger and a horrid mix of other emotions that made her sick to her stomach.

Samantha lowered her eyes. "It's not the same thing, Danny. I didn't sleep with your father. It wasn't sex. It wasn't anything. Just the bite. He came to the club twice. Last night, I told him he shouldn't come back to the club or he'd get caught."

"And later?" Danny said, the hurt showing on his face again as though something had broken inside. "With me? You figured you'd bagged the father, you'd try for the son too?"

"No," Samantha whispered. "I told your father today I couldn't...not with him, not anymore. Even if being with him meant I could give up the club, be part of his staff, be myself again." Her voice broke. "Because I love you, you idiot. You and your silly ideals and your stubbornness, as though you could take all the hurt and ugliness in this sorry, stupid world and make it all disappear under the power of your belief. I love you in spite of what I am and what you are and what I've done, and if that's not enough for you, I'll just have to accept that, because I accept you. I love you. All of you, not just the parts that made me happy. Everything."

Danny didn't look at her, staring down at the roots twisted around his feet. Samantha wanted to reach out to him, but suddenly she felt something like a cold wind through the park, even though the air was motionless.

"Diego," she called.

He was there, stepping out of shadows, still wearing the cloak. His face was as young and guileless as ever, the dark angel she had thoughtlessly rescued from the mob that sought him so many years before.

"Miran-da," Diego singsonged, smirking. "I found something you misplaced."

He stepped aside and Celia stood beside him. She wore a long, blue velvet gown, her spiky black hair calmed into a soft wave around her head. She looked lovely, except for the bruises on her pale arms. The bruises reassured Samantha— vampires didn't bruise after they were turned. Celia was not yet a vampire.

"Let her go, Diego," Samantha said. "She's just a child."

"A young woman," Diego said, running his hand up Celia's arm. The girl flinched, but did not move away. Diego must have rolled her, Samantha thought. "In your time, she might already be a wife and mother, Miranda."

"Stop calling me that!" Samantha shouted, as if it was the worst thing Diego could do to her.

Diego's dark face creased with a cheerful grin. "I always was a man for a bargain, darling Miranda," he said. "Why don't we trade?"

"What do you want?" Samantha asked.

"You, of course," Diego said, still smiling. "It is time for you to take your rightful place as consort of the master vampire, Miranda. Join my kiss and stand by my side, and I will let the little girl go with your boy here."

Samantha shivered. Somehow, she hadn't expected this. She expected violence, retribution for her betrayal in breaking free of the kiss so many years ago and leaving them to Cristoval's deepening madness. But to be reinstated… The kiss would control her every act. Diego would… He could force her to do anything he wanted.

"Oh, God," she whispered.

Celia's large gray eyes flitted back and forth from Diego to Samantha. They had seen so much, but they were still the eyes of a young girl, blameless and afraid.

"You're not doing this," Danny whispered to Samantha. "You have power beyond his. He wants you to increase his power. He'd be unstoppable with you, Samantha."

"I can hear you, boy," Diego laughed. "I can hear your very thoughts."

"Then listen to this," Danny snapped, and flipped him off. Samantha grabbed Danny's arm, but Diego simply laughed.

"He is right, of course," Diego said. "Why do you think you never had a taste for the slaughter, Miranda? Cristoval was a dilettante with pain, but I elevated killing to an art form. What made you hold back when the others leapt forward to join me?"

Samantha shook her head, hoping to keep him talking until the Chain Gang came.

"Empathy," Diego said, answering his own question. "You feel what they feel, even without rolling them. Why, I bet you can feel this little girl's fear from all the way over there."

As soon as he said it, she could. Poor Celia's terror came off her in cold waves, buffeting Samantha as though she were a cork in a terrible sea. On her other side, Danny's dark turmoil provided an even colder balance, and she shivered.

Come now, Miranda, Diego's mind whispered.

Samantha jumped, startled. "It's not possible," she said. "You haven't rolled me."

But that is your power, Diego said.

Samantha shook her head, as if it would clear Diego from her thoughts. "Celia, come to me," she said.

Celia started to walk forward, her steps awkward in whatever shoes Diego had placed on her feet beneath the gown. Her eyes were wide with fear, but beneath, Samantha could see the beauty waiting to emerge. She was like a fragile bird, so close to flying and yet held down by invisible chains.

Samantha sensed the link drawing taut, as Diego made Celia stop. She hesitantly reached out with her mind, to make Diego release her. But the fiery wall of Diego and the kiss fought her back.

So easy, Diego said. *Come now, Miranda. What have you to lose?*

Unbidden, Danny's face in the moonlight rose up in her mind, the tenderness of his touch, the moments they had shared in the twilight bed.

Resolutely, she fought down the images and the feelings they evoked. She didn't want to think of last night with Diego skulking around in her mind. It wasn't his.

"He is human, Miranda," Diego said, his voice cajoling. "He will never understand."

"Come on, honey," Danny said to Celia, ignoring Diego. "Come here."

Celia made it another step. Samantha glanced over at Danny, his earnest face bent on coaxing Celia to him, as though his own feeble human will would be enough to protect her. But she sensed Diego on the other end of the link, playing with Celia, dangling her just beyond safety, and the girl herself, filled with impotent fury warring with her fear.

What have you to lose? Diego said again, and Samantha tried to think of something. Danny was lost to her. Her time on the streets, offering suckjobs to random strangers at the club—was the unlife Diego offered so much worse?

Yes, it is, her sane mind whispered.

Diego's mind turned darker, the ugly mood of a child denied a precious bauble. *If you will not take your place with me, Celia will,* he said. *I sense great potential in her.*

"No," Samantha said, and took a step forward.

"Samantha," Danny protested, but she held up a hand to silence him. She walked to Celia and touched the girl on the side of the face.

"Release her," Samantha whispered, and she felt Diego let go. Celia sagged, as though she were a puppet whose strings had been cut. "Go to Danny."

Celia stumbled over to Danny immediately, and he caught her in his arms. "Samantha, what the hell are you doing?" Danny said.

Samantha took up the last thread of the link she had forged with him, and sent a powerful message through it. *Stay,* she told him, and Danny could not move. At least for a few moments, and that's all it would take.

Samantha approached Diego who stood triumphant before her. Either way, he had won, she thought.

Diego leaned over her. He lowered his mouth to hers, the touch of his lips warm and surprisingly gentle. But it stirred no passion within her, only a tired sadness in the empty hole within her heart. She felt the tendrils of the kiss reaching through him into her mind, reclaiming her.

"Dammit!" Danny shouted, struggling against the message she had given him.

A gunshot echoed across the park. Diego broke the kiss, turning quickly to face Detective Parker who stood at the entrance to the park. She lowered her weapon, which she had fired into the air.

Samantha had to fight a bubble of hysterical laughter that rose up in her chest. It was just like the night before, except for Celia's presence. But through Diego, she sensed the kiss. They were not far away, faceless wraiths waiting for his signal. He had bound them so tightly and controlled them so completely that they had lost the power for independent thought. They were literally extensions of him—it didn't matter that they weren't physically there. They could be there in moments, and they would kill them all. In a moment, Samantha would be one of them.

My God, what have I done? Samantha thought.

"The Vampire Diego, you are under arrest," Parker said, moving forward. She was taking no chances this time, keeping her eyes moving and away from Diego's eyes. Her gun remained level with his head. "You are to be questioned in the murder of Meredith Schwartz and the kidnapping of a minor. Celia, are you all right?"

"I'm okay," Celia said in a small voice.

"What a pleasure, Detective," Diego said, offering Parker a courtly bow. He was suddenly so much like Cristoval it made Samantha shiver. "We were interrupted last time."

"I'd say bite me, but it would be redundant," Parker shot back. "Kneel on the ground, hands behind your head."

Danny finally broke free of Samantha's command, and dashed forward, dragging her away from Diego. "What the hell did you think you were doing?"

"Suddenly you care," Samantha muttered. "Shh, I'm concentrating."

She stared at Diego, and through the tenuous link he had started, she ordered him to kneel. Diego whirled to face her, his knees beginning to bend.

"Kneel," Samantha ordered, the exhilaration of what she was doing overwhelming her for a moment. She fought through the link, fighting to impose her will on Diego as he had imposed it on her.

She took a step forward. "Kneel!" she repeated, and Diego's legs collapsed him to the ground.

His mind surged against hers, fire exploding against the ice of her resolve. Somehow she was able to hold her own against his onslaught, her sadness and anger and fear all bound into a roar of emotion that she used to batter him. In his mind, she saw only emptiness livened by the rush of the kill. She assaulted him with emotion, with feeling, and it was destroying him. He cried out aloud, and dropped his face to his hands.

Sirens wailed in the distance. "Now they get here," Parker groused, circling up near Samantha with her gun still leveled on Diego's prone form. "Do I want to know how you did that?"

"Shush," Samantha said, concentrating on Diego's mind, keeping him constantly under attack with pain and fear and sadness. He writhed on the ground before her.

Flashing lights heralded the police vans. Lieutenant Cox and his officers boiled out of the first van, rushing toward Diego's crushed form. "Chain him!" Cox shouted, and in moments silver shackles were snapped onto Diego's ankles and wrists.

Only then did Samantha release him. Diego's head

snapped up. His eyes burned with fury, a real emotion pouring out of him toward her. The chains shifted as he was pulled to his feet, and she felt the burning pain in his limbs through their link. He tried to struggle, and the acid fire against his skin roared through the link.

"Cut it out, leech!" Cox shouted, kicking Diego in the side.

Despite herself, Samantha lowered her eyes in pity.

Do not pity me, Miranda, Diego hissed in her mind. *I am not done yet.*

"Be careful," Samantha told the officers. Cox ignored her as his men led Diego to the van. Another car pulled up and Freitas was out and running across the park almost before it stopped. Behind her were Robert Carton and Jeff Morris.

"Damn, I missed it," Freitas said, turning to watch Diego being led away.

Robert Carton ran toward Danny, relief clear on his face. But Celia shrank away, and Samantha felt the sudden terror fling outward from the girl.

"Celia?" Samantha asked.

"Him," Celia said, pointing. "He killed the lady the vampires ate."

She was pointing at Jeff Morris.

Morris held up his hands in protest. "I have no idea what she's talking about!"

"He was arguing with her in the car and he strangled her! Then he just ran off when the vampires got there," Celia shouted.

Freitas and Parker exchanged glances and began to move on either side of the others.

"Meredith was killed by a vampire," Robert Carton said, confused.

"They came later," Celia shot back. "Started to eat her, but stopped when they realized she was dead."

Robert turned to face Morris. "Jeff? You didn't, did you?" His face paled, seeing something in Morris' face that the others didn't recognize. "My God, you did," he whispered. "Why? How could you…?"

"It wasn't just him," Samantha said quietly. "Diego made you send the letters, didn't he?"

Morris stared at her, angry confusion warring with haunted fear in his face. Gently Samantha touched his mind, and a tear rolled down Morris' face.

"He's been there for days," Samantha said. "You thought you were going mad, but it was a vampire mind-touch, Mr. Morris. He found you outside the campaign office, he made you send the letters, and then he made you forget."

"He didn't mean to kill Meredith," Danny said, a tone of relief in his voice.

Samantha shook her head sadly. "Yes, he did," she said. "Diego had to cover up for him. But you meant to kill her, didn't you?"

"She was going to ruin everything!" Morris shouted to Robert. "She would have destroyed you!"

Robert's face contorted in sudden misery. "You son of a bitch…"

Freitas was slowly circling around behind Robert Carton and Jeff Morris.

"He kissed her cheek after she was dead," Celia said.

"Shut up! Just shut your stupid mouth!" Morris shouted, and from beneath his sport coat he pulled a snub-nosed revolver.

Freitas and Parker both raised their weapons at the same time, shouting for him to put it down. Behind them, Cox and members of the Chain Gang were running back up the hill, shouting and pulling their weapons.

"Please, Mr. Morris, put it down," Samantha pleaded.

Morris met her eyes, misery and fear brimming behind the tears. "I can't," he whispered.

"Oh, God," Samantha breathed.

Morris' face changed, hardening, creasing into a smooth, chilling smile. "You broke our bargain, Miranda," Diego's voice hissed through Morris' mouth.

He aimed the gun at Celia.

Danny pushed Celia behind him in an instinctive act of chivalry. In one quick lunge, Samantha threw herself in front of Danny and Celia. The report of Morris' gun was echoed by immediate return fire from both Freitas and Parker.

The bullet struck Samantha in the center of her chest, spilling blood down her torso. Its force flung her backward into Danny, collapsing to the ground as he caught her in half fall.

"Samantha," he cried, letting her rest on the gnarled roots of the misshapen tree.

"Need EMS up here now!" Freitas shouted, as she rolled Morris's prone body over. Parker was already moving to Samantha's side.

"She'll be okay, right?" Danny said, his eyes wide with panic. "She's a vampire, bullets don't kill vampires, she'll be okay, right?"

Parker pulled a large handkerchief from her back pocket and folded it up to press it against the wound in Samantha's chest. "Depends on if it damaged the heart too badly," she said. "Their one vulnerable spot... C'mon, Samantha, stay with me."

Samantha stared up at them, the heavy weight in her chest deepening into a kind of peaceful rest. Danny's horrified face, Parker's tense concern and beyond them,

Celia. She was alive and safe, Samantha knew, and the rest was all too quickly forgotten.

"Samantha," Danny whispered, holding her hand. "Please."

"She hasn't fed today," Celia whispered.

Parker glanced up at Celia. "You're right, I don't think she has," she said.

"I don't get it, what does that have to do with anything?" Danny said.

"EMS! Up here now!" Parker shouted, before turning back to Danny. "Vampires are weaker when they haven't fed for a while. Something that a vamp would usually be able to fight off could kill them if they haven't—"

A paramedic team hastened up the hill, but they veered over to Morris.

"Goddammit, help her!" Danny shouted to them.

Cox rolled his eyes from his spot standing over Morris. "Humans first," he said.

Freitas stood up, her hands stained with Morris' blood. In one swift move, she punched Cox hard in the jaw. He stumbled back and tripped over one of the twisted tree roots. He fell hard on his ass, and Parker barely restrained a grin.

A second paramedic team lumbered up the hill. With practiced ease, the larger one with a mustache took over for Parker, sliding an absorbent pad over Samantha's chest. It was stained red immediately.

"Heart wound, severe," Mustache said to the skinny guy who was talking into a hand radio.

"All right, let's get her moving," the skinny one said. They lifted Samantha onto a gurney and carefully carried her down the hill after Morris' team. Danny followed her down.

Parker stopped Celia from following them. "Hey, you

okay?"

Celia turned her large gray eyes up at Parker. The detective peered closely at her face.

"What is it?" Celia asked. "You look disappointed."

"Nothing," Parker said. "C'mon, kid. Let's get you taken care of." They walked down toward the emergency crews, arriving at the bottom of the hill.

The paramedics loaded Samantha into an ambulance. Danny hopped aboard just as they pulled out, his father right behind him.

Danny smoothed Samantha's hair out of her face. "Forgive me," he murmured.

Samantha smiled weakly. "I was going to…ask you to forgive me," she whispered.

Danny lowered his head. "Just stay with me," he said. Samantha's eyes drifted closed and he shook her shoulder. Her eyes reopened, but were clouded and unfocused. "Dammit!"

"We're losing her," the paramedic said.

"Why the hell are we going south?" Robert Carton snapped at him. "Saint Anne's is about six blocks from here."

"Can't take her to Saint Anne's," Mustache said from behind the wheel. "She's a vampire. She's gotta go to Saint Abraham's."

"That's miles away!" Danny shouted. "Goddammit!"

"Rules is rules," Mustache said.

Danny started rolling up his sleeve. "Wake up, Samantha, wake up and feed."

"What?" Robert asked.

Danny stared at him. "If feeding makes her stronger, let her feed."

"She can't roll you, it'll hurt like a son of a bitch," the

skinny paramedic said. "You're fucking crazy, man." He moved up to the front, shaking his head in disgust.

"Fuck it." Danny lowered his arm to Samantha's mouth. "Feed, Samantha."

Samantha shook her head, turning away.

"Dammit, do you want to die?" Danny cried.

Samantha closed her eyes. Danny tried to force her mouth up to his arm, tears leaking from behind his eyelids. "Please," he whispered.

Suddenly, Danny sensed a presence over him. He looked up and saw his father, eyes hollow in a saddened face. Robert Carton leaned down and handed his son a small penknife.

In one quick motion, Danny made a small cut in his forearm, wincing. Blood welled up, rich and thick. Robert turned Samantha's head and opened her mouth. The blood flowed, and instinctively Samantha drank, first in sips, then long draughts. Danny could see a bit of color return to her cheeks. When she stopped, she was breathing more evenly and the blood had stopped flowing from beneath the bandages pressed against her chest.

"Welcome back," Danny whispered, kissing her forehead.

12:51 a.m.

Officer Michael Chapman pulled over his police motorcycle only a few blocks from the small park where some kind of huge shitstorm had gone down. Kelly was in the middle of it, he knew, but no cops had been hurt. Kelly could take care of herself and six other people in a pinch.

He shined his flashlight down the alley between two decrepit warehouses. The van was actually on its side, entirely blocking the alley.

Chapman raised his radio and clicked it on. "Officer

needs assistance on a 10-46, Johnson and Park," he said.

The dispatcher responded, and he swung his leg off the motorcycle, walking toward the alley. He held his flashlight up at eye level, shining it into the toppled van. The back door swung back and forth, but he could see nothing inside.

"Hello, anyone need some help in there?" Chapman called.

"Noooo," came a tenebrous voice, smooth and filled with mad laughter.

Chapman stumbled backward, his heart pounding. The flashlight shook as it illuminated a mad, darkly pale face, emerging from the dark recesses of the van. He seemed young, his eyes filled with dancing glee, and blood was smeared across the lower half of his face.

"Oh, shit," Chapman whispered, frozen in place.

The vampire raised a long, sharp fingernail. "Shhh," he whispered, letting the silver chains fall to the ground.

Chapman glanced down at them, knowing he'd never reach them in time. Then he looked back up.

The alley was empty. No one was there. But somewhere in the shadows, something was breathing.

Watching.

Epilogue

ⓢ

11:45 a.m.

Parker did not do well with the flowers. It was a large arrangement, and she didn't quite know how to hold them. Freitas held the room door open for her.

"Next time, you carry the damn flowers," Parker grumbled.

"I'm hoping there won't be a next time," Freitas said.

Danny grinned as he took the arrangement from Parker. "I see you two are still getting along famously."

Samantha was sitting up, propped on a stack of pillows in her small, dingy hospital room. "Hell, I'm just glad you're both in one piece."

"Ditto," Parker said, sitting down next to the bed. "Boy, they don't give you much space here, do they?"

Danny's smile faded. "Don't get me started."

"Yes, don't get him started," Samantha grinned. "I think he's going to take on vampire health care as his next big cause."

Freitas' smile faded. "Yeah. I'm sorry about the campaign, Danny."

"Well, we had exactly zero chance after one campaign member murdered another," Danny said. "Dad will be happy to hold on to his councilman seat. And I've found...other pursuits."

"I bet," Parker said, waggling her eyebrows.

Samantha pretended to throw a pillow at the grinning

detective. "Not like that," she said. "We're going to open a community center in the neighborhood. One-stop shop for the homeless, drug treatment, job training, child care, everything."

"We?" Freitas said.

Danny smiled down at Samantha, and she smiled back up at him.

"Stop, you're making me sick," Parker said, grinning.

Samantha turned back to Freitas, her mood sobering. "But you've got bad news, don't you?"

"Turn off your mojo, wouldja? It gives me the creeps," Freitas said. "I'm sorry. We haven't found Diego."

Parker leaned forward, her eyes intense. "He killed four police officers, trained members of the Chain Gang," she said. "We've got every cop in town on the lookout, Samantha. Don't you worry."

"No, we won't worry at all," Danny said sarcastically.

Samantha shook her head. "He's gone," she said quietly. At Danny's concerned look, she squeezed his hand. "He didn't bind me into the kiss. It didn't get quite that far. But I can sense that he's gone. Maybe I'll sense it if he comes back."

"You know who to call," Parker said.

Danny wasn't smiling. "Did…did Jeff make it?"

Freitas shrugged. "He made it out of surgery," she said, her voice carefully neutral. "It's not looking good, but we'll see."

"Now we have about four years of paperwork to do," Parker said, standing up.

Danny came around the bed and shook Freitas' hand then Parker's. "If there's anything I can ever do for you…"

"Like what?" Parker said, grinning.

Danny shrugged. "I don't know, get shot at, chase

vampires, bleed a lot. I seem to be good at those things."

Parker cuffed him upside the head. "Just take care of Samantha."

"Hey, I take care of him too," Samantha protested. Danny went over to her and took her hand again.

Parker shook her head. "Disgusting," she said cheerfully, and waved as they went out.

"I don't know," Freitas said, walking with her down the hallway. "Seems to me a certain Officer Chapman…"

"Oh, screw you."

COMING TO A BOOKSTORE NEAR YOU!

ELLORA'S CAVE

Bestselling Authors Tour

UPDATES AVAILABLE AT

WWW.ELLORASCAVE.COM

Cerridwen, the Celtic goddess of wisdom, was the muse who brought inspiration to storytellers and those in the creative arts.

Cerridwen Press encompasses the best and most innovative stories in all genres of today's fiction.

Visit our website and discover the newest titles by talented authors who still get inspired — much like the ancient storytellers did...

once upon a time.

www.cerridwenpress.com